VESTIGES

VESTIGES

PEGGY ANN SHUMWAY

Gilbert, Arizona

SILVEIRA PRESS
Gilbert, Arizona

Vestiges

This book is a work of fiction. Names, characters, businesses, organizations, places, events and incidents either are the product of the author's imagination or are used fictitiously. Any resemblance to actual persons, living or dead, events, or locales is entirely coincidental.

For information contact :
website: http://www.peggyannshumway.com

Cover design by Peggy Ann Shumway
Map design by Steve Chugg

ISBN: 978-1-7360870-1-5 (print)
ISBN: 978-1-7360870-0-8 (e-book)

First Edition: November 2020

10 9 8 7 6 5 4 3 2 1

For Colleen Peppers Moorefield,
who always believed in me, and
Rod Meldrum, Wayne May, and Bruce H. Porter,
purveyors of truths that must be told.

Vestiges Family History

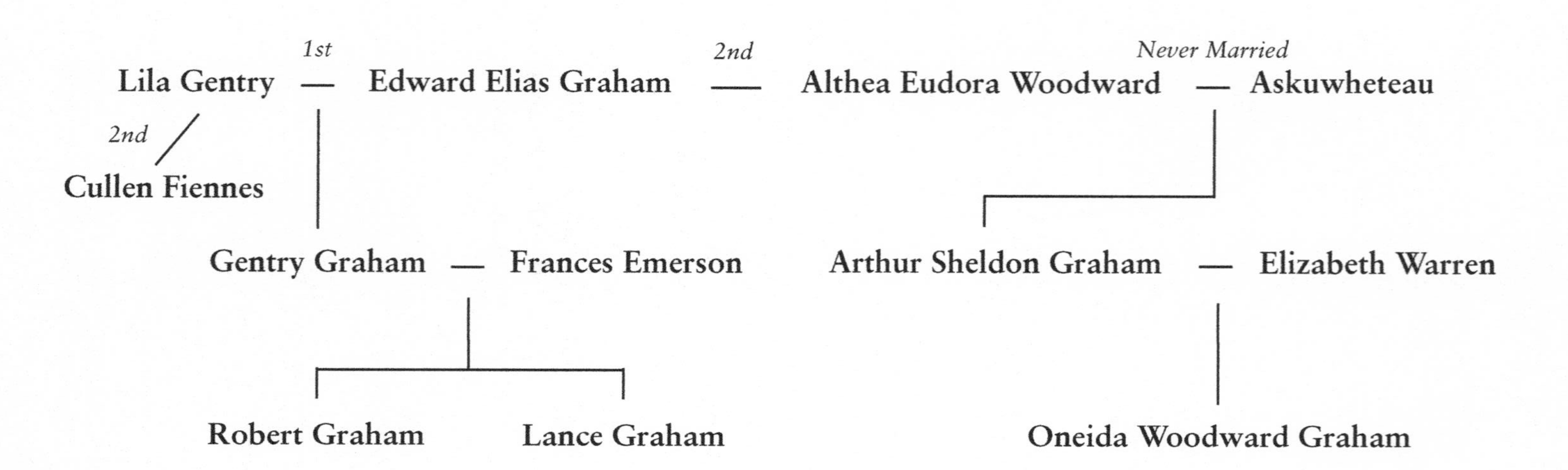

HOPEWELL SPHERE OF INFLUENCE

INCLUDING

SOME NATIVE AMERICAN NATIONS FOUND WITHIN THE SPHERE

Map Created by Steve Chugg 2020

VESTIGE:

A visible trace, evidence, or sign
of something that once existed
but exists or appears no more

CHAPTER ONE

OPPORTUNITY SQUANDERED AND TRUST MISPLACED are dreadful schoolmarms. Neida Graham shrunk under their reprimands the moment the taxi stopped in front of her childhood home. Hopewell's gabled roof pierced the late afternoon sky and cast the dormer windows into angled shadows like two reproving eyes.

"You've been away far too long," the house seemed to nag. And as if the abode wagged a reprimanding finger at her, it breathed in life and flogged her conscience, satisfaction sieving through the holes in the broken staircase—its weed-infested lawns, empty porch, and rusted and sagging fixtures, settling in a frumpy huff.

Well, she was here now. Mr. Warren had expressed the urgency of the situation, and she hadn't slept a moment in thirty-two hours just to get to Gran before it was too late. That stood for something, didn't it? Besides, she wasn't to blame for her father spiriting her away from the place and her life here as a child.

She pushed her way outside the taxi and shook her head at the neglect of this once-grand estate. Such disrepair might have appeared out of place except for the fifteen-foot-high, leaf-strewn, Native American mound that rose from the backyard beyond the balustrade. The Adena and Hopewell cultures had built hundreds of thousands of these pre-Columbian tumuli throughout what was now the United States and Canada, and for almost thirty years, the uniqueness of this particular hill had attached a primeval thread to Neida's heart. She had always intended to return home, regardless of her grandmother's summons. Just not yet, and not under these circumstances.

The taxi driver retrieved her two small bags and plopped them on the top step. Neida hustled to where he stood and handed him his fee plus a little extra. He frowned at the offering in his hand, then whirled around the vehicle, hopped into the taxi, and peeled out down the drive. She gave him little notice as the front door opened and a man appeared on the porch—no doubt, her grandmother's lawyer, Mr. Warren.

The man picked up her bags, one under his arm and the other dangling from his bony hand. He motioned her up the stairs. "Your grandmother is waiting, Ms. Graham. As I said on the phone, we have little time. I'll show you to her room."

He guided Neida across the threshold. Light from several sconces pointed ocher triangles toward the oaken stairwell, spiraling down like a grand twister from the second floor. She hurried up the staircase after the man, although no one needed to show her the way or which room to enter. Still vivid in her mind, her father, in a contemptuous rage, had dragged her from Gran's bedroom and down the stairwell when she was just six years old. Such emotion against a woman who had shown her kindness and love had incited confusion in her young heart, and every detail of that time and place still lodged deep in the recesses of her brain.

Mr. Warren stopped at the familiar paneled door and set the bags near the wall. He peered down at her with a shrug of eyebrows. "Althea asked that I wait here. She'll speak to you alone first."

The weathered handle squeaked as he opened the door, and the ancient hinges protested. On cue, a nurse sitting in a bentwood rocker in the corner rose and breezed past them. Mr. Warren nodded, and Neida bit her lip and tiptoed inside. She barely noticed the door closing behind her.

For over two decades, the memory of Gran's image had lingered as a pleasant dream—the woman's smile, her kind eyes, her mahogany-colored braid, and even her robust body that had squeezed love into Neida each time they were together. Sadness had seemed to lurk in her eyes, the remnant of some deep-seated mystery that Neida had been too young to understand. And now, here, on cloud pillows, Althea Graham lay pale and withered. Her hair, a tangled web of gray, splayed across the embroidered silk. As if the woman sensed herself a spectacle, she fluttered open her paper-like lids and squinted up in confusion.

Neida managed a smile and rushed to the side of the bed. "It's me, Gran. I'm here."

Recognition transformed the woman's features. "Oneida Woodward Graham, about time you came home, young lady."

Her friends called her Neida now, but Gran's use of her full given name sounded right somehow, as though the things that mattered most never changed.

"Come closer, child. Let me look at you."

Neida obeyed, bent to look into Gran's blue eyes that communed a silent language of love.

The old woman's shaking fingers brushed Neida's cheek and touched the end of her French braid that had swung forward over her shoulder. "You've grown into a beauty," she said.

"Your grandfather will be pleased, but why didn't you come back to us sooner?" Her breath came harder now, her voice weaker.

Neida hesitated. "I'm sorry. Papa said ..." What should she tell her? That Gran's own son had sworn to everyone his parents were dead?

Her grandmother's mouth puckered, flattened into a smile. "Written me off, has he?"

"Papa's gone now, Gran, Mama too. They died in a traffic accident out of San Francisco this year. A reckless, drunk driver ..." The words caught, trailed to a whisper.

The old woman's forehead shriveled into a network of lines. "I *am* sorry, dear one, for both of us. Though why didn't you come back to us *then*? Your grandfather and I have waited far too long for your return."

Grandfather Graham had gone missing years before she was born; that much Mr. Warren had reminded her over the phone. Yet, her grandmother made it sound as though he still lived, as though if she'd turn around, he'd walk through the bedroom door.

"I didn't even know you were alive, Gran. Not until your lawyer called me yesterday."

Her grandmother's chin quivered. She sank further into the pillow and closed her eyes. Several seconds passed before she opened them again, so long that Neida jumped when she spoke.

"Grudges are poisonous bedfellows. We're all vulnerable to their infestation, I suppose. But there's no point in sleeping with them, Oneida. They'll only taint you and bring you to do things you wished you hadn't. Your father refused to accept that. Never even made an effort to understand."

"What happened, Gran? Why did Papa take me away from Hopewell and you?"

"That tale takes too much energy to tell. What matters is the Good Lord preserved me until you could come back to claim what's rightfully yours. This house, this land, is your legacy, Oneida. *A trust* ..." Her eyes opened saucer-like to emphasize the last two words, narrowed as she finished her thought, "and I'm leaving everything to you, in your care." She groped for Neida's hand. "Promise me, right now, that you'll accept what your father could not."

Gran's puzzling words, the way she clutched her hand, pierced Neida's heart. She couldn't refuse her.

"I promise."

"Promise me ... use my money ... find the sacred stone box and bring it back. The relic is the key to a past you and the world must respect and acknowledge. Not for fame or glory. Or to pad one's ego. But for honor and regard of those who have paved the way before us. Edward never understood such things, and it's why someone murdered him."

"Murdered?" In the abbreviated stories her father had revealed about Grandfather Graham, he had never shared with her such a portentous scenario. Nor had Mr. Warren mentioned it in any of his conversations with her.

Gran struggled to lift her shoulders toward Neida and, with a last gush of emotion, pleaded, "Remember ... remember, you are *The Awaited One*, the blood of *He Who Watches*. Please honor and reveal the ancient truths." She shuddered and collapsed into the pillow. By increments, her grasp lessened until all pressure dwindled to nothing.

"Gran? Gran!" Neida gasped and fought back the grief rising inside her. Why had her father deprived her of this woman her entire life?

As though she had witnessed the scene through the wall, the nurse bustled into the room. Her shoes squeaked across the floorboards as she passed to the bed. She delivered a consoling nod, checked for a pulse, then closed Gran's eyes and placed the woman's shriveled hands inside the covers. John Warren watched Neida from the doorway, then turned to look at Gran. His face sagged with the tenderness of a long, now severed, association.

Confused, betrayed—*cheated*—Neida escaped the bedside for the window. A large orange moon had risen over the crest in the short time since her arrival, and it bathed an eerie glow over the ruin behind Hopewell. How could a glorious beacon ignite the horizon just as fate snuffed out her grandmother's light forever? Its audacity angered her and urged hot tears to slip down her cheeks.

Movement near the hill startled her. She blinked and pawed at the moisture in her eyes, focusing just east of the mound toward the base of the trees. A blurred figment took shape, a form as real as her grandmother lying on the bed behind her—a stooped, old man. He stared up at her, then leaned back his head and bayed at the moon. The sound penetrated all barriers, vibrated through her core.

She shrieked alarm and turned to the nurse and John Warren, their wide eyes questioning. By the time Neida turned back to the window, the man's somber tune silenced, and, like magnified tunnel vision, his gaze pierced hers, seemed to chop the distance in half, sent a shiver up her spine.

The nurse rushed around the bed, John Warren joining her, but before they reached Neida's side, time seemed to suspend. For in the interlude, the stranger nodded at her and, like some ghostly presence, drifted between the trees and vanished from view.

卌

The apparition outside Gran's window haunted Neida for some time. She was emotional. Gran's death, her plea, and the assertion that someone had murdered Grandfather Graham had all provided powerful catalysts to impact her imagination.

The moon had arced high above the mound before the medical unit finished removing her grandmother's remains. Neighbors and Gran's pastor milled about the house while she just watched the plot unfold in perplexing layers of twists and turns. Mr. Warren coaxed her downstairs to a corner of the parlor and settled her around a small antique table under the muted glow of a Tiffany lamp. He asked everyone to clear the room, then pulled out a document from his briefcase and began his rendition of her grandmother's wishes.

His recitation jumbled inside her head. Constant impressions of Gran in her bed, the life-worn creases of the old woman's face, even the sense of her words, swelled and added to Neida's stupor.

"Miss Oneida, do you understand what I'm saying?"

The lawyer's question jolted her, and she focused on his gaunt features. "I'm sorry. My grandmother's left me something?"

"I said you're an heiress to millions of dollars."

She frowned at him. His disclosure only deepened the upheaval making the pulse at the base of her neck throb.

"I'm what?" she asked a hint of amusement in her voice.

"You're a wealthy, young woman. Your great grandfather turned his father's logging business into an empire after the depression. He sold the company just before your great grandmother passed before him, so he left the fortune to Althea when he died in 1959. Since your grandmother named you as her successor, everything is yours now."

Neida blinked at such a ridiculous fabrication. "But how can that be possible?"

"Well," said Mr. Warren, pushing his glasses up his thin nose, "no one else is left to leave this to, Miss Oneida. You do realize your grandmother was an only child. After your Grandfather Graham failed to come back from his excavation in Ohio, your father grew to hate her. So, she made few concessions for her son. You say he's gone on anyway. Who's left to contest her wishes? I assure you everything is yours."

"But there must be someone else in the family."

He shook his head, a sadness reflected through his spectacles. "Your grandmother left explicit instructions. You're the only beneficiary."

The walls closed in. Mr. Warren's exposé created too many choices, impossible alternatives. They required her to change her well-oiled mechanism of routine affairs. She replayed Gran's last words and Mr. Warren's declaration over in her head. An anthropology professor's stint at an obscure Bay Area university faded under such an endowment. She loved her vocation, had written several books on the Ohlone culture, yet somehow her degree and knowledge, in the few minutes of hearing the details of her Gran's trust, dwindled to nothing extraordinary. In all honesty, she yearned for more excitement in her life than teaching students who took her classes just to satisfy a science credit. She swiveled toward the lawyer and crossed her arms.

"But Mr. Warren, why does Gran expect *me* to give up my life and take up a search? I've built a career for myself. I can't just uproot and leave California on a moment's whim."

Mr. Warren leaned in. His eyes crowned over his spectacles in matter-of-fact pointedness. "The fact is you'll have plenty of money to do whatever you wish. She only wanted what's best for you."

"What's best for me?" Traipsing around the country to search for a stone box that got her grandfather killed sounded like a fantasy to her, or danger if it were true. And Gran had called her such a bizarre name, *The Awaited One*, the blood of *He Who Watches*. She didn't even know what that meant.

"I don't want to sound disrespectful, but was Gran in her right mind?"

Mr. Warren recoiled. "Your grandmother was in perfect mental form, I assure you."

She considered his adamant response. Gran's struggle to lift off the pillow, the way her exertion and whispered utterance pumped life into those tarnished, blue eyes had spoken volumes. And because every syllable, every inflection in Gran's voice, resounded inside her with clarity, she had to agree with his assessment.

Neida rubbed her temples. "I have no idea what to do next."

Mr. Warren threw the trust into his briefcase and sighed. "Althea did love you enough to hunt you down and give you everything she owned. I don't quite understand your confusion."

Neida winced. "You're right. This is an incredible legacy, and I should be more mindful of Gran's generosity. I guess I do have some time off. It won't hurt me to look into Gran's request. But she should have left me a little bit more instruct—"

A howl outside shattered her gripe. She whisked to the window, pulled back the curtain, and scoured the dark void for the source. "Who is that man, and why is he making that racket?"

Mr. Warren's eyebrows jutted inward. "What man? It's just a stray wolf calling for its mate." He closed his briefcase with a click and maneuvered it off the table. He came to her and patted her arm. "I'll expect you at the bank on Friday morning at 11:00. Don't be late."

Neida nodded, followed the lawyer from the parlor to the door, and watched him walk down the steps to his car. *A wolf? No, I saw a man howling outside Gran's window.* She searched the line of trees along the property for the individual, but he wasn't there. The baying wafted to her from some distant forest pocket, and though softer, held the same lamenting resonance as before. Who was the strange man, and what did he want? Neida at least owed her grandmother the courtesy of investigating and, with a bit of luck, finding the relic she had implored her to return home.

CHAPTER TWO

GRAN'S LUXURIOUS OAKEN CASKET started its descent into the grave, and Neida couldn't hold back her emotion any longer. She shook with hushed sobs. Tears streamed down her cheeks until they tasted like salt in her mouth. She dug for the handkerchief in her black suit pocket and dabbed at her face, tried to breathe in the sultry air, but, like lead, it weighed heavy inside her chest. The opportunity to know Gran better dissipated with each inch of the casket's burial, and her resentment for her dad rose in its place to taunt her. He was the individual who had denied her the privilege of such a special relationship with her grandmother. And for what reason? She shook her head. She couldn't do anything about it now. Nor would she ever be able to remedy the violation.

Neida turned away. She couldn't watch a big chunk of her life sinking along with Gran into that dirty, dark hole. She glanced down the row, and her gaze caught on the face of a handsome man staring at her. Something seemed familiar about him. Too familiar. When it occurred to her who he was, she whipped her gaze away to Pastor Will of Newaygo's Baptist Church, well over six feet of him, now standing before her with a patronizing smile. An immaculate tailored black suit wrapped his gangling frame. He patted her hand. "I'm so sorry for your loss," he said.

People lined up behind him then, and though she accepted each condolence from her neighbors with graciousness, she couldn't help but stare at the clergyman, who had moved back by the graveside. He seemed like such an odd man.

The pastor nodded at her and winked, not a cutesy sentiment, but an involuntary flutter of his face. He turned and acknowledged each of the villagers who walked past him. Some flashed their approval, a nod back. Others narrowed their eyes at him as though he represented the devil himself. As soon as the last of the attendees wandered off, he closed in, his long strides carrying him to Neida's side in an instant. He hovered in front of her, too close for comfort.

"I think your grandmother will be pleased with our efforts today," he said.

Neida inched away and craned her neck to look up into his face, far above her own. "And I appreciate your kind words about my grandmother."

He shrugged. "People around here loved Althea. I catered my remarks to those feelings."

His choice of words seemed odd, but she shook them off. "Too bad my father robbed me of the opportunity to know her better."

"Your father *was* a rather headstrong individual."

Neida shook her head. "But I grew up with someone generous to a fault."

"Really?" His question leaned to the incredulous. "That surprises me."

Neida imagined some history lurked between the pastor and her father, but she didn't dare ask about it out of politeness.

"We enjoyed a wonderful rapport," she said. "That's why the facts I've uncovered over the last couple of days make little sense. I can't believe he lied to me."

Pastor Will's eyebrows hiked at her confession. "I believe he loved you, however misguided his motives at times."

"Did he love me? Isn't love based on complete truth?"

"Our Savior is the only complete truth, Oneida. Your father struggled to believe in God, but I'm sure he did his best to love you in his own way."

"But why keep me from my grandmother? Why deny that she was alive?"

"Perhaps he wanted to protect you from something."

"From what? A kind, loving woman?"

The pastor stalled for a moment, then cleared his throat. "Your grandmother once delved into some unsavory business in town. I assume that forced your father to take you away from here—a good thing for your sake. But I'm not so sure about his choice in the state of California."

"What are you talking about? What unsavory business?"

"Forgive me for talking out of school, marring your Grandmother's good name."

Neida stiffened. "I can't believe Gran would act in any way that lacked approval. And everybody loved her."

"Of course, but the unknown can be such a challenge."

Neida eyed the man. What kind of a clergyman was this Pastor Will—pitting her against her grandmother, instigating suspicion? Though the pastor was right about one thing. Since crossing into Michigan's airspace, the unknown had lobbed a multitude of conundrums her way, and they had given her a Texas-size headache.

"I'm going to get to the bottom of a lot of things in this town," she said. "Are you familiar with some ancient stone box my grandmother wants me to find?"

An unreadable emotion flickered in Pastor Will's face a second before it disappeared behind his practiced demeanor. He looked away for a moment, did a double take toward the edge of the cemetery. A hint of displeasure pulled at his mouth.

Neida followed his scowl. A gray-headed man, dressed in a dark suit, watched them from behind a tall headstone. When he realized she and the pastor were studying him, he turned toward the parking lot and disappeared behind the menagerie of cars.

"A friend of yours?"

Pastor Will shook his head. "I don't think so."

She wasn't sure she believed him. He managed to avoid her eyes. "What about that artifact? Newaygo's a small town. You must know something about what Gran was talking about."

When he peered down at her again, his mood had changed, his voice harsh with annoyance. "I know that relic caused a lot of trouble. After Edward dug it up from the mound behind your house and then went missing, Althea talked of nothing else, and I'm afraid misdirected her life because of it. Don't ruin your life too. Don't get caught up in this fairytale. Obsession, well, often tricks the mind and taints reality."

"Are you suggesting my grandmother was crazy?"

"What I'm suggesting is that we focus on what's important and true. Avoid distraction altogether. Show obedience to God and his intentions for our life. And while I'm on that subject, you must worship with us this Sunday, Oneida. Our services are at 9:00 A.M. Your grandmother's pew waits for you to fill it again." He squeezed her shoulder and leaned in; his stale breath caused her stomach to revolt.

She edged away. "Thank you, but I don't attend church. I'm a woman of reason—of proof. Faith in a being we can't see or touch just isn't a part of my reality. My dad was a staunch agnostic, and my mother, an unwavering Christian. Watching their heated debates over the years has left a bad taste in my mouth, and I've sworn off anything that has to do with religion."

Pastor Will frowned and closed in. "But you won't find the proof you seek in the scientific world, girl. What you seek is right before you, and He awaits you with open arms." He finished with a grand gesture, hands spread apart to emphasize the point.

Neida almost laughed. *Is he talking about himself?*

"Your grandmother is cheering you on," he continued, "now that she knows the truth as it really should be. She anticipates you'll understand the one thing vital to your salvation—your relationship with God."

"That was Gran's truth, not mine. I can't ride on the coattails of someone else's conviction. I require evidence. Platitudes are such a waste of time."

The pastor produced a handkerchief and dabbed the cloth against the moisture trickling down his forehead. His eye twitched. "I admit I'm disappointed by your response, Oneida, but if you change your mind, I'll reserve Althea's pew."

"As I said, Pastor, I won't attend services anytime soon."

He eased away and plastered a smile on his face. "I'll pray for you, for your grief and healing. May I give you a ride?" His expression reflected he'd rather face the devil himself than offer her assistance.

"Thanks, but no. I think I need a few moments more."

"Then I'll meet you at your house later." He bobbed his head, turned, and hurried away, almost at a run.

Neida frowned after him. Her agnostic views had upset him for sure. Either that or some other itinerary had transformed him into a man with a purpose.

𝍸

That evening, inside Hopewell, warm bodies and heartfelt condolences swarmed about the parlor. Neida rolled the kinks from her neck and kicked off her shoes just as another well-intentioned villager and his wife sauntered toward her. The man reached to take her hand, then patted it.

"Oneida, the wife and I are so sorry to lose your grandmother. She was a rock of this community with a generous heart. If you need anything—anything at all—please feel free to ask for our help."

Neida forced a smile. Her feet ached, and exhaustion had crept in along her shoulders. She just wanted everybody to leave her alone, allow her the courtesy of falling into bed and pulling the covers over her head. "Thank you for your kind words, Mr. and Ms. …"

"Jacobson. We were your grandmother's good friends. It's such a shame to lose her."

The duo nodded and hurried on, listing toward the food-line tables of finger foods and punch bowls of lemonade. Several Benevolent Society women bustled from the kitchen with tart-encrusted replacements to fill the rank of empty platters that Ms. Jacobson was now depleting at breakneck speed.

Relief set in when John Warren stepped in line. He leaned in and peered down at her over his glasses. "How are you holding up, Miss Oneida? You must be ready for a break about now."

He'll never know how correct he is. "Gran has so many friends," she said. "Well-wishers have scurried out of the woodwork all evening. I don't even know their names."

"You will soon enough. This is a small town. Everybody knows everything about what goes on around here. Just be careful. Your inheritance will make you best friends to some."

Neida peered toward the food table. Ms. Jacobson's plate, in the shape and height of the Hopewell mound out back, promised to keep the woman occupied for a long time. "I guess people act the same way no matter where you hang your hat," she said.

"That's true enough. Have you thought any more about making Hopewell your permanent residence?"

"I've been too busy with Gran's affairs to make such an important decision yet, although this old house and its backyard attraction are beginning to grow on me. But I'd have to figure out just how to break my contract with the University."

"I can help with that part of the equation if you'd like. A contract shouldn't stand in the way of your resolve. Newaygo is a good place with good people. Many of our villagers, including Pastor Will and the good folk of his congregation, will look after you, just as they did your grandmother."

"Maybe so, John, but I'm not sure this town is ready for the likes of me. I got the impression Pastor Will was a bit put out by my California upbringing and my agnostic beliefs. Maybe others would feel the same."

"The town's passionate about their beliefs, to be sure," he said. "But don't let the pastor's doggedness deter you from his friendship or his willingness to be of service. And just look around you. As you admitted only a few days ago, Althea has bestowed upon you a great legacy here, something to provide you security for the rest of your days. That, in and of itself, is a cause worthy of your consideration."

Neida smiled and nodded. "Yes, of course. I have much to consider, and if that leads to a permanent residence here, so be it. As I said, something has drawn me to this old home, and it's conjured up some fond memories of my earlier years."

She could think of one particular happy thought—her cousin, or more accurately, step-cousin Lance Graham. As children, they had wandered and played hide and seek in the fields behind Hopewell, and she had cried for days when her dad had taken her away from her best friend. Neida had caught a glimpse of his handsome face at the funeral. But because of her distraction, she later discovered Lance had disappeared without even talking to her, and it amazed her how disappointed she was.

Her gaze scanned the room and froze on Pastor Will in a heated discussion with the man who had watched them at the cemetery, a familiar association by the look on the clergyman's face.

She leaned into John Warren. "Who's that man talking to the pastor?"

The lawyer found the two men in the crowd. "That's Mr. Blackhour from the Smithsonian. He helped your Grandfather Graham excavate the mound on your property many years ago, and your grandmother had some recent unpleasant business with him. I suppose he's come to gloat."

"Gloat? What kind of unpleasant business did they have?"

"I'm not at liberty to discuss that with you, I'm afraid."

"I'm sorry. I didn't mean to pry."

"That's quite all right. I'm sworn to protect the lawyer-client privilege, you understand. I'm still under contract with Mr. Blackhour. But, if I were you, I'd stay clear of the man. Rumor has it he's dealt in some underhanded, if not dangerous, dealings over the years."

Neida frowned her surprise at the lawyer, though she kept her probe to herself. She turned away, searching for something else to say, but her mind had fogged over, one too many disclosures fighting for space in her brain. Her fatigue had now solidified and weighed cement-like across her shoulders. She craved some alone time. "Do you suppose I would offend anyone if I called it an early night?"

"Certainly not," said Pastor Will, who, from out of nowhere, skirted the lawyer and halted in front of them, though his sparring partner of the last few moments had slipped from the room. "We are an inconsiderate lot to keep you on your feet all day. I'll get the ladies to pack up, and we'll usher everyone out to their cars."

"Thank you," she said, relieved, though, without warning, her knees buckled beneath her.

Pastor Will caught her and directed her to a velvet chair by the parlor's open window. He trudged to the center of the room to clap his hands. The crowd turned with quizzical brows.

"Excuse me, everyone," he shouted above the prattle. "May I have your attention, please? I'm afraid Miss Graham has taken ill. Please kindly exit to your cars so we can allow her to rest. Oneida expresses her appreciation for your support and kind wishes. Please, if you will all proceed to the front entrance."

The room buzzed and bristled with activity, and the crowd began its mass movement toward the parlor door, Ms. Jacobsen guarding her half-eaten plate of food as she squeezed through to the hallway.

Neida relaxed against the back of the chair—her first reprieve of the day—and arched to allow the languid breeze from the window to kiss her neck. John Warren hovered, and his restless fidgeting proved more of an annoyance than what she assumed was his intended help. From across the room, Pastor Will directed gentle commands at stragglers who issued their concerns and desires to help. The parlor eventually settled except for the quiet putters of the church women who removed platters to the kitchen and collapsed the cardboard tables in the room.

Moments later, Pastor Will appeared at her elbow again and adjusted the curtains to allow the night air greater access into the parlor. "Well, John, I believe we've done all we can for Oneida tonight." And to Neida, he said, "I've arranged for someone to prepare your room and usher you upstairs."

Neida peered up at the two men. "I can't thank you enough for your help. I'm sure I'll be fine after I get some sleep and eat some food."

"What? You haven't eaten today?" Pastor Will's brow creased as he waited for her answer.

"A bit. I nibbled on a piece of toast this morning and washed it down with some coffee."

"Shall I fetch you a plate?" he asked.

"No, thanks. I'd rather get up to bed and dive under the covers."

"Then we'll leave you to it. Sally will close you in for the night. I'll check on you in the morning to see if you need anything." He grabbed John Warren's arm and coaxed him toward the hallway. "We'll exit stage right, John. Good night, Oneida," he said over his shoulder.

She raised a limp hand in farewell. As soon as she was alone, she sighed and leaned back again. Though not long afterward, a kind voice at her side nudged her to open her eyes.

"I've prepared your room, Ms. Graham. I can take you up if you're ready."

Sally, she assumed. She nodded, allowing the woman to lift her with a gentle but firm hand on her elbow and lead her toward the staircase. She was thankful for Pastor Will's about-face since their conversation of the morning. His most recent kindness and gentle authority had somewhat quieted her apprehension about him. But why would he have lied about knowing Blackhour? Learning the intricacies of small-town life and the personalities included in such a process would take some time. She only hoped John Warren's opinion about the clergyman—and his reasons for her staying in Newaygo—would prove spot on after all.

CHAPTER THREE

NOW THAT THE ENDLESS PAPERWORK, funeral arrangements, and interment had finally come to an end, Neida found herself suddenly without much to do. But, if truth be told, hunting for lost treasure and hidden truths rumpled her spirits right now anyway. She hoped for a better mindset before Gran's supplication from the grave forced her to face her duty to the woman.

She supposed Gran's donations to the church—the upgrade of the bell tower, the refitting of its oaken pews, and the addition of the stained-glass window splaying rainbows of color over the pulpit—contributed to the pastor's interest in her grandmother's soul. Though no concern of hers, insincerity, in any form, disgusted her.

She imagined Gran's offering had derived from her deep and abiding faith in God. Still, what someone else did and believed held little merit or influence upon the tenets she, herself, had adopted over the years. *I'll form my own opinions. Thank you very much.* Though the pastor's belief about Gran cheering her on toward faith neared the truth, she refused to force piety just because her grandmother wanted her to.

Blame her indifference on her father and mother's constant bickering. Her father had found divinity in their antique business, on golf courses, and vacation retreats. Countless times her dad had suggested that religion proved nothing—did very little for humankind. But her mother had defied his requests to let Neida make up her own mind and had dragged her to church in her youth. Mom had insisted that life's answers lay with an undefinable, heavenly creature who possessed nothing of body, parts, or passions. This philosophy had only conjured up more questions and made little sense to her. So, she had followed in her father's skeptical footsteps for as long as she remembered. Though Neida had to admit her mother's sordid affair with a member of the congregation she attended hadn't helped her opinion about religion either. Dad's hurt over the matter had intensified Neida's feelings about religious pretense. *Organized religion is such a sham!* Besides, life threw out enough tangles without adding God to the mix.

What had been worse was Dad had suffered his battered relationship in silence. "Marriage is a commitment," he had told her. "For better or for worse. Your mother will come around when she gets this nonsense out of her system." He had patched their marriage, despite his wife's betrayal, and his courage had cut Neida to the quick. She supposed that's why she had always favored her father over her mother. She could never forgive the woman as long as she lived. She just wished her dad hadn't abandoned Gran and this beautiful home, a place where they might have enjoyed solace and family connection.

She skimmed over the week's breads and sweets still crowding the sideboard along the parlor wall—gifts from her grandmother's church-going friends. Their donations showed love for Gran and concern for her, though their charity had proven a tad overdone. By the end of the week, she'd have to donate most of their generosity.

She turned her back on the senselessness and distracted herself with an occupation long overdue. For the first time since her arrival, she examined the parlor's furnishings. A velvet settee sat in the center of the room with a matching loveseat angled at its side. Tiffany lamps and an ornate crystal chandelier illuminated turn-of-the-century tables and rugs.

The room exuded character, grandiose by some standards. But the antiquated charm fit Gran's personality as far as Neida remembered her—the in-your-face kind of keepsakes that talked of family, love, and things important to her. The fact that the woman had died with nothing but her wealth, without anyone on which to lavish her affection, except for an estranged granddaughter she hadn't even been sure still existed, stirred Neida's emotions.

She sauntered through the room, felt her grandmother's life in the tatted doilies, the trinkets adorning the dusty furniture, and eyed the intricately carved box on the top shelf above the sideboard. She brought it down, examined the exquisite scrollwork in what looked like deep, rich cherry wood. She rested the box on the sideboard and tried to open it, but the top wouldn't budge. A misshapen keyhole gaped from the top—in the form of a stretched heart if she had to describe it. She assumed Gran had hidden away some treasure inside and had stowed away the key. The mystery piqued her curiosity, but she wasn't in the mood to investigate right now, so she placed the box back on the shelf and moved on in her exploration.

After circling the parlor, Neida paused at the entrance. She had glanced at the library on her endless trips to the mortuary during the week. Now the floor-to-ceiling bookshelves within her line of sight called out to her. She loved books, could spend days in libraries investigating relevant topics, how they shed light on her research. Maybe she'd find pertinent clues hidden there to help her in her hunt for lost treasure.

A musty smell overpowered her when she entered the room. The numberless, leather-bound tomes triggered sensations as close to the divine as she would ever experience. At one end, a section of texts drew her close. She hefted a volume entitled *Vestiges of the Past* and leafed through its gilded pages.

The subject matter required more than just a casual study, especially the notes in the margins. The severe loops and dips of what seemed to be Grandfather Graham's handwriting revealed nonsensical musings, a code of numbers and letters that began and ended the passage on the page. She tried to make sense of the confusing message a moment longer, then shrugged, slipped the book back into the gap, and continued down the line.

Two rows of cases, one above the other, lined part of the south wall. The collection of mound artifacts Neida yearned to play with as a child lay beneath the tempered glass. She lingered in front of some of her favorites—a duck effigy pipe made of soapstone, a mica ornament in the shape of a hand with a cross at its center, copper and flint arrowheads, and a small silver canoe tipped with gold. And she loved the colorful beaded wampum frayed at one edge. To its right, something unfamiliar caught her attention: a clay fragment embedded with chiseled characters. She drew closer to decipher the type of text on its surface.

Several of the shard's markings resembled Sumerian cuneiform, some, Egyptian hieratic characters. The picture-like symbols completed rows across the top, though gouges and chips marred the piece and maimed several toothbrush-looking symbols, unfamiliar to her.

Where had Grandfather Graham found the unusual piece? If that of a Great Lakes scenario, the relic corroborated with other evidence that some indigenous cultures possessed a written language. Sumerian cuneiform and Egyptian writing suggested a Middle Eastern origin.

Then why had Grandfather Graham placed the shard among his Native American pieces, particularly among those items coming from the Great Lakes region? Did he believe the local tribes originated in the Holy Land? She had never found such evidence among the Ohlone tribes, originally made up of around fifty independent nations and thought to be descendants of the Siberians. If this were Grandad's substantiation of the Hopewell's origins amid the traditional Bering-Strait-crossing mentality among scientists, he'd possibly drawn some criticism. Over 4,000 Native American groups had lived throughout the United States over the years, and she hadn't for a minute believed that their origins derived from one amalgamating scenario. Perhaps the answers to the fragment's origin lurked somewhere inside this library. She wished she had known her grandfather. She'd love the opportunity to pick his brain about the relic, as well as some other relevant issues.

In the coming days, she'd camp out at the massive oak desk in the center of the room, though she'd find a more comfortable chair than the leather Neanderthal that swallowed her whole as she sat in it. Neida opened and investigated each tidy compartment of five of the six drawers spanning the desk front. The locked bottom drawer, no doubt, hid another of her grandmother's mysteries.

Gran's list of secrets had continued to grow throughout the week, and now the impulse to uncover what was in the bottom drawer hit Neida with full force. She retrieved the gold letter opener on the desk, though its pointed tip proved too bulky for the lock. She dug for a paper clip and twisted its straightened end inside the keyhole without any luck. She sighed and sat back for a moment, calculating how to open the compartment, then remembered the set of keys she'd found in a bureau during the week and bolted upstairs to get them. When she returned, one key, in particular, smaller than the rest, released the lock.

Inside, green file folders housed utility, court, and miscellaneous records. A single, folded sheet of paper lay askew against the back of the drawer. Neida drew it out to reveal a page of handwriting. The date July 4, 2018, spanned across the top. She turned on the desk's Tiffany lamp and read the almost illegible scribble.

> Time is short. Where did the eighty-one years go? God plays an unfair game with me. My cancer will soon take me from this world.
>
> I've asked Mr. Warren to search for Oneida. I remember the child as if it were yesterday. "Arthur stole—" the ink was too blotchy to read, "from my—" another smudge, "but his threat to keep Oneida away devastated me on many levels. I can understand his contempt for his legacy. But how could he forbid his own child the comfort of family?
>
> I'll pay whatever the cost to bring Oneida home and to retrieve the artifacts. Mr. Warren must understand I am determined. I hope Oneida's reaction proves different than her father's. She

> possesses more courage than Arthur. I feel it in my rickety, old bones. Only she can ...

Neida turned over the sheet to continue reading what appeared to be her grandmother's journal page, but the back was empty. She searched the drawer for another sheet, moved the files, checked in and underneath the folders.

Nothing.

Only I can do what? And what had her father stolen? The stone box? Something else of importance? From Gran? The information she continued to uncover about her father disturbed her more than she wanted to confess.

Other pages, journals—answers—must exist somewhere in the library. Neida folded the page and tucked it inside her pocket, then scoured the bookshelves a second time but found nothing even resembling a journal. Twenty minutes more of searching inside the parlor in table drawers and behind the sideboard partitions provided no clues.

The grandfather clock struck twelve, invoking her to yawn. It was late. What use was there in hunting all night for something that might not even exist? She climbed the stairs toward the guest room. On the landing, her glance swept past Gran's bedroom to another place she had ignored all week. At the far end of the hall, somewhat smaller, with the same weathered green as her grandmother's bedroom entrance, the attic door invited her to explore.

The mystery of what lay beyond the thin panel frightened her as a child. Only once she dared to enter, the day her grandmother took her by the hand and encouraged her up the staircase to show her no monsters hid there but stored treasures waiting for discovery. Gran had reassured Neida she need not fear, yet the menagerie of boxes and bags were big things to a little girl, and she had never ventured inside the room again. She turned the handle, and beyond the door, the stairwell faded into darkness.

Neida dug around for a flashlight in a nearby hall cabinet, climbed the narrow steps, and tried the light switch at the top of the staircase without success. She inched further into the loft, highlighting the interior with the insufficient device in her hand.

Chairs, lamps, boxes, and chests swelled at different levels about the room. Towers of dusty *American Journal of Archaeology* and *National Geographic* publications, sewing patterns, and Christmas decorations hulked like human forms, waiting to leap out at her from the shadows. It reminded her she was alone in the house, and it made her shiver. This time she didn't run, experiencing only remnants of a little girl's fear, perhaps exaggerated by the mystery of the howling man outside Gran's window on the day she had arrived and John Warren's warning about Blackhour. She looked back toward the comfort of the light filtering in from the hallway below, breathed in courage. *Get a grip, Neida.* She bit her lip, sidestepped the paraphernalia, and flashed the beam into boxes as she advanced further into the attic.

An old treadle sewing machine loomed in the corner, and she surmised by its glistening cobwebs that Gran had neglected the apparatus over the years. A beat-up hula hoop leaned against one wall, a relic from her father's past, no doubt. She reached to pick it up and noticed the box of small, leather books just underneath a drop-leaf table. She bent closer to investigate. *Gran's journals. They have to be.*

Neida shimmied the carton into the aisle, brushed off a layer of grime, and leafed through the topmost chronicle. The handwriting appeared faded on the mottled pages, but in a more legible script than the entry in her pocket, the date January 18, 1957, stood out. Adjusting the flashlight, she read:

I marry Edward today. I should be thankful, but my heart belongs to Askuwheteau, the father of the child I carry. He tells me not to worry, that nothing will crush our love, no matter how the white man interferes. Yet, I perceive the pain in his eyes and the anguish in his soul, and as I start my new life with Edward, our hearts will forever cry out for each other. Is it possible to survive such oppressive sorrow?

Neida stalled, reread the passage again. The revelation in her hands set in stone what she would have never guessed: a promiscuous affair with someone whose name sounded Native American. Judging by the date, the relationship resulted in her father's birth. She struggled to breathe. Had Grandfather Graham known of Gran's condition when they married? She searched until she found her answer.

January 20, 1957

My husband is truly kind to take us into his home, especially since Mama and Papa remind me how tainted I am. They only allowed him to marry me because of their relationship with Edward's folks. As a consolation, my parents promise a donation to Edward's excavations in Illinois and to give him a tract of land by the river. Maybe this brings him a trace of solace, marrying someone like me.

We share no love, not that I could ever feel such emotion for Edward, but he'll provide a decent home. He'll open a firm in town and will hire several colleagues to aid him in his work. He plans to call the business Graham & Associates. It's been his dream his entire life.

I'm thankful my stomach is still small. No one will know the truth, except Askuwheteau, Mama and Papa, Edward, and me.

The flashlight dimmed, and the yellow glow muddied the writing. *This won't do.* An examination of the journals required a better forum than a dusty, dark attic. Neida stacked the book atop the others and bent over to heft the box. Bulk and weight made the task impossible. She settled to grab an armload of books and maneuvered around the clutter to the stairwell, where she paused to look back into the obscure corner. She'd retrieve the rest tomorrow. And if the pages she had already read were any indication of what she'd glean, the journals promised to provide her the education of her life.

CHAPTER FOUR

NEIDA AWOKE LATER THAN USUAL the next morning—Friday—with the first of her grandmother's chronicles sprawled across her chest. The sun's fingers poked through the lace curtains of her old bedroom window, warming her face and the colored splendor of the patchwork quilt on her bed.

She could get used to this. Perhaps making Hopewell her permanent residence held some possibilities. It really wouldn't take too much maneuvering to teach at a university here. And even if it took a long time to find a position, she'd never have to worry about money again. That, and the fact she rather liked the pleasant memories the old house brought back into her life, helped her feel contented for the first time in a long while.

Her neck ached from sleeping awry on the pillow. She readjusted under the covers and toyed with a blur of ideas until the memory of her early morning reading pushed her upright, her eyes wide and searching.

She whisked up the book that had fallen to the bed in her haste to sit, flipped through the pages until she found the passage dated March 9, 1957.

> The days are too long. I imagine Askuwheteau chanting under the shadow of Hopewell, waiting for my homecoming. I will return someday, but Edward's work calls us to Illinois now.
>
> We haven't decided on a girl's name. If it is a boy, Edward and I agree to call our baby Arthur Sheldon Graham. Arthur is a respectable name but will disappoint Askuwheteau, I am sure. What could I have done to remedy this? I can't change the way things are. I owe so much to Edward for taking me in before my body betrays me.
>
> Today, Edward told me about a woman he married from Newaygo two years ago—a Miss Lila Gentry. I couldn't believe his confession. I guess we all keep our secrets. His marriage ended in divorce, but he admits he is the father of a one-year-old son, Gentry. Lila forbids him to visit the boy. I wonder why anyone could be so cruel and deny a child his parent.

Neida could relate, but cruel was too light a word to describe her father keeping her from Gran. Even more earthshaking, her ancestry promised to take her in an entirely different direction.

The journal entry from Gran's desk drawer now lay on her nightstand. She reached for it and, in her haste, knocked the paper from the surface. The page glided to the floor like a down feather, slipping beneath the slit at the bottom.

Neida moaned and shuffled from underneath the covers to retrieve the wayward document. She adjusted her weight, and as she pushed the nightstand, she noticed the time on the alarm clock. She gasped and sprang upright, almost stumbling as she ran for the shower. If she hurried, she might make her appointment at the bank where they'd finalize the transfer of estate monies into her name. The journal entry would have to wait. Mr. Warren had told her to be prompt.

After her shower, she slipped into a pair of black dress pants, threw on a red, short-sleeved top and low-heeled shoes, and devoured a couple of slices of toasted, homemade bread downstairs. Neida snatched a last-minute glance in the mirror and sighed at the deep bags underneath her eyes. She grabbed the keys to her grandmother's 1990 Buick from a hook by the door and headed for the garage.

Newaygo nestled in a crescent-shaped valley only fifteen minutes from Hopewell. As Neida neared the township, an occasional rooftop peaked through the trees like a busybody spying on the road below. The Muskegon River snaked toward the north end of town, drawing her forward through the wide streets. Buildings lifted their brick faces and strutted turn-of-the-century style while flaunting flower boxes along the cobblestone-lined walkways. Perhaps Newaygo possessed more qualities than those of her first impression. The township promised to remedy the longing deep inside her, and she had needed such comfort for a long time. And even though she had pledged to herself to withhold judgment until she experienced her first winter here, each day convinced her that putting down roots in Newaygo was a far more logical solution to her life than not.

Her grandmother's bank and its modern architecture paled to compare with the rest of the town's vintage buildings. As Neida admired the adjacent establishments, the words *Graham & Associates* leaped out at her from a small storefront window. She slammed on the brakes and came to a stop. Thankfully, no one was behind her. She squinted to decipher the phrase underneath the title—*Newaygo's Resident Archaeologist*—in smaller print.

She wanted to march inside right now to inquire about the business's origins, but her tardiness checked her enthusiasm—that, and the horn now behind Gran's car, blasting her back to reality. She completed her turn into the parking lot, parked the old Buick, and hurried inside the bank to make her appointment.

Mr. Warren and the bank manager, Sean Riley, a stout, middle-aged man with a balding pate, descended on her as soon as she crossed the threshold—birds of prey with a purpose.

"My dear, Neida," cooed Mr. Riley. "It's so nice to meet you finally. Your grandmother was a fine woman, and although I don't know you personally just yet, I'm sure you possess as stellar a character as Althea did. I'm looking forward to a long, successful banking relationship with you."

Neida managed a smile. "I'm looking forward to it also," she said. She was sure his desire for such a relationship had more to do with the amount of money in Gran's account than just being a nice guy. That thought solidified in her mind once the two men placed the documents in front of her. She gaped at just how extensive Gran's endowment was, far more generous than she had first imagined. She had tentatively decided to make her move to Newaygo only last night, had even made arrangements to fly out to California to test the waters of her decision. Though as she perused the documents in front of her, Neida's priorities jumped high up the scale, solidifying her decision to stay.

After they had finished the last transaction, Mr. Warren offered to give her the VIP tour around town, but Neida asked for a raincheck and issued her goodbyes with a nod and a promise to return. She wanted to investigate what she assumed was Grandfather Graham's establishment, so she left the two men frowning after her. The door swooshed shut upon her heels.

Dodging cars, Neida headed across the street to the opposite sidewalk. Inside Graham and Associates, a man and woman working at their computers glanced up as she entered. A blond woman in a posh, navy blue pantsuit stood and cocked a crooked smile at her. "Hello, Ms. Graham, how may I help you?"

That the woman knew her name rendered her speechless. Neida could only stare.

The blonde raised an eyebrow. "Do you need directions?"

"Uh, no, I'm just curious about the name of your company. A passage in my grandmother's journal says my grandfather opened his business in town many years ago. I'm wondering if this is his firm or used to be, anyway."

The woman's smile stretched wider. "Why, yes, it is. Lance Graham is running it now."

"Lance Graham?"

Neida must have sounded confused because the receptionist raised both eyebrows this time and said, "You remember your cousin, don't you?"

"Of course." Neida plastered a savvy expression on her face and nodded. *I definitely remember my favorite childhood friend.*

"Lance is in now if you'd like to talk to him," said the blonde, though Neida had no time to respond. A door behind the women opened, and Lance, in blue jeans, a grungy tee shirt, and tennis shoes, strode into the front office. He proceeded to the filing cabinets along the back wall, though he didn't look up, just frowned at the paper in his hands, and pulled out a file drawer.

The view from Neida's perspective seemed rather nice. His auburn and gold-streaked curls straggled at the neckline. His broad shoulders hunched over as he dug for files, tightening the shirt across the muscles of his back. Neida couldn't help but ogle.

"Hey, Carl, do we still have the survey of the Bailey project?" he asked in a low, rich timbre. He balanced a cell phone between his ear and shoulder, walked the labels with one finger, then switched to another drawer.

The young man at the computer stopped typing and dashed to the filing cabinet. He opened a third drawer, retrieved the documents in question, and handed them to Lance, a smug expression reflecting his self-importance. "I knew you'd want them again."

Lance took the folder and nodded without looking up. "Thanks, Carl." He slammed the drawer shut with the side of his body, scanning the room in Neida's direction, and stopped short.

The blonde piped up. "Mr. G, you've got company."

"Hey, Bob, I'll call you later." Lance pushed a button on his cell phone, shoved the device into his back pocket, and strode toward Neida with his arm extended. "Oneida, welcome to Newaygo. Please accept my condolences. Althea was an extraordinary woman." His hand—large, warm, and firm—reached over the counter to engulf hers. His chocolate eyes danced as he studied her face.

Realizing the handshake had lingered far too long, Neida whipped her arm to her side. "Thank you." She looked away at the receptionist, at the filing cabinets, at her toes, trying to regain her composure, then looked up to eye each of the faces staring at her. "I feel a bit awkward. Everyone seems to know who I am, but it's been too long for me."

Lance chuckled; his smile lit up his eyes. "Welcome back to small-town life."

"We loved Althea," added the blonde. She reached over the counter and touched Neida's arm. "I'm Kathleen Stewart, but my friends call me Kat. And that's Carl Wiley over there."

Carl waved from his desk and resumed typing again.

"And I'm Lance Graham, owner and proprietor of this establishment. I don't know if you remember the little boy who used to hold your hand and run with you through the meadow behind Hopewell." When she didn't answer, he pointed his thumb at his chest. "That was me."

Happy thoughts flooded her mind again, especially the fact that they had promised to marry each other when they grew up. Her heart raced. She felt her face flush. "I'm afraid that was so long ago," she said, then smiled and fidgeted through an awkward pause.

An expression of disbelief touched Lance's face. "Oh, come on. You remember me. I know you do. Why don't you let me buy you some lunch? See if I can jog your memory and update you on the family."

Carl stopped typing and stood. A frown riddled his face. "What about your appointment with Bob?"

Lance peered over his shoulder. "I'm not meeting him until 2:00." He turned back and smiled, handed the papers in his hand to Kat. "We'll have plenty of time. There's a café just down the street. We'll grab some sandwiches and blender drinks and share stories and witty banter. How 'bout it?" He winked and bounded around the counter, offering her his arm.

Kat smiled at them, satisfaction written across her face. She looked like a cartoon character that had just swallowed one of the artifacts in the display case.

Why not? This unexpected opportunity might offer her more information about her grandparents and the artifact. She shrugged her shoulders at Carl, but instead of taking Lance's forearm, she gestured toward the door.

"Lead the way, Mr. G."

"Have fun, you two," said Kat as they headed out the double doors.

Neida cringed at the woman's words. On the other side of the window, Kat and Carl watched them with probing interest, smiles on their faces. Oblivious to his audience, Lance put his hand on Neida's back and guided her down the street.

"So why didn't you reintroduce yourself to me at the funeral?" Neida asked after Lance purchased two chicken Caesar wraps, a couple of blender drinks, and the River Break Café's homemade blueberry bars.

"Kat and I had a plane to catch to meet with some important clients." He directed her to a small, out-of-the-way table of this refurbished early-1900s architectural gem. Hardwood floors and a rustic wood-block bar provided a dramatic contrast to the brick walls and warehouse-type ceiling.

"Does your work take you out of town often?" asked Neida.

Lance pulled out a chair for her. "Yep, all over the world." He waited for her to sit before he seated himself and attacked his meal. The strong line of his jaw flexed as he took another bite and drag from the straw protruding from his drink. He seemed natural, easygoing. She relaxed and bit into her wrap.

"So, what do you do?" asked Lance. He wiped his mouth on a napkin.

Hurrying to swallow her mouthful, she said, "For work or pleasure?"

"Both."

"Well, for the last six years, I've worked as an anthropology professor at California State University, East Bay, but with my grandmother's endowment, I guess I'm about to become a lady of leisure."

"What's your discipline?"

"Cultural and linguistic anthropology of the California Native American populations. My most recent project was to compile ethnographic data of declining Ohlone populations and determine whether the decrease affects their language."

Lance raised his eyebrows and nodded. "Fascinating. Right up my alley. And for pleasure?"

Neida hesitated and sighed. "What's that? I don't get around much. I have syllabi to prepare, papers to grade, and less-gifted minds to tutor. You know, work."

"Ah, come on. I highly doubt your life is all drudgery."

"Hmm, I do like to hike in my spare time. A creek runs through the hills around the University, and the paths are a joy to explore. There's nothing better than the smell of bay laurel trees and the sound of a murmuring brook beside them." She took another taste of her food.

Lance smiled. "Sounds beautiful. You must remember the attractions around here too. I'll take you hiking with me sometime, reintroduce you. That is if you accept your duties as the proud owner of our local Hopewell mound."

"It looks that way. Gran left me everything, and I can't imagine selling such a gift."

"Althea was a generous woman, just like her parents," said Lance. "They gifted Grandad Graham the parcel of land where he and Althea had built a spread along the river, a place to take his bride and pass along to his son. My father gave me the house when he and mom moved into a retirement community in Grand Rapids just before he died. I'm right down the road from you. We're neighbors."

"That's convenient." She remembered why she liked her step-cousin so much and hoped they'd enjoy some time together again. "Are you familiar with our grandparent's lives together?"

"A little. Granddad Graham married Althea to help her through a delicate situation."

"Delicate?"

"She was pregnant with your father."

Neida gaped at him. "I thought Gran wanted to keep her pregnancy a secret."

"I don't know about that. Lila forbade my grandfather to see Dad because he had married a *tainted* woman." Lance held up his hands in an apologetic gesture. "Sorry—her words, not mine. Althea's heavy involvement with the Ojibwe peeved her. Lila didn't want her son to grow up around 'that kind of people.'" He made quote marks in the air.

"How'd your dad feel about that?"

"My dad couldn't tolerate prejudice. His best friend lived on the reservation. When Dad turned eighteen, he left his mother's home and came to live with Althea for a while. He worked summers at the firm. She had run the business after Granddad failed to come back from a dig in Ohio, and Dad loved the work so much he decided to get his degree in archaeology. He took over the helm after he graduated."

"And you followed in his footsteps."

Lance held up his hands and shrugged. "What can I say? Archaeology runs in our blood."

"Do you know anything about my real grandfather?"

"I think he lived around here somewhere. He left little trinkets for Arthur on their doorstep or howled for Althea from the edge of the forest. I understand his antics annoyed Granddad, big time."

The night she arrived at Hopewell came to mind. "Is the man still alive?"

"Althea never mentioned him if he is. He'd be pretty old by now."

Neida leaned in over the table. "The night Gran died, an elderly man stared up at her bedroom window. He howled like an animal the moment she passed on."

"Do you think he's your grandfather?"

"I don't know, maybe. And there's something else. My grandmother also asked me to find a missing artifact, one that got Grandfather Graham murdered."

Lance put down his wrap and studied her face, wide-eyed. "You must be joking. I've never heard that story."

"At least, that's what Gran told me the day she died."

"What artifact?"

"Some stone box. I assume the relic once belonged to Grandfather Graham. I believe my father stole it when he took me away from Hopewell. Though I'm clueless. I don't even know where to begin a search for the antiquity."

Lance raked his hand through his curls. "Murder ... hmm ... strange that my parents never mentioned the fact. Did Althea explain anything in her trust?"

"Nothing unusual came out in the reading. I did find her last journal entry in her desk drawer and her journals in the attic. I'm hoping they'll give me a place to start."

"Have you asked your father?"

His question shot a tremor through her. She looked away to hide her vulnerability. "No, my parents died in a car accident this year."

A sigh escaped his lips. "I'm so sorry, Oneida. I didn't know."

His large, brown eyes under furrowed brows of apology prompted tears to form. It took a while for her to speak. "I should be in better shape by now. It happened last February."

"That's hardly any time at all. My dad's passing last year still chokes me up. We were close, and it hasn't been the same without him."

A tear escaped down Neida's cheek, and she flicked it away. "All these years, I assumed my father and I were close. This trip to Hopewell is painting a different picture. He wasn't the person he pretended to be. He stole from Gran and told everyone she passed away. What kind of individual does something like that?"

"Sometimes, people do odd things because they're hurting, Oneida. It doesn't mean they're malicious."

She shrugged. "Whatever happened, the reasons must be complicated. Why keep me away from Gran? Or lie to me?"

"Did your dad know about his real father?"

"Maybe, but if he had any clue, he kept the information to himself. Gran's journals sure have opened my eyes to a lot of things, and I think she wants me to understand what happened between her and dad. Just before she died, she pleaded that I'd accept what my father couldn't."

"How about if I help?" He squeezed her forearm. "I have plenty of contacts and the tools to unearth hidden treasure. And maybe we can figure out whether or not someone murdered Granddad Graham."

Neida studied his rugged features, his dancing eyes, and wondered at his genuine desire to help. "I don't cherish doing any of this alone. But are you sure?" He still hadn't let go. She pulled back and placed both hands in her lap and studied them.

"More than," he said. "We can start tonight."

Her head popped up at his suggestion, and when she lacked a response, he smiled a lazy, lopsided grin.

"Well? I won't bite. I promise. After all, we share such a fond history."

She winced. "Uh, I'm not sure that I—"

"Wow ... I'm that forgettable, huh?"

She couldn't help but smile. "No, it's just I'm busy tonight. I have to pack. I'm headed to the Bay Area tomorrow to turn in my resignation to the University. And to ship my belongings."

He brooded a moment, and when he spoke, his expression lightened with his words. "I can go with you. Two would make the chore much quicker. The sooner we get you back to Hopewell, the closer we are to finding some answers."

She'd treasure his help, anybody's help. But she didn't like asking for aid about something so personal and from someone she hadn't talked to in years. "Thanks, but I need to do this myself. And, please, call me Neida. No one has called me Oneida in years."

He nodded, sulked a moment longer—a little boy pout—and finally acquiesced. "I'll dig through my father's papers and things while you're in California."

"Thanks, Lance, if it's not too much trouble."

"No trouble at all. You need a hand. What's family for anyway?"

She could spew a mixed bag of answers to his question, but she only nodded. "I am overwhelmed. If I'm about to unearth something significant in my life, I'm not sure I'm ready for the consequences it might bring. I only hope I can return sooner than later." She sighed and looked up at the ceiling. "I have so much to do."

Lance stood, reached for his wallet in his back pocket, and handed her his business card. "My offer still stands. Hail me if you need anything. I'm only a phone call away."

CHAPTER FIVE

IF ONE TOOK ADVANTAGE of the San Francisco Bay Area's multifaceted offerings, what wasn't to like about the metropolis? Neida had lived there for most of her life. She loved that she could reach various environments and participate in whatever activity suited her mood in just a few short hours. She could surf in the Pacific Ocean, linger in and taste the wine country, ski in the Sierras, or rub shoulders with the diverse coastal Native American tribes to learn about their culture. But, since her return to Hopewell, what had once brought her great satisfaction now rendered her unsure and restless.

Her parents' deaths had prompted her disquiet. Shaking off the overwhelming feelings of loss had proven difficult, and she well knew her healing would take years of discipline. Now, after a week in the Bay Area juggling difficult negotiations with the University and real estate industry, she basked in an elongated square of sunshine reflecting up from the floor of her six-year-old home.

Thoughts of Lance intruded, as they had done since she arrived, and she closed her eyes, imagining what it might feel like if he kissed her. Seeing him again had spurred unrequited emotions to resurface, feelings she hadn't experienced in a long time, due to her last flame taking up residence with a well-endowed blonde he worked with. Neida had yearned to have someone in her life again, someone with whom she could love, respect, and share loyalty. But she doubted such a relationship was even possible. Considering her mother had dishonored her father and that Neida, herself, had never found anyone so committed to her happiness, trusting another man was out of the question. She wasn't about to revisit the same scenario, crying her eyes out for weeks over someone of the opposite sex whose princely charm never quite advanced past the frog stage.

A slight breeze tinkled the chime outside and rustled the mini-blinds, bringing her back to the present. Neida had lodged boxes in every cranny and nook of the house. At present, she sat cross-legged and wrapped wine glasses with newspaper, organizing their placement inside a crate to ensure the least amount of breakage. Since her arrival in Hayward, California, her lagging desire to pack up and leave her friends thumped at her resolve like a woodpecker against a tree.

Her friend Jill, a perky brunette she had worked with at the University for years, was busy removing books from built-in shelves along the living room wall, packing them in small boxes for easy handling. Neida was grateful for her help; if it weren't for Jill's organizational brilliance and the muscle of the rest of her friends, she might have never gotten this far along.

"What about this cigar box," asked Jill? "Should I toss it?"

Neida's head popped up. "No—please—hand it to me."

Jill maneuvered around the clutter of partially packed containers as far as they allowed and leaned to close the space between the box and Neida's hand.

The feel of the cardboard brought back immediate memories of her father. "I'd forgotten I still kept this on the bookshelf. I found it among dad's things when I closed up his house last February."

Neida examined the brown box and its antiquated lettering, its bowing lid, bound by a wide, brittle rubber band. At first touch, the strap broke and shot several feet away. She opened the treasure trove with slow, deliberate treatment and peered at the contents inside.

The jumble revealed a 1776, three heads half-penny—Janus copper, as some erroneously called it—and she held it up for Jill to see. "One of the many reproductions my dad picked up in England. He was so disappointed to find out it was fake."

A folded brochure from the Circle Star Theater's *South Pacific* presentation poked from underneath baseball cards, an unusual, heart-shaped skeleton key, ticket stubs, and Valentine's card she had made in the third grade. She had edged the bit of sentiment with white paper doilies and shimmery glitter, and her dad had displayed the treasure on the bookshelf for months after she had given it to him. Her heart ached to see the treasures again, and she would have slammed the lid shut if not for the old black and white photo that poked out from beneath the pile.

She slid the picture from its moorings. A paper clip attached it to an envelope addressed to her father. She hadn't noticed the photo on her previous perusal of the box, and viewing dad as a toddler in the arms of a Native American man stopped her heart.

"What is it?" asked Jill. "You look like you've just seen a Sasquatch."

"This is a picture of my father as a baby, and maybe my biological grandfather, if I'm not mistaken." She detached the envelope, removed the letter inside, and read it aloud.

> Dearest Arthur,
>
> Let me start by saying I'm sorry, son, for not telling you about your biological father. I can't imagine what you must think of me. I desire more than anything for the chance to redeem myself in your eyes and alleviate your distrust because of what you believe to be true.
>
> It has been days since my phone call to you, and I hope you've reconsidered my request to come to Michigan and meet your birth father, Askuwheteau. I never wanted to hurt you, but I decided it was best to wait until you were old enough to tell you about your genetic roots. I just didn't realize the longer I waited, the harder it would be. You were so close to Edward, and when you heard about his death, your devastation ruffled my heartstrings. I couldn't find the courage to tell you he wasn't your dad. I tried hard to patch up my relationship with him before he left for Ohio, but some things are just not meant to happen.
>
> Please forgive my weakness, and please know how much Askuwheteau loves you. Maybe if you came out to stay with me, you'd realize

just how much. Perhaps you'd even learn to love me again. Please, Arthur, please come home to Hopewell.

Love,
Mom

"Wow," said Jill. "A complicated web."

"You can say that again. I assume this is dad's reason for yanking me to California. It must have hurt him terribly." Neida slid the letter back into the envelope. "This picture just might help Lance and me when I get back to Hopewell, though—that is if I can break my contract with the University." She slid a finger over the elderly man in the photo then replaced it and the letter. She closed the lid and hugged the box of keepsakes to her chest.

"I thought you had that lawyer fellow figuring out your release from school."

Neida nodded. "I do. I should hear back from him any day now."

"I wouldn't worry about the technicalities, Neida. I'm sure everything will work out. Besides, we've come so far packing up your things, and the gang should be here soon. We should get everything loaded into the pod before nine and maybe have some time to party at my house before they leave. You're still staying with me tonight, aren't you?"

"I'd better. I'm not fond of sleeping on hardwood floors or sipping tap water for sustenance."

"Good. We'll eat ourselves into a stupor and have a few laughs."

From where Neida sat, she could see tears forming in her friend's eyes.

"I'm going to miss you, girlfriend," said Jill, holding out her arms toward her.

Neida rose from the floor and leaned across a box to hug her colleague, their embrace, a clutching and swaying of fond memories and friendship. She pulled back and wiped her eyes. "Now, don't get me started. I've barely gotten used to the idea of moving."

"I don't suppose you'd change your mind."

Neida only shrugged and smiled at her.

Hours later, the gang had used every possible crevice and cubbyhole to wedge a life's household into the eight by seven by seven-foot pod in Neida's driveway. The myriad ways to fit round shapes into square holes or how to turn objects at every conceivable angle so they'd stay in their place stunned her. Now that they had finished, trucks and vehicles, one after the other, beeped their horns as they pulled away from the curb on their way to Jill's residence. Neida waved and turned to see what was keeping her friend inside the house.

Jill met Neida at the door. "Man, I'm relieved you still have running water—in more ways than one. I almost didn't make it to the little room." She zipped up her jacket and threw her purse over her shoulder. "You won't be long, will you? I think Reggie's already started the festivities in the back of Bill's truck."

"I have to take a last look around and make sure everything's locked up. Thanks for letting me hole up at your place. My realtor just called a few minutes ago to tell me it'll be a couple more days."

Jill patted her arm. "You're welcome to stay as long as you like. In fact, I'll put in a few calls to your realtor and force her to delay the paperwork."

"Thanks, you're such a loyal friend."

Jill smiled and batted her eyes. "Oh, and don't worry about the pod pick-up. I'll make sure your stuff gets a royal sendoff. Hurry, now." Jill waved over her shoulder and scurried down the sidewalk to her car. And then she was off.

Neida watched the Mini Cooper speed down the road and break—on a run—through the stop sign at the end of the street. By the time Neida entered the house, her cell phone was singing from her purse. She answered it in the nick of time.

"Oneida ... Pastor Will here."

Neida cringed at the sound of his voice and wondered why she had given him her number before leaving Newaygo. "Hello, Pastor. How's everything around your part of the country?"

"Couldn't be better. How are you doing out there in California? Are you packed up about now?"

"We just finished, and I don't have much time to talk. I'm closing up shop for the night and heading over to a friend's house now."

"I hear John Warren's pulled a few strings for you."

Neida perked up with his revelation. "Oh? I haven't heard from him today, but I'd welcome that kind of news. The sooner I can get back to Hopewell, the sooner I can start the search for that artifact."

Pastor Will drew silent, and his pause stretched through the phone a moment or two. "So, you're still bent on searching for the relic," he said when he found his voice.

"Yes, of course, I am."

"For what purpose? It won't bring your grandfather or your grandmother back."

"Look, Pastor Will, I know you disagree with me about taking up this search, so can we just change the subject? Let's agree to stay on safer topics—no religious or antiquity talk, just pleasant conversation between friends."

The pastor murmured under his breath, something she couldn't hear, then he cleared his throat and said, "It's hard for me to sit idly by and watch one of God's lambs head for a dangerous cliff. But for the sake of getting along in the future, I suppose I can try."

Neida rolled her eyes. His drama peeved her, but it was best to finish the conversation on a high note.

"Is there any way I can convince you to join us when you get back?" asked the pastor.

Neida pressed her lips together, stewing over the breach of topic so soon after he said he would try. If she answered now, exhausted, irked, and sweaty, she'd likely bark through the lines.

"I know. I know," he said. "Mind your own affairs, Pastor Will ... but you can't condemn a man for doing his job. Can I do anything at your house or check on your mail for you?"

"Thanks, but John Warren is taking care of that; he has since I left."

"Very well, then. I'll let you get on to your friends. We'll watch for our newest Newaygo resident. Please be careful. Be safe."

"I will. Thanks for calling."

She ended the call and tucked the device and the cigar box inside her purse. Again, she kicked herself for giving Pastor Will her number. She really didn't know what to think of him. One moment he seemed on the level, and the next, he was snooping around into things that were none of his business. She'd have to be more careful with their conversations until she figured out what kind of a person he was.

She made a tour of each room, placated herself with empty closets, and extinguished lights before she headed back into the living room to case the empty bookshelves. Tidbits of newspaper and dust from the top reaches covered the floor. She'd come back tomorrow to vacuum and wash down the cupboards and walls, and then she'd be done with the place—forever.

The finality made her sag. Was she making the right decision? Did an inheritance and a childhood home stack up to a life built around friends and a career? Newaygo now promised unique avenues to explore—a personal mystery and treasure hunt, even Lance, who she had thought about often over the years—adding a sense of excitement and possibility that might have tempted her more had she not sworn off men. She could, at least, look. She saw no harm in that. *I'd enjoy the eye candy*, she thought. Of course, she'd made the right decision to stay in Newaygo, and the sooner she made progress toward her new life, the better. She picked up her purse, took one last look around, then locked up her past behind her.

CHAPTER SIX

THE WEEK SLIPPED BY BEFORE LANCE FOUND TIME to investigate the Graham & Associates storage facility. He'd dig for clues among his father's things for Neida's sake, though, if he were truthful, the hunt and the intrinsic value that Neida's relic promised the archaeological world held an underlying sizzle for him. A bonus: he'd search through libraries and ruins with an attractive woman, one he'd mourned over when her dad had taken her away. Visions of his step-cousin had occupied his mind for most of the week now. He didn't know just how to qualify that yet. He rubbed his thumb over Neida's business card then shoved it into his pocket, out of sight.

Lance stared at his father's containers and belongings that crowded the Graham & Associates' storage facility. He set all insignificant boxes aside—clothing, shoes, and an assortment of magazines. These, he'd deliver to the secondhand store when time afforded. At one end, scuba gear for underwater excavations, pickaxes, hoes, rakes, spades, and shovels leaned against the wall, just where his father had always stored them. Various pieces of furniture hulked throughout the facility, nothing he wanted to investigate now. He targeted his attention on the remaining boxes piled in a corner, almost to the ceiling, and hoped he'd find something—anything—to reward him for his efforts.

One box contained the financial records for his father's business and home. From another, he hefted a baseball signed by the 1987 Tiger's pitcher, Doyle Alexander. He took a seat on the rim of an old chair and leafed through several old photo albums and laughed at the pictures of his graduation from the University. His father had surprised him, and they had partied all night with some of his closest friends.

The abundance of equipment astounded Lance. *Did Dad ever throw anything away?* The items came in pairs, like the animals in Noah's ark: cameras and old film rolls, survey and dumpy levels, compasses and plumb lines.

His dad had buried two open-spooled measuring tapes beneath a basic tool kit, rolled in canvas. It nudged his curiosity. He fingered the rough fabric as though he could intuit his father's life from the fiber. He lay the bag on the cement and unraveled it like a scroll, unveiling one item at a time—a 4-inch trowel, a leaf trowel, a set of calipers, gloves, dental picks, and a magnifying glass, along with a measuring tape and some small make-up brushes. Lance ran his hand over the tools, implements representing a lifetime of discovery and fascination with a world of cultures. A lump rose in his throat. He rerolled the canvas and shoved it back into place.

Several containers housed thousands of excavation-photographs his father and grandfather had documented over the years—images of the Maadi ruins and the dig down in Oaxaca, the Bahamas underwater cave excavations, and the University of Michigan project in Kallithea, Greece. The photos fascinated him. They showed evidence he'd come from a multitalented family. If he became half the archaeologist Dad had exemplified, he might accomplish a quarter of what the man had achieved.

But his respect for his father was more profound than that. His dad had typified courage to stand for truth, no matter what particular scythe swung at his knees. Gentry Graham's brilliance took him to the University on a scholarship. And though a product of a manipulative mother, Dad had defied the woman's ranting, overzealous clout, and withdrawal of financial support. Just on brains and determination alone, he had built up the business far more than what Grandad had accomplished and had committed his time and talents to discover what the ancients had to offer.

Along with his scientific training, Gentry Graham had also left a legacy of deep and abiding faith in God, much different than Lance's grandfather's outlook on life, or so his mother had told him. "Nothing more important than a relationship with the one providing the clues," he'd always say. And his entire character exuded kindness, patience, and the pursuit of right over wrong, influenced by his dad's attraction to anything that built faith. From the time he sat at his father's knee and on into manhood, his dad's research about the Semitic theologies and how they related to the earlier Native American cultures had drawn Lance's interest. And he had continued his fascination within this particular course of study, but taking up the quest with Neida shoved him even closer to that goal.

Deeper in the search, Lance found a manila envelope wedged between a set of photos from a Missouri dig and a site down in the Kentucky Heartland. On one corner, written in pencil, the almost invisible words "Hopewell Excavation" jumped out at him. He frowned and took out the envelope, unveiling several photographs along with a couple of letters. Grandfather Graham, a tall, thin man with a crew cut and horn-rimmed glasses, stood at the peak of an excavation site next to a shorter man dressed in khakis and a baseball hat. They leaned on shovels and smiled as though their discovery warranted find-of-the-century status. Lance turned the picture over and read the writing on the back: *Edward Graham standing next to Thomas Blackhour from the Smithsonian Institution.* Someone had written the date of June 1964 at the top.

The other photos depicted the site from many different angles. One, in particular, shot from above, exposed what looked like skeletal remains. Another, taken at a distance, showed the Hopewell mound behind the old Victorian homestead where Neida now lived. When he flipped to the next photo, he did a double take. A rough, stone box, or casket as some archaeologists referred to these containers, was engraved with some kind of glyphs and lay at Granddad's feet. His grandfather held up part of the lid and pointed at a dangling tree root that, Lance assumed, had broken the cover in two. Unfortunately, the picture's resolution made it impossible to decipher the inscriptions on the box. No doubt, this was Neida's artifact.

Lance looked at the signature at the bottom of the letter. The man in khakis had written the earliest faded page.

> 8 June 1964
> Dear Edward:
>
> I look forward to our rendezvous at Hopewell on June 15. The Institution is quite interested in the stone box and its contents. They'll fund the project and outfit us with all the particulars. A couple of our best technicians and archaeologists desire to witness and support the event. Once we establish the contents, we will ship the artifact

and skeletons to the lab here in Washington, D.C., for further investigation. You stand to take your place among some of the most honored scientists in the field. Congratulations and good work.

Sincerely,
Thomas Blackhour
Office of Anthropology
Smithsonian Institution

The second letter revealed even more.

5 April 1965
Dear Mr. Graham:

I apologize for my delayed response to your letter of November 18, 1964. I realize you are anxious to receive the results of testing on the Hopewell artifacts we shipped to the Smithsonian last June 20, but I assure you these procedures take time and money. A top-notched team is working as fast as possible to comply with our contract, and as soon as we conclude the final test on the tablet and its stone container, I will personally bring you the report.

Coming to D.C. is pointless. Save yourself the time of a wasted trip. These artifacts are a significant find, and we want to take every possible measure to decipher the artifacts correctly before we reveal the information to the world. I'll be in touch.

The same signature closed at the bottom.

Lance frowned at the paper in his hand. For the Smithsonian to get involved at all meant they'd recognized the importance of the find. How strange that the Institution's literature and other archaeological journals had never discussed the Hopewell stone casket and its contents. Something seemed fishy, and grandfather must have realized the deception at the time.

Had the Smithsonian returned the artifacts? According to Neida, Althea accused Arthur of taking them. Nothing made sense. Lance rifled through the picture box a second time, lifted, rearranged, and categorized each packet of photos. Well into the task, oblivious to his surroundings, a rattle at the storage facility door jolted him to attention.

He glanced at his watch—nearly midnight. The rattle came again. *Who would be out here this time of night? And why?* He grabbed a shovel and sneaked behind a couple of bookshelves by the entrance. He waited, listened, tried to calm the thumping in his chest.

A car door slammed just outside, followed by uneven footsteps. Lance gripped the rod in his hand tighter, braced himself for the worst, hoped he'd see tomorrow. More rattling, and then with full force, the aluminum door catapulted upward from the cement. The rollers groaned and scraped along the unoiled tracks until the partition yawned open. The ruined lock lay on the ground.

The storage's disarray hindered the light emanating from the ceiling, casting the burglar's face into shadow. The man appeared taller than most, and muscles bulged from underneath his black suit. Lock cutters dangled from his hand. He darted glances into the corners, eyeing the room with the precision of a bodyguard. Lance swallowed hard. The confrontation would prove one-sided. He squinted into the dark behind the man to see if a companion complicated the equation, lessened the odds in his favor. A second figure stepped from behind the hulk and stared into the abyss.

Lance couldn't believe it. A prowler hadn't come to call, but an interloper just the same. He slunk from his hiding place with his shovel still cocked in front of him for protection and caught the trespassers' attention—and surprise.

"Lance?"

"Grandmother, why are you breaking into the storage facility?"

Lila Fiennes, white-haired and well-worn, wiped the astonishment from her face. A scowl replaced it. "Can't I even check on one of my grandsons? If I left the visits up to you, I'd forget what you looked like."

"You could have found a more appropriate time for a visit and entered through the front door."

Her face shriveled to disdain. "When better than the present? I'm only in town for a couple of weeks. I need to make the most of my time."

Her shrill but manly voice, an unusual characteristic plaguing his grandmother's side of the family, grated on his nerves. It was a harsh reminder of what his father had endured through the years—what they had all endured. His occasional outings to Washington, D.C. as a boy had leaned toward the horrific. Out of respect for family unity, his parents had forced Lance to accompany them and stay with Lila at the mansion she had inherited from her second husband, Cullen Fiennes. Someone had murdered Cullen on the Washington, D.C. streets for no apparent reason, and Lance's grandmother had insisted on their visits from the time of his demise.

Lance's bedroom had been fine, the food, top-notch, but the woman's incessant know-it-all ramblings managed to spoil any possible entertainment. She had spouted research from the books that had landed her great acclaim among her colleagues, and the memories made him grimace even now.

"I'm a busy man, Grandmother."

"Excuses as always, just like your father. Respect requires more of us, more of you, and someday someone will hold you accountable for your insolence."

"How did you know where to find me?"

The woman hobbled inside the storage room, favoring her right side, her cane clacking against the cement. She leaned over to examine a box on the floor and answered without looking up. "From that perky receptionist of yours, though I had to drag the information out of her. It seems your staff possesses an annoying habit of putting a sock in it when Lila Fiennes gets near their precious boss."

That was a lie. Kat had gone out of town to visit her mother for a couple of days, and his grandmother certainly wasn't talking about Carl. He eyed the woman's back. When he surprised her at the entrance, by the look on her face, she hadn't expected him to be here. That fact gnawed at his insides.

"I'll ask again. What do you want, Grandmother?"

"Are you deaf, boy? I have to hunt you down when I can."

"You and I both know that isn't true."

Lance looked over at the thug, still standing at the door. The man's free hand clenched and unclenched at his side. He examined Lance and his shovel, and his legs, thick as two stovepipes, twitched.

Lance repositioned his hands on the shovel and eyed his grandmother. "You want something, something of Dad's, and you'd go to extreme measures to get it."

Lila righted herself, peered over her shoulder with a smirk. "Do you make up stories just to provoke me?"

"You get back what you dish out." He'd crossed the line into impertinence, a place he liked to avoid, but his grandmother deserved little deference, and he couldn't help himself. "I haven't seen you in years, and just when I decide to aid my cousin with an important project, you show up on my doorstep—at midnight—with the hulk here and a pair of lock cutters. What are the chances of that? And what do you know about the stone box Grandfather found at Hopewell? Word travels fast in Newaygo, and you still have a few cronies in town to keep you informed. Isn't that why you're here?"

Despite her cane, she jerked around like a marionette, her eyes wide, her expression crumbling as she spewed her words. "That woman is *not* your cousin, or anything close to it. She's the product of an illicit affair that has tainted this family for years. Edward may have felt the need to rescue Althea from her shame, but I won't have my family sullied again because you want to dig up the past."

Lance leaned into his defense, picked off points in the air with his shovel. "If you're ignorant enough to deem their relationship an illicit affair, you might think twice. Grandfather and Althea never turned their back on Dad as you did. They even gave him a job."

She snorted her disgust. "Your father worked for me. Or didn't you know that? He found the very facts that prove those mound relics are fakes. He hated his father and his cause, who, by the way, was in it for fame and money."

Her words nicked at his confidence. "You're lying. Dad could never work for you. And he loved Grandfather Graham."

"Ask your mother. She'll confirm my story. Your dad wanted to help me. He searched those mounds from the Keweenaw Peninsula to the slums of Detroit just to dig up as much dirt as possible on those hoaxes."

Lance moved one step closer. "I'll admit the relics may include some forgeries, but despite all the books you've written to discredit them, you haven't answered some important questions. Like how does an uneducated forger know an ancient philosophy unfamiliar to anyone in this country at the time? Or how can a mere sign painter know the Greek, Phoenician, and Egyptian languages extensively etched upon the artifacts? James Scotford had to get the information somewhere."

"Don't dangle your fake assumptions in front of me, young man. I'm the expert. Scotford could have copied those characters from any comparative alphabet table, from any number of dictionaries available at the time."

"And know just how to convey the systematic arrangement of the symbols with accuracy? That would have been a pretty hefty feat for someone who was ignorant. Where did Scotford find the time to produce as many dye stamps or character styles used to inscribe the various tablets and relics? How do you explain settlers and farmers discovering the artifacts forty to fifty years before Mr. Scotford discovered his first artifact in 1890? Even Chief Joseph carried an Assyrian cuneiform tablet in a medicine bag around his neck, one he claimed the generations had passed down from his white ancestors."

"You've memorized your lines well."

"It's true. And because of naysayers like you and the books you've written, scientists will never make an effort to find out where the artifacts originated. How can you be so closed-minded?"

"Because of what it suggests."

"And what is that?"

Her eyes narrowed. "That the relics are tools of warped minds and manipulators who would deceive the public just for notoriety among their colleagues."

"That should sound familiar to you. Afraid your colleagues will prove your work wrong?"

"I'll destroy them."

"Destroy the artifacts or the people who uncover them?" Lance doubted she'd resort to violence, but her cause annoyed him. It always had. And she'd not force her way into his life and push him around—or tell him tales about Dad that couldn't possibly be true.

He stepped toward his grandmother, triggering the heavy at the entrance to tilt forward, muscles tensing. Lance didn't care. "Why are you here, Grandmother? You're after something. Tell me."

"Don't order me about, boy. If you insist on bringing to light anything that pertains to those hoaxes, let me warn you now. I'll fight you. I'll shut down your business."

Lila streamed for the door, her cane a useless appendage, her swagger, more abrupt and straighter than when she arrived. The force of her fury peeled the bodyguard from his spot and whirled him about to open the car door. He secured the woman, pointed a last glare at Lance, all steel and promise, and then jumped into the driver's seat and slammed the door. The limousine bolted into the avenue where the buildings swallowed the car's retreat.

Lance leveled his gaze on his hands, tense, white, still gripping the tool in front of him. He breathed a sigh and forced himself to relax. His grandmother had never threatened him before, but the dynamics of this visit had changed things. Purpose drove her actions, and though thwarted, she desired to drive a wedge between him and those he loved. The encounter hovered in the room like an acid cloud ready to rain its poison on the remaining boxes he'd yet to explore. But it was late. He'd replace the ruined lock, bolt the place tight, and return another day, maybe with company next time. But before this adventure was over, he'd figure out what Lila had come to steal.

When he stepped into his house later, Lance's wristwatch beeped 2:00 A.M. His boxer, Pompeii, greeted him, snorting and wagging his nub tail. Lance rubbed the dog's ears and neck, part of the nightly ritual, and threw his keys and the envelope with the photos and letters on the hall table. His cell phone lay right where he forgot it the previous morning, and he cycled through the voice messages as he leafed through his mail.

"Hey, Lance," the fourth message blurted out, "it's me, your long lost, exhausted cousin."

Lance stopped reading, enthralled by her voice.

"This week has whizzed by, and I still have too much to do. I hate to say it, but I'll be a couple of days longer. I need to finish some business with my real estate agent, so I should arrive home on Wednesday. I have some news and something to show you." She paused for a moment, and then, with a tenderness that clutched his heart, she said, "I'm anxious to take up where we left off. See you soon."

He ended the message with a sharp stab of his finger. He looked at his watch again—too late to return Neida's call. He hoped to tell her of his significant discovery and about the strange encounter with his grandmother.

Pompeii barked. Lance looked down at his friend whose whole hind end wagged like a metronome. The dog's face angled sideways in anticipation. The sight dragged him back to reality, resolve spreading to his soul. Forget his grandmother's threats and her stab against his father. Neida needed his help, and he'd give her that help. The night's events proved a point: If the artifact had caused Lila Fiennes to bring out the artillery more than fifty years after its discovery, then its message was far too urgent to remain hidden on a shelf somewhere.

Smiling, he ruffed up Pompeii's ears. "Okay, boy, let's head up to bed." Pompeii jumped at the suggestion, dashed for the stairs, and climbed them two at a time without once looking back. Plodding up after him, Lance deliberated about Neida's delay, his father's loyalty, and his grandmother's ruse. Despite how hard he tried to master an objective attitude, the news and his inability to control any of it haunted him throughout the remainder of his restless night.

CHAPTER SEVEN

DESPITE HIS TOSSING AND TURNING, sometime during the night Lance fell asleep. He wasn't sure for how long, but in the early morning hours, a grueling nightmare intruded and jerked him back to consciousness. He lay in his bed, drenched with sweat, heart racing, and his eyes scanned the darkness of his bedroom for reality. The lingering night vision pushed him to get out of bed and retrieve a glass of water. Standing over his kitchen sink, he stared at the tiled backsplash, inlaid with pyramids and ancient hieroglyphs, as he occupied his thoughts with projects he'd have to complete over the next week. The distraction failed to clear his mind of his dream. When Lance later took to his bed, the impression of Neida far away in California, spurred questions about how she faired, whether his dream was some kind of omen warning him about her well-being. He had to aid her in some way, but so far, she had refused his help. Her flat-out refusal for him to accompany her and hasten her move to Michigan had weighed on him, so much so, he was sure his nightmare had everything to do with her repudiation.

Now that his grandmother was on the warpath, an urgent sense nudged him to rise up and protect Neida from the evil forces already collecting in her absence. And to protect himself. The coming days ahead were sure to be ruthless, and he vowed to never be found without a plan.

The letters in his father's sundries had also augmented Lance's uneasiness. Had the Smithsonian released the artifacts to his grandfather fifty-odd years ago, or had Grandad's efforts fallen through the cracks? Had he died before the transfer had even taken place? So far, Lance's efforts had found nothing to hint at the outcome.

He supposed his position as an archaeologist might enable him to contact Thomas Blackhour with ease, and he hoped the man still lived and possessed ample connections with the Institution. He vowed to call the Smithsonian later in the day. Perhaps he'd shed some light on the relic's whereabouts before Neida returned home.

Exhaustion took its toll about 5:00 A.M., and Lance slipped into a heavy sleep, waking about ten o'clock—two hours past his usual office invasion. He sat up in bed and rubbed his face with his hands. Sluggishness glued his eyes shut, but despite his fatigue, he traipsed to the shower and let the hot water drench him. After dressing, he filled a thermos with freshly brewed coffee, grabbed two pieces of fruit, and headed in for the day.

As soon as he sat behind his desk, Lance called the Smithsonian and asked after Thomas J. Blackhour. He was glad the man still held a position on the board, though Blackhour was unavailable at the moment. The receptionist promised him a call-back later in the day.

Keeping himself busy, Lance leaned back in his leather chair, focused on the transcript from a conference he'd attended a couple of months ago and several other documents that required his immediate attention. About 2:00 P.M. the phone rang beside him, and he answered with his usual casual greeting.

"Mr. Graham, this is Thomas Blackhour returning your call. My secretary said you're concerned over some artifacts in our possession. How may I help you?"

"Yes, Mr. Blackhour. The artifacts in question belonged to my late grandfather, Edward Graham. I understand you were the archaeologist on the excavation at his home in the summer of 1964, and that the stone box and tablet were shipped to D.C. for analysis. I've taken up the search for these artifacts with a cousin who has asked that they be returned for study, as stated in the contract. I'm trying to ascertain whether the relics are still in the possession of the Institution or whether they were returned to my grandfather."

An imperceptible pulse reverberated like the wings of an insect in the moment's pause. Thomas Blackhour answered slowly, an obvious calculated response. "Mr. Graham, I'm not sure I remember the precise excavation to which you refer. We performed quite a few field studies back then, and enormous quantities of artifacts have come and gone within the Institution since that time. If such an excavation took place, those involved might not remember the specific details surrounding the undertaking."

"But I'm certain you headed up the project, Mr. Blackhour. I found two letters from you, telling my grandfather that you'd be in touch with him. You must remember the artifacts since you had such personal knowledge about the venture."

"I'm quite a busy man," said Blackhour, his voice strained. "Please don't assume I retain intimate knowledge about every project I've worked on."

Heat seared Lance's cheeks. Blackhour was being difficult. "But you must have logged in some kind of paperwork on the project, some type of report. Would it be possible for you to search through the historical documents and help us out with this dilemma? I can send you a copy of the letters and a photograph of the stone box, if you like. It's imperative that my cousin and I find the artifacts. It's a matter of great urgency."

"I'm sure it is. Though you can't expect the Institution to answer every request that comes its way. However, since you say I was the archaeologist on the dig, I'll personally look into the records as soon as my schedule opens up. I'll be out of town for a week on important business, but as soon as I return, I promise you, I'll give your request the attention it deserves. 1964 did you say?"

"Yes, that's correct."

"And where did the excavation take place?"

"Newaygo, Michigan. At the Hopewell estate"

"And your cousin's name?"

"Neida Graham. Her grandmother Althea, who recently passed away, was married to Edward Graham, and has asked Neida to make sure the artifact is returned to the estate. Miss Graham asks for your compliance."

"All right, then. I've written down the information. I'll get back to you as soon as I investigate the matter."

"Thank you, Mr. Blackhour. I'll be waiting to hear from you. Have a nice day."

Lance hung up the phone and leaned his cheek into his hand. *That was informative.* He'd be lucky to receive any results from their conversation if he even heard back from Blackhour at all. And he couldn't shake the idea that the man had lied about what he knew. Hadn't Blackhour's letter hinted the Smithsonian was excited about the find? Such excitement and attention usually ensured a personal footnote in the back of one's mind, and even a brief marker written in the history books. He just hoped his inquiry into the matter hadn't started insidious wheels in motion, impossible to turn back. Until he knew what was going on, he'd best keep the call to himself. He didn't want to place undue worry on Neida's shoulders before she even had a chance to settle in.

Neida stepped through Hopewell's door and sighed relief. She parked her luggage in the hallway and headed for the kitchen for some bottled water. The last week and a half's activities released the weight she'd carried for years and had perked up her spirits. She had committed to the move, and with the help of friends, had packed up her house. The pod company promised to ship her belongings across country within the next few days. Her real estate agent assured her he'd snag a buyer by the end of the week, and thankfully Mr. Warren had managed to find mutual grounds to break her contract with the university. She'd find plenty of time now to search for the stone box and her grandfather—if he were still alive.

With water in hand, Neida kicked off her shoes and plodded to the parlor where she settled on the settee. The air seemed chillier than before she left. She removed the blanket from the back of the couch and snuggled under its plushness, adjusting until she found a comfortable position. She had slipped near unconsciousness when the doorbell punctured her reverie. Her eyes shot open. She groaned as she stood and trudged into the hallway to open the door.

Lance gaped at her with a boyish smile, as though he had just unearthed a unique discovery of intrinsic value. He wore a brown tweed jacket and red tie, casual, but dressy. His curls were slicked back, and they looked darker than usual.

"Wow, you're dressed up," she said. "What's the occasion?"

"I met with a new client today. Jeans and a tee shirt make little impression with the well-to-do. They're all about the money, and tweed is the closest thing I own to a business suit."

Neida laughed. "You're not a fan of fancy attire?"

"My motto is *tennis shoes or bust*."

She opened the screen. "Do come in and take off your tie before you break out in hives."

Lance obeyed, sauntered inside, and tugged at the noose around his neck. He paused to peer down at her. "I'm glad you're back, Neida."

Neida unraveled under his intense gaze. She gawked after him as he proceeded into the hallway. It took her a moment before she moved to close the door.

"So, what brings you to this neck of the woods?" She turned to him, wide awake now, donning a veil of composure. "Not that you drove far, considering we're neighbors and all."

He rolled his tie into a ball and shoved the wad inside his pocket. "I took a detour, hoped you were home. Glad that you are."

"Can I get you some bottled water? I'm afraid that's all I have right now."

"That sounds good. Sales pitches always leave me parched."

"Take off your jacket. Relax. I'll be right back." Neida headed for the kitchen. By the time she returned with Lance's refreshment, he had disappeared from the hallway.

"Lance?"

"In here."

She followed the sound of his voice into the library where he examined the display cases along the wall.

"I hope you don't mind my nosiness," he said, without turning around.

"You're welcome to investigate at any time." *I'd cherish his visits*, she thought.

Still jacket-clad, he hovered over the relics, seemingly engrossed in his investigation. She stepped near him, and it closed a void somewhere inside her.

"I've always wanted to examine your grandfather's collection," he said, righting himself. He peered down at her as she handed him his water. "I never found the opportunity."

"As I said, you're welcome anytime."

Lance took a long swig of his drink before he continued. "I've quite a few displays myself. I've collected some fascinating specimens of several ancient cultures. Why don't you come by soon? I'll give you a guided tour."

"I'd like that." She studied him, spellbound by how put-together he appeared in his tweed jacket and open-necked shirt. The pause became awkward, and she pretended to readjust a birch bark basket on its mount. "So, you never returned my call."

"Yeah, I apologize. Kat managed to hustle me from client to dig and then to piles of paperwork without any trouble. However, I do want to show you something."

Neida pivoted around.

Lance didn't say anything, only gazed at her. A grin played with the sides of his mouth.

She shoved his arm. "Do tell. Don't keep me in suspense."

He chuckled and said, "I went through my father's belongings and found an envelope with several photos of an excavation, a dig my grandfather conducted on your Hopewell mound out back. The pictures include an ancient stone box."

Neida gasped. "*The* stone box?"

Lance smiled and brought out a small photo for Neida to view. She took the image from him and examined the man in the picture and the artifact at his feet.

"I assume this is our relic," he continued. "I found two letters included in the envelope. They confirm that Smithsonian archaeologist Thomas J. Blackhour came to Hopewell with a team of technicians in the summer of '64 to examine the piece."

Neida turned to face him full-on. "Blackhour? He was at my Gran's funeral. He watched us from a distance and later carried on a severe conversation with Pastor Will in my home. John Warren mentioned Blackhour had conducted some kind of business with my grandmother recently. He said his attorney-client privileges prevented him from divulging what kind of business that was, but he warned me to stay away from the man. That he might be dangerous."

"Did you ask the pastor about it?"

"Hardly—I'm avoiding him. He's like a one-track record about converting me and how he thinks searching for the relics is going to stir up trouble."

"Maybe I can talk to him and find out what he knows."

She nodded. "Thanks, that would be helpful. Did they find anything interesting inside the stone box?"

"Blackhour's letters mention a tablet, and that he shipped the pieces to the Smithsonian's lab for further investigation." His expression shriveled as he concentrated on the image in Neida's hand. "The letters don't sit well in my gut, though. Blackhour apologized to Grandad for the Institution's delayed report—almost a year later. I can't figure out whether they returned the relics to my grandfather or not. The Smithsonian may still have them. Or maybe Blackhour pilfered them from my grandfather."

"How can we find out?"

"Cold-calling the Institution won't help us," he said with conviction. "They'd be months investigating the matter, if at all. However," Lance held up a finger, "I just happen to know a family acquaintance that used to work at the Smithsonian's SMSC."

"Their storage facility?"

He nodded. "Fitz Emory mentored my father and me, and he's a good friend to our family. He might recall our relics."

"When can we talk to him?"

"I'll make some calls. He lives in D.C., and I'll have to arrange an appointment with him. Oh, there's something else." His face clouded. "My Grandmother Fiennes paid a visit to my storage facility in the middle of the night."

"Is that a good thing or bad?"

"It's not good. I caught her breaking in. And she wants me to believe my father worked for her, that he rallied around her cause. And what's more, she threatened me."

"Threatened you? Why?"

"She's promised to shut down my business if we hunt for the relics."

Neida gaped at him. "Then we'll forget the search."

"I didn't say that. My grandmother doesn't scare me."

"I won't be the reason you lose your business, Lance."

"I'm not going to lose my business. Althea's asked you to search for the relics and bring them back. That's good enough for me." He set his bottle on the case and grabbed her hands in his. "Hey, don't look so grim. I've got a few tricks up my sleeve. Plenty of them. Now, what did *you* find in California?"

Neida paused a moment, contemplating his sincerity, then hurried to her carry-on in the hall. She retrieved the photo and the letter from her father's cigar box and returned to Lance.

She handed him the picture and pointed at the image of the baby. "This is my dad." Her finger glided to the man holding the child. "And I assume this is my grandfather."

"Hmm, the howler," said Lance. "I think I recognize him. He used to come to town often, but I haven't seen him in a while. He does look like a proud parent here."

Neida scowled. "Too bad the feelings weren't mutual. I also found this letter." She slid the missive from the envelope and handed it to Lance. "Gran apologized to him for something that took place between them. She begged Dad to come home so he could get to know his biological father. Do you think someone else around here might know something about him?"

Lance skewed up his mouth, frowned in thought. "I suppose Pastor Will would or Ms. Walden, the old librarian and town gossip. Maybe Wade Newman. He was the sheriff in the fifties and sixties."

"Will you introduce me?"

"Of course, I'll make a few—wait." Lance locked eyes with Neida. "What am I thinking? My mom would know him. I'll call her tonight and arrange a meeting. The first chance we get, we'll take a trip down south to see her. The sooner we have some answers, the sooner we can nip this mystery in the bud."

"Thanks, Lance. How would I do this without you?" The fact is she couldn't have. Gran had dropped a gale-force squall into her lap, and she wasn't sure she could stand up to it. Added to that, Lance's grandmother's threat to shut down his business was a whirlwind in the making. She couldn't let that happen, since she was to blame, though Lance's lack of fear in the matter gave her hope that Lila's bark was worse than her bite.

Lance swept a strand of hair from her shoulder and, as if he had read her thoughts, said, "Try not to worry or think you're at fault, Neida. Believe it or not, I think you and I will make an indomitable team against the elements."

She flashed him a weak smile. *Indomitable* wasn't exactly the word she'd use to describe the yellow streak traveling up her spine.

CHAPTER EIGHT

GRAND RAPIDS SPRAWLED near the Grand River, approximately 30 miles from Lake Michigan. The city ranked the second largest in the state due to the massive furniture industry of the late 19th century. The metropolis, now more economically diverse, boomed with various manufacturers and a thriving tourist trade.

"The Hopewell culture once built hundreds of mounds throughout the area," Lance explained as they drove toward his mother's home. "They're the most well-preserved Hopewell tumuli in the western Great Lakes region. About 40 hills made up this group, and with Grand Rapid's expansion, less than half remain. But it's late. Mom expected us 30 minutes ago. She'll worry if we get sidetracked too long." He drove out of the way to show Neida Millennium Park and promised to bring her back to experience a taste of the famous Norton Mounds up close and personal.

Past the park, Lance turned into a neighborhood with wide avenues and an abundance of shade trees. Oakdale Senior Living

Center, a three-story complex, spread over several acres at the end of the street. The community touted yellow buildings, white shuttered windows, and trellised landings, reminding Neida of something out of New Orleans. A golf course showed green in the distance.

"Let's keep the news about my grandmother to ourselves," said Lance. "I don't want my mom to fret about my security."

Neida shrugged. "Fine by me."

They parked, and Lance guided her along the pathways, sidelined by ivy carpets. An Olympic-size indoor swimming pool—the one Lance told her his mom swam laps in every day—sparkled through a massive window. He directed her to a ground floor suite and rapped with the lion's head knocker. Neida expected someone far frumpier to respond than the same petite, redheaded woman she'd known as a child.

Frances Graham's complexion, smooth and ivory-based, still looked youthful, but with a hint of wrinkles etched around the eyes. Her appearance leaned to the impeccable: pearl earrings, a cream-colored silk blouse tucked perfectly into black slacks. Her hair, cropped to the collar, hung straight and curved about her face in gentle wisps. Her figure was to die for.

"You made it," said Frances.

Lance smiled his apology. "Sorry we're late."

"Come sit with me in the kitchen," she said, motioning them inside. "I'm preparing our supper."

Lance stepped forward, and his mother threw her arms around his waist in a long embrace and kissed him on the cheek. When she let him go, she leaned in and hugged Neida. "Welcome, dear. Lance told me you had grown up to be a beauty. I always hoped you'd find each other again."

Neida flinched at her sentiment and genuine gesture. Lance considered her beautiful, and she wasn't sure what she thought about that, but his sentiment thawed some of the icy edges and cravings inside her, the first inklings of warmth she had felt since her parents had died.

Frances directed them through the Tuscan-style living room, past a rustic fireplace with floor-to-ceiling bookshelves towering on either side. An array of pictures adorned one wall. One, in particular, caught her attention. She'd recognize Lance anywhere. He posed next to another boy in a middle-aged woman's embrace.

"Is that Robert?" she asked Lance.

"Yes, and my grandmother, Lila."

"What's Robert up to these days?"

"He handles security for several state government officials in Lansing."

Frances reappeared from the next room. "Which reminds me, Robert is curious when you'll call him again. It's been a while."

"The phone works two ways, Mom. He hasn't bothered to remember my number in the last couple of months."

"Well, you're both too busy for your own good. There's nothing more important than family now, is there?"

Frances preceded them into the kitchen, and Lance grimaced at Neida behind his mother's back.

A few minutes later, as they ate chicken divan and crisp salads in the dining room, Frances asked, "So, how much do you know about your real grandfather, Neida?"

Neida paused, thinking about what she'd learned over the last few days. "Not much, really. Gran was pregnant with my dad when she married Granddad Graham. I hope I'll learn more about him as I read her journals. So far, the details are rather sparse. About all I know is that his name was Askuwheteau."

Frances pushed back a wisp of hair. "I hope she did write more about him. She didn't like sharing the troubled parts of her life. My husband, Gentry, hated how his mother acted toward your grandmother. Lila considered Althea's relationship with your grandfather as nothing more than an immoral interlude with a savage. She almost owned the local government back then, coming from money and all, and she obtained a restraining order against Edward when he married Althea, so he'd never see Gentry again. But before Edward went missing, Gentry went to see his father. They sparked up a relationship, which lasted until Edward disappeared on that dig in Ohio. As soon as he was of age, Gentry left Lila's home for good."

Lance leaned forward over his salad. "Then, Dad *didn't* work for Grandmother Fiennes?"

Frances's brow crinkled, but she didn't answer.

"Mom?"

"Your father chided himself over that episode. He was a brilliant man, even as a teenager. On the other hand, Lila could convince the most adamant opposition to believe anything in those days. She promised Gentry support and a free ride to the University if he'd become an advocate to her cause. So, Gentry became a bulldog. He found quite a bit of consequential evidence accepted as gospel at the time, and that formed the basis of Lila's first book."

"But I thought Dad believed that the mound artifacts were authentic."

Frances nodded. "He did—later—after he stumbled upon his father's research. Edward's documented quest convinced Gentry of the puzzle's complexity, a far greater challenge and reward than what Lila offered him. He finally broke off his relationship with her, and when she threatened to withhold her support and inheritance, that only made him all the more determined to prove his father's assessments true. He then realized his resentment was damaging to you, so he later tried mending some fences."

Lance nodded. "And that would be our quarterly visits to D.C., his attempt at civility."

"Yes, dear. Your father struggled with those trips, but he wanted you to form your own decisions about Lila."

"Yeah, and that's a bitter pill."

Neida registered the emotion behind his words and nodded at Frances. "I empathize with your husband. My father told me Gran died, and I believed him until her lawyer called me two and a half weeks ago. A lifetime too late. Now I find out my ancestry is nothing like he led me to believe all these years. It's disturbing. Gran wants me to uncover and accept the truth."

Frances patted Neida's hand. "I can't even imagine how hard this must be for you. I never believed the things Gentry's mother said or approved of what she did. Please believe me."

Neida warmed to the kindness reflected in the woman's eyes. "Thank you. I appreciate your sincerity, however, my great grandparents' opinions weren't much better than Lila's."

Frances sat back, and her expression turned reflective. "Althea's parents were wrong, though all their animosity was just the tip of the cat's tail. Your grandfather lived on the Isabella Reservation for years—until his wife died. Then he and his daughter moved to Hess Lake soon after; I suspect to be closer to Althea, but he was probably too hurt and too stubborn to admit it."

Frances stood and hurried to a small cabinet just off the dining room and dug inside a drawer for a moment. She brought a book back to the table as she leafed through its pages.

"Althea once asked me to drive her out to the lake after Dad Graham's disappearance. She needed to turn to someone, to let your grandfather know she was alone again. But that proved a disaster—your grandfather, an aggrieved widow and father, talking to her the way he did. Bless her heart. She cried all the way home. She wanted to reunite with him, but too much had happened by then to make amends. I still might have his address, though." She turned a couple more pages. "Yes, here it is." Frances handed Neida a dingy piece of paper.

Neida examined the handwritten note and wondered if finding her grandfather could be this simple. "May I copy this?"

"Please take it. I've no reason to keep it anymore. If he and his daughter Winona are still around, maybe Lance can drive you to their house. It's not far from Newaygo, and you'll need a man to protect you. Bitterness sometimes rears an ugly head from both sides of the fence."

Neida frowned. Frances's underlying current and tone certainly didn't sound hopeful.

"One of several trips we'll take soon," said Lance. "We're searching for a stone box Granddad excavated from the Hopewell mound on Neida's property. Her grandmother wants her to find it, and maybe her grandfather can point us in the right direction."

Motioning for Neida to stay in her seat, Frances, who had already stacked the dirty plates and silverware, headed for the kitchen sink. "I thought that the stone box and its tablet fell into a black hole or something."

Lance's head popped up. The astonishment on his face mirrored Neida's surprise. He stood and met his mother as she returned to the room, carrying a set of dessert plates. "So, there *is* a tablet inside," said Lance.

"Yes, dear. It sure did create a big commotion among the Native Americans."

"Do the artifacts belong to the Ojibwe?" asked Neida.

Frances shook her head. "I don't think so. They belonged to whatever cultures built those mounds, and to Granddad after he found them, I suppose, though the local tribe felt they owned some claim to them."

Neida gave her a sideways glance. “Why would the Ojibwe claim the relics if they belonged to another culture?”

“Native Americans are touchy about burial grounds and the relics interred within them,” said Lance. “And it’s my opinion that some Mun-dua blood runs through Ojibwe veins as well as through other of the Great Lakes’ tribes. Perhaps they broke off from the mound-builder nation earlier in their history as some believe.”

“Mun-dua?” Neida frowned at the name. “I’ve never heard that term before.”

“That’s what the Ojibwe called the mound-builders,” said Lance. “At least one group of them. They were also called the Puans. Some anthropologists claim the mound-builders were not a single culture or society but a widely detached set of related populations, like the Adena and the Hopewell. It depends on the specific time frame of events what specific group we’re discussing. But I’d like to embellish with my particular theory, if I may.” He took the plates from his mother and set them on the table. Frances returned to the kitchen as he continued.

“Oral history suggests the Ojibwe allied with the Ottawa and the Potawatomi. Together they annihilated the Mun-dua, and many of the Algonquin-speaking tribes claim that same history. According to Native American lore, all the tribes feared the Mun-dua. That’s when the battle for power ensued, and the Ojibwe and their allies destroyed them. Some speculate that the tribes’ hatred for the Puans was so great that after the final battle around present-day New York, they pursued those who escaped to the land southward in Kentucky, perhaps to the Falls of the Ohio. Those remnant people who escaped slaughter assimilated into the Algonquian-speaking camps and adopted their ways. It was their best chance of survival.”

Neida nodded. “I remember the story. Wasn’t this culture a white-skinned, blue-eyed tribe that controlled much of the territory around Lake Ontario? People also called them the Talligewi or the Allegan, and the Native Americans claim giants lived among them."

"One study out of Chillicothe shows the Hopewell DNA ties to the Ojibwe, Mi'kmaq, and Pawnee nations, as well as some other North American tribes. Some samples from the mounds show an Adena origin, and even others imply they derived from an Asian background. Four out of the five tribal DNA haplotypes occur within the test samples."

Neida sighed. "That makes the truth more difficult to uncover."

"I doubt we'll ever know the complete truth. The legends are so mixed now. Even the Dakota led some other cultures from Mexico up the Mississippi River to do their own bit of conquering and assimilating."

"Do any of the tribal chants tell something about who the Mundua were?" asked Neida. "I'm always stunned by how little the Ohlone know about their history. I suppose some of their lack is due to the autonomous villages that made up that culture. After the Spanish displaced the tribes in their missions in the 1700-1800s, the Ohlone lost their identity. The anthropological reports and present-day data are all they have left to tell them who they once were."

Lance shook his head. "The Native American youth around this area show little interest in learning their legends. And with the destruction of these mounds and artifacts, the truth is gone for good. The scientific community just deems the evidence forgeries and calls it a day. Some even manipulate the findings to advance their particular theory."

Neida leaned on her elbows. "You'd think someone would be curious enough just for the number of antiquities that still exist."

"Yeah, treasure hunters out to make a fast buck or museum curators who soon lose interest and stick the relics in a back room somewhere. That's what's so frustrating. President Andrew Jackson's *Manifest Destiny* fueled the attitude that God's authority gave them the right to profit from a piece of property belonging to another. That, in turn, gave Americans the right to drive the indigenous cultures west of the Mississippi, place them on reservations, and take or destroy everything they owned. Although, I'm not saying the Native Americans were innocent in all this. All cultures have made mistakes throughout their history."

Neida sat back. "Then, if the tribes had already destroyed the Talligewi's possessions before the European influx, what would be left to tell their story?"

"Evidence still exists today," he said. "All they had to do back then was dig into those mounds and listen to the tribes' stories to understand the past. Instead, they chose wanton destruction and barbarity to wipe away the remnant people who also believed their Creator had brought them to this land—a people who were here *long before* the white man. Some of the Adena and Hopewell cities became more populated than 4th-century London and Rome, yet until the 1900s, only a handful of scientists cared to connect the dots. It's America's best-kept secret."

Frances came back from the kitchen carrying a chocolate cake, dotted with orange slices. She laid the dessert on the table and used the knife to emphasize her words. "When Granddad found that stone box, the Ojibwe around here resented him. And when Blackhour took the pieces back with him, I thought they'd declare war. It turns out the tribe had every right to be angry. If you ask me, those government men were far from on the level. Dad Graham inquired after the relics a few months later, and those museum people acted like they didn't know a thing. Can you imagine? He trusted those men."

They gaped at Frances.

"Are you saying the Smithsonian lost the artifacts?" asked Neida.

Frances sliced into the cake and placed a thick slab on a dessert plate. "In my opinion, they locked them up somewhere and threw away the key. I suppose they never intended the media to find out about them."

A question mark formed in Neida's mind. "But why would they want to cover up an important discovery? The Smithsonian's motto is the increase and diffusion of knowledge."

Frances shook her head. "Not this knowledge."

"So, they deciphered the language then." Lance leaned in. His eyes glinted. "What was its message?"

Frances paused, holding the chocolate-coated knife in mid-air, and crinkled her forehead. "You know, that's something we never found out. Your grandfather hinted at something earthshaking at first that it would change the face of Christianity, then he totally clammed up about it. He obsessed over Blackhour's double-cross, about not getting his due, and then raced off for a second excavation to that cave and just never came back."

Lance glanced at Neida.

She flashed him a perplexed look and directed her curiosity at Frances. "Do you believe Grandad Graham transcribed the script correctly?"

"He got that language fellow—Rex Willett—renowned in his field. I'm sure he deciphered the language with accuracy, well—as far as we understood such things back then. Then he disappeared in Ohio, too, only nobody knew the location of the cave. We assume they died there. We searched for clues through your Grandad's papers and things for years. Eventually, we just gave up hope."

"Neida's grandmother believed someone murdered Grandad," said Lance. "Have you heard that story? Do you believe the rumor?"

Frances sighed. "I often wondered if Althea believed that claim, though no one could find any proof of foul play. I suppose we'll never know what happened."

Lance rested his chin on his fist. "I wonder why Dad never told me about this."

Frances laid the knife on the rim of the plate. "He'd already beaten that horse by the time you came into the firm. Once your father discovered his dad's notes and that they'd found that symbol on the artifacts—just like the ones on the rest of the Michigan Relics—his all-consuming focus centered on the mound-builders and where they came from."

Lance nodded. "No doubt the symbol is the one solidifying element in all of the discoveries we've found throughout the years. We need to take the time and learn more about what's right in front of our faces."

Frances reached over and patted Lance's arm. "Just be careful, sweetheart. Those relics stirred up a lot of bad feelings in some circles. I suspect that's why they're missing. You still might run into a few kooks who'd frown at your pot-stirring. Maybe even that Blackhour fellow. The subject sure did send Lila into a tizzy. Could be it's the reason someone murdered Cullen."

"Both of her husbands were murdered?" asked Neida. "That's rather odd."

"Kind of makes you wonder who the culprit was," said Lance.

Neida raised her eyebrows and nodded. "It's suspicious for sure."

Lance placed a hand on top of his mother's. "But pot-stirring or not, that won't stop Neida or me. I owe it to Grandad. I owe it to Dad and to all the archaeologists who ever stood up for a true find." He gazed at Neida from across the table. A determined lift of his chin caused the light to sparkle in his dark eyes. "And I owe it to my cousin here, whose grandmother asked her to uncover the truth."

Frances tilted her head, a curious calculation riveting her expression. She eyed first Lance and then Neida.

Neida looked down at her plate of chocolate cake and wished she could dive into obscurity. She treasured the decent and honorable man sitting across from her more than she was willing to admit. Still, whatever conclusions Frances now concocted about Lance and her relationship, she couldn't let that distract her from the task at hand—to find her grandfather. Maybe he'd know where to hunt for the artifacts and, more importantly, why their message caused them to go missing.

CHAPTER NINE

BY THE TIME THEY HAD FINISHED TALKING to Lance's mother, the hour had precluded an excursion to Hess Lake. Frances made up the couch for Lance and put Neida in the spare bedroom for the night. Neida had enjoyed herself, and in the morning, she hated to leave, but her hunt for her grandfather was foremost in her mind. After an exchange of hugs and well wishes, she and Lance promised to be careful in their searching and that they'd return as soon as their hunt for hidden treasure ended.

Thunderstorms accompanied them on their ride north. Neida settled into the seat of Lance's jeep and soaked up the scenery. Once they hit Newaygo, all of ten minutes passed before Hess Lake, gray and choppy, appeared through the haze under threatening clouds. They speculated whether they'd find her grandfather alive or whether his daughter still lived at the address Frances gave them. Yet, as consolation, the ride allowed Neida to explore more of Michigan, even if from behind the car window and under sporadic, torrential rains.

"So, what is this symbol your mom talked about last night?" she asked.

Lance hunched forward and peered at the road through the quivering veil of water that drenched the windshield. "It's the sign of the Creator. It's a cuneiform style of writing similar to that of paleo-Hebrew that we find on most of the Michigan Relics. The Ojibwe still use the symbol in their sacred lodges today."

Neida studied his profile. A Hebrew origin made perfect sense. She had toyed with the theory when she discovered the cuneiform piece in her grandfather's display case at home. "Then you're suggesting that both the Hopewell and the Ojibwe were of Semitic origin."

"Both their DNA samples match a rare Haplogroup X gene sequence that originates in Europe, North Africa, Western Eurasia, and among the Druze. The latter group lived primarily in Syria, Lebanon, and Israel. Ojibwe and Mi'kmaq oral traditions suggest the tribes anciently traveled across the Atlantic to North America, and the Ojibwe hieroglyphs on their birch bark scrolls, confirm those legends."

"How can the Smithsonian ignore such powerful evidence?" she asked.

"I wouldn't say *ignore*. I think my mom is right. They've probably just buried the facts. When farmers first plowed up the mounds, they found an abundance of artifacts and mound formations that defied explanation. Some archaeologists believed the Mun-dua a highly advanced race that came here apart from the Native Americans. Like Cyrus Thomas and John Wesley Powell of the Smithsonian, other scientists concluded the mound-builders and the natives were one and the same. Powell, who was the son of a minister, already believed the Native Americans were savages, and he didn't appreciate how much the Institution had spent exploring the mounds. He wanted to keep the research in a comprehensive Amerindian study."

"Someone must have continued to analyze the evidence," said Neida.

"Yeah, but more and more scientists stopped seeking the truth and got in bed with the Smithsonian, even though evidence abounded against their scientific bullying. Some mounds corresponded in angles and trajectories found in the Egyptian pyramids. These people even tracked the moon's motions and delved into other advanced technologies, but the Smithsonian, along with popular opinion, just explained it away. Heck, the U.S. army plowed under the oil lamp and menorah mounds years ago, and I've even heard the Smithsonian dumped a boatload of artifacts into the ocean."

Neida frowned. "Again, I find that kind of story hard to believe."

"Oh, I have no doubt it's true."

"The Ohlone were mere hunters and gatherers," said Neida. "If the Mun-dua showed such advancements, you'd think someone would stand up to the railroading."

"A few did, but most were either incompetent or eventually refused to go against the established theory. And academia only held on to these opinions throughout the years. If we find this stone box and tablet, we'll fight against harsh opposition, trying to convince anyone they're real."

"I'm sure. Come on, changing the face of Christianity? That smacks of a fairytale. That religion is all a bit of regurgitation, don't you think?"

Lance turned off the highway into a forested neighborhood and stopped on the side of the road. He faced her, his voice reflecting annoyance. "May I ask why you find Christianity so hard to believe?"

"Christianity is unoriginal. Equivalent doctrine exists in pagan religions throughout the world."

"Did you ever think with the multitude of stories running rampant that they might derive from one true source? You've studied language and how man alters the essence of a dialect through his migration patterns or population shifts. Facts transform in the same way. Remember the telephone game we used to play as kids? By the time the communication transfers from the start of the line to the end, the gist of the message alters."

Neida pointed at his chest. "That's exactly my point. Heaven, hell, sacrifice, the immortality of the soul all belonged to earlier Pagan faiths. There were many crucified Gods: Khrisna, Esus, Quexalcote. I think Christianity and Judaism are just man's attempt to grasp for explanations of what he can't explain."

"But you're a scientist, Neida. It seems to me you might test some of those theories you're so adamant about believing. Every culture known to man has similar creation and flood stories within their histories. Some people even believe those gods you just mentioned quite possibly describe Jesus Christ himself. Perhaps in your examination, you'd find that Christianity contains more meat than what you might suspect."

Neida huffed. "My mother crammed quite a few unfounded beliefs down my throat when I was a child, but I refuse to cleave to any fabrications no one can prove. A god who exists everywhere and nowhere at the same time is a mass of confusion to me."

Lance leaned closer. "Somewhere in the middle of man's grasping lies the truth, Neida. The various ideologies can't all be right—or wrong."

"But how does this doctrine relate to a people who arrived in this country *before* the time of Christ? How could their beliefs change our understanding of Christianity?"

Lance let out an exasperated sigh. "Even Abraham believed in Christ. All the Old Testament prophets testified of him. And the prophet Jeremiah foretold God would scatter the House of Israel throughout the world. If the Great Lakes cultures, like the Mundua, prove to be the Phoenicians or Copts or some other Semitic peoples, they'd leave artifacts behind depicting their particular philosophies. They might even be what Christ referred to when he said, 'other sheep I have, which are not of this fold.'"

Neida grimaced. All this talk of shepherds, scattered people, and trite beliefs gave her a headache. "Well, whatever the artifacts advocate, I'm going to need proof before I cave to any preconceived notions."

Lance raised his eyebrows. "What if those preconceived notions, as you call them, offer a different view to modern Christianity, a purer form of belief. Take the Michigan Relics. Farmers first documented these artifacts in the mid–1800s, years before James Scotford and his buddies made their discoveries."

"Who's James Scotford?"

"He excavated over 500 mounds in the early 1900s, with the help of Michigan's former, discredited Secretary of State and a Catholic priest. Popular opinion believed Scotford forged and planted his fakes throughout Michigan. Even his relatives signed affidavits claiming they saw and heard him pounding away on the counterfeits at night."

"And you *don't* think forgery is possible?" She couldn't believe he could be so gullible.

"Scotford and his buddies may or may not have been profiteering, but with the discovery of 3,000-10,000 artifacts or more, I'd bet most of the pieces are real. At the very least, they provided the sources for some of the forgeries. And farmers found the relics in 27 different Michigan counties and even in

Illinois. I don't care what the skeptics say; our treasure is real. And you and I are going to prove the facts beyond any doubt."

At least he had the decency to include her in the equation. She'd have to remind him who first instigated the search for lost treasure.

Lance turned to face the steering wheel and placed his hand on the key. "Our methods of analysis are much more sophisticated now than at the turn of the 20th century. If I could only get my hands on that stone box ..." His voice faded into silent contemplation as he stared out the window. He finally set the car in motion, and they traveled the rest of the way in silence.

Neida's aspiration to uncover the artifacts promised to plunge her into something far deeper than what she first assumed or that of a rudimentary hunt for lost treasure. She also wanted to understand why the antiquities were so important to her grandmother and what part she, herself, played in the puzzle. She wasn't ready to believe the relics held any religious implications. Whatever they discovered, she hoped she'd find her grandfather alive and well.

By the time they found the small, cottage-like cabin abutting the shore, the weather had worsened. They parked in front and stared at the dirty white house with its two large, paneled windows and three rain-soaked steps leading up to a red front door. The porch roof provided insufficient covering in the slant of the storm. At the yard's end, the rutted mud formed several significant pools that drained toward the beach behind the house, where glimpses of the lake poked through the forest.

"My mother issued me the warning again, just before we left."

Neida turned to Lance. "What warning?"

"To make sure I came with you today, to protect you."

"Ah, she did mention something like that last night."

"Mom said that, even as a little girl, your Aunt Winona acted downright nasty when my mother took Althea to see Askuwheteau."

"Why?"

"I guess she's overprotective of her father. She attempted to push your grandmother off the porch."

Neida sighed and studied the house again. "Maybe time has softened her feelings. That is if she even lives here anymore."

"Well, there's only one way to find out. Are you ready?"

"As ready as a one-legged man in a butt-kicking contest."

Lance chuckled and patted Neida's leg. "I'll get your door."

He barreled out of the jeep to Neida's side, keeping his head down against the pelting rain. As she exited, he used his jacket to shelter her back and directed her through the sludge to the slight cover of the overhang. A sliver of the mini-blinds inside the house flicked closed. Someone had watched their approach. Neida hesitated, her courage suddenly waning.

They worked at removing the mud from their shoes, but the porch mat had well-served its purpose. The small rectangular carpet oozed with layers of gunk, which stuck to their soles no matter how hard they tried to wipe them free.

Neida knocked. The door finally cracked open, and a round-eyed child peered out at them. He said nothing, only gawked.

"Is your mother here?" asked Neida.

The little boy shook his head.

"How about your daddy or your babysitter?" asked Lance.

The child turned to someone just out of view. Without warning, a woman pulled the boy out of the doorway and came back to scowl through the small opening.

"What do you want?" The shadow inside concealed the woman's face, but her aggression stabbed into the dim light outside.

"My name is Neida Graham, and this is my cousin, Lance Graham. We're sorry to disturb you, but we're searching for my grandfather and his daughter. Are you Winona? Is this the home of Askuwheteau?" Neida stumbled over the name.

The woman opened the door further. Her face clouded, making her deep-set eyes sink inward, emphasizing her frown. "I *am* Winona, but *you* are not part of this family."

Neida whipped out the picture from her purse, protecting the surface against the rain, and held it out for Winona to see. "Is this elderly man your father?"

Winona examined the image. "Yes." Her voice rose to a dare.

"The baby he's holding is my dad. My grandmother swears your father is my grandfather."

"Think what you like, but you will never be my father's grandchild. You must earn that right. Now go away and leave us alone."

The offending sentences jabbed at Neida as hard as the spiteful rain. She pushed against the closing door. "But is he still alive?"

The partition slammed shut in their faces.

Neida tensed. After coming this far, she refused to allow such hostility to inhibit her from her goal. She put the picture back in her purse and knocked on the door again.

Lance squeezed Neida's shoulder. "Come on. Let's get out of this deluge."

She knocked again.

"Neida ..." he said with emphasis.

She sighed and acquiesced, allowing him to usher her through the muck back to the car. He helped her scrape some of the mud from her shoes with a stick then closed her in. He sprinted around to the other side and repeated the process for himself. Once inside, they sat in silence for a moment. He turned over the ignition just as something moved by the trees.

Neida grabbed his arm. "Lance—"

He peered at her.

"Look over there, by the side of the house."

He followed the direction of her pointing finger. A stooped man shuffled out from behind the shrubbery. He motioned for them to wait.

The rain obeyed his gesture too, lessened until the swipe of the wipers revealed only a misty smattering on the windshield.

Neida squinted to examine the man across the yard, the very one that had stood outside Gran's window the night she died. "That's my grandfather."

"He looks kind of like the guy who used to come into town." Lance turned off the motor.

They hastened out of the car, ignoring the mud, sloshing toward the man who now motioned for them to follow him.

He led them past the main house to a small lean-to hidden by a circle of trees behind the property. He wiped his shoes on the mat and entered, leaving the door open. Neida and Lance glanced at each other. They, too, cleaned their soles and ducked through the entrance after him.

The dark interior swallowed visibility. Only an insignificant window on the far wall shed diffused light into the room. When Neida's eyes adjusted, the old man materialized again, his image sharpening when he turned on the light. He sat on a bed in the corner, nodded at two chairs pushed up to a small table in the center of the floor. "Please sit," he said.

They situated themselves in front of their host. Once seated, Neida studied him. Deep lines etched his face, though his complexion seemed lighter than she expected of someone claiming his heritage. His high cheekbones and the deep Nasolabial folds on either side of his hawk-like nose painted a classic Native American picture—much like what stared back at her in the mirror every day. In the dim light, his eyes appeared dark, a strange shade of gray, and they pierced into Neida as if he were as curious about her as she was about him. Though silvered, his hair still showed streaks of black and hung in a long braid down his back. He wore a coarse poncho over his loose-fitting pants and denim shirt, and his shriveled hands and cuffs barely protruded from under the covering. He appeared much different than the image in her purse, but she would recognize him anywhere. He was an older version of her father.

"You're my blood grandfather, aren't you?"

He remained silent for a moment, then lifted his chin as he studied her. "Do you want me to be?"

She yearned to uncover her past and to belong, and the words rushed out of her. "Yes, more than anything."

A hint of a smile raised his cheekbones, and he nodded. "That is good. The ancestors have beckoned you back from your father's world. You have listened and obeyed their wisdom."

"You were outside Hopewell the night Gran passed away," said Neida.

"Althea called to me, and I went to meet her."

Neida frowned. "She called you on the phone?"

He shook his head. "You do not understand."

"Gran was in no shape to use the phone. And I stood at her bedside. I saw you—heard you from her window. You never came to her."

"Appearances aren't always what they seem. Your grandmother summoned me, and I sang to the fathers as they guided her over the threshold into the *Land of Shadows*."

"Into the Land of Shadows?"

His face remained patient, but his eyes reflected sorrow.

Shame pierced Neida to the core.

"The place you call the afterlife," he said.

"Yes, I know. How did you know Gran was dying, or to come to her just then?"

He raised his chin again. "You ask too many questions. You have much to learn."

His second reference to her ignorance made her grit her teeth, but she quelled her emotions and chose her words with care. "Then, please, enlighten me."

Askuwheteau lowered his head.

"I've been away too long," she continued. "I'm ignorant of the past, about how you and Gran met. Until two and a half weeks ago, I knew nothing of my true heritage."

The old man lifted his gaze to Lance. He studied him with intensity.

Neida grimaced at her bad manners. "I'm sorry. This is Lance Graham, a step-cousin. He's the grandson of Edward Graham—my white grandfather. He helped me find you."

Lance nodded in greeting.

Askuwheteau acknowledged him in return and only considered him a moment longer before he shifted his gaze back to Neida. "Treat your heritage with respect, Granddaughter, and accept your responsibility to The People. Our Fathers named you, and this name tells you of your purpose—to perform a great service to those who came before. Since the Creator brought our people to this land, they have passed down the prophecy until now. Our Fathers mean for you to complete what they foresaw."

Neida knew his reference to the Fathers was just Native American superstition in play, like those among the Ohlone. But she wouldn't, couldn't, tread disrespectfully over his beliefs. "Please tell me what the name Neida has to do with my purpose?"

Askuwheteau's mouth flattened into a firm line before he spoke. "Why do you call yourself Neida?"

"My friends call me that. They have for years."

"Your given name is not good enough for you?"

"No, I like my name. The shorter version is just easier, I suppose."

"Easier is not always better. That which the ancestors gave you implies you are here for a reason."

Neida opened her mouth to ask him to explain, but he held up his hand to silence her.

"It is enough. What good is the wisdom of a teacher if the student is unable to hear his words? You must learn in layers, like the crest behind your home that teaches history from the inside out. I know many questions burn in your heart, so I will tell you only the information you need to know. Your father did not understand or care about The People. His ways were the white man's ways, yet his blood is of noble ancestry, and because of that, the fathers found favor with him. They blessed him with you and whispered to him your name."

"What does my name mean?" She couldn't help but ask.

He waited a long time to respond, no doubt, to teach her patience. "You are Oneida, *The Awaited One*. Do not treat the name lightly. You are to return to our people that which many have dared to rob from us."

On the night she died, her grandmother had called her *The Awaited One*. The significance hit her now. "Are you *He Who Watches*?"

Askuwheteau nodded. "All our names have meaning."

"What was taken from the tribe? The relics Gran told me about?"

"Some answers are for you to discover for yourself. That is the way you remember things of importance."

"But—"

"It is enough."

Neida stared at her grandfather, her mind bursting with questions. "I'm sorry, Grandfather. I have to know. Gran asked me to find the artifacts and bring them back. Do they belong to The People? Lance, show my grandfather the photo of the box," she said as she looked to him for support.

Frowning, Lance hesitated before he dug into his jacket pocket to present the picture. Askuwheteau turned away from the offering.

Neida took the image from Lance's hand and held it closer to her grandfather. "Is this the relic? Do you know where I might hunt for it?" She didn't want to seem impertinent, but she needed some answers.

Lance rose and touched Neida's shoulder. "Come on. Let's go now."

"But—"

"It's *time* to go." His emphasis cut off the rest of her sentence.

She peered up into his face. The gravity in his expression made her close her mouth.

Lance took the picture from Neida and returned it to his pocket. He held out his hand to help her up.

She stood and followed him to the door, where she stopped and pivoted around. "Please forgive me, Grandfather. I'm only trying to do as Gran asked me. I need to know if I'm on the right track, where to begin."

Askuwheteau lifted his head, and the lamplight caught the surface of his tear-filled eyes. His shoulders bowed under some invisible weight that seemed to push them down. "Begin in your heart," he said. "It knows the road to follow."

Lance pulled on her arm, and Neida walked out into the storm, more confused than when she arrived.

"Begin in my heart?" Neida asked for the umpteenth time as she and Lance, shivering and dripping rain, stepped through Hopewell's front door. They entered the parlor where Lance placed logs in the fireplace and prepared to light a fire.

Neida stood in front of the settee and watched his back. She wondered at his silence, just as she had her grandfather's. Lance had kept to himself in the car while she complained about the strangeness of their visit, the audacity of Winona slamming the door in their faces, the relentless rain, and her ruined shoes. His indifference confused her.

"Aren't you going to say anything? First, my grandfather's snub, and now yours. I've been talking to myself all morning." Tears stung, but she forced them back and released a frustrated growl.

Lance swiveled from the fireplace, his face wrinkling with concern. He rushed to her and pulled her into his arms, his warm embrace swallowing her whole. She wanted to lean into him, but in her awkwardness, she pushed at his chest and tried to step away. He refused to let her go, so she finally ceased fighting and rested her head against him.

After a stretched moment, he stepped back and cradled her face in his hands. His mouth rearranged into a boyish grin, just like it used to when they were kids. "I *almost* said something back there," he said, "but you're an *ace* at talking to yourself."

She couldn't help but laugh. Lance's chocolate eyes flashed with his smile, reminding her to relax. The moment's tirade now seemed pointless, and embarrassed, she lowered her head and rambled into his shirt. "I *was* on a roll, wasn't I? Sorry, I never could hide frustration well."

He lifted her chin again. "I hope you didn't think me angry with you back there."

"The thought *did* cross my mind."

"I've rubbed shoulders with many of the tribes' elders. A more patient approach gets you a lot further than probing. When he's ready to tell you more, he will."

Even as a little girl, her curiosity demanded explanations; she had lost a few friends that way. Neida shook her head and sighed. "My grandfather must find me a disappointment—an impatient academic who needs proof to believe anything, whose blood is a mixture of two different worlds at odds with each other. No wonder, he cried."

Lance chuckled. "Don't be so hard on yourself. He's proud of you and, I'm sure, pleased that the prophecy will now come to pass. Wouldn't you be, especially if your people had passed on the tradition since the time they had come to this land?"

Prophecy? More like unproven wishful thinking. Neida smiled and peered into his eyes. They were deep and comforting, and she wanted to crawl inside and take shelter there. And then she realized the moment's intimacy, his warm hands on her back and shoulder, the way he gazed at her. She felt her cheeks sear. She stepped away, searched for a neutral topic, a place to focus her attention.

"So, where do we go from here?" She hoped he'd understand she meant hunting for artifacts, not the intimacy of the moment or the closeness they once shared. She had to stay neutral when it came to Lance.

He remained silent for a moment, little creases furrowing his forehead, though his gaze locked onto hers. "I guess I'll call my grandfather's friend tomorrow."

"And that's our last lead. What if the man is dead? How will we locate the relics then?"

"Trust me. We'll find the artifacts. You can bank on it. One thing's for sure, *Oneida Graham* ..." He grinned as he emphasized her given name. "I'll be right by your side through our entire hunt for treasure. I give you my word."

"Really?"

He nodded.

"You may get sick of me."

His impish grin widened. "Never. I'm looking forward to it. More than you know."

CHAPTER TEN

THE DAY AFTER MEETING NEIDA'S GRANDFATHER, Lance went into work for a while to check his father's research. But as he sat at his desk and poured over document after document—his efforts soon proved a useless undertaking. Neida's image clouded out the words on each page, became an annoying distraction. His spark for her had reignited, but the real question begged whether he should allow himself the indulgence.

From the moment she arrived in Michigan, Neida's uniqueness had captivated him—the way she leaned her head to the side when she entertained an idea, how the black luster of her hair intensified her ebony eyes and fair complexion. She was his equal—intelligent, inquisitive, determined, and though she had lived thousands of miles on the other side of the continent, she had chosen a field of study very close to his own. Neida had gotten under his skin, he well knew, and few women affected him that way, only one other in his lifetime. The distraction would only complicate things now, might insight gossip over too close a family tie, even though their gene pool relationship was unrelated.

He refocused his attentions on his studies, though not for long. A knock sounded before Kat leaned into the office. "Mind if I bother you a second?"

He motioned her to enter. Kat crossed to the desk and placed a couple of documents in front of him.

"What's this?"

"The contracts for the Williams and Beckett digs. You need to sign them today so that we can organize the help before Labor Day."

"Is everything in order? I don't want to hire the guy out of Lansing again. He was a punk and did shoddy work. I've got a business to run here and a name to protect."

"I'm one step ahead of you, Boss. No punk allowed, and a new guy ready to take his place. All you need to do is sign the papers."

He grabbed the expensive gold pen from his dad's unique desk set and scrawled his signature in the usual places. "Thanks, Kat." He handed her the documents and, once again, immersed himself in his father's notes.

Kat's movement toward the door spurred his memory about his morning's mission, and his head shot up. "Oh, Kat ... do me a favor, would you? Look up Fitz Emory's number. Call him and transfer him over, please?"

Kat pivoted around as she approached the door. "Fitz Emory? Your grandfather's friend? Is he even alive?"

"That's what I hope to find out."

"And about what topic should I inform him we're calling?"

"Ask him if the Smithsonian is still hiding treasure from the public these days."

Kat raised an eyebrow.

"Never mind, just tell him Edward Graham's grandson needs to talk to him about an important matter."

"You've got it."

The door closed, and he refocused his attention. The phone beeped five minutes later, and he hit the speaker button. "Yes, Kat."

"Fitz is on the line now."

"I appreciate your help."

A second later, he heard familiar heavy breathing in his ear.

"Fitz, Lance Graham here. It's been a while."

"Well, I'll be," said the raspy English accent on the other end. "How long has it been?"

"The last time we talked, my dad and I were digging up trouble on the Keweenaw site. Fifteen years now, I think."

"How is your old man, anyway?"

Fitz's question conjured up a recurring ache in Lance's chest. "Not as well as I'd hoped. Dad passed away last year."

"Passed away? Why didn't anyone tell me?"

"We tried to, but your secretary told us you were in Europe and unreachable."

"Dash, I would have liked to have been there. He was a good man, a tad more level-headed than his father."

Lance swallowed his emotion. "Yeah, we miss him, but I'm not calling about my dad. I want to ask you a favor."

"Why certainly. Anything. Name your deed."

"I've discovered some information about a stone box and a special relic it contains. Granddad found the piece in the old Hopewell mound on his property, and the facts point to a Smithsonian cover-up. I wanted to bend your ear about the dig. I thought you might remember something."

Fitz whistled long and low. "Ooh, my boy, some things are better left hidden, if you get my drift."

"So, you *do* recall?"

"Of course, I do. The experience shoved me knee-deep into a dark and dirty episode, one that's haunted me for over fifty years."

Lance sat forward in his chair. "Care to explain?"

Fitz paused for some time before he answered. "We'd better discuss this in private, lad. The phone tends to sprout ears."

"Then, may I fly out to D.C. to discuss the subject with you?" He refused to back down, no matter how dark and dirty the episode.

"Are you sure you want to dredge up this can of worms?"

"More than sure."

Fitz grunted. "It's your funeral ... and possibly mine, if anybody finds out I've enlightened you. But I'm an old man, and I'm tired of carrying around their nasty little secrets. Be a relief to lighten my load."

"So, where do we meet?" Lance asked.

"Meet me at the Castle grounds next Monday at 10:00 A.M. by the Fountain Garden. A smashing rendezvous to rat the skunners out."

"Do you mind if I bring a friend?"

"You don't quite understand the scope of the deed I'm talking about. This topic involves dangerous men and comes with a steep price if the wind blows in the wrong direction. You'd better let your friend appreciate what he's getting into."

"We'll see you next Monday."

Fitz chuckled. "You Grahams always did possess the grapes. It's Monday then."

"At 10:00 A.M. sharp." Even though Lance wished him a good evening, the line went dead without the man ever hearing his words.

卌

Neida poured over Gran's journal, read another dead-end passage, then rested her head against the sofa. She enjoyed learning about her grandmother and her father as a child. How strange that her entries lacked any mention of Grandad Graham, and she wondered how much the other journals might teach her about the events surrounding the artifacts' discovery. For an experience as earthshaking as Frances described, Gran must have recorded her thoughts about the event.

The phone rang. Neida sighed and rushed from the settee to answer it.

"Oneida," said the man on the line. "I hope I'm not disturbing you."

Neida drooped when she recognized the voice. Pastor Will had called her every day this week. His constant interruptions annoyed her, and she refused to hide her irritation this time. "Well, I *am* resting," she said. A little manipulation of the truth wouldn't hurt. She wanted to get back to the journals.

"So sorry—I'll be brief. I'd like to invite you to the potluck we've scheduled for tonight. We have some good cooks in the church. You won't regret participating."

Neida tensed at the suggestion. She'd just have to cut his expectations off at the pass. "Thanks for thinking of me, Pastor. However, I've already made plans. Maybe some other time."

"Then, is there something I might do around your property? Life can be difficult without a man to do the heavy work. I'm pretty handy with a saw."

"All fine on the home front too. I appreciate your call. I better go now." She waited for him to sign off, but his voice fell silent.

"Pastor Will?"

The pastor cleared his throat. "Are you, by chance, avoiding me?"

She paused, stumbled for an explanation. "Uh, no ... I'm busy right now, that's all."

"Oh? I thought you were resting."

Neida clenched her teeth at the faux pas, searched for words. "Yes. Yes, I am. But I'd just like some space if you don't mind. I mean, with Gran's passing and all. I'm sure you understand."

"And again, I don't mean to press, but talking about your grief might help."

The guy's persistence irked her to overflowing. "I'll talk to you later, Pastor. I'm fine. Thanks for calling."

She hung up before he protested further.

Neida went to the kitchen to get a soda and took the refreshment back to the couch, picked up her book, and found the passage where she'd left off. After she digested several more entries, a determined knock at the front door jolted her.

Lance had called her earlier, excited about something he wanted to tell her, so she hurried to answer the summons. As soon as she opened the door, she stepped back in surprise.

"Winona. What are you doing here? Or, uh, please come in."

Neida pushed the screen wider to let her aunt enter. The woman's face was still soured and brooding but softened from the last time they'd met. Despite her aunt's resentment, she showed Winona to the parlor and directed her to the settee as she cleared Gran's journals to the side. "Please have a seat."

Winona didn't budge from her position behind the sofa. "I'm not staying. I'm only here because my father asked me to apologize. But understand, I'm not ashamed of what I did. He is old and lives by the ways of the elders. He thinks I should treat you with respect and to honor your purpose among our people. I tell him we must be wary of outsiders, that you will take everything we have, but he is stubborn. He believes you are *The Awaited One* and that you'll bring light back to our nation."

Neida stiffened at Winona's shoddy opinion of her character. "I don't want to take anything away from The People, especially from you and Grandfather."

"You appear at my door, claim my father is your family. You would take all that I have."

Neida crossed her arms in frustration. "If you feel so adverse towards me, why did you even make an effort to come?"

"I told you. My father asked me to apologize."

"Despite what you think of me, I only wanted to get to know you both. I didn't even realize Gran was alive or that you and Grandfather were my family until Mr. Warren summoned me to Hopewell. Perhaps you can appreciate my desire to remedy the lack."

"Why?" Winona rushed around the sofa toward her, her face distorted with resentment. "How can anything be made better because of it? You understand nothing of The People's ways. You grew up in the white man's world, learned traditions that poison the waters, the skies, and the land. Your people steal what they want, whenever they want, and leave us only the reservations where they expect us to live. I won't let you take the one thing I have left. I'll protect my father, even if he *is* willing to trust you."

"No doubt, you felt the same about my grandmother."

Winona's expression furrowed. "She groveled at my father's feet and begged him to take her back. Askuwheteau, the watcher of sacred things, is not to be tossed aside and taken back at anybody's whim. I'm glad he broke her heart."

Neida studied her aunt for some time, finally issued a sigh. "Winona, your anger is poison, the same toxin of which you accuse the white man. If The People hold a double standard, you are no better than those committing the same offenses. We won't resolve a thing until one or the other rises above such hatred."

Neida stood taller. "I possess the blood of both The People and the white man. It wasn't my choice, but perhaps if I use the best from both sides, I can make a difference. I only want to discover who I am and the purpose of my being here. Please, let me get to know you. You are the family my father deprived me of all my life. Please don't do the same." Neida held out her hand toward her aunt.

Winona lowered her gaze to Neida's offering of love. Her eyes filled with tears. After several seconds, she reached out, seemed as though she'd take Neida's hand, but a knock at the door shook her. She dropped her arm to her side and said, "I have to go." Embarrassment hampered her voice. She dashed from the parlor.

By the time Neida reached the front door where Lance stood on her threshold—surprise written on his face—Winona had swept past him and had sprinted halfway down the walk.

"I must be seeing things." Lance closed the screen. "That woman is the express image of your aunt."

Neida nodded. "My grandfather asked her to apologize to me."

"Did she?"

"Hardly that, though I might have convinced her I'm not the ogre she thinks I am. Your knock came a few seconds too early."

Lance winced. "Sorry. My timing stinks."

An old Ford truck raced past the house. Neida watched its retreat down the drive as she continued her explanation. "She thought I wanted to take Askuwheteau away from her. Can't she see how anxious I am to have family in my life again, that my intentions are honorable?"

"Give her time. She'll warm up."

"Whether she does or not, she won't keep me away from my grandfather."

"Hey, she realizes she can't stop your relationship with him. Her father raised her to respect the decisions of her elders. Her coming here today proves that fact. If your grandfather wants you in his life, she'll possess little clout on the matter."

Neida sighed and closed the door. "She doesn't even know me. How could she make such terrible assumptions about my intentions?"

"That's my point. Winona doesn't know you, and I doubt you'll win her over easily. People believe what they want, despite the facts staring them in the face."

"I can't understand such ignorance. Seeing ..." Neida stressed the word "is believing."

"How can you trust that?" Lance asked with mirth in his voice. "The world's a complicated place, Neida. Nothing is black and white. A shade of gray lurks somewhere behind the scenes. You know, doubt, fear, hope, faith. It's called theory, and people rarely check the facts. And their indifference keeps the formula interesting. It's what makes us who we are and the world a more colorful place in which to live. Even science would fare better with a tad more faith."

"Faith?" She scowled at the word. People like Pastor Will catered to faith, not intelligent individuals who think for themselves. "Don't you believe scientists should hold to the results of their observations—hard facts?" she asked.

"Yes, of course. But you know as well as I do that the analysis of our theories can never be considered final. We continue to test them, and we modify the results as we discover new data. Pre-conceived beliefs only prejudice those results." Lance inhaled and sighed. "All I'm saying is sometimes we need to analyze our hunches with an open mind. Find a little hope, a little faith. Isn't that the whole premise behind the scientific method of inquiry? We question and create a hypothesis, give our predictions, then test the snot out of them with a hope we'll find some answers."

"Hope has nothing to do with it," she said with emphasis. "That's putting the cart before the horse, don't you think?" She headed for the parlor, wasn't about to fall into his spiritual trap.

Lance followed on her heels. "But don't you hope, just a tad, when you test your theories about the Ohlone and their language?"

Neida shrugged. "I don't feel any particular way. I wait for the facts."

Lance grunted. "I've grown up around the sciences all my life, avenues dominated by testing evidence and theories. I've seen too many miracles amidst the specifics to write off the inexplicable. Solid facts aren't the only bearers of truth, Neida. Faith is the essential element in such a process, and grasping makes a man ask questions. It pushes him to work hard for the rewards until he believes and hopes for things he can't see or touch. That's what my father taught me over the years."

Neida tsked. "You sound like Pastor Will."

"Then I'm in good company."

Neida focused on the firmness of his jaw, the sincerity radiating from his eyes. *Why does he buy into all this stuff?* she wondered. She often wished she could trust in the unknown as he did, but she never had. Never would. How many times had her mother insisted that God built people into far more than what they could create themselves? Neida couldn't ignore the many inexplicable occurrences existing in the world, like the powerful draw that had pulled her toward Michigan or the change of character that some of her mother's converted friends had experienced. Drug addicts and released convicts among the bunch had turned to charity and kindness just by believing in a God they couldn't prove. She supposed these anomalies from the norm could be considered faith, but she'd need a lot more proof that God was at the foundation of those transformations before she'd admit such things to herself or anyone else. And she didn't want to argue right now, just craved to hear his news.

"I don't know, Lance. I'll think about it awhile. Let's just change the subject. What were you so excited about over the phone?"

They settled on the sofa. Neida curled up against the arm. Lance only grinned at her.

When she gave him a *you'd-better-spill-your-guts-right-now* evil eye, he blurted out his report.

"Fitz Emory is alive, and he knows about the artifacts."

At last, they were getting somewhere. "Does Fitz know where they are?"

"He wouldn't tell me over the phone. He said it's best to speak to him in person."

"Then, when do we meet with him?"

"I've booked us on an early Monday morning flight for D.C. We'll rendezvous with him at the Smithsonian Castle at 10:00 A.M. I hope that's okay?"

"Of course, it is, but what did he say?"

"There's a lot more to this Smithsonian cover-up than I thought. He suggested some shifty characters are involved, and they made the relics disappear back then, people who might still be alive and averse to anybody knowing the truth."

She could think of two. "Like Blackhour? Maybe even Lila?"

"Or maybe others," he countered, obviously willing to give his grandmother the benefit of the doubt. "Perhaps I should take someone else with me in your place. Or go alone."

"Don't be ridiculous, Lance. I'd never forgive you."

"I'm serious. If what Fitz says is true, these people are heavy hitters, Neida. Our hunting for the artifacts might draw unwanted interest."

"You mean like Blackhour's," she repeated. "Think about it. If foul play is involved, we need to uncover what happened and handle it."

"I doubt either of us is ready for that," he said.

He was right, but she had to convince him she was braver than she felt. "I refuse to be chased off by thugs who want to play cloak and dagger. I took some self-defense classes at the University. A foot to the knee works wonders in crippling an enemy."

"But I'm referring to criminal intent, Neida, men with guns and silencers, who aren't afraid to use them."

"What's the worst that can happen if we talk to Fitz?"

He stared at her. "You don't want to find out."

"At the first sign of trouble, we can go to the authorities."

"What if the first sign of trouble is one of us getting shot? What if the authorities are on the bad guys' payroll?"

The ideas sent shivers through her. Her mind went blank.

Lance reached to touch her arm. "Look, you're my family. I can't let something terrible happen to you."

"That's not going to happen."

"You don't know that."

"Do you honestly think your grandmother would hurt us?"

"I wouldn't put it past her."

Neida paused. He sounded almost sure, but the flicker of his eyes as he turned away crumbled the validity of his words.

"And we don't even know anything about Blackhour's involvement yet," he added. "I don't want to be responsible for your demise before I figure out why you tilt your head to the side when something peeves you."

His comment stopped her retort. "I tilt my head to the side?"

"Big time."

His response made her laugh, but she shook off the mood. "You're my family too. If you get hurt, I couldn't deal with the guilt. Let's stick together on this one. Two heads are better than one, right? Besides, Fitz is just dishing out a trumped-up fantasy. It's been over fifty years, for crying out loud. Who's left to care about any of it?"

He shook his head. "A pragmatist to the end."

"A die-hard," she said with emphasis.

"Just promise me if we do run into trouble, you'll let me take you as far from Washington, D.C. as we can get. I've some places where we can hide and several trusted friends who'll help us."

"I promise."

"We might have to stay more than one day but keep your carry-on light."

Neida lunged forward and threw her arms around his neck. She sat back with a smile, too excited for embarrassment. "Thank you, but you do realize I'd have shown up even if you denied me the opportunity."

Lance smirked at her and nodded his head. "Yeah, I'm well aware of your determination, Missy. I just hope you won't regret your decision come Tuesday morning."

CHAPTER ELEVEN

NEIDA ARRIVED IN TOWN ON SUNDAY MORNING to get a few supplies for her trip. To her surprise, when she hit the main drag, Newaygo bustled with activity. In her anxiety for the excursion to Washington, D.C., she'd forgotten Labor Day weekend. The Logging Festival was in its second day of events. The town engaged itself in sidewalk sales, arts and craft booths, inflated play areas for the kids, and in setting up the range for the fireman's water battle. Others were making last-minute preparations for the parade set to march through the heart of the township in the afternoon. Roadblocks cut off her usual route and forced her to park about a quarter of a mile from the drugstore.

A slight chill nipped the air, and she thanked a last-minute intuition for bringing a warm jacket and comfortable shoes as she meandered by the attractions and entered Brooks Park in no particular hurry. As a former resident of the Bay Area, she had never learned the ambiance of small-town living. In San

Francisco, a constant array of festivals and attractions lay in every direction out of the city. The sheer number of attendees made the outings impersonal and hectic. Here in Newaygo, she belonged to something special, had become a vital part of the whole. People nodded as they passed her. She recognized several familiar faces, almost an impossibility in California's urban sprawl.

She spotted the clingy Pastor Will talking to one of the craftsmen. His continued calls throughout the week, and at the most inconvenient times, had rubbed her raw. Despite her many reminders to sidestep unacceptable subjects, he preached religion, invited her to outings, and asked her the strangest questions. She wanted to avoid him today, so she ducked behind the nearest tent available and headed down a different aisle.

Kat waved to her from a display booth that brandished colorful advertising about egg-carton creations for sale. Carl was unloading a box of additional artwork and looked up long enough to smile and nod at her.

When Neida stepped up to the booth, Kat stood to hug her. "Hey, Hon. I'm glad you've come to enjoy the celebration."

"I actually forgot about the festival this weekend. I'm only here to buy a couple of things, but I'm glad I ventured out. This event is fascinating. The town gets involved."

"Yeah, we're proud of our history. Folks come from all over the state to celebrate our heritage. It's a lot of fun too. Once you experience the party, you'll never want to miss it." Kat straightened one of the sculptures, then picked out a Native American woman in full ceremonial costume and handed the figure to Neida. "Enjoy. I'm late in giving you a housewarming gift."

Did she ever forget anything? Kat was the most organized and efficient soul Neida knew, and her friend was starting to give her an inferiority complex.

Neida stared at the treasure in her hand. The sculpture was fashioned together with pieces of an egg carton and painted with an artist's skill. She turned the artwork over in her hands, examining every minute detail, down to the last feathered trim on its dress. She had never encountered anything so unique. "Did you make this?" she asked, astonished.

"My daddy took up the hobby when the government put him out of work for a few months. He made so much money selling these things that I wanted to learn the craft myself. I dabble with them in my free moments."

"Thank you. Your artwork is incredible. How do you find the time to do this with helping Lance run the business and all?"

Kat beamed. "Kind of puts a different perspective on what small-town folk can do, don't you think?"

"We're not some old hole in the wall," said Carl, turning to join the conversation. "We've got culture, heritage, and talent."

Neida feigned shame, placing the back of her hand to her forehead. "That'll teach me to underestimate the neighborhood."

"Stick around for the parade, too," said Kat. "You'll be dazzled. Lance sponsors the Hopewell float. He decks it out with a mound, and some of the Ojibwe do their ceremonial dances on top. You'd like it."

"Hmm, I wonder why he never told me about it."

Kat leaned in and whispered, "Lance sometimes rides the float. I'm sure he'd be happy to see you." She finished with a wink.

"If I didn't know better, Kat, I'd think you were trying to set us up."

The woman smiled with mischief. "He is the most eligible bachelor in town, and from what I understand about your life in California, you're short on commitments. Since you and Lance were kissing cousins as kids, well ..." She raised an anticipatory eyebrow.

"Sorry, I *am* committed to someone." Neida hated to lie to her, but she wanted to close down Kat's matchmaking business in its infancy.

Kat's smile faded to disappointment then reappeared as she stared over Neida's shoulder. "Speak of the devil."

Neida twisted around. Lance strolled toward them, but with the last person who she hoped to encounter in tow. Pastor Will conversed with Lance and focused his beady little eyes on her, drills mining for oil.

"Here she is," he said when they stopped in front of them. "I've been searching for you, young lady. I hoped to extend you an invitation to the Church's tug-of-war next weekend, but Lance tells me you're going out of town. Where are you headed?"

Lance animated, more than willing to share the information. "We're meeting one of—"

"—my cousins from California," Neida interrupted. "Up north." She smiled at Lance, who frowned with confusion. Kat, privy to their plans, raised an eyebrow and glanced at Lance.

"Where up north?" the pastor asked. "You mean in Michigan?"

Again, his persistence. What she did five minutes from now, or at any time, for that matter, was none of the preacher's business. And the constant twitch of his eye creeped her out.

"Our plans are unsure," said Neida. "My cousin will call us and let us know where to meet her."

"But I thought you were flying to Washington, D.C.," said Carl. "Isn't that what you told me, Kat?"

"We've had a change of plans," said Neida, stepping on Kat's answer, the only explanation she could think of at the moment. "Now, would you all please excuse us? I've some important matters to discuss with Lance about our trip." Neida hooked arms with Lance and dragged him away from the others. "We'll catch you later."

"How long will you be gone?" Pastor Will called out after her. "Do you need someone to keep an eye on your place?"

She pivoted around and walked backward. "No, thanks. All taken care of."

Once they were out of earshot, Lance frowned down at her. "What was that all about?"

"I don't trust the man. He's a bit nosey lately, and I'd like to avoid him."

"Why do you distrust him so much? He's a good person. He watches over his flock, that's all."

"I'm not part of his flock, and I never will be." The words tumbled out from the sensitive place inside her, and she checked herself. "Religion was part of my mom's and grandmother's worlds, not mine. I've told Pastor Will to forget trying to convert me, but he's quite a determined man."

Lance chuckled. "You're right about that, though lying to him isn't necessary."

"Maybe we'd better not let anybody in on our plans, Lance, especially since your friend warned us against digging up the past. Did you tell anybody else besides Kat and Carl?"

He shook his head.

"Don't you think that's wise? I mean, with dangerous men involved. If someone mixed up in the scandal back then still lives in this town, we can't be too careful."

Lance watched her for a moment. "Yesterday, you were ready to jump into this project with both feet. Today, you've screeched on the brakes. You sure you want to come with me? I can get Kat to go in your place."

"I'm not screeching on the brakes. I've had some time to sleep on the idea, that's all. And I agree with you about the danger. Until we know what we're up against, we need to proceed with caution. Pastor Will and everybody else in this town are suspect, in my opinion."

Lance shrugged. "Okay, but I still think you're on the wrong track about him."

She had to change the subject. She pretended to glare at Lance. "So, I hear you're a man with a lot of secrets."

"Secrets?" He frowned his confusion.

"Kat said you sponsor a Hopewell float and that you even ride on it sometimes. Why didn't you tell me? I wouldn't want to miss one of your crowning achievements."

"Oh, that. I had some tasks to finish up before we left and didn't know whether I'd find the chance to participate this year. Not that the project is my crowning achievement. My father sponsored the float years ago, and I've continued the tradition for the last few. It's a way to keep up relations with the tribes."

"I'm impressed."

"If that's all I need to do to impress you, my work will be easy. Even though the assembly of one of those floats takes a lot of man-hours, we're all close friends by the time we place the final strawberry plant. Every one of us would do it again, despite the problems."

"You're lucky. I've missed out on that kind of camaraderie in California."

"Didn't your parents take you to the festivals when you were young?"

"If they did, I don't remember."

"Well then, I'll re-introduce you once we get this artifact business completed."

"Which reminds me ..." Neida opened her purse and handed him the money for both of their plane tickets. "I'm funding this project, Lance. Since Gran asked me to use her means to find the stone box, I'm making good on her request."

Lance examined the cash in his hand and then Neida. His mouth skewed into a pout. "How noble of you, however, I can help out if you don't mind. I'm not exactly destitute, coming from the same family and all."

"Oh, no, I didn't mean ... well, my grandmother insisted."

"I know. I know. I just wouldn't want you to think I'm after your money or anything." He winked and flashed an exaggerated smile.

She laughed, searched for something witty to say, and then focused on her aunt sitting behind a basket-weaving stall across the alley.

Lance followed her line of sight. "Do you want to talk to her?"

Nodding, she flashed him an apologetic smile. "I think I'd better. Would you mind if I catch up to you in a few minutes? Even though she's the one with the issues, if I take every opportunity to get on her good side, it'll make getting to know my grandfather a lot easier."

"I'll be helping with the company float. Meet me at the park entrance afterward."

She waved over her shoulder and headed for the booth.

Winona's barbed glances reached her from several yards away. Neida kept walking anyway. Whether the woman wanted to meet with her or not, she was determined to make an effort.

As she approached the stall, Winona gestured her away. "If you're not buying anything, move on. I've got customers who need the room."

Neida glanced around. Only one shopper showed a half-hearted interest in the white birch bark baskets for sale. "All right, how much is that large basket behind you? That'll look perfect on my library shelf."

Winona's scowl hardened. "That one is not for sale."

"The basket is not for sale or just not to me?"

"What's the difference? Your money is no good here."

The woman who eyed the table of goods glimpsed up at them and hurried away to the next booth. Winona glowered after her, then turned to sneer at Neida.

"How can I prove I'm sincere, Winona? I've already told you I don't want to take anything away from you or The People. I'm hunting down an artifact Gran asked me to find. Maybe you can help me." Neida retrieved the picture from her purse and pointed to the stone box lying at her grandfather's feet. "Do you recognize this relic?"

Winona scanned the photo. Her frown dissolved, and she gasped. "Where did you get this?" She took the image, examining it closer.

"It was my Granddad Graham's photo."

"That box disappeared many years ago. Your white grandfather brought in some fancy government men to examine the relic, and I never saw it again after that."

"Did the piece belong to the Anishinaabe?"

Winona's chin trembled as she raised it. "I didn't say that. The box belongs to those who built the mounds, certainly not to your white grandfather. He robbed the sacred ground and disturbed the spirits buried there."

"But he breached the mound so he could find out more about the ancients who built the structures in the name of science, to preserve the past." Winona's prejudice would be challenging to conquer. Neida had to figure out a way to gain her trust.

"His reasons do not matter," said Winona. "He took away something no one can return."

"I'm going to find the artifacts. I promise."

"I'm not talking about the artifacts. People like your grandfather stripped that piece of the earth of its purpose, and with it, they stole my father's honor."

Neida frowned. "You know, that's something I don't get. If the Anishinaabe wiped out the mound-builders, and the Smithsonian took the artifacts away, why would the elders dishonor *He Who Watches*, especially if the items belonged to their enemy?"

"You don't have a clue about any of this or about who you are, do you?" asked Winona.

"Why don't you explain it to me then?"

Winona shook her head. "That is not my place. That mound on your property has more significance in your life than you can ever imagine. It is one of the last hills that holds evidence of a nation far greater than you suspect. But the white man never believes what we say. In their stubbornness, they hold on to made-up stories and flaunt their superiority because they refuse to believe what might be true. If they had only shown faith and goodwill toward our views over the years, we might have coexisted in peace instead of being at odds with each other as we still are now."

Neida didn't know what that had to do with her. However, something in Winona's words scraped against a raw edge inside her. Her dispute almost leaned to the impasse she and Lance had argued about over religion, and she wondered if all the adamant beliefs she'd adhered to throughout her life had inflicted damage on everyone in her line of fire. She hoped not. And now, she had to prove she only wanted to help. "If I can find the relics and bring them back, will that make a difference to Grandfather? Will my efforts restore his honor?"

"Maybe in his mind, but in my opinion, it is too late for that. No one is left to care."

Neida pulled back and peered through the crowd with exasperation then turned to her aunt again. "I've got to try, for Grandfather's sake, and to understand who I am, as you so eloquently put it."

"Why do you even care? You have been away since you were too young to understand such things."

"I told you, I want to know what my purpose is here. If my white grandfather caused Askuwheteau to suffer, then maybe my actions can right that wrong. Even as a little girl, a force pulled me toward this place, and I'll do anything to understand what that power entails."

"Huh, you hold such high hopes for a half-blood."

The derogatory remark hovered in the air, the sharp edges refusing to dissolve. Neida squared her jaw. "I'm determined to convince you of my love. I've wanted a family more than I can say. I need you. You and Grandfather are all I have left in the world. Please let me into your lives."

Winona's dark eyes swirled with emotion, then took on shades of amber in the morning sun. She stared at Neida as though she calculated the price of such a request. She shoved the picture at her, and just as Neida thought she'd lost the battle, Winona grabbed her hand.

Neida peered down at the connection, then back up into her aunt's eyes, accepting eyes. For the first time since she met her, Winona's hostility retracted like a cat's claw.

"I'm not saying you have convinced me yet, Oneida Graham, *The Awaited One*. But, if what you say is true, for my father's sake, I will help you in any way I can."

CHAPTER TWELVE

"SO HOW DO YOU THINK YOUR AUNT will help us?" asked Lance as they placed Winona's birch bark basket next to the others on Hopewell's library shelf.

"She'll fill in the blanks as we hunt for the relics," said Neida. "So far, she's confirmed that she and Askuwheteau watched the excavation from the edge of the forest. The delegation examined the find for days. When the Smithsonian failed to decipher part of the language, Grandfather Graham went to the reservation hoping the tribe could interpret the characters."

"Were the Ojibwe any help?"

Neida shook her head. "Winona insists the Ojibwe have forgotten most of the language. Maybe they didn't want to cooperate. I don't know. But just on principle, they admonished Grandfather Graham for his desecration. They demanded he hand over all the antiquities, but of course, he didn't, which provoked antagonism after the Smithsonian took the pieces away."

Lance's jaw worked as though he chewed on her words. "So, how and when did they decipher the message then? They needed to work fast, considering the Institution left nothing behind for Granddad to examine."

"Your mom told me they had photographed and deciphered the script later. The evidence must be hiding around here somewhere."

"Have you found any notes in the house?"

"Not so far."

"Do your grandmother's journals explain anything?"

Neida sat on the edge of the library desk with her arms folded. "You'd think a scientist would keep copious notes about something as important as this. His colleagues were bound to want an explanation."

Lance walked to the archaeology books and removed one from the shelf. He raised the tome with emphasis. "My father used to scribble his discoveries in the margins of some of his most prized textbooks for safekeeping. He'd include the book's number and page where he'd come from and where he'd continue the thread. He'd eventually document the whole picture throughout several volumes. The process fascinated me. I loved reading his annotations." Lance returned the book to the shelf and turned around.

Neida clutched the edge of the desk. Her heart raced. His words brought her back to the night she first explored the library.

"What's wrong?" asked Lance.

"Your grandfather kept notes like that too." Neida rushed to where Lance stood, read the titles of the books, and retrieved the specific edition she reviewed weeks ago, combing through its pages. "When I first came to Hopewell, I found this volume and noticed Grandad Graham scribbled in the margins. It looked like a bunch of gibberish, so I thought nothing of it."

Lance peeked beneath the cover of the book. "*Vestiges of the Past*. Sounds like an appropriate title."

"I don't believe it. Look here." Neida pointed at Edward Graham's comments and read them aloud.

> S2:115 Some kind of cuneiform writing. Another unfamiliar tongue—no clue. Rex Willett says he'll give a go at the language. Q8:40

Lance took the volume from Neida to the desk and turned on the light. "Hmm ... S2:115 ... Q8:40. My father used the names of shelves instead of letters."

Neida examined the oak ledge in front of her, and the title *Archaeology* engraved on a gold label below it. She crossed to her grandmother's desk and pulled out a piece of paper and pen from the top drawer. "Let's do this as systematically as we can. Start over at the end." She pointed at the west shelves. "Read me each shelf name."

Lance hurried to the last bookshelf and began shouting out titles. Five minutes later, they had listed twenty-six names.

"*Quantitative Reasoning* is our pick for Q," said Neida. Lance found the designated marker and retrieved the eighth book. He hefted *Psychometric Testing* and thumbed through until he reached page 39. He paused and glanced down at Neida, who had joined him.

"And on page 40 ..." Lance turned the page. "Bingo."

Neida read the familiar scribble aloud.

> A7:200 June 15: Smithsonian arrived today. Blackhour seems knowledgeable enough, though something isn't quite right with his methods. He's excited about the find—wants to test in D.C. as

> soon as we discover what's inside. Opening the casket tomorrow, June 16. L18:126.

She bit her lip. "This system doesn't seem efficient. What if someone inadvertently switched a book's position or added additional volumes?"

Lance used his finger to mark his place, closed the cover, and examined the spine. "Look. Granddad marked references like my father, at the bottom of each book corresponding to its location on the shelf." He pointed at the tiny handwritten Q8 penned under the author's name.

Neida studied the shelves in her line of sight, searching for other numbered texts. "We've got to read the rest before we leave tomorrow."

He grimaced. "This could take us all night, and we fly out of here at six in the morning."

"Don't you want to uncover the whole picture, at least from granddad's point of view? We might find pertinent information before we talk to Fitz tomorrow."

"You're right. Who needs sleep?" He hurried to the shelf marked *Languages* and found the reference L18.

By midnight, they had scattered books across the library desk and on the floor surrounding it. They had gleaned a full fifteen pages of entries, though they still had a lot to examine to complete the puzzle.

Neida kept mulling over one annotation in particular. "I don't understand this," she said, rubbing the back of her neck. "None of Grandad's comments suggest he ever deciphered the language. Take this entry."

> Rex working on translation. Smithsonian no further. Blackhour gives nothing but excuses;

no report forthcoming. Got a strange feeling about this.

Lance pulled out his cell phone and texted a message. "I'll ask Kat to get Cory Willett out here while we're in D.C. He's a good friend. And he's studied his grandfather's research."

Neida yawned and rubbed her eyes. She had curled up in the office chair, and exhaustion now numbed her senses.

Lance smiled down at her. "You sure you want to keep at this?"

Neida nodded. "I wish my grandmother owned a scanner."

Lance flinched and gave her a sheepish grin. "I own one."

She scowled at him. "Are you serious? And when were you going to tell me this?"

He ignored her sarcasm, just stacked several volumes in the crook of his arm. "Let's take the books to my house. We can at least get the entries copied before we leave. My machine copies to my computer."

By 2:00 A.M., they managed to duplicate all of Edward Graham's notations. They didn't bother to read the passages but concentrated on digitalizing their grandfather's words. After copying the last notation, they sat on Lance's sofa with Pompeii sprawled at their feet. Neida laid back her head and closed her eyes.

Lance yawned beside her. "I've changed my mind. Sleep sounds pretty tempting about now."

Neida nodded without opening her eyelids. "You think Pompeii would care if I crashed on your couch? I couldn't make it home if I tried."

"He won't mind a bit. He's been dreaming of dog bones for some time now."

She didn't respond. Who would have thought they'd find such important leads hours before they left for Washington, D.C.?

How ironic that the answers had lurked on her grandfather's library shelves all along.

Lance stood. "I'll wake you when it's time to go, which I'm afraid is less than an hour from now."

His words garbled in her head. She mumbled a reply. As her mind faded toward unconsciousness, she barely noticed Lance lifting her legs to the couch and tucking a blanket around her before he left the room.

ᛘ

They scrambled to make their flight out of the Fremont Municipal Airport. Lance had overslept, allowing them only a few minutes to change their clothes, pick up Neida's bag, and take Pompeii to Kat's house. To Neida's disappointment, in their haste to get to the airport, she left her cell phone behind on her bedroom dresser, and now she felt like a one-armed woman without her lifeline. Lance reassured her she could use his device if she needed it. That was some consolation. But in her mind, such forgetfulness loomed over her like a premonition of things to come. They arrived at the airport only forty-five minutes before their plane took off. They rushed through security with only a few minutes to spare.

Lance stored the digital copies on a thumb drive in his backpack. They'd brought a couple of her grandmother's journals as well. Neida had hoped to read the entries during their short flight but sitting next to Lance had proved too comforting. They both succumbed to their exhaustion soon after the plane reached altitude.

The Washington Dulles International Airport swarmed with activity when they picked up their rental car a few hours later. Located in Chantilly, Virginia, it was one of three major airports in the Baltimore–Washington metropolitan area and served over 21 million passengers a year. By nightfall, it would draw a hive of returning Labor Day vacationers, and the sooner they completed their business here, the better. After signing the contract for a Jeep Cherokee, they set off for the heart of Washington, D.C, 26 miles away.

Neida reflected about what had jump-started the last few days' events—her grandmother's plea, the subsequent journal entries, Askuwheteau's admonition to begin in her heart, and the annotations in Grandfather Graham's textbooks. And now their anticipated meeting with Lance's friend conjured up oversized butterflies inside her stomach.

She still harbored skepticism about Fitz's hype. Why would a stone box and its ancient tablet pose such a threat that someone would commit a crime over it? The Michigan Relics proved that if scientists deemed their findings as forgeries, the public soon lost interest. What possible reason had caused the Smithsonian to go to such lengths to keep the discovery a secret? She imagined the relics had slipped through the cracks or ended up on a forgotten shelf somewhere. And the most imminent and challenging obstacle ahead would be to convince the Institution to allow them access to the treasures—to persuade them to hand them over.

She examined Lance's profile: his wilted countenance, his disheveled hair—much like her own frayed demeanor. A day's growth painted his jaw in shadow, and his puffy, red eyes rendered his face paler than usual. He clutched the steering wheel and stared at the open road in the distance. The sight tugged at her compassion, and although she wanted to touch his cheek and run her fingers through his hair, she shoved down the urge before it made her do something she'd regret.

They both perked up when they arrived at the National Mall at 9:45 A.M. and found their target. Constructed of red Seneca sandstone, the Smithsonian Castle appeared as if someone had dropped it in the middle of the American sprawl right out of 12th-century Normandy.

"It looks better than its pictures," said Neida. "It makes me imagine we're time traveling." Despite her occupation, her only visit to the museum was as a young girl on vacation with her parents. The memory had faded, and she felt exhilaration at the prospect of exploring such a magnificent landmark once again.

Four red sandstone pillars ushered them from Independence Avenue into the Enid A. Haupt Garden. At the agricultural wonderland's ground level, the landscape spread over four-and-a-quarter acres of rooftop above the subterranean Ripley Center and the Sackler and African Art museums. They walked around the Fountain Garden, where hawthorn trees hung over granite seating. Turn of the century iron furniture and granite vases dotted the path. They found a bench, and Lance motioned for Neida to sit.

"Fitz will meet us here." Lance rubbed his hand over the stone underneath them. "It's not too late to change your mind, Neida. I can't be sure about the outcome of this meeting."

She hated to repeat herself, but the man just wasn't getting it. She fussed with a disobedient lock of hair dividing Lance's forehead. "Again, you've forgotten that Gran and I are the reason we're here. I've come this far—willingly—and I'm not about to change my mind now. We've got to stick together, chase down the ghosts as a team. Who knows, this may be a dead-end, but wherever the day leads us, let's rely on each other to get over the rough spots. Agreed?"

Lance's gaze swept over her face. He nodded. "So, why do I feel like I'm pushing you over the edge?"

"Didn't you hear anything I just said? I'm the one who instigated this."

"And if I had any sense, I'd take you away before the fun begins."

His overprotective attitude bothered her. She could very well take care of herself. "I'm here for a lot more than curiosity or obeying my grandmother's wishes," she said. "I'm here to understand what freak of nature sucked me back to it. An unknown force has lodged in some deep dark place inside me, and before it eats me alive, I need to discover why."

Lance focused into the distance over the top of her head. He frowned and stood, squinting toward the entrance.

His intenseness made the hair on her nape spike. "What's wrong?"

"I thought I saw something." He ran his hand through his hair. "Man, I'm already expecting the worst and seeing things to boot."

"What did you see?"

"I thought I saw Pastor Will at the entrance. But that can't be."

Neida rose and perused the garden. "I wouldn't put it past the man to follow us here."

"That's ridiculous. Why would the pastor do that? My imagination is just playing with me."

"I don't know. The man's sure been hounding me lately." She turned back and leaned into him, patted his chest. "But you're right. We're both tired. Let's take a deep breath and take one step at a time."

"Well, now, if this isn't a cozy little scene." The English accent startled them, and they turned to a tall man with horn-rimmed glasses and long, silver dreads. He hurried toward them with his hand out.

"Fitz, it's good to see you. It's been too long." Lance shook his hand.

The Englishman smiled a row of crooked, graying teeth. "You were barely out of high school the last time I laid eyes on you. But you've grown into a fine fellow."

Neida couldn't help but gawk. Fitz Emory's bony arms, leathered with age spots and wrinkles, dangled from under his shirt sleeves. His butt, almost non-existent, leveled the plane of his back, sagging his pants, though a leather belt kept his faded blue jeans at a respectable height and the ends of his denim shirt tucked inside. His green plaid sweater vest appeared too small but seemed the only thing almost normal about his appearance. No one from that generation wore high-top Chuck Taylors, especially a pair as stained and mottled as Fitz's.

"And who is this lovely?" Fitz directed a long, pointed nose at Neida and ogled her over his glasses with piercing, blue eyes.

"Fitz, this is Neida Graham. Sort of a cousin."

"Sort of, you say. That's convenient." His mouth puckered as he spoke, as though he sucked on sour candy. He winked and offered to shake her hand. "A little hanky with your panky, is it? Makes the job a tad more pleasant, I dare say."

Neida bristled at the innuendo.

Fitz turned to Lance. "Have you warned Neida about the consequences of being here?"

"More than once," said Lance.

Neida crossed her arms. "Mr. Emory, I don't know what Lance told you, but the only results I'm interested in are those surrounding the acquisition of that box. I'm here because my grandmother asked me to find the artifacts and bring them back. And I'm more than determined to honor her request. I'll discover the truth, whatever that entails, and I hardly think the interpretation of these relics will be a threat to anyone."

Fitz chuckled and slapped Lance on the shoulder. "By Jove, she's a Graham through and through. Can't detect the danger for the thrill of the hunt. But none of this Mr. Emory claptrap. Call me Fitz."

His jovialness waned, and he stared off into the distance, scanning the grounds. "I think we should walk," he said. He made a sweeping gesture with his hand.

Lance peered over his shoulder at the entrance. He hustled Neida behind Fitz away from the castle and toward the Moongate Garden.

Fitz's long strides kept a fast pace, and she hurried to keep up. Further down the path, the Englishman finally stepped in line with them again and addressed Neida.

"So, dear girl, you want the truth, do you? What version would you like me to entertain you with?" His knotted finger pushed up his glasses in one swift motion.

"I'm not here for you to entertain me," she said. "The only version I'm interested in is an accurate one, backed up by facts."

"Don't peruse the news feed much, do you, my dear? People around this part of the country tend to make up their own sordid accounting of the truth, as long as it benefits them. Why are you and your grandmother so determined to find these artifacts, anyway?"

"I don't know if Lance told you, but my biological grandfather is a member of the Ojibwe Nation. Years ago, Askuwheteau watched over the mounds around Newaygo, and after the artifacts went missing, he lost his honor among The People. I suppose they no longer trusted him. I want to right that wrong."

"And you honestly believe you'll accomplish this just by exposing old pieces of metal and stone?"

"That's my hope."

Lance peered at Fitz on the other side of Neida. "If the relics enlighten us about the mound-builders' beliefs, the whole world should learn of its message."

Fitz sucked in his cheeks. “I hope this search to restore honor and understanding is worth the price of opening Pandora’s Box. I may be an old relic myself, but in my estimation, honor, understanding—truth for that matter—rests on far more significant ideals than physical proof.

“A bloke needs to hold himself to a model of conduct and listen to his gut, despite the rubbish people throw at him or what rewards they dangle under his nose. Although, I dare say, your grandfather was quite caught up in the excitement back then but couldn’t have stopped the artifacts from disappearing even if he tried. Too many fingers in the pie, so to speak, and it doesn’t matter a fig how much proof we hold in our hands anyway, does it? People believe what they want just to avoid examining the facts and their misguided hearts. If you desire the truth, my dear Neida, you’ll need to look far beyond the Smithsonian warehouse to the root of what’s truly going on.”

Again, there was that same theme, listening to one’s intuition and the facts versus refusing to examine one’s heart. Neida was beginning to think some force was playing dirty with her mind, that its message kept repeating because it was something she needed to learn. “That may be, Mr. Emory, but we need to start somewhere, and you and the Smithsonian are where Lance and I will begin.”

“Right. So how would you like my help?”

She brushed back a strand of hair whipping in the breeze against her cheek and explained. “You worked for the Institution when Thomas Blackhour shipped the artifacts here to test them. As far as our research reveals, they never returned or reported on the goods. Lance believes you might know what happened to them.”

“Yes, I worked at the Research Branch in the Bronx back then. My crew logged and stored all the antiquities in the warehouse. That is until the Institution completed the SMSC in 1998. That was a promotion, I can tell you. They made me somewhat the storage facility's overseer, and I earned every penny in the enormous task we completed moving the relics from New York to their new home. Took us five years."

"So, the stone box and its contents are at the SMSC?"

"Quite."

"And you know where the objects are?"

"I was one of the original four who crated them up and stored them in the "no man's land" section of the Bronx warehouse. You could say we took the misplaced objects and misplaced them somewhere else." Fitz laughed at his clever joke.

Neida didn't get the humor. "Why would the Smithsonian do that?"

"I wouldn't quite deem it the Smithsonian's idea. They knew nothing about the antiquities. Rather, the young upstart and ruthless swindler, Thomas J. Blackhour, stole them from your grandfather and possessed the money with which to carry out his evil plan—and, I might add, the company to do his bidding, including that assistant, Stephenson, stuffed in his pocket. Blackhour proved a mighty slick manipulator back then. Still is, if you ask my opinion. He stole plenty of artifacts from the Smithsonian in his day and sold the pricy objects to buyers all over the world. I caught him in the act once. And I hear someone else found out about it too. That someone is blackmailing him now, someone who wants those artifacts as much as you do."

"Do you know who?" asked Lance.

"I can't help you on that matter. All I know is that Blackhour is panicking and scrambling to hunt down the culprit and the goods. It's hilarious, really. In the first place, that Stephenson fellow never told the chap where he hid the goods. And just to add a little fun to the mix, my friend and I moved the artifacts to a new location years ago—to make sure he'd never find them again even if he tried to hunt them down. A jolly good show, if I do say so myself. I planned on returning them to Edward, but he never returned home to retrieve them.

"The four of us got paid a big bonus that year, and Blackhour remained oblivious to the fact that we duped him. I'm one of three still privy to the scheme back then, though my friend and I are the only ones aware of their exact location. We didn't bother to share our little secret either. The other bloke was a nephew or some such relative to Blackhour's cohort."

"How do you know all this?" asked Lance.

"Let's just say, I have a few fingers in the pie myself, a few birdies watching the store for me, though I've lost my rank for admission to the premises in recent years."

"Can we access the relics?" asked Lance. "Can your friend remove them from storage and ship them to Michigan for us?"

Fitz stopped in the path. Surprise transformed his features. "You want us to steal them? I don't know, that changes the scope a bit. Security is quite tight these days, more so than when I worked at the farm. Not a fan of spending the rest of my earthly existence banged up, either. I'll have to think on that one."

"Fitz, we need your help. No one else is as familiar or has the contacts."

"But I'm not fond of dying either. I kind of like the old tabernacle of clay."

"What is so important about those relics?" Neida asked, her voice rising again. "Why would someone kill you over them?"

"Oh, lass, riches, power, and manipulation are formidable motivators in the minds of the wicked."

Lance stopped and balled up his fists. "You're right. I can't ask you to do this. We'll find another way."

Fitz stared at him without expression, and finally, with a sudden suck of his cheeks, he pursed his lips and peered over his glasses. "Now, wait a minute. I suppose I have some friends that owe me a favor. They might be able to smuggle the relics out for me. Do you have somewhere to drop them?"

"No, we still need to find a hotel."

"Inform me when you get settled. If worse comes to worst, I suppose I can get my associates to deliver the crate to my house. I'm only a few minutes from the Mall over in Georgetown." He dug under his vest, pulled out a business card, and handed it to Lance. "Make sure you find an out-of-the-way hole in which to fall. And from now on, pay cash wherever you stay. With what we're about, you don't want a paper trail leading to your whereabouts. It may take me a few days, but we'll work out the details."

"Honestly, is this charade necessary?" asked Neida, more agitated than before.

Fitz's jagged teeth warped into a smile. "Well, you know what they say: better to be safe than sorry." He paused for a moment, then leaned toward Neida. "You truly don't have a clue about the severity of the situation, do you, my dear?"

Lance cleared his throat. "I've been trying to explain it to her, but she just won't listen."

Fitz slapped Lance on the shoulder again. "Well, no matter, she may get the gist of it soon enough. And if the facts are told, by the time she gets those artifacts in her pretty little hands, the truth will seem a tad uglier than it is now."

"We'll manage," said Neida.

Fitz only nodded a twisted smile and continued down the path at a faster pace.

CHAPTER THIRTEEN

AT FOUR O'CLOCK IN THE AFTERNOON, while touring the *National Museum of the American Indian*, Lance's cell phone startled him. Neida had paced a few feet ahead, where she viewed a display about the Blackfoot Indians. He retrieved the device from his back pocket and walked in the opposite direction to answer it.

"Hello." He covered his ear to block out the noise around him.

"You've got to be the luckiest bloke I know, old boy."

"How's that Fitz?"

"I called in a few favors this morning, and your precious stone box will be delivered to my door by 7:00 tonight. The lads from the SMSC cherished the opportunity to get me off their backs finally. A friend of mine will bring it in one of her trucks after work. Neida's ancestors are smiling on you, Lance. Perhaps Neida is your good luck charm."

Lance nodded and turned to glance at Neida, who examined a hide robe. "She is," he said. "What time do we show up at your place tonight? We want to examine the items right away."

"Oh, you'll have to wait to disassemble the goods, I'm afraid. The crate can survive the test of Hercules, and I don't own the materials to open the casing for you right now. But I'll enjoy the company right enough. I'll ship them to Michigan for you tomorrow."

Searching the crowd, Lance spotted Neida hunched over a glass display. He continued a few more steps in the opposite direction. "How about 7:30?"

"You know where I'll be."

Lance couldn't believe their luck. "Fitz, I owe you."

"Let's just say my family owed yours a lifetime of favors. Tis nothing. Ta 'til tonight."

Lance repocketed his phone, pivoted around just as Neida advanced through the press, and stopped in front of him. "Anybody I know?"

"Fitz swears your ancestors are pulling for you, Neida. They'll deliver the artifacts to his home tonight. We'll meet him there at 7:30."

"How did he arrange it so quickly?"

"As long as I've known Fitz, he accomplishes tasks faster than most guys think about starting. He'll ship them for us tomorrow."

"So, we'll leave for home in the morning?"

"No, my friend will fly us out tonight."

"But don't we need to investigate the artifacts first?"

I'd rather take you away from D.C., as far and as quickly as possible. He almost told her so, but he wanted to avoid her wrath. "No, we'll have to wait for the unveiling until we're home. The seal is pretty tight, and we best transport the relics to a controlled environment anyway."

"Why go to Fitz's at all then?"

"I want to ask him a few questions. And we'll need instruction on how to open the crate. Let's get a bite to eat first. Then we'll take the car back to the airport and grab a taxi."

"Thanks, Lance," she said, her voice tender as she caressed his arm. "If it weren't for you, I'd still be wondering how to begin. When this is over, I'll treat you to a big steak dinner with all the trimmings. Although that wouldn't be enough appreciation for how grateful I am."

"I can think of a just reward," he said, pointing to his lips.

She shot him a shy smile. "Uh, well ..."

Lance chuckled. Neida turned red without the slightest effort, but he'd spare her further embarrassment. "Onward, my dear Neida," he said, mimicking Fitz's accent, which made her laugh. "Our adventure is about to begin." He grasped hold of her arm and ushered her toward the facility door. He only hoped the rendezvous with Fitz proved event-free, that they'd return home before something went wrong as his intuition had been warning him all day. But with the lump in his stomach already producing moments of nausea, he doubted they'd arrive in Newaygo unscathed. He'd never told Neida that his friends had dubbed him *The Prophet* because his instincts proved right more times than not.

"Where are we going," asked Neida when Lance headed in the opposite direction than that of the airport. They had just finished some fish and chips at a small, fast food restaurant. She glanced at her watch to see how close they were to their rendezvous with Fitz. "Don't we need to drop off the rental car and get back?"

Lance kept his eyes on the road and turned into a row of offices where he parked the Jeep. He turned off the ignition and scooted around to face her. "There's something I have to tell you."

The look on his face scared her. "Okay, I'm not sure I want to hear this, but I'm all ears."

"When you were in California, I called Thomas Blackhour and asked him if the Institution still possessed the artifacts. I suggested he might search the records and get back to me about their location."

She swallowed back an expletive. "What was his response?"

"Well, he gave me the runaround, said he couldn't recall the excavation, but he promised to get back to me."

"When Hell freezes over, I'll bet. Of course, he knows about the dig. Why are you only telling me this now?" She tried to calm her annoyance. He should have told her as soon as she returned home from California.

"At first, I just wanted you to get settled in. But the more we discovered about Blackhour, I wondered if telling you was the smart thing to do at all."

She sighed. "So, now Blackhour knows we're searching for the relics—a man who stole them from our grandfather in the first place, possibly a felon who will do just about anything to cover his tracks. I told you he was at the cemetery."

Lance scratched the back of his head, growled, and pounded the steering wheel. "Look, I thought I was helping—making some progress. I didn't know Blackhour's part in all of this at the time. We might as well confront him face-to-face now."

Her stomach flipped. "And why would we do that?"

"To make him think he's in control—that we're still in the dark about the goods. If we throw him off our track in the beginning, maybe he'll leave us alone. I talked to Pastor Will the other day about Blackhour, and he told me the man had asked him a lot of questions about you and about why you were searching for the artifacts."

"Well, I vote to keep our distance, especially now that Fitz is delivering the artifacts. I see no advantage in inviting Blackhour's notice—or his irritation. We'll end up nose-deep in the mire, right in his backyard."

"That's not going to happen, especially if you appear as a damsel in distress."

"I'm not a stellar actress, Lance. He'll read my face like the lousy poker player that I am." Neida sat in dazed silence. Her imagination conjured up a multitude of dangerous scenarios that awaited them if they got too close.

"Please, just do this for me," he said, breaking into her thoughts. "We don't need someone hounding us or confiscating the prize before we even find out what it's about."

Neida closed her eyes and reopened them, inhaled a cleansing breath. "I hadn't planned on facing my demise so soon."

"Just follow my lead, and you'll do fine."

"I'm not so sure about that."

Inside the plush office, the walls, painted in muted earth tones, were lined with case after case of Native American artifacts. Grand flagstone tiles led them through a massive lobby to a desk with a large brunette woman sporting an earphone, her fingers nipping over her wireless computer keyboard. She continued typing for a few seconds before she peered up. Her smile pleated the lines around her eyes. "Good afternoon, how may I help you?"

Lance handed her a business card and leaned in over the waist-high desk ledge. "We're here to see Mr. Thomas Blackhour."

"Do you have an appointment?"

"No ma'am, but we spoke with him in recent days, and we have urgent business to conclude."

The woman continued to smile, but she shook her head. "Oh, I'm sorry. Mr. Blackhour's schedule won't permit walk-ins. I have him booked through the end of the month, I'm afraid. But maybe ..." she searched the screen, tapping the down arrow over and over, and then paused to peer up, "I can schedule you sometime in late October."

Lance scratched his chin and smiled. "We're only here for today. Can you just let him know Lance and Neida Graham are here to see him? I'm sure he'll squeeze us in."

The woman flashed him a doubtful scowl, pushed a button on her console, and waited for someone to answer on the other end.

Lance turned to Neida and raised his eyebrows.

"Yes, Mr. Blackhour," said the receptionist a moment later. "I have a Lance and Neida Graham here to see you on an urgent matter. I've told them your schedule is too tight today, but ..." Her eyes widened. She peered up at Lance in surprise. "Certainly, Mr. Blackhour. Right away, sir." She hung up, rose from her chair, and motioned them to follow.

"This is highly unusual, you understand," said the woman. She led them down a narrow hallway with several pictures depicting Native Americans in various impressive headgear. At the hall's end, the receptionist opened a rustic door and walked into the office ahead of them.

"Your guests, Mr. Blackhour." She brandished her hand toward two chairs in front of an elaborate oaken desk, then left the room. Blackhour watched them with intense curiosity, and despite his gray hair, his youthful face and toned physique surprised Neida. At the cemetery and in her house, the man's appearance seemed far different than that of her current impression.

"We're sorry to drop in on you like this, Mr. Blackhour, " said Lance, "but Miss Graham and I were in the neighborhood.

We thought we'd inquire about your search for the Hopewell artifacts—thought you might have made some progress. We're anxious for the relics' return. Neida's grandmother was most distressed about their whereabouts."

Blackhour focused on Lance. His elbows dented his padded armrests, his hands covering his mouth to hide all expression except for the dullness of his eyes. "As I told you on the phone, Mr. Graham, I've been away for a week. I've yet to find a moment to investigate your particular case. I hope you didn't come all this way just to hurry things along."

He lowered his hands and leaned toward Neida. "Ms. Graham, my condolences to you for your loss. I understand from your cousin that you've recently lost your Grandmother. I'd hate to think Mr. Graham dragged you all this way, especially in your time of mourning, for what might be a lost cause. I'm no longer working in the field, you understand, and my position on the board takes up most of my time in committee. Like I told your cousin, I'm not sure I even remember the excavation on your property."

"No, of course not," Neida said, shaking her head. "Lance and I are here on other business at the moment, and we're taking in a little sightseeing in our spare time. I haven't been to D.C. since I was a little girl."

"And how are you finding our fair town?"

"I'm enjoying the museums, of course. I only wish we'd have time to give the sights a respectable amount of effort. I don't know when I'll get back to this part of the country, and cramming in so much, in such a short time, is not as satisfying as I had hoped."

Lance adjusted in his seat and cleared his throat. "Mr. Blackhour, we won't take up any more of your time, but if you can give us any indication of how soon you'll address the issue, you would relieve us both."

"May I ask why the urgency?"

Lance stalled.

Blackhour's eyes narrowed as he waited for an answer.

"There are complications to Althea Graham's trust, and they require the artifacts to ensure a quick settlement of affairs. Our hands are tied until we locate the items in question."

Neida marveled at his ability to fabricate an excuse. She would have stumbled over an explanation without the chance to think it through.

"Then, by all means, I'll expedite my search," he said. "I should report back sometime next week. Does that sound acceptable to you both?"

Neida nodded. "Thank you. I can't tell you what this means to me."

Blackhour stood and reached to shake both of their hands. His cold, large fingers upon her skin sent a shiver up her spine.

He smiled down at her. "Thank you for stopping by. I hope the rest of your trip provides you far more than you expect."

Minutes later, the lingering chill of Blackhour's handshake and his foreboding words terrorized Neida's heart. *Far more than I expect. What did he mean by that exactly?* And he had lied. Why else would he forget the excavation after his recent business with her grandmother on the same property? Why, at Gran's funeral, did he ask Pastor Will about who she was and about something of which he claimed to be ignorant? Lance was delusional to believe they'd thrown Blackhour off their track. They had only exacerbated their predicament by coming here. They were sure to face Blackhour's retaliation—even revenge—and that, set in motion by their single, impulsive blunder.

ᛁᚻᛇ

At seven twenty-five, Lance and Neida exited a taxi outside of Fitz's neighborhood. "We'll walk the rest of the way," he said. "The less attention we draw, the better."

Lance claimed he'd been to the man's house as a kid, but as confident as he sounded about the location, they needed more direction than a childhood memory. They walked for a while, backtracking several times until Lance found his bearings again. Her feet ached, and her thin jacket proved ill-equipped to deflect the wind. The clouds brewing above them for the past hour threatened rain.

"Maybe we should ask someone, Lance."

He kept walking. "I recognize where I am now. Fitz's house is a few streets away." He picked up his pace, and Neida pushed herself to keep up with him.

The neighborhood reeked of money. Most of the homes they had passed at the beginning of their journey into the area were modest brick structures, but as they advanced further into the tract, the buildings grew more extensive and more custom in their architecture.

At one corner, Lance slowed and studied the street. Without warning, he sprang from the sidewalk and pulled her behind a screen of rhododendron bushes. He peered around the foliage again at the scene beyond.

"What's the matter?" asked Neida. Her heart slammed against her chest. She clutched Lance's arm for courage.

He turned, slipping his backpack from his shoulder, and took her hands in his. "I want you to wait here. I'll go through the back and determine if it's safe but stay out of sight. A black car is parked down the street, not far from Fitz's place. Someone's sitting inside."

Neida's heart skipped. She shook her head. "You're not leaving me."

"You'll be safer right here. Stay behind the bushes." Before she countered him, he set off beneath the cover of the towering rhododendrons.

She peeked after him, watched his retreat. The sedan faced her, and through the dark windows, she detected a man's form. The car door opened midway into Lance's advance, and he withdrew further into the bushes, causing her to lose track of him. Seconds later, he came into view again just as he scaled a brick wall and disappeared on the other side.

The car door slammed shut soon after, causing her heart to beat high in her throat. She pulled further back and studied what she assumed was Fitz's medieval-style home faced with wainscoting and multicolored stones. The Smithsonian had paid him well. Either that, or he was filthy rich. Massive, lush grounds enhanced the structure, and the house sat behind a wrought iron fence where two dark forms, ferocious dogs by the sound of them, paced and whined outside the front door.

A blast of wind rippled over her, prompting her to pull her jacket tighter. The longer she waited, the more her anxiety mounted. Minutes had passed since Lance's disappearance over the wall, but his absence seemed like an eternity. If the sentry decided to drive the neighborhood, her exposure would draw his attention for sure.

She inhaled courage, slid Lance's backpack and her purse further into the bushes. After eyeing the black car, she made the plunge, hugging the rhododendrons along the same path Lance had traveled only moments before. At the fence, she paused. He had easily pulled himself over the barrier, but nothing seemed available for her to copy his efforts.

The movement inside the vehicle thrust her further into her limbed fortress. Through the stiff covering, she assessed the direction of the man's gaze. Moisture dripped down her cheek. She wiped at the trickle, and when she lowered part of the bush for a better view, blood covered her fingers. She gasped, now aware of the intensity of the branches stabbing her back and scratching her face, though she dared not move.

The lookout cased the neighborhood—a slow twist of his head. The door opened again. He stepped out of the car and swept a pointed search along the line of properties. The moon hung low in the sky and illuminated his muscular frame. He exuded trouble from every pore, and she hated being so close.

Classical music pierced the wind's howl. The man pulled out a cell phone and answered it.

"Yeah? No, he's not out yet."

Fear grabbed Neida. Someone, she imagined a-not-so-friendly sort, had already invaded the house. She had to warn Lance and Fitz if it wasn't too late already. The man glanced in her direction, forcing her to freeze in place.

The stranger leaned against the car's roof and took out a pack of cigarettes from inside his coat pocket, then lit one. "How would I know?" he said into the phone. He flicked his match stub to the ground. "The artifacts never showed up. But Telly will make him spill his guts. We've been watching the place as Blackhour asked."

Neida struggled to breathe.

The man swiveled and leaned against the car, craning his neck to blow out a stream of smoke. The vapor frenzied off with the breeze.

Neida searched behind her. An electrical box jutted from between the bushes close to the fence. Using the man's distraction and the fierce sound of the wind, she climbed atop the metal casing, using the rhododendrons to hoist herself up. At the top of the brick wall, she shimmied around until she found momentum to push off into the yard on the other side.

The impact shot sharp pains through her cold legs. She winced but stayed low and gaged her situation, hoping for the absence of ravenous dogs on the attack. Low-glowing patio lights lit the way to another wall and the stone house that rose above it from the other side. Disappointment stabbed her. The yard where she crouched belonged to a different property than Fitz's. She'd have to scale a second barrier, and only one tree appeared high enough to use as a ladder.

She dashed across the yard, watched the door and the massive glass windows of the house for signs of light. To her relief, the interior remained dark. She inhaled a frigid breath and wedged her foot into the junction of the lowest hanging branch. Her hands ached from the cold, and she struggled to hold on, but her concern for Lance pushed her upward, one limb at a time, taking her to the top of the brick fence where she peered over the partition toward the black car. The rhododendrons hid it from view, another break, since that meant the man couldn't detect her either.

Neida examined the yard below. The landscape, typically Italian, boasted formal walkways and geometrically shaped bushes. They led to a gaping side door. She hustled over the fence to the carpet of lawn—experienced another spike of pain—then dashed to the entrance and closed it behind her, unwilling to become a ready-made feast for Fitz's dogs.

Dim light led her through a formal hallway adorned with a gallery of family paintings. The sound of a struggle scudded into the corridor, conjuring up images of a perilous dance on the other side of the wall. She approached the entryway, heart slamming, and chanced a glance around the door frame to judge the scene inside.

A man's broad shoulders and wide back almost collided with her face. He pivoted an inch, and Lance's feet flailed into view, heels scraping the wooden floor, breath obstructed under the stranger's massive hands around his throat.

She searched for something to use as a weapon. Grabbing a brass statuette on the hall table, she lunged and bashed the back of the man's head. He grunted, then crumbled, falling on top of Lance.

Neida hurried to free him, failed to budge Lance's frame from under more than six feet of muscle and bone. The brute reminded her of a Mafia heavyweight—big muscles, pocked face, and stubby, fat fingers. She switched her position, tried pulling on the attacker's arm until she moved him several inches from where he lay. Stepping over the human mound, she fell to her knees at Lance's side.

"Lance, Lance, are you okay?" Her voice, a mere whisper. She touched his cheek, his hair, trying to provoke a response.

Lance's chest heaved. He touched his throat, opened his eyes, and looked into Neida's face. "I thought ... I told you ... to wait outside," he said between gasps.

"A lot of good that would have done."

He clutched her hand and helped himself to sit, winced with the effort. "Help me up. We've got to get out of here."

She wedged an arm under his shoulder, anchored herself as she rose to bear most of his weight, allowing him to stand on his feet. She glanced past him into the next room and almost collapsed at the scene. Fitz leaned back against a suit of armor, a spear point projecting through his body out the front. His eyes bulged his expression, pure horror.

She cried out and whirled herself away.

"I'm sorry, Neida. I didn't want you to see that." Lance wrapped his arms around her shoulders. She leaned into his chest, clung to his back in sheer fright.

"We've got to go."

"Shouldn't we call the police?" She refused to unlatch her fingers at his coaxing.

"We can't take the time. We need to get out of here."

He pried her arms from around his waist and pulled her down the hall out the back door. The dogs' silence put her on guard as Lance guided her through the garden paths to the fence. With new-found energy and breath, he linked his hands together and boosted her to the top of the wall, pushing her legs around and over. She teetered, prepared herself for the pain of the drop, but froze as two sets of snapping fangs reflected in the light of the moon. They raced toward Lance.

He jumped, caught the edge of the brick ledge just in time, and struggled in his weakened state to pull himself up. One of the dogs leaped after him and snagged his pant leg in its strong jaws, dragging him back down again.

Neida groped for his hand. A section of the pants fabric ripped free, and Lance hoisted himself to the top again. The animals fought over the shredded cloth but realized they'd missed their target and slammed against the wall in a frenzied volley. Neida struggled to hold on. She held her breath and tugged Lance up the bricks. His feet scuffed for traction until he reached the top, and they both jumped to safety on the other side.

Scaling the next wall proved less difficult. They managed to ease silently down behind the bush's cover. The sentry's attention focused on Fitz's property line, where the dogs' snarls lobbed over the partition. Lance yanked on Neida's sleeve, and she followed him, keeping to the shadows, frozen puffs of air dissolving behind them in their race around the corner.

They grabbed their bags, ran through the maze of streets, and didn't look back until they reached a bus stop on the main road. The Metro had just pulled away. They sprinted after it with flailing hands, shouting for the driver to wait. He complied. They darted for the open door and paid the fee, then collapsed into a seat at the front of the empty bus.

"You're lucky I caught a glimpse of you in my mirror," said the driver without turning around. "I can't see a thing out the door this time of night."

"Appreciate you stopping," said Lance.

They rode in silence, forever it seemed, passed the menagerie of neighborhoods and storefronts, across the Potomac into D.C. again, on a course toward Foggy Bottom.

Fitz's contorted face had seared into Neida's memory. She doubted she would ever forget the shock of it, now locked inside of her forever. Her grandmother must have understood the dangers they'd face in their hunt for the stone box. Why would Gran ask her to carry out such a feat, and for what? Was the relic's message worth losing one's life?

Her grandfather's last instruction seemed pointless too. *Begin in your heart. It knows the road to follow.* All the roads that faced them looked rather bleak right now. She shook her head and closed her eyes against the undulating wave that washed over her, dragging her out to sea.

"We can't go home, Neida," said Lance, hastening her drowning.

She turned to him and searched for meaning in his eyes.

Without further explanation, he reached for a piece of paper in his pocket and handed it to her. She held the blood-splattered missive at the edges, slapped a hand to her mouth as she read the note.

> Grahams,
>
> Stop looking for the artifacts. If you ignore my warning, you'll end up like the Englishman, skewered by your stupidity. And I will find you. Watch your back.

Neida lowered the death sentence into her lap. "I don't believe this. Is this tablet an actual letter from God, or something?"

"Whatever it is, now that Blackhour has the relics again, we'll never find them."

Neida spun to face him. "But he doesn't have them."

"He doesn't? How do you know?"

"Just before I climbed over the fence, the guy outside told someone on the phone the relics are missing. What are we going to do?"

"You're sure?"

She nodded.

He slid his arm around her and pressed her against him. "We'll hide out tonight, and in the morning, we'll find a way to my cabin in northern Michigan. We can read the rest of Granddad's notes there and determine our next move."

Neida pulled away. "No, let's go to Askuwheteau. He'll tell us more about the past."

"Do you think that's wise? If we lead Blackhour to him, we'll put your family in danger."

"Something tells me he's the person we need to rely on."

"Okay, but let's find a place to spend the night. I can barely function, as it is." He brought a hand to his throat and winced as he gingerly touched the tender places.

"What about your friend, the pilot?"

"I'll text him to sit tight until I contact him."

Neida leaned against Lance and rested her head on his shoulder. He wrapped his arm around her back, and she clutched his waist. Would she ever return to Hopewell again or appreciate the mysterious mound that had held her hostage her whole life?

She sighed and nuzzled even closer. Everything had taxed her mettle lately. Perhaps a tad bit more belief in her ancestor's watchful care or Lance's dependability might provide the medicine for the anxiety she felt. Nothing ever seemed to rile her grandfather, and perhaps his mountain of faith had been the reason for that. She could learn from such wisdom. But for now, she had to get control—at least find faith in Lance and herself. Whatever force had led her to Hopewell and this threatening mess, she hoped it was powerful enough to push them down the unknown road looming ahead of them.

CHAPTER FOURTEEN

NEIDA AWOKE THE DAY AFTER their escape, aware of warmth, of someone holding her hand. The sensation startled her to consciousness and forced her to open her eyes.

She lay on the bed right where she had dropped when they had arrived at the small Maryland motel the previous night. Lance had slept in a chair, but sometime during the night had scooted closer to watch her up close. Sadness, mingled with exhaustion, emphasized the shadows of his face. Awake now, she scrambled to sit, searched the room for sense and place.

"What time is it?" she asked.

"It's about three."

Since the sun intruded through a slit in the curtained window, she realized he meant in the afternoon. "Three? Are you kidding me?"

Neida lunged from the bed and tried to straighten the wrinkles from her clothes, though her efforts proved futile. She glanced in the mirror and, not liking what she saw, retrieved the brush from her purse to comb the tangles from her hair and clasp her mane in a band.

Lance stood and approached Neida from behind. Their gaze locked in the reflection of the glass. She ached to spin around and throw herself into his arms, lavish in the comfort there, and she was sure he'd respond in kind. But dredging up unsure territory wasn't smart. Not now. Not after what they'd been through.

Footsteps sounded on the landing outside, followed by an impatient knock and the intrusion of a key. The door opened, and a leather-faced maid halted when she realized they were inside. She scowled and spoke with a thick accent Neida couldn't place. "How long are you going to be? I can't wait any longer. You'll have to pay for another day."

Lance nodded. "Could you please come back in a few minutes? We'll be out soon."

The maid grunted, mumbled something under her breath, derogatory by the sound of it, but she retreated.

Lance returned his attention to Neida. His jaw and top lip receded under his stubble, and his hair spiked sideways where he had slept hard against the chair back. "We need to talk."

His words pricked like daggers, and though he spoke the truth, she dodged their sharpness and headed for the bathroom. "Half the day is gone. We don't have time to talk. We need to get far away from this place." She clipped her sentence with the click of the door. Leaning against the cold wood, she listened for a response that never came.

Neida zipped through her toiletries and applied a light layer of lipstick. She re-tucked her unused nightgown, and her change of underwear inside her oversized purse then scrutinized the image staring back at her in the mirror.

How had she overlooked the signs of her heritage? She traced her high cheekbones, contemplated her deep-set eyes. Though her skin paled to other Native American complexions, her hair grew thick and black, raven black, just like her father's.

She touched the scratch on her forehead. The bruise stood out over the pallor of her complexion. She tried to lift the new lines forming around her eyes, signs signifying the impalpable future ahead of them. She'd slept most of the day, but exhaustion weighed on her like a heavy blanket. Only a miracle, or luck, would instill normalcy again, and those wells had run dry long ago.

When she found the courage to go out to Lance again, he sat at the small table next to the window scrutinizing the motel grounds through a slit in the drapes. He got up and met her halfway across the room.

"I've called my friend. He's asked us to meet him at a private airstrip in Virginia. He'll fly us to my cabin where I have a stash of money and plenty of food. My family has always made sure the cabin's stocked for emergencies on a moment's notice. With any luck, we'll leave for Hess Lake before the end of the week. We'll keep away from major airports and public places, stay out of sight. We should be able to avoid a tail."

"What if when we get there, Winona turns us away?"

He smiled and peered down at her. "Whether you think so or not, Winona does have a heart. And she'll honor her father when Askuwheteau takes us in. Try not to exasperate your grandfather with questions, though. He'll give you pertinent information in his own time. And I'll be using your full name, so I avoid ticking him off." He had a grin on his face, but he issued his statement with candid aplomb.

"I'll behave myself. Askuwheteau's the only family I've got now. I don't want to solidify his disappointment in me."

"Hey ..." Lance moved in. "Your grandfather's expression lit up as soon as you walked into that room. He loves you. He realizes you're important to The People. I think he'll cherish taking you in and educating you."

She closed her eyes, opened them again. "One layer at a time? Come on, Lance, his methods will kill me. We need as much information as possible, as quickly as possible."

"At least we have Grandad's notes," he said.

"I wish I had the rest of Gran's journals. We should have scanned those too."

"I could call my brother and have him bring them to us at the cabin."

"Would he do that? Your mother hinted that he was annoyed with you."

"He'll help me. He always does. Since I'm the younger brother, he hovers over me like the Great Protector. That usually involves issuing advice, admonishing me on how better to live my life, and whatever else he thinks I need to hear."

"What if someone's watching the house?"

Lance shrugged. "He'll figure a way to sneak them to us without a tail."

Neida put her hands on her hips. "I hate this. I just got used to the fact I'm a landowner. Now, I can't even step through my front door. I may never see Hopewell again."

Lance cupped her chin. "You'll see Hopewell. A force brought you there, and the same force will take you back to it again."

She sniffed, almost drowned in the reflection of his brown eyes. He looked like an angel smiling at her. For a moment, she wondered if he *were* a figment of her imagination. Who in their right mind would volunteer to be by her side after what they'd experienced the previous night? His lips hovered close to hers;

his breath warmed the contours of her face. She felt tempted to close the gap, and she would have, except he stepped back and took her hand in his.

"Don't worry, Neida. I'm here for you. Your grandfather isn't all you have left. And your ancestors will make things happen. They'll guide us to where we need to go."

She wrinkled her nose at him and pulled her hand away. "There you go again—forces and mysterious powers. It's like voodoo. It's like Pastor Will and his faith talk at the funeral. Though I'm beginning to think all this mumbo jumbo might hold some merit."

Lance stared at her, seemed to be on the verge of divulging some furtive detail about his philosophy, but he only smiled. "You'd be surprised at what faith can do for you. Now get your things. Dave expects us before nightfall."

"How will we get there?"

"I found a farmer down the road this morning who understands the value of a Suunto X6HRT. He traded me his old tobacco truck for it."

"You bought a truck this morning? With your watch?"

"Not just any watch. A Suunto X6HRT. I guess he wants to check his heart rate and barometric pressure. He'll never get lost in his fields either. That compass helped me more times than I can say. Though he got the better end of the deal, I think. That truck looks like it's on its last legs."

"Why would you sell such a valuable device?"

"The watch is replaceable, Neida. You're not. I'm taking you away from here today, right now. So, no more talk. My friend will be waiting." He hurried to gather his backpack, then went to the door and turned with an expectant look on his face.

She tsked and pressed her lips together. She couldn't stop the train wreck even if she tried. With a frustrated sigh, she picked up her purse and dragged past Lance, though more than grateful that he promised to stay by her side.

卌

Their luck worsened several miles' drive down the beltway. The truck's tire blew and forced Lance to coax the limping vehicle to the shoulder. He pounded the steering wheel hard with his fist and mumbled, "Yeah, that farmer definitely got the better end of the deal."

They lost a couple of hours hitching a ride on the back of a flatbed truck to and from a tire store some distance away. Later, the tobacco truck overheated as they crossed the border into Virginia. They passed another hour immobilized, cooling down until they could add water to the ancient radiator, then chanced the remainder of the trip.

They ran out of miracles after they crawled into the mountains and hobbled off the main highway into a forest-hidden field. A cloud of angry vapor roiled up from under the hood, and the vehicle sputtered and jolted to a stop. Neida's hope sank. That's when she spotted the Cessna waiting for them at the end of a dirt runway. How odd the way things often turned out, but she wasn't about to question the forces of the universe now.

"Why would someone need an airstrip in the middle of this wilderness?" she asked.

"The state used to mine salt up here, and this runway served as their lifeline. Dave found the spot on one of their hundreds of camping trips to the mountains."

"Dave?"

Lance nodded in the direction of the plane. "My friend, the pilot."

The dwindling light provided little comfort. By the aircraft's appearance and the excuse for a runway, Neida hoped his friend kept a miracle in his pocket.

A few minutes later, she found out that Dave, a squat little man with a leather jacket and baseball hat covering his shiny bald spot, came highly skilled. He taxied to the runway's end and used every inch of the bumpy strip to get the Cessna off the ground and over the trees. Neida hadn't realized she'd stopped breathing until Lance took her hand in his and squeezed. "Hey, relax. Dave's about the best there is. His dad was an ace pilot in Nam and taught him how to fly."

Dave shrugged, and even within the tinny sounds of their headgear, his reply sounded heavy with humility. "I get by in a pinch. By the way, Lance, I called your brother as you asked. He'll be at the cabin with the goods."

"The journals?" Neida shot Lance a sideways glance. "You weren't kidding. He'd drive all that distance without question."

"Well, he'll fly," said Lance. "He's a pilot too. He'll arrive even before we do."

She hadn't seen Robert since they were kids. If he turned out half as amiable as Lance and his mother, she'd like him. He'd gone out of his way for her. His kindness had already chalked up some points in her book.

Once her flight jitters settled, Neida found little problem dozing. With all the car trouble out of D.C. and the previous night's atrocities, their plight had depleted her energy more than she realized. She awoke to a shake of her arm.

Lance pointed out the Cessna's window. "My cabin's down there somewhere."

She yawned and stretched in a snapping of joints and examined the void below her. Nothing, endless nothing. "Is it safe to land?" Just as she spoke, two long rows of lights appeared below and edged up a dark runway.

"Signs are favorable. I hope Robert's lit a fire." Lance handed her a parka from the back of the plane. "Better put this on. It's much colder up here than in Newaygo. Oh, and Neida, let's keep our plans to ourselves. For right now, I don't want Robert to know our business."

She nodded, though she couldn't understand Lance's secrecy. If Robert handled dangerous situations daily, his help might prove invaluable.

Several minutes later, Dave landed the aircraft, dead center, inside the runway lights. By the time the plane's engines had faded to silence, and they descended the Cessna steps, two headlights raced toward them from between the trees.

A mother of pearl Esplanade stopped in front of them, and a muscular man lit from the driver's side to open the back door of the vehicle. He helped an elderly woman step to the ground. She grabbed a cane from the seat, thumped it in front of her, and maneuvered around to face them. Her body wobbled as she advanced toward Lance, her cold stare fixed upon them both.

Lance's face clouded when she stopped in front of him. "Grandmother, what are you doing here?" His jaw worked in and out with anger.

Every inch of Lila Gentry's stance, her stiffness and formality, exuded a foreboding threat, intimidation to seriously regard. Even in the dim light, her silver hair and gaunt complexion emphasized her pinched face.

"Is that any way to greet your favorite grandmother?"

"I expected Robert."

The woman's manly chuckle made Neida instantly dislike her.

"He asked me to help," she said, her gruff voice growing cold.

"Yeah, well, you shouldn't have troubled yourself. The trip is too taxing."

"For an old hag, you mean. You ought to realize by now I get around. I've got pilots and drivers who take me anywhere I want to go. Besides, Robert seemed adamant I bring you a box. Must be pretty important with how secretive he was. What's inside anyway?"

The driver retrieved the package from the car and shoved it at Lance.

He accepted the receptacle and snapped a response, "That's none of your business."

Lila turned to regard Neida from head to toe and back again. Her probe burrowed deep, and a snarl curled her thin lips. "And this is who you profess to be part of our family?"

Neida shivered at the harsh scrutiny and barbed assessment.

"Don't get too comfortable, young lady," said Lila, leaning toward Neida. "You'll never be a part of this family. Your grandmother thought she owned Edward. And you plan to take her place and convince my grandson to follow in his grandfather's footsteps. Make no mistake. I'll ruin you if you search for those forgeries."

Neida backed away from her angst, stepped closer to Lance. The woman's words flitted in the space between them like quivering pieces of ash.

Lance grabbed his grandmother's arm. "I appreciate you venturing up here for Robert. However, I'm sure you need to get back as soon as possible." He ushered her toward the car.

Lila pulled to a stop and smiled. "Why would I do that? And after coming all this way. This is the perfect opportunity to have our little visit since you're never at home."

"I don't mean to be rude, but we came up here to be alone. I didn't expect company."

"Like your pilot, here." Lila jerked her head toward Dave.

"He's leaving in the morning."

"What a coincidence. So am I. We'll have a cozy little reunion tonight. Better hurry inside, though. We'd don't want the girl to freeze out here, do we?"

She limped to the car, where her bodyguard rushed to lift her onto her perch and shut her inside. He eyed them all, a dire warning, before he stuffed himself behind the wheel and closed the door. The darkened, back window opened halfway, and Lila leaned out her head. "Meet you back at the ranch." She chuckled low in her throat before the pane rose again, and the car sped off, disappearing through a line of trees.

"You never told me you had such strange relatives," said Dave, scratching underneath his hat.

Neida's panic, along with the cold and exhaustion, severed a nerve. "Why didn't she give us a ride? Is the cabin far?"

When Lance failed to answer, Dave patted her arm. "No worries. Lance's place is just through those trees."

That fact consoled her, though she shied away from the cozy little *visit* Lila promised back at the ranch.

Lance grabbed Neida's hand. "Let's get to the house. She's up to no good. I never trusted the woman, and I don't intend to now." He tugged her forward, and the trio headed for the trees.

"We'll take turns as sentry, Dave. Until she leaves tomorrow, I want to understand her purpose for being here. And Neida, the sooner we drop off the face of the earth, the better. Too many people know our business right now."

His words sat like lead along the edges of her nerves. It was true, Lance and Dave provided her a measure of safety, but she couldn't shake the notion that they sprinted toward a future far beyond their control.

They dined on tuna sandwiches and bottled water before bed. Lance handed Neida the box of journals, telling her to guard them with her life, and left Dave with his grandmother as he directed Neida to a spacious room at the top of the stairs. Inside, he removed dust covers from the furniture to reveal a vintage dresser, side tables, and a four-poster bed adorned with an antique quilt. Spode accessories and hand-woven pillows accented the room. The effect appeared warm and inviting. Too bad the visit was under less than restful circumstances.

"I'll keep the first lookout," he said. "While you and Dave sleep, I'm going to bend my grandmother's ear a while, figure out the reason she's here. I don't understand Robert. He knew the secrecy of our getting the journals. Why would he just hand them over to our grandmother or send her in his place?"

"Maybe you should call him."

"The reception is nil up here. I'll have to use the plane's radio, see if I can make contact with anyone who might know if Robert filed a flight plan."

"You think your grandmother had some involvement with the mess we're in?"

"That's something I intend to find out."

Neida frowned at his confidence. "She's not going to tell you whether she's a buddy of Blackhour's. Maybe we should sneak off in the night while she's asleep."

"I wish we could. But we need to rest, and I want to get to the bottom of this. You try to sleep some too. In the morning, we'll head for one of Dave's camping sites north of here. It's quite some distance from the state parks and not easy to get to, but no one will be able to find us there. We'll head for your grandfather's once we lay low for a couple of days."

Neida sighed, helplessness rendering her at a loss.

Lance reached to touch her forehead and let his fingers linger near the tender place over her eye. "I'm sorry," was all he said before he left the room.

Though she tried several times, Neida couldn't sleep. Her mind wandered to Fitz's demise, then to the conversation in the living room downstairs. She paced the floor for an hour, but the activity failed to help relieve her anxiety.

On one trip across the bedroom, the container of journals snagged her attention. She hurried to the dresser, brought the box to the bed, and tore at the tape holding the package together. When she pulled back the flaps, she scowled at the contents.

Neida disemboweled the box and checked each book, *Wuthering Heights*, *Jane Eyre*, and *Treasure Island* among them, but none of Gran's journals. Lila had lied, stolen her grandmother's things, and now she hoarded them someplace or had destroyed them. They'd never find her grandmother's words again.

She rushed to the door and tiptoed to the stairwell. Calm conversation wafted up the banister. She took two steps at a time to the bottom, slowed, and breathed in courage before she walked into the living room. To her surprise, Lance and Dave stood over a map sprawled on the coffee table, but Lila Gentry was nowhere around.

"Lance?"

The men looked up.

"Where's your grandmother?"

"She slipped out the back when I showed you to your room. She and her heavyweight are long gone."

"I thought she planned to stay the night."

"Just one of her lies."

"Why didn't you come to get me?" She didn't let him answer. "Lila took my grandmother's journals, Lance. They aren't in the box."

He shook his head, put a finger to his lips, and led her outside. When they were free of the front porch, he turned to her. "You can relax, Neida. I just talked to Robert. It seems my grandmother disabled his plane today, and he's spent the afternoon repairing the damage. He's on his way with the journals now. He believes Lila overheard his conversation with Dave and decided to check things out for herself. She must have put the box together as a ruse for taking Robert's place. And we found this." Lance dangled what had once been a square device in front of her, its casing and miniature radio transmitter smashed to pieces.

Neida couldn't believe it. "She bugged the place?"

"She's thorough, to be sure. But we're not waiting around for her next surprise. We keep an old trailblazer up here for emergencies. Dave's going to get the vehicle running. As soon as we round up some supplies, we'll leave."

"But I thought Robert is on his way." Her head spun with the turn of events.

"He'll meet us at Dave's cabin. Once we get the journals, we'll head out the long way to Hess Lake."

"Are you sure Robert picked them up?"

Lance nodded. "Positive. He retrieved the books himself, and he hasn't let them out of his sight since."

"And no one suspects he's doing this for us?"

"You mean, except for my grandmother? Not as far as we can tell."

"Don't worry, Neida," said Dave, as he came outside to join them. "We're safe. We've swept the house for more bugs and checked down the road a bit. Lila's gone back to the hole she slithered out of. But we can't be too careless with our conversation inside." He slapped his hands together. "Guess I'd better attend to the Trailblazer now. As soon as I get the car running and check the plane for any tampering, I'll let you know."

Neida liked Lance's friend. "Thanks, Dave. I can't tell you how much I appreciate all you've done for us, but will you be safe? The last guy who tried to help us ended up on the wrong side of a spear."

Dave walked backward toward the side of the house. "Don't worry about me. I'm known to hide away for weeks, especially when I need to escape my wife." His last comment produced a smile. "I'll be fine. I'll come to get you in a few." He turned and strolled into the dark.

Neida turned to Lance, who appeared more spent than before. She could relate. A short time ago, she lived a quiet existence in California, ignorant of her heritage and the elusive artifacts that had kept them running for cover. And just how long they'd continue to slip from the grasp of their enemies, especially without knowing who those enemies were, was anyone's best guess.

Lance leaned in. "Why don't you go rustle up some trail food inside the pantry? Two meals a day for at least a week should be sufficient. I'll gather some money and clothes we can use." He inched closer and caressed her shoulder. "As soon as this is over, I'm going to take you on a long vacation. Maybe hike the back hills of Michigan in the spring." He paused and glanced down. When he looked up again, his brown eyes sparkled with emotion. "I want to know you better, Neida, like when we were kids. More, if you're agreeable."

After a slight hesitation, she brought her hand up to caress the side of his face. "After this is over, you'll probably want to stay clear of me. Remember what they say about harrowing circumstances throwing people together. If our lives settle down, we may find we don't even like each other."

"I hardly think that will happen."

To be honest, neither did she. Neida smiled and patted his chest. "Why don't we wait and see how the artifacts crumble." She headed for the kitchen, and despite the fact she'd sounded so sure of herself, she shoved away the emotions flowing upward from her toes.

CHAPTER FIFTEEN

DAVE HAD BUILT HIS CABIN by special permit through the favor of a ranger friend. The handcrafted dwelling lay far from the walking trails of Michigan's Upper Peninsula in the Ottawa National Forest. By early morning, Neida and Lance had traveled a considerable distance north on US 2 near Besseme, up The Black River Scenic Byway, and continued west past the Great Conglomerate Falls.

Miles later, after they parked, Lance retrieved the backpacks from the Trailblazer's storage compartment. He helped Neida slip into the straps of one of them and donned the other pack for himself. He guided her down the trail—about three-fourths of a mile over rolling, forested land.

"How are you doing back there?" he asked a few minutes later. Lance glanced over his shoulder but continued in strides that forced Neida to increase her pace.

"Slow down, will you? It's been a couple of months since I've walked a trail. I'm a bit out of shape."

Lance stopped and turned around with a sheepish grin. "Sorry, you'll find I'm relentless in the wilderness. There's something about the air that pushes me into overdrive. We've got several miles yet to go, and I'm anxious to meet up with Robert."

"I can't imagine a place to land an airplane up here." Neida finally reached his side. She was panting a bit more than she expected and tried adjusting the heavy load on her back.

"There isn't. Not where we're going. Robert will have to hike in, just like we are."

Neida rolled her eyes. "Perfect. That's wonderful." Her trouble had caused everyone to jump through hoops.

"What's wrong?"

"I haven't even seen the guy in years, and he'll trek the wilderness and endanger his life to bring me a mountain of books on his back."

Lance laughed. "You worry too much. He doesn't mind. Believe me." He adjusted one of her straps then headed down the path again, just as fast as before.

Neida sighed and hurried after him.

They walked several more hours, and she wondered if he knew where he was going in such dense surroundings. He surprised her miles later and led her into a clearing where a small rustic dwelling nested against a tree-laden embankment.

"This is unexpected," said Neida. She studied the rustic bungalow. "No one would even know the cabin is here."

"That was Dave's plan. He built it himself. It's his refuge away from the wiles of the world, though the ranger's permission only allows him to reside here a couple of weeks at a time."

The cabin door opened. Although darker in features, a man stood Lance-like in the entrance. He peered through the rank of stately trees that separated them.

Chuckling, Lance grabbed Neida's hand and guided her toward the porch. As they approached, Robert's smile cracked and swung into a wide grin. She eyed one man and then the other; over the years, they'd grown to look so much alike.

"Do I have to travel hundreds of miles for you to visit me, little brother?" asked Robert.

Lance matched his brother's smile and let go of Neida's hand. He jumped on the deck, and the two men embraced, slapped each other's backs, and stepped away to examine the other. Their eyes danced, almost as if their last encounter spanned years instead of months.

"You're looking a bit pudgy through the middle." Lance poked at Robert's gut. "Has your cushy security job kept you from the trails?"

"That, and Deandra's cooking, will be my undoing," he said, patting the excess at his front. Robert turned rapt attention upon Neida, causing her cheeks to burn. He shoved Lance aside and walked to the edge of the deck to help her up. "Extraordinary! Our long, lost cousin."

"It seems so," said Neida with a nod.

Robert guided her back to Lance, gawking at her as he did so. He socked his brother on the arm. "Mom's right. She's done nothing but tell me what a looker Neida is—that she grew up into a beauty. No wonder she hopes something's going on between the two of you again."

Lance flinched. "That's my brother. Not a bashful bone in his body. Comes right out and gets to the point."

"How else?" said Robert. "You can't protect the clients I have by pussyfooting around. A hard-nosed approach is the only method to handle surveillance—and life."

"At the very least, I'll know right where I stand with you." Neida grinned at him and pumped his hand.

Robert continued to gape and didn't let go. "You always knew how to pick them, brother, scratches and all."

Neida touched her damaged face with her free hand and shook her head. "Uh … no, Lance and I aren't—"

"Yep, she's got my seal of approval."

"As if I need your approval." Lance detached their hands and whisked Neida inside, whispering "sorry" before Robert followed them and closed the door.

Although the cabin seemed small, the interior design leaned to the grandiose. One wall flaunted oversized rock and a floor-to-ceiling fireplace. Unstained paneling completed the other three walls, and massive beams spanned the length of the vaulted ceiling. A stairwell ascended behind a railing to the highest point where she supposed a loft hid from their view to her left. A rustic, horned chandelier hung low at the center of the room.

"Electricity runs this far out?" asked Neida. The possibility amazed her.

Robert thumbed toward the outside wall. "Nah, they own a generator."

Lance helped Neida slip off her backpack and put it with his in the corner. She held her hands toward the fire to warm them. The day had turned crisp, and since removing her gloves, the elements had sucked not only warmth but moisture from her skin like a slow drain.

As soon as they sat on the sectional surrounding the fireplace, Neida asked, "So, did you bring the journals?" She'd not rest until she saw her grandmother's words again and tucked them away in a safe place.

Robert rose and retrieved a box from the sideboard. "Per my baby brother's instructions, here are the years 1957 to 1965. Not an easy task to pack them across this terrain, mind you, but doable. I've locked up the rest of the journals, but if you need them, please ask."

Not that she distrusted him, but she unfolded the flaps to remove the first of several chronicles as the men carried on small talk. She caressed the leather, slowly unboxed all of them before she went to her backpack to retrieve the two volumes she had brought with her. When she came back to the couch, under Lance and Robert's admiring examination, she nodded satisfaction at Robert. "Thank you. I'm indebted to you."

Lance glanced at his brother. "She can't believe you'd bring them all the way up here."

Robert's face shadowed in the light of the fire. "Why wouldn't I? On the whole, the Grahams are a bunch of trolls, but a few of us possess some redeeming qualities. Besides, I had a little vacation coming." He smiled the same boyish grin that often played with the corners of Lance's mouth.

Neida patted one of the journals. "These are invaluable to our research. You'll never understand how much."

"Must be some big trouble my brother placed on your shoulders," said Robert. "Dave acted pretty reticent when he called me yesterday. You can trust me, Lance. If you're in danger, I'll do anything to pull a few strings, use my influence. Just ask."

"I know, Robert. I'm not questioning your loyalty. For reasons I can't explain, I won't allow you or Mom to get involved."

"I'm already involved. What's going on?"

Lance sprang from the couch and hovered near the fire, his back rising and falling as he inhaled a long breath. He remained silent for some time before he turned around. "We're on to something Granddad uncovered, and someone will do whatever is necessary to keep us from our goal. Since Granddad disappeared all those years ago, I'm beginning to suspect foul play—to make sure his discovery stayed buried."

"You can't be serious," said Robert.

Neida studied Lance. How much of their agenda did he plan to reveal?

Lance's shadow flickered on the wall on the other side of the room. "I'm dead serious. I want you and Mom as far away from all this as possible."

"Sounds as though you need the local authorities involved. Is this about the artifacts Granddad found? Mom said you were looking for them."

Lance nodded.

"I've got contacts, people who can help. Think of Neida. Think of Mom if you go and get yourself killed. She's already worried since you didn't call her when you said you would. I don't want that burden on my shoulders. I'm here for you, bro, whether you like it or not."

Robert appeared sincere, and he demonstrated a deep love for his brother, but Lance could hold out all night. She frowned at him, annoyed. "Why don't you let him help us?"

Lance ran a hand through his hair and lowered his head. After a lengthy pause, he looked up at both of them. "I'm going to regret this."

Robert jumped up, animated. "You can count on me. I'm already investigating who turned Neida's house into a heap."

Lance sighed and rolled his eyes. "Thanks, Robert."

"What?" he asked with his palms facing up.

"My house is in a heap? What do you mean?" The revelation weighed like cement in Neida's chest. She couldn't breathe.

Robert's eyes softened. "I'm afraid someone's turned your house upside down, destroyed the library mostly, but left nothing unturned. After the law snoops around and we hunt down the perpetrators, we'll have to hire a contractor to clean up the place."

"You mean, whatever's left to clean up," she added. The cement solidified sharp edges and all—her grandmother's antiques destroyed, her Grandfather Graham's precious books and artifacts, violated by some unknown hand.

Lance crossed the room and parked himself next to Neida. He touched her knee, but his concerned gesture did little to relieve the flood rising inside her.

Robert coughed. "Listen, Neida, the fools that committed the deed wanted pay dirt. Do you keep important documents filed somewhere in the house? Do you know of anything that might lead us to these slime balls?"

Neida shrugged. "Maybe in Grandad's research. Maybe in my grandmother's journals." She placed her hand on one of the volumes.

"Well, we lucked out there. I went back last night to check if I'd left anything behind. The house was trashed by then."

Her spirit sank at the word "trashed." She pulled away from Lance, stood, and plodded to the fire to get warm.

Lance lit from the couch after her. He rubbed her shoulders then turned to his brother. "Okay, Robert, you're in, but you can't tell anyone where we are. Until we find the artifacts, no one knows what we're up to, not even Mom. Promise me."

Robert frowned. "I'm insulted. I've handled some pretty dangerous scenarios in my day, those that require discretion. And I've always had your back. Always will. So, you've got to tell me everything. Where will you be staying?"

"We'll leave in the morning and drive until we find a place. We'll contact you when we solidify our plans."

Despite the sincerity of his delivery, his manipulation of the truth almost choked Neida.

Robert joined them at the fireplace. "Promise me you'll play it safe, little brother, and protect our cuz here. Call me as soon as you get settled."

Neida stared at the floor, avoiding both their eyes. Lance's lie about their plans just proved that Robert would wait far longer than he had any idea.

ᛐᚼᛍ

Sleep eluded Lance that night in the cabin. The three of them each took one of several single beds ranked in two rows the loft's length—the men on one side of the room, and Neida on the other. Lance extended a rope between walls and draped a blanket for Neida's privacy. He hated her passing the night alone with her thoughts.

He wished things were different. That Robert was different. Unfortunately, Robert had hurled the news about Hopewell at Neida without once weighing the repercussions. It would take days for Lance to reassure her and to repair the damage.

The fire sizzled and spat, and had simmered down to smoldering hot spots behind the grate downstairs. Though the cabin had turned cold, the earlier blaze had consumed all dampness, and the dry air seared the back of Lance's throat.

He rolled to sit on the side of the bed, and when no one stirred, he crept to the head of the stairs and descended to the lower level, avoiding the groan of the bottom step altogether. The embers' soft glow in the fireplace guided him to the small burl table and lamp next to the couch. He turned the switch, bathing the room in dim hues.

Lance shuffled through the journals still stacked where Neida had left them until he found those pertinent to the investigation. He retrieved the computer from inside his backpack and hurried to the couch to wrap up in a wool throw, and then pulled up the scans from Granddad's library on the screen.

This opportunity was his first chance to view the annotations, and though he knew he should wait for Neida, urgency compelled him to examine the data anyway. He reread one particular entry they had discovered the night before they left for D.C.

> A7: 200 June 15: Smithsonian arrived today. Blackhour seems knowledgeable enough, though something isn't quite right about his methods. He's anxious to test back in Washington as soon as we discover what's inside. Opening the casket tomorrow, June 16. L18: 126.

He switched to the next passage, to the specified date:

> L18: 126 Opened the casket at 10:00 A.M.—Stephenson, Blackhour, Rex Willett, a few others, and I all present. Cement holding sides together and topmost stone to box—a type of heated limestone mixed with sand and gravel—used organic agent for waterproofing—testing in D.C. to determine materials and susceptibility to acid degradation. Lid carved, rounded in middle, and flattened out to sides. T10: 45

The next annotation continued the thought.

> Rex trying to decipher writing on top and sides of stone casket—looks like a mix of hieroglyphs and hieratic, Coptic, Phoenician, Egyptian, even

> unknown characters, toothbrush in form—hard to determine at first glance. Removed lid—copper tablet set on two carved stones—raised from bottom—one symbol consistent on all. Looks similar to Hebrew.

"What are you doing?"

Lance, so engrossed in his reading, jerked in his seat when the voice shot through him like an electric current. The computer almost toppled from his lap. He spun around to Neida, who leaned over his shoulder from the back of the couch. "Don't scare me like that," he said a little too sharply.

"Sorry, I heard you get up." She looked chagrined. "I haven't slept all night. Thought I'd come down and keep you company."

Neida's hair hung loose and poured over her shoulders, dangling against him in disarray. It surprised him and melted the moment's annoyance. Ever since she came to Michigan, she'd braided her tresses or caught the stray ends in a band. Now, she appeared as the most beautiful creature he'd ever seen. A blanket draped around her back, and she clutched it in front of her in a modest fashion. The top of a flimsy nightdress poked out where the wool overlapped.

"You must be freezing. Come over here and cuddle up next to me." He opened up his wrap, and she skirted the couch, plopped next to him, and snuggled closer without hesitation. In the swoop of an arm, he swathed the throw around her shoulders, closing her against him.

Her nearness and the way their bodies touched under the blanket distracted him. *Man, she smells like Heaven.* Their eyes met and locked. Her mouth hovered just inches from his. Lance's gaze traveled to the luscious curve of Neida's lips, felt her warm breath caressing his mouth, inviting him to close the space.

Before he could, a succession of Robert's short snores scudded over the railing from above, and the shock of it forced them apart. They looked at each other for a moment—Neida's eyes as large as platters, her mouth skewed in mocked surprise at the noise. They stifled their laughter, and despite how much he still wanted to kiss her, the moment had passed. He was forced to turn his head away and concentrate on the computer as a ruse to regain his composure.

"So, have you discovered anything helpful?" Her voice strained with embarrassment.

Lance looked up, but she focused her attention on the computer now. The depth of his disappointment surprised him.

"Neida ..."

She only shook her head. "Please, don't say anything."

He sighed inwardly and pulled his arm from around her shoulder to right the laptop and tap the finger pad. The scan flashed on the screen, and he cleared his throat. "I think you'll be interested in this entry. Rex Willett was present when they opened the casket."

Neida leaned in to read. After finishing, she sat back and tilted her head. "Hmm, they couldn't decipher the language yet."

Lance found the next section and read it aloud.

> Tomorrow penetrating tumulus deeper. Searching for skeletal remains under what's left of wooden platform. Blackhour taking samples back to lab at end of week.

"I wonder if Blackhour shared even a smidgen of the data with Grandad," said Neida.

Lance shrugged. "The letters suggest months passed by without a word." He picked up the 1964 journal and handed it to her. "Why don't you check your grandmother's entries for clues?"

Neida searched until she came to the date in question and shared the passage.

June 16, 1964

What an eventful day. Who would guess our little mound out back could create such a stir? Several technicians accompanied Thomas Blackhour to investigate thoroughly. I'd never seen Edward so excited as when they found a copper tablet inside the stone box. The earlier tablets Edward discovered were usually clay or slate and buried underneath the dirt with no protection around them at all. Rex is trying to decipher some of the characters the artisan etched into the metal, but thus far, I don't think he has a clue. Edward was so sure they'd figure out the language.

On another note, I met Askuwheteau at the edge of the forest. He was with the young girl again. They both viewed the unveiling without expression. They must have been devastated about the museum men and Edward cutting into that mound. I saw them from my bedroom window, and I couldn't stand it any longer. I drummed up the courage to go out and talk to them. The youngster scowled at me. Askuwheteau frowned, as though he thought I should stop Edward from the desecration. Tears eventually ran down his

> cheeks, and all he said to me was, "Your husband violates sacred things."
>
> I didn't know what to say, but his sadness pierced my soul. I wanted to wrap my arms around him, but too many years have passed since we were together. He hates me now. And the little girl just kept glaring at me. Edward refuses to abide by my pleadings to give up this treasure hunt, and because I married him and turned my back on Askuwheteau, my grief is unbearable.

Neida stared at the page; the anguish of her grandmother's words tightened a sensitive place inside her chest.

"Your Gran still loved Askuwheteau," said Lance. "Is the little girl who I think she is?"

"Winona? I assume so. I wonder if Gran realized she was his daughter." She leafed through additional pages. "There's not much more here. Her next entry talks of mundane things. Nothing else refers to the dig, except she says the men from the museum went home."

Lance switched to the next scan on his computer:

> June 17. Dug deeper into mound today—found skeletal remains that disintegrated when exposed to elements. Also, found arrows and copper spearheads, tools, pottery vessels. The mound design suggests higher development than the Adena culture unearthed in Ohio. Blackhour beginning to annoy—follows me around, hovers as though I'm hiding artifacts, information. Smithsonian packing up all evidence to remove

> to D.C. Worries me. Rex working around the clock to decipher language before the museum carts off tablet and stone box.

"Sounds shady."

Neida and Lance looked to the loft. Robert leaned over the railing and frowned down at them.

Lance minimized the screen then peered up again. "Sorry if we were too loud.

"Nah, I wake up several times a night," said Robert. "Too many things on my mind. Bugs the heck out of Deandra. She never gets any sleep because I fidget." He hurried down the stairs to the bottom. "But what are you reading? Did I hear that Granddad found a graveyard with the copper tablet? In his backyard? I wonder why Dad never told us about this."

Lance shut down the computer. Robert's eavesdropping would trigger a billion questions he refused to answer right now. "I suppose both Granddad and Dad spent their days trying to convince their colleagues to study the Michigan Relics, but society refused to listen; no one ever listens. Someone probably killed Grandad because of it. And now we're clueless over a people who lived and breathed right where you stand."

Robert stepped closer. "Do you really believe the information got him killed?"

"I'm just guessing. We don't know that for sure."

"Let someone who's trained in this sort of thing figure it out. Like me. Do you want to risk your life—and Neida's—over a hoax?"

"The Michigan Relics aren't hoaxes, Robert, at least not all of them. I'm convinced granddad and dad both found proof of that, and I'm taking up where Dad left off. Now, it's too early. Neida and I are going back to bed. And I suggest you do the same. We've all got a long day ahead of us."

Lance grabbed the computer and scrambled out of the blanket. He motioned for Neida to stand and whisked her past his brother up the stairs. Just before they reached the landing, he stopped and peered back over the railing.

Robert frowned up at them. His dark robe, tied tight, forced his paunch to balloon over the belt. "I think you're chasing trouble, little brother. And for what? To tick someone off? Why don't you let *me* handle it? I think you're in over your head."

Lance gritted his teeth, clamped his lips together to avoid a retort. His opinion would make little impression on a man who thought he held all the answers, one who often showed overzealousness in his methods. He didn't need his brother running the show either. Their situation needed a calm head and patient resolve.

Besides, Neida was watching them both. The argument had probably surprised her. He hoped the rift would dissipate after a good night's rest, but for now, he doubted even a machete could cut the tension that followed them to their beds.

CHAPTER SIXTEEN

THE TRIO LEFT THE CABIN by 5:00 the next morning. They had decided to take the long way home to introduce some unpredictability into their plan. The trip to Hess Lake promised to take over twelve hours, not including stops.

To Neida's relief, after they drove Robert to his plane, Lance hugged his brother and wished him a safe journey home. Optimism swelled inside her as they commenced the long ride back to Lower Michigan.

But the elation lasted for only a brief time. As Neida and Lance reached the outskirts of Rockford, Illinois in the afternoon, Lance still had spoken little. The last few weeks had taught her to take his silence as thinking time. The previous night's incident with Robert no doubt had caused his present mood.

"Want to talk about it?" Neida asked when he turned off the car in the Rockford Café's parking lot.

"Talk about what?"

His attempt at ignorance wasn't fooling her. "Something's bothering you. You haven't spoken a sentence to me since we left this morning."

He leaned against the headrest. "I'm sorry, Neida. I'm trying to figure out the last couple of days. First, Lila appears from out of nowhere and disappears as quickly, and then Robert's act last night."

"How did he act?" she asked, frowning. "He seemed pretty normal to me. I couldn't quite understand why you were so upset with him. Was it because he asked about our business? He seems like he wants to help, and a man in his position might understand how to do that, and know the individuals to contact."

"I told you, the fewer people savvy to what we're doing, the better off everyone will be. Robert tends to shoot from the hip. You heard him. He doesn't appreciate the importance of our goals, and he's quick to criticize anything that contradicts his philosophy or life choices."

Neida shrugged. "Well, you understand your brother better than I do, and certainly, I'm no judge of character, but please try to remember we're searching for these artifacts because my grandmother requested it. Somewhere along the way, this became your quest to inform the world, instead of honoring a promise."

Lance twisted in his seat. Anger furrowed his face and turned his voice to steel. "In case you've forgotten, someone has murdered my friend and grandfather. Thieves ransacked your house, and a thug almost crammed my Adam's apple through the back of my neck. That makes this quest a heck of a lot more important than just honoring a promise."

The fire in his eyes scorched her, increasing the emotion his words stirred within. She shoved herself outside and ran. A car door slammed behind her, then another. Halfway across the parking lot, Lance caught up to her. She veered and dashed for the highway to keep distance between them.

"Wait, Neida," Lance called out behind her. "Please wait."

She stopped on the median strip of the highway, the lanes momentarily devoid of cars, and whipped around to him as he joined her. A vision of him blurred through her tears.

"I'm sorry." He clasped her arm.

"I'm as anxious as you are, Lance." She punctuated her words with her finger. "I don't know who to trust. Or where to go that's safe. I can't even return home."

Lance placed his hands on either side of her face and stared deep into her eyes.

She stood still, fought off the need to run, balked in the offered intimacy.

Cars now sped past them; a horn beeped. Neida didn't care. He tried to draw her close, but she pushed him away. A man yelled out from his car window, "Get a room."

Lance kept his eyes on her. "I'm sorry I took my mood out on you, Neida. I promise that stops right now." Concern pleated his forehead. "I didn't mean to run the show either. I thought we both wanted to find the artifacts for the same reasons."

She sniffed. "We do, but you've got to remember who asked me to do this. My grandmother begged me, and I promised her I'd find the artifacts. I need to keep my word."

"I know. Can we at least try to find out what Grandfather Graham discovered? That's just as important too. Whatever answers those artifacts hold, I believe they'll satisfy your grandmother's request and teach us what we want to know."

The way he gazed at her, with pleading, puppy-dog eyes, calmed her. "I want to grasp the answers as much as you do, Lance. Whether or not I trust the premise of what the artifacts contain is unimportant. Fact or fiction, right or wrong. I'm in this for the duration."

A blast from a passing truck jolted them both. Lance laughed with embarrassment. "I think we'd better get back to the sidewalk."

She nodded and allowed him to slip a protective arm around her shoulder. They stepped onto the highway as Lance checked for oncoming vehicles and held her back. "Wait. Let's let this van pass first."

A black Dodge Caravan had turned into the road from a row of businesses several yards away, the tinted glass swallowing the driver in darkness. They waited as the van sped up. Then, without warning, the wheels veered, steering a mass of steel and rubber in a direct line toward them.

Someone from the sidewalk screamed, "Look out!"

Lance reacted, heaved Neida out of the vehicle's path, and forced her to dive through the air just a second before he followed. They slammed into the pavement, rolling like pop cans across the street. Every turn dented, each scud crushed another part of her body until the tumult ended abruptly and she lay stunned under Lance's protective frame.

A string of events unfolded at the edge of her consciousness—the van sped away; people ran out of establishments. Somehow the traffic stopped. In the haze, someone called 911. A robust biker with a full beard and bandana encircling his frizzy hair lifted Lance and aided him to the curb—came back and, with gentle power, carried Neida as though she were air and placed her next to him. Gravel clung to Lance's bloody abrasions, but she sagged against him anyway.

The man with the bandana shook his head in the direction of the fugitive van. He turned back and gaped at them, a colorful expletive punctuating his words. "Are you two okay?"

He didn't wait for their answer. "Just sit tight. An ambulance is coming."

Every inch of her body ached like what she imagined roadkill felt like, but she somehow managed to sit upright. She rearranged a stray lock of Lance's hair with her bloodied hand, not that the neatness gesture mattered. Blood matted his curls, and a dark bruise now formed on his left cheekbone.

His intense stare frightened her. At first, he almost peered through her, and then he reached to clasp her nurturing fingers and held her hand to his chest. "I'm sorry. I got careless."

"I'm all right," she lied. "Once the paramedics come, we'll be all right."

He shook his head. "No, we need to leave now."

"But you're hurt worse than I am."

"If we end up in the hospital, we'll become targets for sure. Our assailant might come back to finish the job."

Sirens wailed in the distance.

"What do we do?" she asked. "Everybody's watching us."

Lance struggled to stand. Grunting and wincing, he straightened his body and reached for her hands to pull her up. "We'll make a run for it."

He scrutinized the biker. The man sucked on his cigarette and exhaled a stream of smoke, staring at the approaching medical unit, a tiny flashing of white and red that raced toward them from 200 yards up the road.

Lance grabbed the stranger's hand. "Hey, thanks, man. Appreciate your help, but would you mind running a diversion for us? Not fond of answering questions, if you take my meaning."

The biker's smile slowly formed under his grizzled beard. He nodded. "Gotcha, dude. Been there a time or two myself."

"Do you know a place where we can pick up a reliable vehicle? Cheap?"

The man pointed down the road to the south. “There’s a small mechanics shop about two miles that way called Roy’s. Ask for Mad Dog. Tell him Spud said to fix you up.”

“I owe you, man.”

“Just make all my noise worth it.” The biker nodded, sprinted away, and pointed to a side street. “Hey, over there,” he shouted. “Those are the guys in the black van. Let’s get ’em.”

Onlookers whirled to where the biker pointed. Lance and Neida inched away, and they ducked behind a parked car. Several men joined Spud, and the bystanders moved toward the new attraction, intercepting the ambulance as it slowed to a stop up the road. With siren blaring, a police car whizzed by to the head of the crowd, parting the sea of confusion. Lance and Neida hobbled toward their vehicle almost undetected.

Once they climbed inside, Neida slumped low in the seat and spied the commotion outside the window. The paramedics lugged out medical gear and now searched for their victims. Someone pointed at their Trailblazer. Lance turned over the ignition, edged onto the road, and picked up speed.

Neida checked Lance often to make sure he remained alert. About a mile down the road, he brought up a hand to touch the blood coagulating on his cheek and winced.

His pain made her more aware of her own. “You okay? You want me to drive?”

Though she sounded brave, every fiber of her body revolted, and she hoped he’d refuse. Her adrenaline had dissipated, and she rubbed her screaming shoulder for relief. She doubted it would ever heal properly.

Lance shook his head. “Keep an eye out for Roy’s.”

Neida took out a bottle of water, wet several tissues, and leaned to dab at Lance’s abrasions.

He flinched and pulled away. "Watch the road," he barked. "Someone may be waiting for us up ahead. The sooner we switch vehicles, the better. Inform me of anything unusual."

Neida almost laughed at his request. "Unusual, huh? Has anything been usual since I returned to Michigan?"

He didn't answer.

She opened the passenger mirror and dabbed the dirt and blood from her face and neck, though her attempt did little to remedy the damage. They continued in silence.

The garage appeared a mile farther down the road. *Roy's Chop Shop* reeked of heavy biker clientele. Harleys leaned on their stands outside windowless, gray walls. Their polished bodies gleamed, and their chrome trim sparked flashes of sunlight into Neida's eyes when Lance turned the Trailblazer into the driveway. They parked in the only available space and headed for the metal door with the word *Office* painted in black letters on the outside. No one sat at the desk, so Lance led Neida around the corner toward the roar of a motorcycle engine.

Inside the garage, a man in greasy overalls straddled a Harley and revved the machine, listening with his head cocked to the side. When he saw them, his pinball-size eyes, too small for his face, glinted with mischief, and he grinned a mouthful of rotten teeth as though he mocked and assessed them in some way. He continued to work the bike underneath him. Neida resisted the urge to cover her ears.

The mechanic finally cut the engine and leaned forward across the handlebars, dangling his blackened hands over the wheel. "You're not supposed to be in here."

Lance ignored the reprimand. "We'd like to speak to Mad Dog."

"You're still not supposed to be in here."

"Well, if you tell us where we can find the man, we'll leave."

"I'm Mad Dog. Now leave." The man tilted his head—a brazen taunt.

Lance squared his jaw. "Spud sent us. He said you might fix us up with a vehicle."

Mad Dog's gaze traveled up Lance's length and stopped at the red and purple bruise that puffed his face.

"Appears you ran into a bit of bad luck."

Lance nodded. "We've experienced better days."

"You say Spud sent you."

"He helped us out, provided some background noise so we could escape awkward questioning with the authorities."

Mad Dog chuckled. "Then you come highly recommended. What kind of vehicle are you looking for?"

"Something reliable and cheap."

"You got cash or anything to trade?"

"A Trailblazer out front."

"It's not stolen, is it? I've got enough trouble of my own."

"Free and clear," said Lance.

Mad Dog nodded. He flung his blond braid behind him, hiked his leg over the bike, and motioned for them to follow. He led them through the back door of the garage, where they stepped into a yard cluttered with scrap metal and an array of junked cars. Ushering them to the rear of the property, Mad Dog stopped next to an old Chevy truck, patches of chipped, red paint marring its surface. He opened the door to let them investigate the interior.

"It may not seem like much, but she's as reliable as they come. I'll take your Trailblazer for the exchange. She's got all her parts, and the lights work. Nothing mechanical will get you pulled over. Don't know where you're going, but you could drive to California and back without any trouble in this baby. I did the overhaul on her myself, and I stand behind my work.

I'll even throw in the rusty hammer in the back. You might need protection from the looks of you."

Neida peeked into the truck bed. The tool, pressed against the side, had caused rust to grow underneath it, telltale evidence it had been there for a while. She struggled to picture Mad Dog standing on reputation, but she believed him. He seemed to honor a code that he and his friends like Spud recognized among each other. For reasons she couldn't understand, the club and their odd system of ethics opened to include them, at least for this one instance.

"We'll take it," said Lance.

Mad Dog nodded. "Let's go inside and finish up the details."

Hours later, the sun had descended into the horizon somewhere within the state of Indiana. As Mad Dog had promised, the truck's lights illuminated the road after sunset, and the new rubber underneath them hugged the roads with precision.

The last part of the trip proved too much for Neida, and she fell asleep somewhere out of South Bend. She lay sideways on the small seat with her head butted against Lance's leg and dozed to the hum of the engine.

Neida woke when Lance's voice penetrated the fog of her strange dream, and to a gentle shake of her shoulder. "Hey, we're here."

Neida stretched and yawned, a painful experience. She sat up with a grunt to ascertain their location. She almost didn't recognize Askuwheteau's small home. The moon cast the structure in long shadows across the yard. A light lit the interior, and a speckled glow splintered through the mini-blinds. It seemed like years since they had knocked at the red door. How would her grandfather react when he beheld them again, two battered and uninvited guests on his porch asking for shelter? The awkwardness of the scenario and her advanced hunger pangs caused an uprising inside her stomach.

"What time is it?" She rolled her neck.

Lance winced as he plucked his cell phone from his pocket and looked at the screen. "It's almost eight."

"I hope my grandfather is still awake. Winona might boot us off the porch, and then where would we go?"

Lance leaned over the steering wheel. He yawned and worked the apparent stiffness from his back. He opened the door and paused as he regarded Neida. "I have some prospects, but the sooner we identify where we stand, the sooner we'll locate a pillow. My body mutinied somewhere back at the border, and I can hardly see with all this swelling."

Neida scrutinized his face in the light of the cab. The swollen parts had grown two sizes larger over the afternoon, and it made her winced just looking at it.

At least this time, they walked across the yard without slipping and sliding in the mud. Since their last visit, the ground felt hard under her feet, would be an impenetrable embankment as soon as the weather brought freezing temperatures.

Lance knocked softly. As they waited, Neida leaned against him for support.

Seconds later, the door opened, and Winona stared at them in horror. "Oneida, what happened? Are you all right?"

"Where's grandfather? We need to ask a favor—one I hope you'll both consider before you answer."

Winona raised an eyebrow. The same skeptical mistrust of their first meeting slid across her expression. "We don't want trouble. By your looks, you require too much from him, Running Deer, and me. You'd be better off to take your problems to the white authorities."

A rustling sounded behind Winona, and Neida leaned sideways to peer around her aunt.

Askuwheteau stood in the living room, stoop-shouldered, staring at them. "I will hear their words," he said. His tone, though undemanding, imbued authority. His dark eyes explored Lance's face. His lips parted in surprise when he eyed the scrapes and bruises upon her own. He advanced toward the door, motioned them inside, and gestured toward the divan against the wall.

At least they had made it this far. The opportunity to sit lessened the chances of them imploding on his floor. She almost sighed with relief as she sank into the cushion.

When Askuwheteau spoke, he stared at Neida, though his comments issued a gentle reprimand at Lance. "You've brought my granddaughter through an ordeal today. Please rest. Tell me of this favor."

Neida sucked in courage. "As I told you, we're searching for the stone box Gran asked me to find. Someone wants to keep us from our goal. They've murdered one of Lance's friends, and today, in Illinois, they tried to run us over with their vehicle. Someone trashed my house. We can't go back to our homes, not until we figure out who these people are and what they want." She paused, unsure of how to ask for sanctuary; emotion welled in her eyes.

"You can't stay here," Winona blurted out. "Father, tell her they can't stay. They bring bad luck. They'll endanger our home, and I won't allow harm to come to my grandchild."

Askuwheteau turned to Winona. "As I won't allow harm to come to mine."

He approached them and examined Neida's damaged cheek with his wrinkled hand. He motioned to Winona. "Daughter prepare a slippery elm poultice for their wounds. Set up a bed for Oneida on the couch and one out back for her friend."

Winona's expression hardened, but she nodded and left on assignment as her father asked.

Askuwheteau's gaze followed after her. When she had disappeared around the corner, he turned to Neida again and spoke with gentle encouragement. "What is it you want me to do." His kind eyes invited her tumble of words.

"Lance and I need shelter for more than one night. Will you allow us to stay here until we can resolve our trouble? We made sure no one followed us. Please, we've nowhere else to go."

Askuwheteau's dark eyes penetrated her layers, shattering the fear and vulnerability that pooled inside her. "A journey for the truth is often a difficult path," he said, "but a direction we must follow. That is the only way to find balance and to understand the Creator's plan for us." He placed his hand atop her head. "You are welcome. Consider my home your own."

He turned to address Lance. "Your passage in the coming days will require patience. When the path appears rough, rely on the strength inside you." He nodded and reached for Lance's hand and placed it upon Neida's. "Trust each other. Help each other. If you are united, you will arrive where the journey asks you to go."

How could he discern what lay in the future, as if he were some kind of mystic? And would their road be as horrible as all he described? Neida almost asked, except Winona returned to the living room with blankets in her arms.

The woman frowned at her father, holding Lance and Neida's hands together. Bitterness tainted her voice. "The poultice will soon be ready. I'll prepare your bed now and show you how to apply the medicine. Come with me." She motioned at Lance.

Askuwheteau stepped back.

Lance, with effort, rose and nodded his appreciation. "Thank you both for allowing us to stay."

Askuwheteau plodded to the hall entrance. He turned around and shook his head. "Winona and I do not determine whether you remain here or not. This journey is yours to discover. I've only accepted my part along the road." He scanned each of their faces before he turned and disappeared into the room beyond their view.

CHAPTER SEVENTEEN

SOMETIME DURING THE EARLY MORNING, excruciating stiffness had set into Neida's muscles. The poultice had helped alleviate the burn of the abrasions on her face and limbs, but the deeper tissues cried for attention. She surrendered her attempt at sleep, and just before dawn, struggled out of her makeshift bed, dressed, and wrapped a couple of blankets around her shoulders. She limped out the back door into the crisp morning air.

The lean-to behind the house sat quiet and almost invisible in the pre-dawn. She hoped sleep now relieved Lance of the last few days' nightmares. When they parted at the hut entrance the previous night, his face displayed the same exhaustion that wearied her. Heavy bags, swelling, and bruising distorted his features, and she vowed to lay low for the next few days. They needed to function with some normalcy before they hunted for the relics again.

Descending past the shelter, she continued toward the lake. She stepped with precision in the diffused light. The intermittent flashes of sky spiked through the canopies above her head and provided increased visibility as she neared the shore. The sound of lapping water drew her closer. When she finally broke free of the trees and stepped into a small cove, she marveled at the scene before her.

The promise of daylight painted traces of pinks and yellows along the horizon, highlighting homes and docks along the curved shoreline. Each residence twinkled with signs of occupancy and reflected undulating light upon the water. Neida sat on a bench nestled against the scrub lining the cove and studied the sky.

Almost five weeks had come and gone since she'd returned to Michigan, though the passage of time seemed like forever. Disaster had been rampant, as though her presence in the state of Michigan had ignited her misfortune. Nothing even close to the chaos she had experienced here had befallen her in California—ever—and she was grateful, at least, that they were still alive.

The sky's pink hues were now turning to orange with the increase of light, and the lake's expanse caught fire with color. Though the morning felt cold, traces of summer still lingered. She breathed in a lungful, endured the aching in her body—not just the physical pain, but uncertainty, fear, and the consequence of little sleep. Tears spilled down her cheeks, surprising her, and she cursed herself for such weakness.

A limb cracked behind her. She whisked around to a blurred vision of her grandfather, who watched her from the edge of the trees. She turned away to wipe her eyes with the back of her hand, breathed in the frigid air to gain composure. Soon after, he shuffled around the bench and sat next to her.

"It is too cold to swim." He issued the simple declaration without fanfare. He didn't look at Neida, just removed the towel draped over his shoulder and handed it to her. She took the offering, dabbed at her nose and face, then leaned into his chest.

He tilted his head against hers and patted her arm, communicating the depth of his sentiment far more than words. They sat huddled for some time, and when the sun had spilled over the edge of the horizon, he finally spoke.

"A thief steals joy from my granddaughter's heart," he said, empathy in his voice.

She nodded against him. "You once told me to listen to my heart—that it would show me the road to follow. Lance and I have traveled over many roads lately, each becoming worse than the last. A man died. Someone almost victimized us, yet we're no closer to finding the artifacts than when we began. We've run out of options. I can't even return to my lovely home."

She sat back and paused for a moment to swallow the grief forming in her throat, then tried again. "I hate to rely on others' hospitality. I would never forgive myself if I put you and Aunt Winona and little Running Deer in danger. You are my only family now." She looked up at him.

Her grandfather viewed a distant place on the horizon. The morning rays emphasized his profile: a strong nose and an abundance of wrinkles etching and sculpting his features. Pride held his chin high, and she tried to read the history written in his expression.

"The most difficult journeys hold abundant answers," he said. "It is hard to view solutions when the unknown casts shadows in your way. But you must continue forward, Granddaughter; walk to the edge of the light and step into the darkness. The Creator who walks before you will guide you. He'll help you recognize and understand the rewards of your journey. They wait for you a few paces beyond that which you can see."

Neida repressed her comments about his philosophy on faith. She stared down into her lap and sensed him watching her.

"You do not believe in such things," he said.

Neida shook her head. "No, Grandfather. I don't. Faith makes little sense to me. Give me facts, something tangible, and I can understand. Talk in abstractions and, well ..."

He nodded as though he understood. "Then, your road will be difficult. Our eyes rarely discover heaven and earth's greatest mysteries, Oneida. We discern these things within our hearts." He placed a hand on his chest. "Do you not trust your heart?"

She didn't know how to answer. How could she rely on her heart—a fickle and vulnerable entity that threw out concrete facts for incomprehensible emotions, made her yearn for inexplicable things? "I trust what I can see."

"What do you see when you behold a wolf in sheep's clothing?"

Her retort stuck, dwindled to nothing. Life often threw out red herrings, theories changed, appearances weren't always as cut and dry as she first assumed. Still, her heart's quandaries caused her discomfort and made her balk when she tried to deal with them. She could never depend on anything responsible for such confusion and pain.

He patted her hand again. "Close your eyes, Granddaughter. Trust your heart. It is the wiser of the two."

Somehow, she knew he was right. Nothing in the last few weeks had been as clear-cut as they seemed. She had been operating on the fumes of her intuition, and she hadn't even realized it until now.

"But you didn't trust *your* heart when it came to Gran. Did you even love her? You married another." The words tumbled out before she could stop them.

The etching around his eyes deepened, and he turned to the horizon again. "It is impolite to speak of the dead, but I will tell you about this matter. This thing you call love is like a garden. It draws us toward the planting. I was young, and the day I met Althea, the promise drew me in, and I followed, a willing gardener. I planted my heart with her—forever.

"But the planting requires a competent gardener and makes no promises of the harvest. Sometimes our field is fertile, and the roots of love sink deep. Sometimes the ground of circumstance is too strong for the seed, and the roots cannot grow." He held his fist upright to animate his story. "I nurtured those seeds for as long as possible before the wind of truth blew and sent them to a place where they could take root." He dropped his hand, and his brow furrowed. "I allowed your grandmother to blossom in someone else's field because she was happier there."

Neida shook her head and caressed her grandfather's arm. "You've got it all wrong. Gran honored her parents, and she obeyed them. That's why she married Edward Graham, but she never stopped loving you."

The line of his chin hardened. "How can your absence over the years teach you her heart's story?"

"I found Gran's journals in the attic at Hopewell. She wrote about you often. She expressed her sadness and loss over the years."

He lifted his chin a little higher. A slight tremor rippled across his jaw.

"I'll prove it to you. Let's go back to the house. I'll show you her words."

He shook his head. "The past takes care of itself. Sometimes it is enough only to believe."

She smiled and leaned against him again. He was a wise and proud man, and much like his budding faith and hope at the beginning of his story of unrequited love, she was now beginning to cultivate that faith required to allow her own field to blossom. Her soil, stony and unforgiving, had kept his words of wisdom from taking root at first, and had she not experienced the miracle of surviving the events of the last few days, she would have forever let her seeds of hope fall on infertile ground. It would take her years to become skilled at such untested and unfamiliar expectations and learn all that her grandfather so readily embraced. Even though she now longed to understand what faith entailed, she still wasn't ready to divulge to anyone that its stirrings rumbled inside her. She shook off the impression, arose, and faced him. "Lance and Winona must be wondering where we are by now."

He stood. "Oneida, do not worry so much about the way to turn or what has led you to this place. You will be safe with us. The Creator has spoken this to my heart." Assurance radiated from his eyes. He held out his hand in the direction of the trees, waiting for her to proceed. After a moment's pause, she entwined her arm through his and ushered him toward the house, basking in his company, as she now knew he reveled in her own.

When Neida and Askuwheteau sauntered through the door, Lance bounded from the couch and met her at the living room entrance with a smile. "We've found the relics," he said, relief and excitement aggrandizing his delivery.

Neida narrowed her eyes at him. "What?"

"A caller contacted me fifteen minutes ago. She'll meet us on the Mall just outside the *National Museum of the American Indian* by 10:00 tomorrow night."

A disturbing tremor shot through Neida. "But we'll be completely visible there. Did this mysterious caller leave a name?"

"No, but just from the details of what she said, she's the one Fitz had asked to deliver the artifacts to his home. She heard about his death on the news, and she's scared, so she called us."

Neida frowned. "That sounds like fiction to me. Would Fitz give someone your number? What if this is a ploy to draw us out?"

He shook his head. "She knew too many things about Fitz to be a fraud, and she sounded pretty distraught over his demise."

"Yeah—the whole world's a stage, and great actors all. Why call us? She doesn't even know who we are."

"She wants to unload the artifacts. And she wants justice for the crime."

"And she expects *us* to wield the sword? That's asking a lot. I don't know, Lance. This coincidence seems all too strange. We can't trek to D.C. without some assurances."

Lance sighed and raked both hands through his hair. "I realize we have to use our common sense, Neida. But the woman didn't leave her name, so I can't look her up online. And what if this is our only chance to get hold of the artifacts? If we don't at least take a chance, we may never find them. The caller did call Fitz's dogs by name, and I doubt that one of Blackhour's thugs knows that Fitz owns a home around Lake Michigan, but *she* did."

"Is that enough to believe her?"

"I think so. My dad and I spent a summer or two vacationing with them. The caller mentioned Fitz had lots of fond memories of our time together, including the tire swing we rigged from a tree."

"Then I guess we can at least make the trip and check it out. But we need to make the rendezvous as safe as possible. Maybe we can pick up one of Fitz's dogs for protection," she said as she gave him a facetious smirk. The memory of shining fangs in the moonlight made her shiver.

Lance ignored her last comment or, perhaps didn't realize she was joking. "The news report says they've already roped off the area and taken the dogs away. At least, that's what the caller said. No doubt, the police have found a few extra fingerprints as well."

"Our fingerprints?" *That's all we need. To be hunted by the police.*

"Ours, as well as others," he said. "But unless you've committed a crime in the past, I doubt you'll be on the grid."

Winona, who stood behind Lance, picked up Running Deer, who had just exited the bedroom, groggy with sleep, rubbing his eyes.

She approached them, her voice turning cold. "If this predicament of yours is as dangerous as you say, you can't return to our home."

Askuwheteau turned and shuffled into the kitchen. He opened the refrigerator to retrieve a carton of orange juice and poured himself a cupful. As he drank, Neida hurried to his side.

"What's your opinion, Grandfather? Do you think this is a ruse? Would you rather that we stay away?"

He lowered his glass. "You must trust your heart, Granddaughter. I cannot tell you what to do."

Lance joined them, and Winona followed close behind.

"If we *do* pick up the box, we'll disappear for a while," said Lance. "You've already shown us unbelievable kindness. We wouldn't presume to bring trouble to your door."

Winona pressed a hand to Running Deer's head and pulled him closer. "Father, surely this is wise. You must agree."

Askuwheteau cupped Winona's chin and looked to the boy snuggling in her arms. He ruffled the toddler's hair. "It is Oneida's path. She and her friend are welcome in my home for as long as they desire to stay."

"But Father—"

"I will speak of this no more."

Winona glared at him. She reeled around and stomped off toward the bedroom.

Neida watched her aunt's angry retreat then turned to her grandfather. "I didn't mean to worry her. If this is on the up and up, and we pick up the artifacts, we'll go somewhere else to examine them."

"It will be better for us to investigate the items in a lab with experts in the field," said Lance.

Her grandfather shrugged, and his gaze bore into her as he spoke. "Winona's tongue is swift. She worries for her grandson and me, but wherever this journey will take you in the future, your refuge will always be with us, with your family. Winona will one day understand the wisdom of my words."

Neida smiled, grateful for his patience and generosity. Maybe the spirits had tipped him about the outcome of their imminent adventure. Not that she'd believe in such communication, but his confidence and open invitation relieved her. "Thank you for your understanding," she said before she threw her arms around him and almost knocked him off balance.

ᛏᚻᚢ

The trip to D.C. was uneventful. Lance let Neida drive a good portion of the way. She claimed it had been too long since she'd been behind the wheel and that she wanted him to doze and rest his bruised body. He had to admit, he felt relieved. The extra sleep seemed to restore his spirits, and he almost felt invigorated. Several times, Neida caught him staring at her, and though, at those moments, she seemed more aware of him and a little self-conscious to boot, he hoped she understood how attracted to her he was, even reciprocate his feelings.

By nightfall, just before 9:25 P.M., Neida found an empty metered parking space along Jefferson just outside the *National Museum of the American Indian.* Small groups still roamed the grounds, although the museum had closed hours before. After feeding the meter, they hurried across the street up the few steps to where water cascaded from the curvilinear building into a rocky creek bed below. The rushing water calmed Lance, despite his frayed nerves. He pulled Neida toward a landscape wall near two towering totems. The talismans posed an intimidating display of greeting to those who cared to enter the path, and the surrounding hardwood trees would at least keep Neida hidden away from the street.

"I want you to stay here," Lance said. "I'll meet with the woman alone, just in case. There are plenty of people around, and rangers are still casing the area if you need assistance."

She pulled a face. "I'm going with you, and don't try to stop me." She waited with hands on her hips for his answer. "Come on. Two of us would stand a better chance if things go wrong, Lance."

He regarded her for a moment, but ignored her comments. "If anything happens, if I haven't come back by 10:45, you dash for the car and drive like mad to your grandfather's place. Promise me. The trip won't be easy; you'll have to keep your eye out for anything out of the ordinary, but if you can get to your grandfather, you'll be safer there."

Neida shook her head.

He placed his hands on either side of her face to stop the movement. "Don't argue with me. Just do what I ask. I'll be back in about a half-hour."

The way she studied him with moon-sized brown eyes and pouting lips lured him like a magnet. He couldn't help himself. He kissed her full on the mouth, inhaling every luscious scent of her, coaxing the very feel of her lips to memory.

She sagged in a moment's surrender, then pushed at his chest and jerked back. Shock, yet something else he couldn't read, pulled at her expression. "Why did you do that?" she asked, the sound of her voice more confused than angry.

"If this is a trap, I refuse to sprint to my grave without a souvenir to ease the pain." He didn't wait for her reaction, just whirled about and pushed toward the street again, kicking himself across Jefferson at his knee-jerk attempt to keep her close. He didn't want to force his attentions on her, but she'd never know how important she'd become to him—again.

He crossed the graveled easement, continued across the sparsely tree-lined carpet of lawn, and found a bench where he'd wait for his contact. He sat back, searched his surroundings, and almost jerked off the bench when Neida appeared from out of nowhere. He hadn't even heard her footsteps following behind him, a warning that he'd have to be more careful.

She edged around the bench and sat beside him.

He expected her reproach for kissing her only moments ago, but instead, she peered at him, her eyebrows hiking for emphasis as she spoke. "I told you. I'm coming with you. We've got to stick together on this one. Besides, I'm not waiting in a creepy, dark corner of D.C. so someone can shove me in a car or shoot me and drag me behind the trees."

He shook his head in exasperation, struggled to push away his own anger. Once again, she had defied his admonition to stay out of danger. "You're as stubborn as they come, Oneida Graham."

"And then some," she said.

He strained to listen, scrutinized the spectacle around them, then pulled from his jacket pocket a knitted beanie with wide colorful strips and placed it on top of his head.

Neida peeked up at the hat and bit back a smile.

"What? You don't like my hat?"

"It's quite becoming," she said, her smile stretching wider.

"My contact and I agreed on out of the ordinary, though I hope she'll find us sooner than later."

Lance had assured Neida the caller's intentions were honorable, but the cold call *did* unnerve him. Neida's valid point fossilized inside his stomach every time he thought about it. Fitz had insisted on their discretion. Why would he give the woman his phone number unless he trusted her without question? And now, Neida was knee-deep in danger, smack dab in the middle of the battleground right alongside him.

He swallowed hard and wedged his hands under his armpits to get warm. "You cold?"

"A bit."

He felt her body lean closer, and he slipped an arm around her shoulder and rubbed it to cause friction. "Keep your eyes peeled. She should be here any minute."

He rechecked the time on his cell phone: 9:58, only five minutes since his last glance. The breeze ate through the layers of his jacket, and his hands hurt. Everything hurt. The stiffening chill made his jaw quiver, severing the thin thread of his patience. *Neida must be even more miserable than I am*, he thought. How much longer would they have to wait?

Rustling from behind startled him, and they both whipped around. A woman stepped out from behind a tree pulling a cart behind her. Strapped to the device, a crate, a little larger than a suitcase, weighed down the transport. As she drew closer under the LEDs, her chubby, lined face came into clear view. She wore dark-rimmed glasses, squares that magnified her crow's feet and wary stare. She approached with caution.

"Lance?"

"Yes."

Her posture relaxed, though her movements remained defensive. "I wasn't sure. I didn't expect anyone to be with you."

"This is my partner," he said. He wasn't about to give the woman Neida's name.

She rolled the cart from the green to the sidewalk and stood before them, her gaze shooting constant glances into the dark beyond the lampposts. When she turned and examined their faces, her words caught, then spilled with concern. "You're hurt. What happened? Are we safe?" She scoped the area again; her head jerked with each trajectory of her neck.

"That depends on if anyone's followed you here?"

She turned back and shook her head. "No. I'm sure of it. But Blackhour must know by now I've taken the artifacts. He'll find me soon enough."

"Why would he presume you're involved?" asked Neida. "I thought he's ignorant about the artifacts' location."

"He knows I worked at the facility. He spotted Fitz and me kissing at a Smithsonian party once and made a wisecrack about policy. Fitz loathed the man, and since he had a soft spot for Edward Graham and his artifacts, he made sure we moved the crate to another location. A sure tactic against Blackhour's greedy little hands. When Fitz asked me to retrieve the items and bring them to you, somehow, our operation leaked to the guy who helped us hide the relics in the first place. Maybe someone bugged the phones. I don't know. He's been snooping about, asking odd questions. He was Stephenson's relative, and he's on Blackhour's payroll, the monster who murdered my Fitz."

"Are you quite certain Blackhour's involved?" asked Lance.

"Of course, he's involved. I heard him talking to my co-worker the other day. Since the relics failed to arrive at Fitz's house as planned, they'll figure out who's got them." Her unsteady breath sawed into the silence around him.

Neida stood, and the woman stepped back as though she prepared to run.

"Please, I won't hurt you," said Neida, raising her palm to comfort her. "What's your name?"

"Amanda ... Johnson."

Lance rose from the bench to join them. "If what you say is true, Amanda, then you're out of a job." *She was more than out of a job.* She could never go back, might get slapped in jail for taking the artifacts off the premises—or worse.

She sighed and slumped forward. "What am I going to do?"

"We'd cherish another assistant at the lab in Michigan," said Lance.

She straightened, eying him with surprise.

"You've taken a big risk to help us," he said. "We'd like to return the favor."

Amanda stepped away from him and shook her head. "No. I've lived here all my life. I've got family and friends. I only want to get rid of this thing and find a safe place to hide."

"Just come with us until the threat is over," said Neida. "You'll be safer that way."

Amanda darted wary glances behind them again, then shoved the cart toward Lance. "I'm sorry. I can't. I have to go." Amanda whipped toward the trees. She glanced behind her at Neida and Lance as if she expected them to chase after her.

"Call us if you need anything," Lance shouted after her. He sighed his frustration, chagrined that the woman refused to think smart about her predicament. "And be careful," he tried again, but his words flitted into the breeze, hurling down the walkway toward the capitol building.

They waited until her form faded into the night. Lance checked the area for rangers then grabbed Neida's arm. "Let's get this crate to the car—now. Who knows what surprises might be lurking in the shadows?"

They hurried toward the trees as fast as their load allowed. Though small, the heavy crate snagged and stalled in every rut along the path. At least Amanda had provided a smart way to maneuver the relics. Lance hoped deciphering the language would be as easy, only he hoped it wouldn't take too long. Every second counted in their race against Blackhour.

CHAPTER EIGHTEEN

NIGHT BREEZES WHIPPED AGAINST NEIDA'S CHEEKS as they hurried toward the truck. She stretched her neck to peer into the distance, but it was just too dark to see beyond the trees. Pounding sounded against the bones inside her ears. Her head hurt, and she huddled against Lance to stay warm. The stillness unnerved her, and though she wanted to throw her arms around Lance's neck and apologize for how she had reacted to his kiss, she kept pace with his every step and didn't make a sound. She had hurt him, for sure, and the emotion had caught her off guard, but now was not the time for apologies.

The crowd along Jefferson had thinned over the last twenty minutes. As they neared the vehicle, an underlying rustling registered nearby, fading into nothingness. She scanned the ground toward the Mall and back toward the empty sidewalk alongside the museum, scrambling and panting to keep up with Lance. A lone straggler hurried toward the building's rear entrance. Her nape hair spiked until he called out, "Hey, wait for me," to someone further on down the River Walk path.

"Relax, Neida," said Lance beside her. "We're almost there."

"I'm trying."

A prickle of eyes traveled down her back. She scanned the area. This time, the rushing sounded from across the street inside the shrubbery next to the museum access. Lance's head jerked toward the noise, validating her fear.

She squinted into the void between the trees, saw nothing. Only the slight movement of branches swayed in the breeze.

Lance pulled her faster toward the truck. She glanced back as a dark figure hopped through the bushes and ran across Jefferson, following their same course. Neida's foot caught on one of Lance's heels. She almost tumbled to the ground but kept herself upright with the aid of the cart handle.

Another glance back. To Neida's horror, the shadowy form had increased his speed.

At the truck now, Lance grunted to lift the cart and crate into the bed. He unlocked his door and shoved Neida into the cab, plowed in after her, then locked them inside.

Their pursuer sprinted toward them now, almost at the vehicle's side.

Lance fumbled to insert the key. The engine failed on the first try, engaged on the second. He stomped on the accelerator, and the truck lurched from the curb, inciting the pursuer to race and jump on the back, reaching over the tailgate to pull the crate toward him.

Lance swerved left, right, then left again to shake him, but the hooded man clung to the edge with one hand, started to unlock the tailgate with the other.

No! He'll get the crate! Neida removed her seatbelt, climbed over the seat, and opened the cab's sliding rear window to either side.

"What are you doing?" Panic heightened Lance's voice. "Don't. The artifacts aren't worth it."

She begged to differ with him.

He reached over the seat with one hand and grabbed for Neida's leg.

She kicked from his grip and pushed with her feet, jutting her head and torso outside. The wind whipped at her face and thrashed the hair from her band. Shimmying through the small opening, she supported herself on her hands to maneuver her legs free of the cab. She lurched forward, grabbed the cart's chassis, and rolled the crate closer.

The man growled and heaved himself inside the truck. Despite Lance's maneuvers, he balanced himself and lunged at Neida. She bolted sideways, almost tripping over the cart. She tried kicking at his knee though missed her target, allowing him to grab her arm and swing her around hard, slamming her into the side of the truck. She caught the edge, almost tumbled out of control, and only Lance's swift tactic in the opposite direction saved her from catapulting over the side.

Then she saw the rusty hammer in the corner, Mad Dog's prophetic donation. She dove for it.

The man reacted, tried to beat her to her goal, but Neida was closer and plucked it up.

As he reached her, he gripped her arm, yanked on the tool with his free hand, causing the hammer to slip. She fought to hold on. Inhaling, she reached up to pull the tool's handle with both hands, and with her weight, kneed him in the groin. He doubled over, and the hammer wrenched from his grasp. Again, she almost propelled over the side as she ripped free.

"Neida!" Lance's bellow issued through the open window.

She steadied herself, kept her focus.

Though writhing, the man dove at her again.

She stepped back, fell to her knees, and swung the tool with all her might at his knee.

The sound of bone crunching and a scream assailed the air. He toppled sideways, hit the tailgate, and hurled over the edge. His body thumped as it hit the street, bouncing along the pavement until it tumbled to a stop.

Panting, Neida collapsed onto the truck bed and closed her eyes. She barely budged as Lance floored the truck around the corner and sped toward the Michigan lab.

卌

Lance insisted on driving and broke the speed limit on their way back home. He had only stopped long enough to secure the crate and Neida safely inside the cab and for a brief catnap when he could barely keep his eyes open. For a good portion of the trip, Neida butted her head against his leg as he stroked her hair.

"I thought I had lost you back there," he said, choking on the last couple of words.

She reached to grasp his hand, and their fingers intertwined. She clung to him for some time but didn't say a word.

After crossing the border into Michigan the next morning, Lance meandered through various townships, weaving through small neighborhoods where they lingered and double-checked approaching cars to make sure they hadn't picked up a tail. For extra caution, they waited for night's cover before they chanced the rest of the trip and ventured into Newaygo. By the time they reached the township around nine that evening, Neida's energy had hit bottom. Her mood took a free-fall. She sunk in her seat and hoped the darkness provided sufficient cloak to conceal their faces as they drove down State Road. Though she ached to go home again, Lance avoided Hopewell and its general vicinity.

Turning off the main highway, Lance headed for an isolated area. As he curved to a familiar road, Kat's cottage-like house rose from out of the dark. Lance drove down the narrow access along the home's length and maneuvered the truck toward the wilderness beyond the house where a sizable facility took shape. In their previous haste to leave town, Neida failed to notice the expansive warehouse covering part of Kat's back acre.

Lance parked in the rear, beeped the horn twice.

Seconds after the summons, the warehouse's steel door cracked open and swung wide. A man propped the entrance ajar with a wedge and plowed across the yard as Lance exited the truck and hurried to retrieve the crate from behind the seat. Neida joined them.

The man approached and clasped hands with Lance. "You finally made it. Good thing you let us know you were on your way, or I'd have called out the dogs." He nodded at Neida. "Let's get this inside. You never know who might decide to take a midnight stroll." Darting glances over the compound, he guided them toward the building.

Lance coaxed Neida forward and into the warehouse first. They paused within the hallway where their guide kicked the wedge inside and allowed the door to slam shut behind them.

Lance motioned with his head. "Neida, this is Rex Willett's grandson, Cory. He's our resident paleographer and a crackerjack at deciphering languages. He puts his grandfather's talents to shame."

Cory smiled his apology. "Don't listen to him. My grandfather was the best of his time. I'm only here to continue his work. We've so much more data and the tools to aid us these days." He nodded at her again. "I've anticipated your help, Neida."

She liked his deep voice and the humility of this graying, middle-aged man. He smiled with his eyes, and she soaked up the immediate warmth in his presence.

"So, this is the little jewel causing all the trouble," said Cory, glancing down at the cart. "And by the look of both of you, it hasn't been an easy task to find it."

"Trouble doesn't even describe half of the trials we've been through in the last couple of days," said Lance. He swept a curl from his forehead and sighed. "Do you have a magic wand hidden somewhere in the lab, something that might change our luck?"

Cory smiled. "We'll see what we can find."

The warehouse's interior surprised Neida. Though the building appeared crude from the outside, someone had built up the core at great expense. An outer corridor and a multitude of offices circumnavigated a central laboratory enclosed by walls of thick glass.

"Wow," said Neida. "This setup is quite impressive."

Lance nodded at the core. "You'll find extra security systems, surveillance cameras, emergency supplies, along with double-steel doors and locks. If Blackhour even thinks to cross the perimeter of the compound, we'll know about it. We can lock ourselves inside this place for weeks, and he and his misfits would never breach the fortress."

Neida frowned her confusion. "And this is part of Kat's property? Why would she have a laboratory like this behind her house?"

Before Lance could answer, a swarm of activity unfolded inside the lab. At the heart of the bustle, the sight of one individual, eye to a microscope, stopped Neida in her tracks.

"Kat!"

Almost as if she had heard her name, Kat glanced up and waved.

Lance smiled. "I don't remember if I told you, but Kat not only runs my office, she comes from a long line of archaeologists and paleographers. This was her father's lab. He worked for the U.S. government on some pretty secretive projects. She's one of the best partners an archaeologist can acquire."

"Then why does she always refer to you as Boss?"

Lance chuckled. "When we first joined forces, I acted a little overzealous with her. She called me Boss to bring me back down to earth, and the name stuck."

"Can't say I disagree."

Lance rolled his eyes.

Kat rushed to open the lab door. A world of weight slipped from Neida's shoulders the moment the woman put her arms around her and hugged the tension away.

"It's about time you two showed up. I've gnawed my nails to the nubbins." She scrutinized their faces and stepped forward with alarm. "What in the world happened? Where did you get those bruises?"

"We had a bit of a run-in with a van, but we're fine," said Lance.

Kat raised an eyebrow. "Care to explain?"

"I'll fill you in a little later." Lance shrugged and turned to Neida. "Are you still doing okay?"

She nodded, though she felt anything but satisfactory.

"Well, then, let's get this crate front and center," said Kat. She directed them to the workstation waiting for the central attraction.

Neida was amazed. Kat had equipped the cleanroom with every conceivable technological device, and a handful of technicians and assistants puttered at various tasks around the lab. Moments later, they secured the crate in place and threw out ideas of how to penetrate the casing. Well into the fray, Kat motioned for Neida to follow her to an out-of-the-way corner.

"You sure you're all right?" she asked when they were far enough away from the others.

Neida sighed. Kat would call in the National Guard if she knew about her last dance with danger. "I'm a little stiff," she said, "but I'll survive." She needed to change the subject. "Who's watching the store while you're away?"

"Carl. He remembers every little detail. Kind of takes after me. And he always thinks on his feet. Since we've been a little preoccupied with these artifacts, he's contracted with some of Lance's colleagues to take up the slack. I'm thankful we hired him. Now, would you please explain these bruises to me?"

Neida glanced toward Lance and Cory, who tried to rip the crate's rubberized sealant away from the seams—an unsuccessful attempt. "So much has happened since we left, more than I can explain right now. But someone is on our trail and has tried everything to prevent us from accessing those artifacts. Once we see what's inside that box and whether it's still in one piece, we might understand what all the fuss is about."

"Well then, come on. I think those boys need a woman's touch."

She ushered Neida to the workstation, where Lance tried to pry off the sealant with a sharp probe. He stabbed at the adhesive, then stood back and shook his head. "Man, Fitz didn't exaggerate. This stuff's impenetrable. Not only did they nail the crate with a gazillion staples, but the compound adheres to the wood like solder. Maybe we should try a solvent of some sort."

Kat nodded at the crate. "I'll get the boys to analyze the goo and find something that'll do the trick."

Lance laid the probe on the counter, his face straining under the intense light of the lab. "Do you mind if Neida and I grab a little shut-eye?"

Kat smiled. "Way ahead of you, Boss." She gestured at the corridor behind them. "I've set up a couple of rooms on the south side. I brought in cots, some fresh clothes, and a few sundries. The shower is at the end of the hall when you're ready."

"You will wake us as soon as you get this crate open, won't you?" Lance asked with a stern look on his face.

Kat nodded and raised her right hand. "I promise. No peeking at the good stuff until both of you are front and center. The world's been oblivious to this discovery for thousands of years. Except for your granddaddy and Blackhour, of course. What's another hour or two more?"

Lance expressed his thanks, then directed Neida out the lab door and down the hall.

Now that she was home—well, almost home—this fortress, surrounded by trusted men and women, eased her fears. She looked forward to some needed rest.

About five in the morning, Lance shook her awake. "Neida, Cory wants to see us right away."

She sat up and yawned off her stupor. She had been so exhausted she hadn't even remembered entering her room or lying down on the cot. And now the bright light of her quarters overpowered her, and she squinted to protect her eyes. "Did they open the crate?" she asked with another yawn.

Lance held out his hand to help her up. "They're waiting for us. They removed the box a while ago, but it's time to delve a little deeper."

Neida grunted from her cot and hobbled her injured body down the hall after him, where a technician let them into the lab. They headed for the specimen table at the center of the room, where someone had strapped the rough, stone box firmly in place on rubber racks. A cement of sorts connected the four pieces of granite. The lid, rounded at the center, narrowed to the edges; its two chunks, once a single stone, fitted together in concert at the break. She surmised the ancients had initially cemented the cover to the bottom to form a watertight seal to protect the treasure inside. Marring hinted at the exact location where it seemed Blackhour's technicians had compromised the original closure. The strange characters etched into the lid and on the sides made Neida quiver with anticipation.

"Is everyone ready?" asked Cory.

Kat handed gloves to Neida and Lance, and they hurried to put them on.

Cory motioned the technician to proceed, and the man removed the top pieces and placed them on another rack next to the box. They all leaned in to view the contents: a copper tablet, or at least the appearance of one. Oxidation had disfigured and painted the entire plate green with corrosion, but the relic seemed no thicker than heavy paper and about eight inches wide and ten inches long. What appeared to be an outline, perhaps a map, spanned the upper third of the tablet. Many characters etched the surface, but the decay filled in the grooves and the depressions, making a decipherment impossible.

Cory lifted one edge of the relic and exposed two stone blocks underneath. "We've got something big here. Not the same shape, but this reminds me of the Tookabatchas' records."

"Tookabatchas?" Neida had heard of the tribe but knew little about them.

Lance examined the specimen without looking at her. "The tribe's priests possess two plates of brass and five of copper with ancient inscriptions on them."

"Where are those plates now?" she asked. "Has anyone translated them?"

"The Tookabatchas once lived in Alabama until the government drove them into the Arkansas Territory, but no one can touch the treasures," said Cory. "The natives are pretty prickly about those relics and only bring them out once a year for their *Green Corn Celebration*. They're for priests' eyes only. The tribe claims the Creator gave the antiquities to their ancestors."

Lance rubbed along the casket edges. "If the people who buried this tablet felt it important enough to put this piece in a stone box, they meant to preserve it. They deemed it sacred."

"Have they ever discovered any relics in boxes like this before?" asked Neida.

Lance nodded. "A few. The natives fashioned most of the tablets from clay, stone, slate, or flint and buried them without protection. The ancients didn't use a firing process on the clay samples either, and as a result, the relics crumble easily. We're probably dead-on about this tablet's importance. Not only did they protect it, but they used material that would last through time."

Cory examined the piece closer. "They found plates like this from King Darius's reign. He ordered his royal proclamation engraved in three different languages on plates of pure gold and silver. They buried the tablets in a stone box, much like this one. Old world meets North America."

"They'll burn all the history books," said Lance.

Neida shook her head. "Not if it's a hoax."

Cory squinted at Neida. "Are we entertaining a skeptic here?"

"I don't know. We'll see. It depends on this little green thing and whatever the characters on this casket say." She touched the surface again.

Cory lifted the tablet and twisted it around between his fingers, examining the corrosion. "It'll take a while to clean this up." He nodded his head toward the lab door. "Go do whatever you need to. Breakfast should arrive by the time you get back. It's Kat's café today. She cooks the best omelets around. We thought ordering food in town and for a crowd might call attention to what we're doing here."

"Good thinking." Lance turned to his partner. "As long as you don't mind cooking, my dear."

Kat still beamed from Cory's compliment. "Fine by me."

"Then it's to the showers. Ladies first, of course." Lance placed a hand on Neida's back.

Neida faked a pout, but the sentiment was near truth. She didn't want to miss a second of this mystery. She longed to get her hands dirty and help discover this unique part of history. "Don't do anything important without me, boys." She glowered at them. "This is *my* party, remember?"

Lance turned her about and gave her a shove. "Then you had better get a move on, Missy. You don't want to be late for your festivities."

𒌋𒌋

Neida showered and found her way back to the lab in less than an hour. As soon as she walked through the entrance, the smell of omelets, bacon, and freshly brewed coffee drew her in.

"Grab some food," said Cory. "We're just about finished with the cleanup."

Lance had already helped himself to the counter of food. Lab beakers of orange juice sat like science projects next to the fare, and Neida served herself a healthy portion of fruit, bacon, and one fluffy omelet.

"This is the best I can offer you today," said Kat. "I've got to get into the office by nine. If the cots get too uncomfortable for you, I'll bring in some mattresses."

Lance glanced up from his meal. "Everything depends on how long it takes us to decipher the tablet."

Kat snatched a piece of bacon from the tray and pointed the strip at him. "Then it's business as usual. I've moved your truck inside the storage compartment." She turned to Neida. "If you need anything, Hon, please let me know. I'll do my best to fill your order." She took a bite of bacon and headed out the lab door.

Being sequestered on the outskirts of town might turn out better than Neida had hoped. She enjoyed Kat. They hadn't had much time to develop their friendship since Neida had come to Hopewell, but she looked forward to a more relaxed atmosphere so she could discover more about her. Kat's efficiency baffled her, and Neida wondered what it would take to tap into her superwoman mentality. Somehow, she doubted she'd ever make the grade, but she already considered Kat a true friend.

During breakfast, Neida's thoughts turned to her Grandfather and Winona. She hoped for their safety and had worked up an urge to talk to them. Lance sat across from her on a lab stool, devouring a second omelet and paid her little mind. She soon mustered enough courage to ask. "I'd like to call my grandfather. Would that be possible?"

Lance stopped chewing, swallowed his mouthful before he looked up. "My cell phone is traceable."

Neida grumbled. "Haven't they hooked up a protected line here?" Her words spewed harsher than she intended.

Lance set his fork on his plate. "Relax, Neida. Cory's office has a secure phone. As soon as you're finished with breakfast, we'll call them and put your mind at ease."

She nodded, almost satisfied. Maybe they could bring her family to the lab. This steel warehouse on the edge of nowhere seemed to hold the security of Fort Knox.

A lab technician barged through the door, carrying a tray of breads and some drinks. "We have muffins and more coffee here, and a newspaper, if anyone's interested."

Neida ran over to snatch the publication from underneath the man's arm and returned to the counter. "I don't even know what's happened lately. I've been dying to find some news feed."

"I've got dibs on the sports page." Lance reached for the paper.

She pulled the periodical away from his fingers, playing with him as she took her time to hand him the preferred section. She searched the headlines for the highlights.

Turning to the second page, Neida stalled on a photo of a familiar face. The title read, "Woman Mutilated, Drowned in D.C.'s Reflective Pool."

She scanned the story. The name, Amanda Johnson, popped off the page. She read the first paragraph of the article and covered her mouth, almost vomited up her breakfast.

Lance looked up from the sports page and frowned at her. "What?"

She just stared at him, mouth agape.

"Neida, what's wrong?"

"They've killed her."

"Who's killed who?" Seconds later, as his frown transformed into understanding, he turned the paper around to read the article. As soon as he had finished, he shook his head.

"They cut off her hands, Lance, and they drowned her. And they're blaming it on gang violence." Neida's stomach tightened. "What is so important about these stupid relics anyway?"

Her outburst drew the technicians' stares. She sprang from her chair and rushed from the lab. Lance held up his hand on the other side of the glass to stop her, but she ignored his plea and ran down the hall.

She didn't know where to go to get away from the sick feeling inside her. She stopped at the end of the corridor, tried to force the visuals out of her head, but instead Amanda's mutilation came to the forefront of her mind—and Fitz's demise right on its heels. The lab door opened and closed again, and the sound of footsteps approached her from behind.

"Neida ..."

She whirled around to the familiar voice. "I've got to call my grandfather—right now, Lance." She pushed against his chest. "Now."

He nodded. "Cory's office is right over here." He directed her down the hall to the fourth door and opened it to reveal a space the size of a large closet.

Cory had stacked boxes halfway to the ceiling, and a menagerie of papers, trinkets, and scientific instruments cluttered the desk. A small, black phone poked out from under a pile of sketches. She sat in the leather chair, shoved the mess away, and removed her grandfather's number stuffed in her pocket so she could tap it out on the console. Lance leaned against the office wall and studied her. She turned from the intensity of his dark eyes that seemed to plead with her to use discretion.

A picture of two little girls frolicking on a lush lawn on top of Cory hung from a shelf. She shook her head. The men and women who had volunteered to decipher the tablet had families of their own, everything to lose. She feared for them. Did they even understand what havoc surrounded the project?

The phone clicked on the other end. Winona's greeting sounded abrupt as usual.

"Aunt Winona, this is Neida."

"Where are you? Is everything okay?"

"I can't tell you where we are, but we're fine. Are you and Grandfather all right?"

"Yes ... why?"

Neida paused, kept Amanda's demise to herself. She didn't want to give her aunt further reason to resent her.

"Are you sure everything's okay?" asked Winona when Neida remained silent. "What are you not telling me?" The woman's grandson whined, Neida imagined in her arms.

"We ran into another snag, that's all. I just wanted to check on you both."

This time Winona's voice rankled with harshness. "We're fine."

"Do you know of any place you could hang out for a while? I'd breathe a little easier if you and grandfather dropped off the radar for a few days. At least until Lance and I figure out our dilemma."

"You're scaring me. Father isn't well. Besides, he won't leave this place."

"Can you convince him? In fact, why don't you let me talk to him?"

The line went silent for a couple of seconds before Askuwheteau answered.

"Grandfather, you're not going to like this, but I need you, Winona, and Running Deer to pack up and go somewhere else for several weeks."

When he answered, his voice hinted annoyance. "Why do you continue to ask this of us?"

"Someone has committed another murder. I can't be sure what these people know about you, and I won't put you in danger."

"We will stay here. Our ancestors will protect us."

Not that ancestor gibberish again, she thought. She checked herself, though each word continued to escalate until her delivery reached a crescendo. "Oh, Grandfather, you've got to think of Winona and Running Deer. Your life is in danger. Why can't you all go away for a while until we've removed the threat?"

Lance leaned against the office wall, shaking his head.

She had stepped over the line into disrespect, but she refused to accept her grandfather's pigheadedness. His belief might get him killed. Couldn't he see that?

"You stand at the edge of the light, Granddaughter. Your heart fails you because you allow fear to guide your footsteps. It is time to let go of unbelief and step into the darkness. The ancestors will provide you a solid ground to walk on, or they will teach you to fly. But you must make an effort."

Her grandfather's words stunned her. She searched for something to say.

"Do not worry about us," he continued. "We will stay here. I'll plead with the spirits for your safe return. Come home to us with wings. *Baamaapii*, Oneida."

The line went dead. Neida lowered the handset, clutched it until her knuckles turned white, and her hand shook. Lance took the phone from her, replaced it on the charger, and waited for her to speak, but she could only stare at him, unable to form the answers to the questions in his eyes.

CHAPTER NINETEEN

THE FIRST DAY OF DECIPHERING PROVED SLOW. They examined the box initially. Cory used illumination to create shadows across the stone, throwing the letters into sharp relief. The resident photographer on the project took pictures in contrasting light angles to make the less discernible images more visible. He spent the next few hours dumping the photos into Photoshop to combine and layer the data, increasing its readability. Although she still felt a cloud hanging over her about her grandfather's stubbornness, the scientific process took her mind off her disappointment, even thrilled Neida as nothing else could. She took notes on every step of the procedure.

They repeated a similar routine with the tablet. Using fiber-optic light, the technician shot high-resolution photos and then built accurate composite pictures to make the text speak to them. Stacks of Rex Willett's notebooks rested beside the artifacts. Cory pointed out the cipher's intricacies, and they hashed over the facts for hours.

The strange toothbrush characters were impossible to decrypt, considering they had no basis for a translation. Nothing they tried cracked the puzzle. The mysterious symbol of the Creator remained the one commonality between the relics.

By 7:00 P.M., exhaustion took its toll, and Cory called an end to the day's hard work. "I want you back here by 8:00 tomorrow morning."

The whole company sighed in combined relief, and one by one, the technicians exited the glass doors and left the building. Lance and Neida headed to their rooms in silence. Halfway down the hall, Lance yawned. "I don't know about you, but I'm exhausted. I think I'm going to take a shower and hit the sack. Do you mind?"

Neida examined his face. Creases etched deep under his bruised eye, and he almost appeared dazed as he watched her. The sight tugged at her heart. "Yeah, I'm rather tired myself. I'll see you in the morning—bright and early."

They parted. Neida had almost sauntered to her door when Lance called out, "Hey—"

She pivoted around.

"Promise me you'll get some sleep. We've got a heavy day tomorrow."

She nodded, waited until he closed his door, then went to her room. In truth, she couldn't sleep even if she tried, not with the news about Amanda and after a day of following Cory around the lab. Figuring out the complexities of this ancient text filled her with adrenaline. She'd stay up all night to view the newest procedures bring the script to life. If that wasn't hope and faith in something unknown, she didn't know what was.

She switched on the light and stared at the uninviting cot set up in the corner. What would she do to pass the hours? She didn't want to read or listen to music on the iPod Kat had brought her earlier in the day. Maybe she'd walk the narrow passage to Kat's back door and intrude upon her hospitality once again—satisfy her need to talk. But her new-found friend had appeared as pale and tired as Lance when she'd left. Kat had cooked for the crew, shipped in supplies, and headed one experiment after another. She had probably fallen asleep fully clothed.

At least Kat enjoyed the luxuries of home. Neida yearned to sleep in her bed at Hopewell, to make Gran's house her own. She ached to know what Blackhour and his colleagues had done to her grandparent's belongings. She couldn't bear to think of the violation and what repairs she'd have to make once she stepped through Hopewell's door again.

And then a thought occurred to her.

She stood motionless, trying to remember the day—Gran's journal entry on the bedside table, how her clumsiness had knocked it under the nightstand. What if Blackhour had found it? He'd learn about her grandfather, which would lead them to Winona and her grandson too.

She went to the door and poked her head out to peer down the hallway. Cory had gone home, and the night light illuminating the lab's interior appeared to be the only evidence of life left inside. Lance hadn't come down the hall to the showers yet. He too must have taken a nosedive into his cot and had fallen asleep. But she had to discuss this problem with him, and as soon as possible. She inched down the hall and rapped on his door.

He answered right away, gazed at her, his shirt buttons undone to reveal his carved, bare chest.

The sight stunned her. She forgot what she was going to say.

"Do you need something, Neida?"

She searched her mind for coherent thought. "Umm, yes. I've just remembered leaving behind an important document in my bedroom at Hopewell. It points to my Grandfather,

Winona, and Running Deer. Somehow, we've got to retrieve it before Blackhour finds it and hunts down my family."

He frowned at her. "And how would we do that? Somebody already trashed your house, and I'm sure, is surveilling it. It would be suicide to attempt a rescue. I imagine Blackhour's already found the evidence anyway."

Neida looked down, searched the facility floor. Tears burned at the edges of her eyes. She knew he was right, but she had hoped for some miracle he might suggest, something that she hadn't thought of yet. She hiccoughed a sob and closed her eyes.

Lance stepped into the hall and engulfed her to him.

Her hands slid around his waist and clutched his back. She rested her cheek against the soft hair of his chest.

"I know this is hard for you," he said into her ear. "But you've got to hold on, Neida. I can't promise you guarantees. You'd see right through my pretense. But this is where faith steps in and carries us forward with hope. You have to believe your family will get through this."

She stepped back, withdrew her arms, and shook her head. "I'm sorry. I just can't put my mind around such feeble assurances. It's meaningless to me." She hadn't meant to sound so peevish, but his continual talk of faith always managed to sidle its way near her emotions. She shook her head again and started for her room. "Never mind," she said over her shoulder.

"Neida ..." came his exasperated response behind her.

She closed the barrier between them before he could say anything else and leaned against it. Several seconds passed before she heard the click of Lance's door. She pulled herself to the cot, inhaled a rush of air that hardened like ice inside her chest, and sagged against the wall. Then noticing one of her grandmother's journals lying beside her, she took up the beckoning book to soothe her nerves with Gran's words.

Neida curled up and opened to a random passage, read slowly, cherishing every sentence. Here was evidence her grandmother made the best of her separation from Askuwheteau. And she had eked out her survival when she learned of Edward's death. Life dealt the woman misery, had exacted heartache and pain on everyone and everything dear to her. How was anybody ever supposed to trump a lousy hand when frustration made them too wary of playing the game?

Neida turned the page, and her eyes fixed on a crude table blocked out between two paragraphs. The table's five rows each contained symbols representing translations in different languages. The first row consisted of the original toothbrush characters. The second row resembled Egyptian, the third, Greek, and the fourth, an abbreviated form of the Greek above it. The last row, an English translation. Nothing in her grandmother's passage referred to the table or explained why she had kept it there. Gran had just wedged the information between paragraphs, like a random doodle, while she rambled on about everyday occurrences.

Neida leafed through the rest of the journal. Several additional tables and random characters, including their translation beside them, appeared further into the text. Some lay in the corner of a page, yet others lay between words. No explanation accompanied any of them.

Lance needed to know. This discovery couldn't wait until morning, either, not if the information promised to help them translate the tablet. She grabbed the book to her chest and dashed to Lance's room. She placed her ear to the cold metal door and listened for signs of life inside.

Silence.

She could almost see Lance's frustration with her seeping from beneath the door. She rapped anyway. "Lance, can I talk to you? It's important."

He didn't answer.

She knocked louder. "Lance, I found something. Please come to the door."

The cot squeaked, followed by a rustling on the other side of the partition. After a brief pause, the knob turned, and Lance peered through the opening. He wore a scruffy tee shirt this time, and his face sagged with fatigue. "Yeah? Can this wait until morning?"

That, a direct stab to her heart, made her pause. Then she shoved the volume at Lance in hopes the distraction might curb his annoyance. "I found translations of the symbols in my grandmother's journal."

Lance switched on the light, took the book from her, and studied the page. After several seconds he glanced up, his face wiped free of irritation. "Did you examine the other journals?"

"Not yet. They're still out in the truck. But these tables are scattered throughout the pages. Maybe Grandfather Graham asked her to keep the information for him. No one would search for the key in her journals."

"You might be right. Do you mind if we take a closer look at the rest?"

She shook her head and pivoted to take a step, but he grabbed her arm. She peered down at his hand and back up into his eyes.

"Neida, I appreciate your concern for Askuwheteau's safety, but our anonymity is crucial. If what we discover will lock away Fitz and Amanda's murderers, we have to act with some forethought. It's not just you and me involved in this anymore. It's Cory and Kat and the technicians, maybe even their families at risk. Can you understand my concern?" He reached to caress her cheek. "And I don't want you hurt. Your grandmother would never forgive me."

She brought up her hand to enclose his. "I know, but I only wanted to protect my family."

"You just found something to make our work a lot easier. I've got a feeling this hunt for treasure will be over much quicker than we first assumed. You'll be back with your family before you know it." He hiked his eyebrows, motioned with his head toward Neida's room. "Wait for me. I'll get the rest of the journals from the truck."

He squeezed her arm, then grabbed a jacket and shoes from inside his room and hurried toward the warehouse entrance. She watched him retreat down the corridor and out the steel barricade separating them from the world outside. She turned for her room and paused at the entrance, snatching a last glance down the hall. Even though they had found a way of deciphering the text, a sick feeling inside reminded her that her family was still unsafe and, despite their caution, that this new avenue might tip over the first domino in an unending line of disaster.

Cory and the technicians filed through the warehouse door before 8:00 the next morning. Kat had provided another feast, although abbreviated this time. Neida beat Lance to the lab and helped herself to the fare. He joined her several minutes later, her grandmother's journal wedged beneath his arm and his hair still slicked to his head after his morning shower.

Puffy bags and his bruises stood out like black paint under his eyes. Their journal-reading vigil had lasted well into the early morning hours, and to her disappointment, without them garnering any other information. Lance had fallen asleep on

Neida's cot sometime around four A.M., and she hadn't the heart to wake him or send him back to his room. So, she had camped out in the chair. And though she had gleaned little sleep herself, their discovery once again filled her with excitement.

Lance sat on the stool opposite Neida and rested his chin in his hand. "What vitamin regimen are you taking?" he asked. "How did you possess the energy to walk to the lab after reading the whole night? I fought my way out of bed this morning. The old eyes refused to open." He yawned and rubbed his face. "I'm just sorry I occupied your bed, though. Where did you sleep?"

"I didn't really sleep at all. I can't wait for the amazement on Kat and Cory's faces."

"Let's eat breakfast first. I'm starved. If we're to make some headway on the deciphering process today, I want to proceed on a full stomach."

Kat bustled through the lab entrance and presented the technicians with another platter of scrambled eggs and toast. She set the tray on the counter and hurried to where Lance and Neida sat, a frown pulling at her mouth. "Aren't you a pretty picture this morning, Boss? What did you do? Walk the streets most of the night?"

Lance smirked at her. "Greetings to you too, my dear. I was in Neida's room all evening if you must know."

Kat's brows shot up. She glanced from Neida to Lance and back again.

Neida shook her head and waved her hands. "Don't get the wrong idea, Kat. We've been scouring my grandmother's journals. We've discovered something that will be of interest to you."

Kat's expression transformed from surprise to deep interest. "Anything we can use?"

Neida sat up with her shoulders back, anticipating the reaction to her news. "We found a key to the script."

Without turning around, Kat shouted, "Cory, you better get over here."

Cory, who was examining the computer images they'd taken the previous day, glanced over at them. "In a minute," he said. "I'm on to something right now."

Kat pivoted around and pointed her finger at Lance. "You're on to something, all right, but you'll find the information over here."

Cory's brows bunched over his deep-set eyes. He strode across the lab and parked himself on a stool next to Lance and scratched his head. "Okay, you've got my interest."

Lance slid the journal over to his friend. "Take a look inside."

Cory flipped open to the first marker, examined the page, and his mouth gaped wide. He whirled in his seat and held out the book. "Where'd you get this?"

"Neida's grandmother. One of several journals, although this is the only one that contains a key."

"This cipher, with my grandfather's notes about the inscriptions, will cut our work in half."

Lance nodded. "It's a start, anyway. We need to figure out where the map leads us."

Cory bookmarked the journal page with his finger. "From what I've surmised, we're looking for an Ohio cave." He shot from his seat. "Do you mind if I take this to my computer? I want to make some comparisons." He didn't even wait for an answer.

Neida leaped after him. She'd not miss out on the analysis or the experience of a professional paleographer in action. Lance followed behind.

They settled in front of the monitor, and when Cory realized he'd picked up an audience, he found renewed energy. "The artifacts we've discovered to date begin with the sign of the Creator. Most of the time, the name is positioned at the top, the highest of all that follows. Henrietta Mertz called the figure *The Mystic Symbol.*" He pointed at the character.

Neida remembered the woman. Henrietta Mertz had worked as a patent attorney and codebreaker for the U.S. government's cryptography department during World War II. "I've read some of Mertz's work," she said. "She corrected the Smithsonian about the writing on the Bat Creek Stone being Paleo-Hebrew and not that of the Cherokee language. It translated to something like, *for Judea*, I think."

Cory nodded. "Right, but later scientists considered the piece a fake because it matched a similar inscription in a Freemason book. No surprise there. We lost a great boon to our cause when Mertz died. What's significant about the *Mystic Symbol* is that it suggests a definite hierarchy in the heavens, a Creator above all, written as the tetragrammaton HWHY, the shortened form of the Hebrew word, *Yahweh*."

Lance and Kat joined them along with several of the technicians.

Cory sat forward like an excited schoolboy and pointed below the marking with the tip of his pencil. "These two figures caught my attention," he said.

Neida examined the stylized hands, one slanting to the right and the other to the left.

Cory tapped the images in succession on the screen. "These characters represent paths leading in opposite directions. I've made just a rough guess at this point, but I believe the translation begins: '*Yahweh* provides two roads to pursue.' Pay special attention to these mirrored images on either side of the hands."

"The shepherd's crook—the Egyptian symbol for rulership," said Neida.

Cory turned to her, smiling. "That's right."

Neida touched two other symbols on the screen. "So, what are these other characters right next to the stylized hands?"

"They're the symbols for the *son of the right hand* and *son of the left*, two subsidiary gods or sons of *Yahweh*. This one that's to our left of *Yahweh* translates as the Hebrew word *daq*, meaning small, bruised, you know like the Genesis 3:15 translation—whose heel will be bruised, but who would bruise the serpent's head. We know this to be the good messiah. The Copts called him *Little Yao*. And the image to our right of *Yahweh* represents the counterpart, *Samma-el*, *son of the left hand*, or the Satan. Those little coffee table or house-like symbols are also Egyptian characters translating to *heaven* or what is above it, like the throne of heaven."

"So, I think the passage reads, '*Yahweh* provides two directions or roads to follow. On the right of God's throne, follow the righteous son or the Messiah who reigns there, and on the left, follow the evil son.'"

"The Messiah and Satan, two distinct children of a supreme being at odds with each other," said Lance. "Now, that's an interesting concept."

Neida rolled her eyes at his obvious slight against her beliefs or lack of them but didn't rise to the bait. "The tablet's use of multiple languages must be significant," she said.

Cory turned to them with gusto. "That's the beauty of this piece. Trade and the massive influence of these old-world philosophies at the time of the 4th-century Copts traveled across all borders. If these people came out of the Holy Land, their language would reflect a multi-cultured society's diversity. And as soon as we crack the rest of this script and what the language reveals, life, as we seekers of truth understand it, is going to change."

"Let's get started then." Kat gestured at the group. "Back to your stations, everyone. Cory has a lot of work to do here, and you've got some more to clean on our stone box. I want an impression of the exterior by 5:00 this evening."

When Cory, Lance, and Neida were alone again, Cory crossed his arms in front of him. He swiveled on the stool to face Neida. "I hope your grandmother's journal will fill in the rest of the gaps."

"This is fascinating, Cory, my man, but breakfast awaits us, I'm afraid," said Lance. "Keep us updated, will you?" He pointed at his favorite lab table and addressed Neida. "Care to join me while I eat? I need to talk to you."

Neida wanted to learn more. If she could, she'd glue herself next to Cory and shadow him all day. However, Lance's expression appeared strained. She nodded and went to sit at their usual counter space and waited for him to return with another plate of food.

"I know that look," said Neida when they had settled on their stools. "What's going on?"

Lance's eyes focused on his breakfast a moment longer, then peered up at her. "Cory is sure to break the script and map soon. We'll leave for Ohio once he does. I don't know how long finding the site will take us, but the journey will be difficult. Do you want to go with us? Or would you prefer to stay here, where you'll be safe?"

"We've already been through this. You know the answer to that."

Lance cleared his throat and gave her a cheeky smile. "I've got a pretty good idea, but you've never been on a dig inside a cave before. The task can be grueling—lots of bugs, spores, and holes to fall through, maybe even a cave-in. I'll teach you a few basic principles about how to climb before we go. You've got to do everything I say to a tee. One false move inside that cave, and you might fall to your death."

"I'll obey. If there's something significant hidden away in that Ohio cave," said Neida, "I want to be there to unveil it, even if I have to climb into the deepest abyss in the state."

He studied her for several seconds, then picked up a morsel of egg and put it into his mouth. "I'll ask Kat to bring the climbing wall along with some rope and harnesses from storage. We'll start today."

She didn't expect such a suggestion, and so soon. She hadn't any clue what spelunking entailed, but to develop a new skill lifted her spirits. "I'll be ready, Mr. G."

He finished his eggs, and as his fork clicked against the plate, a smirk slid across his features. "Get some sleep first, would you? I don't want to rescue an addle-brained female, dangling at the end of a rope."

CHAPTER TWENTY

NEIDA PEERED UP AT THE WALL DETERMINED. "Okay, I'm ready to climb."

Lance tightened the slack in the rope and shouted down to her. "On belay."

"Climbing."

"Climb on."

Neida grasped the polyurethane ledge with her chalked hands, pulled herself up several feet, and paused. After several more steps, the lead, too taut, knocked her off balance. "Watch me," she said, as she began to tilt backward.

Lance tried to correct the line without success.

"Falling," shouted Neida as she lost her grip and footing. The rope caught her weight as she fell against the wall, swinging her arms, flailing as she tried to secure herself again. She was thankful the floor wasn't too far away. She hoped she'd get the hang of this sport before she faced the real test of skill. On one of her topsy-turvy passes past the middle, Kat appeared below her, worry etching her face.

"Hi, Kat." Neida waved from her precarious position. "Here to see the fledgling fall out of the nest?"

Kat didn't even crack a smile. "Hey guys, I hate to interrupt, but can you come down? We've got a problem."

"Give us a minute," said Lance. "Neida, I think we've practiced enough for today."

She agreed. Her body ached. Muscles she hadn't felt in some time screamed for relief.

Ten minutes later, they had rappelled down, removed harnesses and rope, and the three of them started packing away the equipment. Even though Neida and Lance stood on solid ground now, Kat's face still pinched as though something weighed on her mind.

Lance finished tucking away some of the gear and glanced up at his partner. "What's going on, Kat? Neida's safe. You can stop worrying now."

"I wish I could, Boss, but Pastor Will paid me a little visit tonight."

"Did you forget to send in your donation again?" Lance flashed her an exaggerated smile.

She ignored his lightheartedness, her mouth taut. "The pastor asked a lot of pointed questions as if he expected me to tell him where you are. He said Blackhour is in Newaygo. He's occupying the church. As soon as the pastor sneaked away from Blackhour's thugs, he came directly here. It sounds like they're searching for you and the artifacts. I can arrange a lab down Grand Rapids way if you'd like. I'll insist Cory pack up the crew and head south with the stone box and tablet tonight."

Lance secured a backpack over his shoulder and shook his head. "We've almost cracked the script. If we stopped now, we'd be days setting up the lab again."

"But they might drop in at any time," said Kat, emphasizing each word.

Neida's stomach tightened, and a hint of a headache pressed in the middle of her forehead. Her adrenaline rush of the last few hours tumbled to the bottom, just like her fall against the wall.

Kat helped Neida don one of the other packs on her shoulder. "Carl said a stranger came into the office the other day. He seemed eager to talk to you and asked a lot of questions. That scares me, Lance. I won't go back to work anymore. If he's one of Blackhour's boys, they might follow me home. A little inconvenience seems worth the caution, don't you think?"

"We'll be on our way to Ohio soon," said Lance, stuffing the last of his rope in another pack and lifting it from the ground. "I'm not ready to run when we're so close to some answers."

"Do *I* have any say about this?" Neida placed a hand on her hip and scowled at them. "Kat's right, Lance. We've witnessed for ourselves that these men are capable of anything. They'll hunt for us until they get what they want."

Lance shot her a confident smile and pointed at the walls. "Remember we're sitting on top of a fortress. We'll be safe enough right here."

Kat picked up the last pack and swung it over her shoulder. She shot him a strange look. "Well, I hope you're right, Boss."

They followed her to the far end of the building and stashed the equipment in a steel storage compartment. After securing the doors, Lance turned to Kat. "So, where was the pastor headed?"

"I'm not sure, but he was in an all-fire hurry as though the devil himself nipped his breeches."

"Did you check out front after he left?"

"Yeah, he was alone."

"What if his visit is a trick?" asked Neida. "Maybe Blackhour sent him here to draw us out?"

Kat shrugged. "I don't know. He seemed quite annoyed about Blackhour."

Lance placed a hand on Kat's shoulder. "We'll be fine. Have I reminded you lately how much I appreciate you? I owe you the world for everything you're doing for us."

Kat smirked. "How about that equal share you've always promised me?"

"Yeah, you earned that a long time ago."

"And then some," she said with emphasis.

He gazed at Neida; his expression animated with emotion. "You okay with the plan?"

If the currents running through her body indicated her mood, Neida felt anything but confident about the arrangements, though she refused to admit her fear. This work to uncover her grandmother's desires was too important. She shrugged. "I guess—for now—yet the sooner this project is finished, the better, in my opinion."

"Then let's go visit Cory. Maybe we can hasten his work along." He nodded toward the corridor leading to the lab. Kat led the way.

That night, Neida sat up on her cot and placed a finger under a section of text she'd been studying. Grandfather Graham's quirky notation, the lead they had searched long and hard to find, shot electricity through her. She rechecked the scan, and the next few, each page building her excitement.

"Eureka," she shouted.

Lance didn't answer or move. She peered up from the document to eye her companion leaning sideways in a chair, asleep. The scans they had printed in the lab lay in disarray on his lap.

She bounded from the cot and crossed to where he dozed. Up close, just the sight of him made her pause. She'd come to adore the man—handsome, courageous, intelligent, and kind, the type of man she needed in her life but was too marred from past relationships to disclose. She pushed back the familiar wayward curl from his forehead. Restlessness, and something else she declined to identify, welled inside her. She pushed the emotion away.

"Lance ..." She shook his shoulder until he moved.

"Hmm?" His eyelids fluttered open, and he yawned himself to consciousness. "What's the time?"

"Time to leave for Ohio."

"Did you find something?" His eyes widened, and he sat higher in the chair.

She smiled down at him and shoved the scan in front of his face. "I'll let you be the judge."

Lance adjusted the paper to reading distance, skewed the page sideways, and read the notation aloud:

> Take SR50, drive halfway between Chillicothe and Hillsboro, just west of the Highland/Ross county line and southwest of Seven Caves. A mile past the Cave Road sign, follow trail south and descend to waterfall. Found eighth cave, deepest of all. Seems unexplored.

Lance shuffled the papers in his hand to the next scan.

> Entrance just beyond waterfall. Dolomite walls rise about one hundred feet. Use caution—

> springs, sinkholes, and several dead-end cave entrances—wildlife in abundance. Find hemlocks at the base. White cedars at *cliff's edge on top. A* micro-Canadian ecosystem—need to pack warm clothes. Look for rare Sullivantia Sullivantia. Vertical dolomite dense with bulblet ferns, ginger—entrance hidden, but just east of the center point. Somewhere up top—moon entrance. Search for opening next trip.

Then on to the next scan.

> Beyond the moon's light, discovered tunnels that lead to room beyond throne. Statues and mural. Symbol of Creator painted over central figure. Markings on feet, wrists, and hands significant. Find release latch on right foot. Launching expedition to document all.

Lance glanced up, astonished. "So, he found a room? Does the next scan reveal anything else?" He peered around her to the pile of papers on her cot.

"The next few scans only mention the particulars of equipment, nothing more. My grandmother's journal wasn't any help either. It did say Edward left for Ohio."

Lance examined the entry again. "At least this gives us direction. Hmm, statues and a mural painted on the cave walls. And a release latch on the central figure's right foot." He glanced up at her with his eyebrows arched in the peculiar way he adopted when proving a point. "It even says there are markings on the figure's hands, wrists, and feet. A depiction of Christ, maybe?"

Neida snatched the scan from his hands. "Don't be absurd."

"I'm just keeping an open mind," he said with his palms raised toward her. "The theme does corroborate with other Michigan Relics."

"They're fakes, remember?"

Lance grumbled. "If they're fakes, then why is Cory pouring over an ancient relic tablet in the lab right now? An artifact our grandfather found buried under rotted roots inside ash layers ... among skeletal remains ... in a mound behind *your* house. You'd dismiss tangible proof because it might lead to the natives' foreknowledge of Christ?"

"They *didn't* believe in Christ."

He stood and gazed down at her. A mixture of pity and conviction radiated from his eyes. "I've never told you how the Ojibwe pronounce the characters of the Creator. '*Yod-Hey-Wav*,'" he said with weight. "What does that name sound like to you?"

She comprehended his meaning, but she wouldn't answer him.

"Sounds an awful lot like *Jehovah* to me."

Neida placed her hand on her hip. "*Jehovah* wasn't the New Testament Christ. Even I know that." She braced herself for more about this fictional character, and just as she feared, he continued to expound.

"Then you're mistaken. In the Greek Old and New Testaments, *Kyrios* means *Jehovah* or *Yahweh*, translated as the Lord in English. That same text uses *Theos* for *Elohim*, more accurately, *Ho Theos*—The God, in English. *Theos* always refers to the Father." Lance leaned closer. "In Corinthians 8:6 Paul said, 'There is one God, the Father ... and one Lord, Jesus Christ.' In the Greek, they use *Theos* in that passage to mean the Father, and *Kyrios* when they refer to the Lord Jesus Christ. That's two separate beings mind you. Somewhere along the way to modern Christianity, people lost this understanding."

She opened her mouth to counter, but he cut her off.

"Ask *He Who Watches* about the Creator. He'll tell you about the sandaled visitor who came to this land to visit every tribe in the area. He traveled to the western part of this nation and into Mexico—even beyond. The Natives tell stories about how the Creator came here to do His Father's work."

She crossed her arms. Visions of her mother sermonizing to her came to mind. "Since when did you become a theologian? Spouting the Bible non-stop? Our work is a scientific investigation, Lance, not some camp revival."

"Even some of the experts consider the whole picture, as should we. Science doesn't hold all the answers, Neida. Think about it. Has academia ever verified how the earth's formation occurred? Or how man came to be?"

"We have theories."

"Right. We cling to theories—expand them by our imaginations and guess upon guess. Scientists are experts at disproving a hypothesis, but you know as well as I do, they can never prove an assumption entirely true."

"We come pretty darn close." She couldn't refute his logic, and she didn't know why she continued to fight him about the possible existence of God. Over the last few days, the premise had inched under her skin like a revelatory tick, sucking the lifeblood from her convictions, until she wasn't sure what she believed anymore.

Lance's expression softened. "Haven't you ever wondered why the answers are so hard to find? Perhaps truth requires much more of us, the one thing you keep saying you don't trust—faith—believing in things we don't see tangible evidence for. I've got news for you, Neida Graham. You're full of faith, but you're so determined to prove me wrong, you fight me like a polecat, letting off a stink when I get too close to your true feelings."

And still, he went on.

"If you're skeptical about finding the artifacts, why do you even bother searching for them? Why did you press on after we found Fitz at the end of a lance or read about Amanda's death? It's because you want the results as much as the rest of us. You yearn to believe there's something or someone in the universe who *does* have the answers. You're so full of hope, you're clueless about what to do with the evidence, and you push the facts and everybody around you away."

Neida clenched her fists. "You're quick to put words in my mouth—thoughts in my head. You haven't a clue what I believe." Her resistance and limping fortitude jumbled inside her head, endangering her past beliefs, and it made her angry. Caving after years of building arguments against matters of the heart would wield the final blow and prove her weak.

"Embrace the concept, Neida. This knowledge can enlighten and empower you. Science might let you down, but faith takes you to roads you've yet to explore."

Neida blew out her frustration. They didn't have time for this—to hash over man-made philosophies and legends no one could prove—or to discuss what she did or didn't believe. They had to find the cave and figure out the things Grandfather Graham understood and let the rest of the world in on the information before the knowledge fell forever silent.

"Why do you buy into all this confusion?"

"It's not confusion." He placed his hands on her shoulders. "Ask your grandfather. He'll tell you some stories."

"Indian folklore is anything but reliable in the scientific world—talking animals and ancestors who teach you to fly. It's like something out of Camelot. Merlin and King Arthur."

Lance shook his head. "All folklore and legend hold some basis of truth, Neida, no matter how strange the details sound. Humankind might skew evidence over the centuries, but facts exist at the root of every fantastic narrative. Is burying ancient remains on the backroom shelves of museums in our best interest? No, it isn't, and neither is sweeping information passed down for generations under the carpet. They all work together, Neida. They help us piece the answers into something concrete."

"I still don't buy it," she said, yet his theory was screaming at her to take it to heart. "Cory's no doubt finished his translation on the tablet while we're arguing about monsters and goblins and how they can lead us to the truth—or take us away from it."

He pulled back, and a wall rose between them. She had built the barricade with haughty determination, one brick of stubbornness at a time.

Then a thought hit her. She wasn't arguing with Lance. She was arguing with her mother, against the constant shove down her throat of impalpable things—dogma that had caused her to adopt a hardnosed outlook most of her life. Hadn't she felt a change inside her of late? Hadn't she felt a more open approach to the facts they had gleaned? Yes, her practiced pragmatism had forced her to anger, which was the least of her intentions, especially when Lance desired nothing except to help. She opened her mouth to apologize, but he cut her off with his curt reply.

"Then, of course, don't mind me. Since you've figured out the whole of it, let's proceed to the lab." He whipped around toward the door.

His remark stuck in an uncomfortable place inside her, as had all his words. Though he'd ventured far closer to the truth than he understood right now, the opportunity for confession had passed. She swallowed her apology and followed him down the hall in silence. Would she ever learn to tread lightly around others' convictions? For that matter, would she ever be gentle with her own?

CHAPTER TWENTY-ONE

WHEN NEIDA AND LANCE ENTERED THE LAB, Cory sat hunched in front of the computer screen, pointing at a character on the monitor. Kat stood next to him, but her attention focused in their direction as they approached.

"Hey, you two. Where've you been? You're missing out on all the fun."

"We've stumbled on some fun of our own." Lance rattled the paper in his hand, though he referred to much more than the scan. The fun never ended with Neida's hardheadedness.

Cory swiveled in his seat. "You found the directions." A statement rather than a question.

Lance nodded. "Now, *you* need to figure out what the fuss is all about."

Cory adjusted the laptop toward Lance. "I can do better than that. Take a look."

Lance leaned over his shoulder and examined the characters layered to fit one on top of the other in perfect contrast against the light behind them.

"What are we looking at?" asked Neida, stepping closer.

Cory's nervous energy showed evidence he'd stumbled onto something big. He pointed at the foreign inscriptions on the right side of the screen.

"I did a comparison of several languages we know from past discoveries--the five plates from Cuenca, Ecuador, some middle American script, ancient Semitic, Egyptian, and Cypriot texts. Compare the similarities with the Michigan inscription. They range from 50% to 90% relationship. They're almost identical to the Semitic and Cypriot symbols, more so than in any of the other languages. Although this isn't conclusive proof, the data show whoever inscribed this plate came from the eastern Mediterranean. The American inscriptions use syllabic or ideographic characters, but we'll need a lot more comparisons like these before we completely understand the language."

"Then you haven't deciphered the tablet yet," said Lance, his hope sagging.

"I didn't say that." Cory looked smug. "Narrowing the locale to a specific time and place helps us use the belief system of that people to understand our conclusions. Exploring their religion and folklore gives us a better grasp of the whole picture."

That was the exact premise he had just described to Neida. He peered at her to see if she realized it, but she avoided his eyes. Lance turned back to the images. "What does this inscription tell us?"

"You don't believe the language a fake then?" Neida asked before Cory could answer.

Cory shook his head. "No way. The doctrine found on this tablet is a perfect match to the Copt philosophy." Cory adjusted himself on the stool. "In the 4th century, it seems the Nicene Council played into the Roman emperor Constantine's hope to come to an understanding of who the God of the Bible was.

Constantine was a pagan and only converted to Christianity at the end of his life, and then, for political reasons. He didn't care what the bishops decided. He just wanted them to come to a consensus. *Homoousion* was the order of the day—that only one God exists in substance, essence, and nature—three in one and one in three or what we know as the *Trinity* today. It was a confusing concept, almost overturned several times, and no one successfully questioned or defied the ecclesiastical leaders' final decree. Those who tried, like Bishop Arius, a priest in Baucalis in Alexandria, Egypt, were considered heretics and were exiled from the church."

"They even burned some at the stake," said Lance.

Cory nodded. "Perhaps mayhem ensued, and our little group of Coptic Christians believed Bishop Arius's theories and escaped religious persecution. As I told you during our last meeting of the minds, most of the Michigan tablets and relics show the mark of the Creator at the top. The symbol represents an all-powerful or *highest Yahweh* who sired two sons, the *son of the right hand*, the l*ower Yahweh* or good Messiah, and the *son of the left*, the Satan or evil Messiah."

Neida frowned. "This is confusing."

Lance leaned against the counter and folded his arms. "Not as confusing as the Trinity. Yet except for a few modern faiths, most Christian theologies still believe in the doctrine."

"There's another reason I find Christianity so hard to believe," said Neida. "If a true God does exist, wouldn't sects be more in agreement with each other? It seems to me everyone is just making up the story as they go along."

Lance nodded. "Mankind is flawed, to be sure. Selfish motives, like politics, power, money, and evil intentions often control public opinion. Religious interpretation is no exception to the rule. And it makes our job of digging up the past more difficult. We wade through the various creeds with careful examination but are still only able to present theories and our best guesses."

"Well, I think our little group of Michigan Relic creators catered to the Copts ideology," said Cory. "You have to agree with me, Lance."

Lance shook his head. "I have a different take on the puzzle than you do, Cory. The creators of the Michigan Relics may be a separate group from these mound-builders, either that or the Hopewell may be an earlier group of Semitics who believed in such a theology. Think about it. Your theory still doesn't answer the question of the older skeletal remains that the ancients buried in the mounds before the time of Christ. And the Native Americans who annihilated the culture swear the Hopewell were in this country long before the 3rd century CE. They could have been the Essenes, a sect that studied all religions and languages and extracted the great scientific truths from everything around them. They believed themselves the guardians of divine teaching. And they lived at the same time as the Hopewell."

Cory frowned. "Weren't they a celibate bunch? That's a far cry from the Hopewell lifestyle." Cory shook his head, as though shedding his confusion. "Well, whatever peoples *they* turn out to be, the early pioneers and farmers who uncovered the artifacts weren't buying the fact that an earlier Christian people had beat them to the promised land. Or that they had written on tablets about their particular theology."

"Did you find any redundancy on the tablet?" asked Lance.

Cory shook his head. "Many of the Michigan scripts use different styles than this one, although the characters never change. The symbols can appear thin and messy or fat and precise. Some sprawl across a passage, others are grouped, suggesting many people authored them. Yet, they all contain a consistent pattern of manufacture. We're working with a definite language here."

Lance nodded. At least they had authentication on their side. "Tell us about the tablet itself."

"As far as the boys were able to determine, the copper came from the Keweenaw Peninsula, rather than from another country," said Cory. "This metal was cold-forged instead of using today's methods of hot work. The process ranged from room temperature to several hundred degrees. I'm sure they used a variation of bending, drawing, heading, and extrusions to get a diverse range of shapes for other objects."

"What tools did they use to inscribe the material?" asked Neida.

"In this case, copper engravers," Cory said with conviction. "The cutting points of this tablet were blunt. Thus, the neater form of writing, and with regular spacing, but without hesitation as a copy might indicate."

Neida tilted her head to the side. "So, there are no puddles or lack of cohesion to suggest forgery?"

Cory shook his head. "Not a one."

Neida pressed closer. "What if a forger invented a language system? Could he attain fluency sufficient to create a near-perfect inscription?"

"Scotford and his buddies didn't have the time. Most of the tablets use several different Semitic forms of writing. The inscriptions read from left to right, some right to left, but others boustrophedon. Look, I'll show you," Cory said, pointing to a few lines. "These read up one line, and down the next, one string is read from right to left, the next row from left to right."

Cory turned around and examined them over his spectacles. "Scotford received little education. To understand these language idiosyncrasies or these people's religious beliefs, well, it required someone quite knowledgeable—certainly not a bunch of farmers or the Christians who settled here in the dawn of this country. In my opinion, very few possessed the ability to read and understand what these artifacts suggest. A Gnostic text called the *Pistis Sophia*, containing this philosophy, wasn't even translated into English until 1895, and a forger would make a lot more errors as they copied the characters and beliefs to all the relics we've found."

The lab phone rang, and Kat left to answer it.

Lance's impatience welled up inside again. They needed to get to the meat of the writing and head out for Ohio today. "Tell us what the inscription says. And were you able to decipher the script on the outside of the stone box?"

Cory whipped around to the computer again. "Have no fear, my boy." He picked up his pencil and switched to another picture. "The image you see here *is* from the outside of the box. Examine this line."

He paused for a moment, distracted. Kat had appeared again and placed several manuals into a backpack on the floor. Lance recognized the strain around her eyes, the pallor in her complexion hinting something worried her.

Cory, oblivious to her anxiety, turned and continued his explanation. "It seems—"

Kat cleared her throat. "Cory, I hate to interrupt your lecture, but since you've determined a translation now, and Lance knows the directions, we all better get to Ohio. You can educate Lance and Neida later. We've got a ton of work to do before we find the cave entrance, and since Blackhour may already know where it is, we might experience a little interference in the process."

Cory's expression morphed to understanding. He closed out the computer program, slipped off the stool, then squatted to help Kat place the rest of the manuals in the bag. "I'll tell you more on the way out of here," he said without looking up.

Lance examined the little folds of worry creasing Neida's forehead as she watched the technicians, Cory, and Kat disassemble the lab in seconds. The best thing to do was get her away from here and occupy her mind with specific tasks so he could ask Kat for an explanation. His frustration against Neida's stubbornness dissipated; his role of protector took over.

"Neida, do me a favor. Go and pack just the essentials for our trip. I don't know how long we'll be in Ohio. Stuff whatever you can carry in the backpack we provided you, but don't forget your grandmother's most helpful journals. We might want to reference them from time to time."

"What's going on, Lance?" The creases on her forehead deepened.

"We've got a lot of searching ahead of us if we're to find that cave entrance."

Her jaw tightened. "I won't move until you tell me what you're hiding from me."

"I'm not hiding anything from you." He spoke the truth because the specifics eluded him at the moment, though he'd find out soon enough. "Please, just hurry. We'll leave within the next few minutes."

Neida didn't say anything. She turned and hustled toward the lab door, peered back over her shoulder just before she passed into the hallway.

Lance waited for the door to close behind her before he questioned Kat. "So, who was on the phone? The way you've hustled the troops, I surmise there's a problem."

Kat nodded. "A car has been parked down the street all day. A few minutes ago, reinforcements arrived, and they've moved out back, ready to charge the castle. We'll take the alternate route. You best get your things and hurry Neida along."

The alternate route. Lance looked in the direction of Neida's exit. "How long do we have?"

"We'd better leave pronto. Now, go. Get your things and swallow that papa bear instinct. Neida's got more inside her than you think she does. Your feelings for her will have to wait until all this mess is over." She patted his arm then hurried away, hastening the technicians.

They had already gutted most of the evidence of the lab's operation. The treasure's only salvation lay in a safe underneath the floor. But would the relics survive? Would they escape? That thought made him rush through the lab door as though the devil himself followed fast on his heels.

Neida hurried to keep pace with Kat and the technicians who moved down the tunnel without a word. Lance followed behind her. What kind of secret projects had Kat's father worked on that the government would build surveillance monitors in what resembled a war room with revolving walls, narrow underground tunnels, and locked doors threading away from the lab. The experience touted a virtual scientific anomaly straight out of *James Bond*. She almost asked Lance for enlightenment, but red lights began to flash on and off around them, and her question fizzled to nothing.

Everyone craned their necks heavenward and stopped to listen, a moment's hesitation before Kat motioned them on. Neida's heart continued to pound at the base of her neck, and a strange dread rose in her gut. She'd always experienced panic in narrow places, even as a little girl.

Lance must have sensed her struggle because he placed a hand on her back and nudged her forward. "C'mon, Neida, only a few more yards."

Several minutes later, they emerged amid the trees from what appeared to be a ranger station situated at least a half-mile downriver of the lab. She sucked in the freshness of the night air, couldn't get enough of it, and tried to gain her composure.

Two Range Rovers waited in the brush. Once Lance closed the station door behind them, Kat hustled them to the vehicles. The staff placed their backpacks inside against computers and other technical equipment, then piled into one of the cars.

Kat loped toward them with a severe expression, devoid of her usual enthusiasm. "I'll ride with you two," she said as she approached. "Cory and the crew will head out first. We'll man the rear. I want to make sure we don't pick up strays along the way. We should reach Ohio by early tomorrow morning if we drive straight through."

Kat placed an arm around Neida's shoulders and opened the car. "C'mon, Hon. The sooner we get to Ohio, the sooner all this mayhem stops. You'll see Hopewell again before you know it."

Neida shoved down her fear, hustled into the back seat, and Lance slipped behind the wheel. Once Kat secured Neida's door, she skirted the vehicle and jumped into the front passenger seat. Cory and the technicians raced ahead and turned onto the highway. Lance shoved the car into gear and accelerated after them.

CHAPTER TWENTY-TWO

AFTER MIDNIGHT, they stopped to refuel the Range Rovers in Toledo. Kat had thought of everything. The vehicle's glove compartment had built-in safe boxes with enough cash to finance their trip. Using credit cards was out of the question now, and they had quite a few items to pick up after leaving much of the necessity behind in the lab.

The morning had brought crisp temperatures and frost to the roads. The moment Neida stepped from her sanctuary, the chilled air blasted her in the face. She tugged her jacket a little tighter around her body and hurried inside the convenience store to find a magazine to read and a snack to tide her over until breakfast.

When she returned from the ladies' room, Kat, Lance, and the technicians still debated outside. She had caught the essence of their conversation on her way into the store. They haggled over the logistics of setting up a base camp and how those who stayed behind might proceed. Judging by their heated debate, they'd yet to reach a decision. The technicians were the lucky ones. They'd find warmth and safety—and anonymity. She almost wished she could volunteer for the job.

The magazine rack displayed various women's fashion and home décor favorites and several men's fitness, hunting, and fishing periodicals. One, in particular, caught her notice. The name Chillicothe sprawled across the cover in white letters. She picked it up and leafed through the colorful pages, decided to purchase it. At least she'd educate herself on the area where they'd hole up for the next few days or weeks, or until the fair weather thumbed a ride south for the winter.

The door chime rang, and Lance and the crew barreled toward the restrooms. Some helped themselves to the coffee and the doughnuts inside plastic bins. The clerk, animated at the commotion, watched the isles and the newcomers like a kid choosing the flavor of his first Popsicle. When Neida finished her shopping and approached the register, she placed her items on the counter and reached for her wallet.

"You folks just passing through?" asked the clerk.

She looked up at the pimply-faced youth to answer, but Lance stepped up to the counter next to her and cut off her reply.

"Yep, just passing through." He placed a couple of doughnuts and two steaming cups of coffee on the counter. "I'll get this," he said to Neida and pulled out his wallet.

His vagueness was smart. The less revealed, the better—in case Blackhour followed their trail.

The clerk scratched the soul patch on his chin and searched for the magazine's bar code before he scanned the item. "You headed for Chillicothe?"

"Could be," said Lance.

"Lot of interest that way lately," the young man said. "A few heads are haggling over the earthworks, trying to guess what they mean to the rest of us. Looking for some ancient road the local tribes built, I hear. Dude, went all the way to Newark, they say." He looked up. "That'll be $15.85. You scientists or something like that?"

"Something like that," said Lance. He passed the clerk a twenty, who returned the change. Lance handed Neida her purchases before he retrieved his refreshments and headed outside.

Not anxious to face the cold again, Neida took a sip of her hot coffee and hunched her shoulders before following Lance to the car. He opened the door for her. She scooted onto the seat, careful to keep her drink upright, and waited for Lance to close her in. Instead, he motioned her over, slipped in next to her, and shut himself inside.

"What are you doing?" she asked, feeling a jolt when his arm touched hers.

He held the cup near his face, the palpable steam stroking his chin and cheeks before he cast a sideways glance. "Just taking a break. Thought we could talk while Kat buys up the establishment."

On the other side of the store window, Kat clutched an armload. She still managed to reach for something else on the shelf.

"She's always prepared, isn't she?" asked Neida.

Lance chuckled. "Never met anyone like her. She's one step ahead of you even before you decide which way to go."

"So, what do you want to talk about?"

Lance shook his head and smiled. "Don't you ever just savor a moment? Sit and enjoy someone else's company?"

"After what we've experienced? I'm not in a reflective mood."

"Too bad. The stillness offers insight. When we're reflective, the powers that be can talk to us."

She eyed him with raised eyebrows. "The powers that be? You mean the force of the universe, the cosmic energy of time and space, right?" She couldn't help but smile, though their well-worn disagreement sat around them like an elephant inside the car.

He ignored her taunt and looked down at the magazine on her lap. "There's a magic about Chillicothe and the rest of the Scioto and Ohio River valleys. You can find more earthworks per square mile there than in any other part of North America. The locale served as the heartland of the prehistoric Woodland cultures. We've only now discovered the spiritual nature of these monuments and how they relate to today's tribes."

He leafed through the periodical with his free hand. He stopped at a full-page spread displaying several tumuli rising from the mist at sunrise. "There's Hopeton and Mound City," he continued, "Seip Mound and its earthworks. And Story Mound. What's fascinating about these ruins is that the culture laid them out in various shapes—circles, squares, octagons, and ovals. They calculated their huge centers to the moon's trajectories." He pointed at the page open on Neida's lap. "They buried their dead in these conical and loaf-shaped tumuli, and roads connected them with the larger geometric earthworks."

With his explanation, the structures on the page took on an ethereal quality. Who would build such magnificent traces of their day-to-day lives only for some other culture to obliterate them without explanation from off the face of the land? Nothing of the Ohlone culture compared to the magnificence of what they were about to uncover within this Hopewell territory, and it thrilled her. Neida shifted in her seat. "What road was the clerk talking about?"

Lance sipped his coffee again, then placed the brew in the cupholder. He balanced his doughnut on top and turned to her. "Archaeologists believe the Hopewell used the highway for ceremonial and spiritual pilgrimages. The Shawnee, Delaware, and Miami tribes who lived around here too also refer to the

White Road in their traditions. We're not sure if their stories refer to the Milky Way or rather denoted something earthbound, like the Great Hopewell Road. Maybe both." Lance looked past her outside the window. His gaze fixed on some vision transforming into the tangible that only he could see.

She examined his profile, amazed at his extensive knowledge on the subject, a discipline that seemed to be changing her world. "You truly love your work, don't you? I envy you. You travel all over the world, dig into other cultures—a far cry from the classroom. At the University, our most exciting event in the field involves work on an Ohlone dig, but I've always wanted to get my hands dirty on something like what we're doing now. You might call me an armchair archaeologist."

Lance closed the magazine on her lap. "Well, you're about to get your wish. You'll dirty much more than you bargained for before we're done with this place."

"How long do you think this will take?"

Lance shrugged. "It's hard to say. We'll find a motel in Toledo for the day. You and I need some warmer clothes, and the technicians have to purchase a few more items for our trip. This is our last big stop before Chillicothe, and we don't want to draw attention to ourselves once we hit town."

"But shopping shouldn't take us all day."

"I thought we'd pour over the rest of the scans and your grandmother's journals too. Glean as much as we can before we plunge into our work."

"May I call my grandfather sometime today? Before we leave for Chillicothe? To see if he's safe?"

His forehead creased, and she surmised his answer even before he spoke.

"I'm sorry. We just can't chance it. We're in a race for results now."

She lowered her head and closed her eyes, shut out her disappointment. She ached to the bone to know just a tidbit of information about her family. The desire reached inside her to a hidden place of longing and immediately enticed feelings foreign to her—emotions of love and connection that pierced deep. They opened a fresh wound that she didn't know how to dress, and it made her shiver. The cold only added a layer to her pain.

Lance moved beside her, and before she realized what he was doing, he confiscated her coffee and doughnut and placed them in the other cupholder. Sitting back again, he slipped a warm arm around her shoulders and pulled her close, doctoring her throbbing soul.

She burrowed her head underneath his chin, where she remained still for some time. A slow thaw caught hold, imparting safety, contentment—and, to her surprise—an abandonment she had yet to experience since she had reacquainted herself with Lance. Whether her weakness was the result of the exhaustion of the last few weeks, the comfort of the moment, or just the scent of him, she tilted back and, without a second thought, kissed him, a gentle caress against his mouth.

He jolted in surprise.

"Thank you, Lance," she whispered.

"For what?" He met her gaze, uncertainty in his expression.

"For being here. You've helped a blind woman feel her way through the dark, to uncover the possibilities, even when they seemed illogical or impractical. I couldn't have done any of this without you."

"You would have found a way to proceed."

"Not the same." She closed her eyes for a moment and sighed, reopened them. "You've moved me forward, kept me at an even pace. You've supported me, despite my orneriness. And I owe you an apology." She sighed in frustration at how hard it was to get her words out. "I guess what I'm trying to say is I'm glad you're in my life. You're ..." she breathed in courage, "important to me."

An intensity replaced puzzlement in his eyes. His gaze shifted to Neida's lips, lingered there, and back up to penetrate the barrier between them. He closed the gap until the warmth of his words skimmed across the surface of her mouth. "You don't know how long I've waited for you to say that."

Her heart pounded; she couldn't breathe.

His lips parted and enveloped hers, tender and warm at first, then he pulled her closer, and all barriers shattered. She sagged against him. Their kiss intensified, and she slid her hand into his hair, where her fingers intertwined with his curls.

Without warning, reason intruded. Neida pushed at his chest, tore herself away from their embrace, and placed a hand over her heart to settle her emotions.

Lance searched her expression and frowned at her. "What's wrong?" he asked.

She shook her head. What should she say? That she wanted him, but that her heart needed an overhaul, that her completeness in his arms lay victim to the gaping mouth of her distrust of men. "Lance ... I ..."

The back door of the Range Rover flung open, and the interference severed them farther apart.

"Ooh-wee, baby, it's cold outside."

Neida whipped around to the voice and watched Kat pack her purchases with precision next to the equipment in the storage compartment. She seemed oblivious to the dynamics in the seat in front of her. Either that or she chose to ignore them out of respect for their privacy.

"That kid in there. Let's just say his elevator is a tad short of reaching the top," said Kat.

The woman glanced up at Lance, who sat like a statue, although from Neida's perspective, the passion on his parted lips, the confusion on his face, was evidence he struggled for control and understanding. The cold rushed through the opening, thrashed at them along with Kat's next words.

"Do you want me to drive now, Boss?"

"No, I'll drive." Lance shoved the door wide and slammed it, then bolted from the back to the driver's side. Kat forced the rear gate shut soon after, both impacts reverberating inside Neida, joggling her from her muddled state to coherent thought again.

What had possessed her to kiss him, anyway? For almost two months now, she had vowed to suppress all attraction for Lance, but he had become friend, mentor, and companion to her in this wild pursuit of discovery. Every day, she grew fonder, relied on him more, but tonight, she had forgotten her resolve. She mentally kicked herself for such stupidity. She wasn't prepared to handle a relationship adjustment right now or her fickle nature.

She lowered her head and calmed herself, though Kat's incessant gabbing made concentration difficult. The woman had gained a second wind at the rest stop. As Lance drove out of the parking lot and barreled down the road after the technicians, her ramblings picked up speed.

"You okay, Hon?"

Kat's volley over the seat was like a blast of cold air to the face. Neida glimpsed up at the woman who frowned at her. She managed a smile. "Just listening to my teeth chatter, is all."

"Here, let me crank up the heat." Kat busied herself with the thermostat.

Neida's attention shifted to the back of Lance's head, the way his hair tousled in silky waves, the same softness her fingers had explored just moments ago. Despite her resolve to never go there again, she longed to repeat the last few shared minutes with him. The closeness had liquefied the last icy edges of her soul.

She shook the thought away, readjusted her legs crammed against the seatback, and rolled the kinks from her neck. When she opened her eyes again, she gasped. Nothing prepared her for the shock of Lance watching her in the rearview mirror and how it immediately stopped her mind and heart.

Lance rested his cheek in the palm of his hand and read his grandfather's entry a third time. The words still refused to stick. Distraction numbed his brain in the form of Neida. She sat opposite him at the motel table, her eyes glued to her grandmother's journal, her finger moving over the page in front of her. He had yet to confront her about their early morning kiss and why she had pulled away. The longer they avoided the topic, the more agitation derailed him.

Kat had accompanied them all day on their various outings. They had gone to the mall to make sure they found ample layers for their subterranean journey and to grocery stores for sufficient food to feed the crew. Then Kat directed them to a home supply center for drills and other tools to go along with a supply of dynamite they had brought with them. Now, Kat puttered with a camera and lens lying on the bed, and Lance managed his impatience about her relentless drive akin to a hornet captured in a jar.

Neida was right about one thing. Shopping for clothes and equipment took up only a portion of their day. He itched to get her alone before he trudged next door and passed the hours with Cory talking technicalities.

He studied the top of Neida's head, her black, plaited hair draping over her shoulder. He reached for her fingers, resting on the table. "Neida, why don't you and I take a walk? We need a break."

She retracted her hand. Her body language screamed that to be with him—alone—was the last thing she wanted to do.

"I'm kind of tired," she said.

Lance glanced at Kat to see if she had heard the interchange. By the expression on his partner's face, the answer was clear.

Kat stood, retrieved the camera, and announced, "Hey, I think I'll go next door to give those boys a hand. I know Cory. He's jabbering on about some tangent. He'll delay us from packing up before dark. I'll be back in a little while, Hon," she said to Neida. "Maybe we can squeeze in a bit of girl talk before we hit the hay."

Neida popped to attention. "Do you need help?"

Kat shook her head. "Not right now. It'll take a while for me to steer Cory back on task. And the technicians, well, only egg him on into telling stories, and they never get anything done. When we're ready to pack up, I'll come and grab you both." And then Kat hurried outside.

Kat's wake sent silent ripples throughout the room. By the look on Neida's face, her patience had capsized, and her willingness to talk bobbed like some drowned piece of flotsam.

Lance struggled to keep the edge out of his voice as Neida sunk into her chair. "Can we talk about this morning?" he asked.

"What's there to talk about?" Her gaze remained fixed on the table.

"The fact that we feel something for each other."

She raised her chin. "I'm not ready to dive into that subject."

"Come on, Neida. So, am I to presume you were only hoping to rip out my heart for the sheer pleasure of the sport? Is this your usual practice—to entice men until they're close enough to drop them on their heads?"

"It's not like that."

"Yeah? What is it like?"

"I've considered this from every angle. A relationship between you and me could never work."

Lance frowned, let his disappointment—rage—boil up inside him, and this time, the sentiment spilled over, unchecked. "Why do you overanalyze everything you get your hands on? You're like some obstinate teenager who thinks she knows more than anyone else. Life's too full of promise, Neida. Sometimes you just need to grasp onto an idea and believe in the premise, run with it, no matter how far-fetched. Often, that something turns out to take us to levels we never thought possible."

"That hasn't been my experience."

Lance shoved himself away from the table and clamored to stand. "My case in point. You're too stubborn. You're too determined to prove everything. Do you want proof you and I will be good together, a neat little package tied up with a bow? Guarantees don't exist. Neither do pat answers. Sometimes we have to find guts enough to take a leap and treasure the possibilities."

Tears brimmed in the corners of her eyes. "And then what? I've watched too many of my dreams chop me down at the knees. Stab me in the heart and leave me for dead."

He felt sorry for her. She suffocated in practicalities, anticipated future failures. All she had to do was breathe in the possibilities. "You'd never succeed as an archaeologist. You'd wait for the bones to pop up and invite you to dig."

He stormed to the door and addressed her back. "You lack the one thing required of you, Neida. Faith beyond what you can see—in science, yourself, and your relationships. Until you discover that, you'll never believe in anything worthy enough to make you whole."

His comment had surely hit home, but he didn't care. He refused to let her dangle hope in front of him, play with his emotions, and then snatch the reward away like some wishy-washy prima donna.

He growled out his frustration. "I can't do this. I'm going to see what Cory needs. At least *he'll* accept what I have to offer. Just be ready to go by 4:00 in the morning. We've got a long day ahead of us tomorrow."

He flung the door against the wall and plodded outside. He was done trying to convince Neida of anything.

CHAPTER TWENTY-THREE

THEY REACHED CHILLICOTHE in the early morning and found an out-of-the-way motel where they set up computers and secure phone lines for safe communications. Neida's energy waned. She had cried herself to sleep long before Kat came back to the room. She woke during the night and stared into the darkness for hours, remembering Lance's spiteful words. She had seldom taken chances on anything or anyone, and now she had alienated the one individual she'd never meant to hurt. *Why did I have to kiss him?*

Lance showed politeness and professionalism the entire morning. His underlying rancor recurred in how he refused to look at her, in how he passed the hours with the crew rather than spend one moment longer in her presence. While they worked to set up the computers, she found a corner of the room to curl up by herself and read more about the town.

Chillicothe, located along the Scioto River, once thrived as a center for the Hopewell people circa 200 BCE. They had constructed mounds for ceremonial and burial purposes. They had also established trade routes to the Rocky Mountains and beyond, into Canada and Mexico. Though a significant entity in North America, the Hopewell had, without explanation, disappeared around 500 CE. The Shawnee later settled the area and named the place *Chalahgawtha*, meaning principal town. That's what the settlement had become. It served as Ohio's first and third Capital in the early 1800s. Its leaders had built up an impressive university too. She wished they'd wiggle out enough time to explore the city.

But as soon as they had set up ground control, Kat hurried them along. She directed the men to stuff four large packs in one of the Range Rovers. Lance pointed the vehicle west toward State route 50 and Paint Creek.

Cory sat in the front with Lance, and Kat joined Neida in the back. She welcomed the company. Kat's constant stream of words distracted her, and she chided herself for falling asleep and missing out on her friend's offer of girl talk the previous night.

About halfway between Chillicothe and Hillsboro, Lance slowed. "I think the Highland/Ross county line is somewhere near. Watch for the Cave Road sign."

They all inspected the sides of the thoroughfare for their mark, and five minutes later, Cory located the placard. Lance pulled over and let the car behind them pass. They sat at the edge of their seats now, eyeing the shrubbery, searching for the trail that would take them off the highway.

Lance rolled down his window, inching the car forward, and leaned his head out, causing a cold breeze to blast into the back. Neida adjusted her collar tighter around her neck and anticipated the hike through the elements for the next day or two. Even Lance might cool off, and the fresh air would lift her spirits.

Cory spotted the narrow opening in the forest first. Kat shrugged into her jacket and picked up her gloves. "Well, let's get cracking, shall we? I think we'd better park it off the road, though, or we'll be sitting ducks for sure."

Lance drove further up the highway and steered into a recess between some trees and wedged the Range Rover as far into the shrubbery as possible, leaving enough room for all of them to get out.

Neida exited the car last, and everyone had donned their gear by the time she reached them. The remaining pack lay on the ground. Lance glanced at the bundle, then at Neida, but instead of helping her, he locked the doors with a click of the remote and trudged after Cory to wait for them a few yards away.

Kat stared after him and shook her head. "What is wrong with him? Here, let me help you put this on, Hon. It's easier with a second set of hands."

Neida hunched her shoulders to bear the full weight of the load. She was out of condition, for sure, but she'd prove to them all she could keep up. She only hoped she hadn't forgotten her lesson on how to scale the side of a mountain. She imagined the information would come in handy further on into their adventure.

They climbed from the ravine through the feathery foliage of arborvitae trees and checked for cars before they ventured out onto the highway. Cory dashed to the opposite side as though his pack sprouted wings. He headed into the narrow gap, pivoted around, and motioned for the others to follow him. "Hey, what are you guys waiting for?" he said with a smile. "We don't have all day."

They all plowed after him, though he was like a kid, energized and bouncing down the trail, making it difficult for the women to keep up.

Once the forest had swallowed them from sight, Neida relaxed. Vitality invigorated her and replaced the doubt she'd harbored over her abilities. Every step forward seemed to lighten her load. Their expedition suspended on the perimeter of the world—on the edge of the Appalachian Plateau, to be exact—a place far more impressive than the brown hills surrounding the California university where she used to hike.

They wound their way over the limestone ridges dotted with chestnut oak and Virginia Pine in clear view of Rocky Fork Creek below. They made exceptional time. They climbed into the gorge past bronze grape fern, jewelweed, and the last lingering traces of Queen Anne's lace to the symphony of the rushing sound growing louder and more intense the deeper they traveled into the terrain. By the time the foursome reached the lower altitudes, their moods lifted. Lance even talked to her while they rested by an embankment of trees. Neida wasn't about to question his change of heart. She concentrated on the sandwich Kat had provided and basked in a ray of sunshine, reaching down through the canopies above.

The air turned humid and dense and hung on them like a shroud as they ventured on. The rushing became a definite roar by the afternoon. Neida gasped as she stepped through the trees into full view of the creek, its impressive spread, wide enough to resemble a river. The waterfall cascaded in undulating foam from the ridge at least 100 feet above. An eagle circled over their heads, its span vast, its form embossed against the blue sky. She followed the flight path until the cliff snagged her gaze, and the bird disappeared over the top.

After the four investigated the area, they regrouped along the denser bank. They had found a cove of sorts. Thousands of years of whittling and receding water had carved a natural hollow into the rock face. Trees and shrubbery provided the perfect screen of protection from the elements and onlookers who might view the terrain from the opposite side of the waterway.

"We'll make camp here for the night," said Lance. "Tomorrow, we'll hunt for the entrance. Granddad's notes say we should find it someplace between those two walls of limestone just east of the waterfall."

Kat placed her hands on her hips. "We still have some daylight, Boss. With the four of us, maybe we can find the cave opening before the end of the day."

Lance opened his pack. "I'd rather set up camp and venture inside in the morning. I'd feel better if we first hide from unwanted company."

In all the excitement of the hike, Neida had forgotten the threat of dangerous men on their tail. "Do you think Blackhour is already here?" she asked and scoured the line of trees behind her.

Lance shrugged. "Maybe. Though I refer to the four-legged animals, the kind that stalks the woods at night." He detached a rifle from his backpack and caressed the surface with reverent strokes. "I packed this baby, just in case papa bear pays us a visit."

Neida studied his smile. She couldn't tell if he were serious or not.

"Oh, don't listen to him." Kat swatted the air. "No use in getting yourself into a tizzy now. We'll just hang our food up high and keep the fire burning bright. The critters will keep their distance if I have anything to say about it."

Though Kat sounded confident, Lance's comments forced uneasiness to creep back inside her. Neida continued to peer over her shoulder for the rest of the day.

They searched for the cave entrance an hour before sunset without success. The lack of light forced the team to return to camp, where Neida helped Kat prepare their evening meal. After dinner, they secured their food high up the rock wall before Neida settled in Kat's two-person tent and read her grandmother's journal under the low glow of lantern light. She fell asleep sometime after midnight.

Cory's booming laughter jolted her from sleep the next morning. Neida sat up, found her bearings in the firelight that flickered patterns through the tent walls. Kat had rolled her bed and taken her pack. Neida hoped the team wasn't stewing and waiting for her to make an appearance. She struggled out of the sleeping bag, shoved her feet into her boots, and donned her jacket before she pushed her way outside.

The pre-dawn showed pink through the tops of the trees. Kat, who hunched over the campfire, sautéed what smelled like fresh trout, while Lance and Cory huddled around the flame. They warmed their hands, whispered, and laughed at something Cory said, and the divine smells increased the pangs inside Neida's stomach. As she sauntered toward the fire, they whirled about and watched her approach.

"Well, she's come back from the dead," said Cory. "Though you shouldn't sneak up like that. Lance, here, might have shot you for a bear."

They all laughed.

Neida sat next to Lance, who gave her a thin smile. "Why didn't anyone wake me?" she asked.

"Once we find the mark, our destination is that-a-way." Cory pointed upward. "We thought you might need the rest before you tackle the hard stuff."

Lance peered down at her. Again, his voice sounded kind, almost as if he'd forgotten their exchange of words at the motel. "If we can't find the mouth of the cave, we'll search for the second entrance somewhere up top. I don't think Granddad ever found it. The directions aren't in any of the rest of the scans. He might have died before he had a chance to explore."

Neida swiveled to scrutinize the dark chasm of the cliff face. A nameless excitement settled in her stomach at the thought of scaling the jagged giant. She righted her neck and leaned into the warmth of the fire.

"Last night, I finished the rest of my grandmother's journals and found nothing there to help us, either."

Kat slapped a portion of fish into the men's containers. "It certainly will be an adventure," she said. "You want to bring me your mess kit, Neida? I'll divvy out some grub to you. There's nothing like fresh fish on a cold morning—thanks to fisherman Cory here. The moon had them hopping into his net all morning."

Cory beamed, and Neida retrieved her kit and returned to the fire in seconds. The delicious meal filled the void. Afterward, Neida washed the dishes while Kat and the men broke camp and stuffed their packs again. It seemed the placement of equipment and how much they could fit inside each bag required science.

The dark heads of the trees soon brightened, highlighting their huddled forms against the ridge. The foursome set off for the two limestone walls. They investigated a good portion of the morning, hugged the craggy towers, and searched for an opening in the rock walls. They decided to split their task in half. Lance and Neida investigated the waterfall's surface, while Cory and Kat chose the more rugged west side dotted with sparse foliage. So far, they had found no signs that Blackhour and his men had beaten them there, though the threat sat like a pall over their examination.

Again, Lance's palpable silence pricked Neida's insides. She thought he'd put his anger behind him at breakfast, though she surmised he'd only pretended civility to save face in front of the others.

They rested among a dense stand of pines and snacked on Kat's leftover fish that they had stored in their cold packs.

A slight breeze rushed through the canyon, and icy fingers breached Neida's long johns, making her shiver.

Lance glanced at her with a rueful expression. "Once we get inside, the wind won't bite so much. But it's a different kind of cold inside the earth. It settles in your bones and makes you ache."

Neida nodded. She had already imagined the worst. And if she was going to survive this adventure, she had to do whatever she could to soothe the breach between Lance and herself. She didn't want him to be angry with her, and he had been right about her seeking guarantees in their relationship. Somehow, she felt confident that Lance would never dump her for a buxom blond like her previous boyfriend. Lance was too good of a person to do something so disloyal. In fact, he was the epitome of devotion and honor. Still ...

"Lance ..."

He peered up at her, his eyes devoid of expression.

She took a cleansing breath and made the plunge. "I can't begin to express my apology for seeming not to care about your feelings the other day. I'm not the type of person who leads men on. I meant what I said that night, but I'm confused. You *are* important to me. Yet, despite my real and deep feelings for you, my past pain keeps surfacing and resurfacing, and I just can't handle trusting someone right now. At least, not until I come to terms with those feelings. I hope you understand. Honestly, I didn't mean to hurt you, and before I upset you again, I thought you should know why I'm so unable to commit."

He stared at her for a moment before he spoke. "Well, I'm not Superman, if that's what you're hoping. My feelings took a hit the other day, and my ego is a bit bruised. And I'd like to ram my fist down the guy's throat who hurt you so much that you can't even trust anyone. But I'm not like that guy, Neida. I never will be. I'm just a man who's found his equal, a match in just about every way—brains, vitality, love for old things and old people. Except I'm not so fond of that pragmatism you cling on to like a little girl who cleaves to her doll. We're opposites in that realm. But I get it. Althea dumped a lot on your shoulders, and I want something you're not ready to give. Though it would be an exercise in futility if we harbor hurt feelings forever. Newaygo's too small of a town." He held his hand out to her. "We're going to have to trust one another through the uncertainty that lies ahead."

Neida eyed the peace offering extended in front of her, then nodded and accepted his handshake, "I really am sorry for everything that morning, Lance."

He started to pull away, but she wouldn't let go. She slid her thumb over the back of his hand and studied the pain in his eyes. "Please, say you forgive me for wanting something I have to deny myself. I don't know what's come over me lately."

Lance shrugged. "The same thing that's come over me, I guess, but I won't kiss you again. I promise, unless you want it first." He studied her face a moment longer then turned away to explore the canyon walls.

It would take more than a moment's apology to return to the previous normality between them; she could see it in his eyes. But she hoped she had at least smoothed his ruffled feathers enough that they could carry on a decent conversation together.

Neida sighed inwardly and fixed her focus on a place several feet up and frowned toward a depression in the contour of the wall. "What is that?" she asked. She rose and darted up the slope to where a massive boulder sat precariously on a ledge.

Lance ran up after her. Grunting, he wedged himself behind the obstruction and poked at the crumpled pile of rock behind it, almost an invisible entity from the floor below. "This is the original entrance. Look at the outline around the fallout. This used to be open. I'm sure of it, though it doesn't appear we'll get past this mess." He bent down and tugged until he freed a bit of cable from under the ruin and held it up for her to see. "Part of a blasting cap. This was no accidental cave-in." He tossed it over the side and manipulated himself from the tight space. "C'mon, we have to tell the others."

Lance pushed past her and ran to the bottom again, studied the opposite ridge. He pulled a whistle out from underneath his jacket and blew on it. The shrillness assaulted the space around them, and Neida winced and slapped her hands over her ears. The sound echoed between the walls, softening and fading to nothing in the distance.

She flitted to the bottom to join him again, concerned. "If Blackhour's near, won't he hear the whistle?"

"Maybe. However, Cory and Kat aren't far away. As soon as they get here, we'll set off for those bluffs ahead and climb to the ridge. Somewhere up top is our ticket inside."

Five minutes later, Cory and Kat emerged from the trees. Lance gave them a tour of the cave-in, and when they joined Neida at the bottom again, Lance knelt to write in the dirt.

"Here's where we are. Here's the waterfall. If we can find a gradual incline somewhere close, we'll circle back once we reach the top. Just remember our position to the waterfall. That'll give us our bearings of where to start our search."

Cory took off his cap and scratched his head. "You think Blackhour will know what to search for?"

Lance stood and kicked the soil over his illustration. "That's hard to say. Unless he's been inside or someone told him about it, Grandad buried that information in the pages of his library books fifty years ago. He'll have to search for the entrance, just like we do."

Kat took Lance by the shoulders and twisted him toward the bluffs. "Well, let's not stand around and haggle over it, boys and girls. We've got a lot of ground to cover, and we want to get inside as soon as possible."

Cory donned his backpack again and took up the lead. The rest of them followed him through the canyon.

Neida breathed a sigh now that she and Lance had patched up their rift, but a new kind of nervous energy settled in her gut. The limestone walls were high and hard to climb. Her rock-climbing experience prepared her for little, nothing like this. She was on edge to be so inexperienced in a place where the others might not be able to help her during the roughest parts of their adventure. And the cave might also offer a few tight spaces—nooks and crannies that would cause sheer panic and disfunction inside her as they journey ahead. To be honest, Neida didn't know how she would survive this plunge into the earth, but she had already committed, and she couldn't turn back now.

An hour later, Cory found the perfect place for an ascent with minimal use of rope. She followed Lance, placing her boots up the angled surfaces with care; each step a head-on collision with the unknown.

What had Gran been thinking? The woman couldn't have been clueless about shady individuals destined to steal or destroy the artifacts for whatever cause. And if her grandmother knew anything about where the tablet led, she must have realized cave exploration was chock full of bats and sinkholes and a multitude of other dangers that would face them inside.

Whatever outcome their expedition promised, Neida knew Blackhour would be at the heart of most of it, and that was a thought she refused to cozy up to now that they were so far from home.

CHAPTER TWENTY-FOUR

THE CLIMB TURNED OUT EASIER than Lance expected, and they reached the first crest in no time. To find a sinkhole sufficient enough for them to shimmy through into the bowels of the earth was another matter altogether. They tramped the same scrub twice over, from the ridge to the center in all directions. If they didn't find their target at this level, they'd have to climb to the next until they did. The sun baked them to overdone; the wind sucked their skin dry. Still, he pushed them on—for Neida's sake. Cory and Kat had experienced many such adventures during their careers, but Neida's nerves appeared frayed with the threat of Blackhour's appearance at any moment. He refused to drag out the search any longer than he had to.

He applied himself to the task again, hacking at a clump of vines with his machete, then halted when he discovered a cluster of walking ferns. He bent closer to examine the telltale evidence of cave terrain, confirming he had found his mark.

His chest drummed, and the rhythm kept beat with each additional slash of his blade, each tug of undergrowth. He heaved a final stroke and froze. An opening yawned just yards in front of him.

"I found it," he yelled out and dashed to the crescent-shaped fissure.

Cory first approached at a run. His teeth gleamed white in the afternoon sun. "Finally—progress." He stooped to make an examination. "It's smaller than the other entrance, though."

Lance prostrated himself on the damp ground and examined the worn edges of the sinkhole. "But big enough for you and me to get through, I believe, even with our packs on."

"What about us?" asked Neida as she and Kat came to a stop next to Cory. She grinned and shifted her weight with enthusiasm like she hadn't a care in the world.

"I think we can accommodate you," said Cory, looking up at them with a smile.

Though the entrance appeared smaller than any he had attempted before, Lance refused to let the fissure's restrictiveness stop them now. The prize awaited, and Neida deserved this; they all had earned the reward.

The shaft of light from the outside overpowered everything inside. It reflected off the cave floor like a beacon, whitewashing the walls. He sat back and shook his head. "I can't see anything. We'll have to rappel inside to make any sense of it. I'll go in first, size up the cavern, and if everything seems doable, then you can help Neida." He glanced at Cory. "Make sure she's safe before you proceed."

Cory and Kat nodded.

Neida's gaze rested on each of their faces. "Hey, I can handle myself. This is the easy part."

"Don't get cocky on me, Neida," said Lance. "Nothing is easy about rappelling down inside a cave."

Cory patted her on the back. "No worries. Lance will break your fall. And we'll tumble down, right on top of you." His chapped lips cracked into a grin beneath the makings of a gray-specked beard.

Several minutes passed as they secured harnesses and readied the ropes. They donned gloves, neoprene socks, Cordura oversuits, and hard hats. Lance rechecked his and Neida's gear for the third time. "I'll be below you," he said. "And Kat will have your back. You can do this, just like we practiced in Newaygo." He squeezed her forearm. "Just let me know if you get in a jam."

Cory glanced over his shoulder and back again. "What was that?"

The wind blew strong where they stood. The nearby treetops' crackling sent off false impressions, yet another sound intruded, deeper, and more repetitive. Lance followed the path of the flattened grass from the cliff's edge. He didn't detect anything. Still, he'd already learned what could happen when he let down his guard.

Kat motioned at Lance. "We best get moving. I don't know how, but Blackhour's been one step behind both of you throughout this journey. The sooner we get inside, the better."

Nodding at Neida, Lance stepped over the side and sat back into a rappelling position. At that second, just beyond the ridge, a helicopter pitched over the distant edge. The transport hovered for a moment, then made a pass over the cliff and disappeared from view.

Lance readjusted his grip. "They've spotted us. We better hurry. Remember your brake hand, Neida." He nodded and lowered himself through the aperture. Releasing tension in quick bouts, he eased down the cave wall to the floor where he freed himself from his rope and peered up. The activity above him dimmed in the light streaming in.

"Okay, Neida. Your turn." The line tumbled over the side, and he adjusted it, shouted up for her to proceed. Her form inched over the edge with baby steps, started and stopped, and finally froze as gravity took hold.

Kat's gentle voice echoed down to where he stood, coaxed Neida on, but he heard the panic in her tone.

"C'mon, you can do it, Hon."

Lance struggled to discern the cavern's interior. The blaring light vanquished full visuals of his surroundings, so he refocused on Neida. "Lean back into your harness. Ease down, steady, steady. Keep your brake hand in close to control the descent."

Neida appeared to conquer her fears in short time. She edged down the wall, a swift scale to the bottom where he helped her off the rope. As soon as her feet touched the floor, a sick pallor took over. He'd witnessed the same in the tunnels on their escape from the lab—claustrophobia. The malady was sure to hinder their progress when they needed all their wits about them.

Kat and Cory descended to the cave floor next, just as the helicopter's roar reverberated outside and in the hollows around them. To Lance's disappointment, the company in the transport had circled back.

Lance filled his lungs with the dank air and placed his hand on Neida's back. "You okay?"

She nodded with a weak smile.

"Just stay close to me. Whatever you need, I'm here for you. We all are."

The helicopter's thumping continued outside, and the trickle of water and flapping bat wings resounded from further inside the cave. Lance squinted toward the circumference of the chamber again. The wet walls gleamed; tiny streams flowed from a place in the rock above and out through cracks around the floor's perimeter. Formations hung over them, and thousands of years of deposits jutted up from the base like glowing icicles.

The central cavern needed no light at all. The interior swelled with the single shaft streaming through the sinkhole. The room seemed more massive than it had appeared from above. Lance hoped that at least this section of their journey would give Neida the ability to breathe.

"We've got to get out of sight," said Lance.

Cory took out his notebook and leaned in closer to the light's beam to read an entry. "The translation talks of three statues guarding the room called Sacred, pointing the way to living water. I don't see any of that in this chamber. Maybe there's a tunnel further on."

Voices outside suggested the uninvited party loomed almost on top of them. Lance grabbed hold of Neida's arm, and they all dashed to stand out of sight against the cave walls and stared up at the sinkhole. Lance's pulse raced. No one appeared. Still, he waited. He didn't dare risk detection by moving too soon.

Kat leaned toward Lance. "It won't take them long to find the opening."

He shook his head and placed a single finger over his lips to hush her.

The voices outside drew closer. Seconds stretched into minutes, and then the words Lance dreaded shot down from above.

"They're already inside. Cut the ropes." Four severed lifelines soon writhed from above into a pile at their feet.

Neida stared at Lance with wild eyes and a face devoid of color.

"Okay, lower them in," said someone. The command echoed around them.

A flurry of movement from above preceded the appearance of something large that dangled at the opening for a moment and blocked the light. Then the bulk swayed and twisted with the momentum of a send-off. The shapes descended toward them with steady jerks at first, then hurled to the ground and landed in a pile at the bottom.

As soon as Lance recognized the men, he wedged Neida against the cave wall. Neida squirmed and tried to break free, obviously identifying the pastor and the man tied against his back. She almost slipped from his hold, and it took all of Lance's force to keep her confined.

Neida grabbed and tugged at his hand, then gasped the single word into his palm. "Grandfather—" The rope end dropped from above on top of the men. Neida closed her eyes and sighed.

Lance pressed the weight of his body against hers and whispered in her ear. "Stay here, Neida. I'll go get them." He nodded at Cory and Kat, a signal for them to grab her and keep her from following.

Lance waited until the sounds receded. Watching the opening above, he inched out to the men, shielded his eyes against the light that blinded him. He couldn't tell if anyone watched from above or not. He hoped they didn't see him either because he needed to get to Neida's grandfather.

The pastor's face seemed dazed. Scratches and bruises covered his arms, but he appeared fit enough. Battered and weak, Askuwheteau's shallow breaths came fast, and his bloodied features proved he had endured harsh handling. The old man glanced up at Lance with sad eyes, though he said nothing.

Lance brushed the dirt from his face and whispered close to his ear. "Don't worry. I'll get you out of here." He straightened Askuwheteau's body carefully, then untied Pastor Will's hands and feet and asked, "Do you think you can help me?"

Pastor Will blinked, and his eye convulsed. "I think so," he said. Though in his dazed state, he paused for several seconds, his affirmative answer failing to register.

Lance again motioned for the clergyman to clasp Askuwheteau under his other arm. Pastor Will snapped to the present, and they dragged him closer to the cave walls. Cory rushed to lift the old man's feet, and the three maneuvered him the rest of the way into Neida's embrace.

Neida stroked her grandfather's cheek and frowned down at him. "Where's Winona?"

Askuwheteau shook his head.

"Blackhour's men took her and the boy hostage," said Pastor Will. "To force your grandfather to lead us here. And now he intends to blow this sinkhole shut."

"You Grahams never know when to quit." The voice was Blackhour's, dropping down on them from above.

They all squinted up at the entrance. The silhouette against the glare made the face hovering there a black blur.

"Maybe now you'll realize some things need to remain in the past," he continued. "And when I blow this entrance shut, I'll at least bury part of my troubles forever." The blackened face disappeared from the opening.

Solutions coursed through Lance's mind. He wasn't about to stay around for the fireworks. Besides, the beam's glare through the fissure was lessening with the earth's rotation. They'd be in plain sight before too long. He moved closer to Cory and whispered. "What does my grandfather's notation say, Cory? Beyond the moon's light, there are tunnels. And the tablet suggests *Yahweh* presents two directions for you to choose. On the right of his throne, the reign of the righteous son ..."

Cory nodded. "Yeah, and on the left, the reign of the evil son."

"Hmm, look at the pattern the light's shaft creates on the cave floor."

Cory smiled. "It's a crescent moon." His head punctuated the beat of his whispers. "Beyond the moon's light ..."

They searched the circumference of the room one increment at a time, and when Lance found what he was looking for, he pointed toward the rock structure at the far end of the cavern. The path rose to a higher plateau where two portals pierced the cave wall beyond. "Aren't those a couple of passages on either side of that formation? I don't know about you, but that rock construction looks an awful lot like a throne."

"You're right. The tunnels, the *son of the right hand*, and the *son of the left.*" Cory's voice tapered to a whisper. He stared, mesmerized at the back wall.

"What do you want to bet the room called Sacred is down that corridor to our left," said Lance, "on the right hand of whoever sits on that throne."

Noises outside drew close, and Blackhour's voice tumbled down once again.

"It pains me to seal off this entrance, to destroy valuable artifacts that can bring a good price, but you've left me no choice."

Lance swore under his breath. "C'mon. Let's get across that ledge and into the tunnel before Blackhour blasts us there."

"What about my grandfather?" Neida asked in hushed tones. "How will he make it across the ledge? The incline is too narrow for him."

Askuwheteau stirred. "Go. Leave me here. Do not worry about taking an old man with you."

She shook her head. "We're not leaving you."

Askuwheteau's eyes glowed. He brought up a hand and cupped her cheek. "Walk into the darkness, Oneida. The Creator will light your path. He will help you accomplish what He sent you here to do. The message of the Prophecy is your purpose now and has been since your birth."

Neida peered up, desperation in her eyes. "Lance, tell him we aren't leaving him."

Lance winced, and solutions spun into something tangible in his mind. He produced a thin rope from his pack. He squatted next to Neida and addressed Askuwheteau. "Do you think you can walk?"

The old man nodded. "But I am too slow."

"Cory let's get the ropes. If we knot them together, we'll turn them into a brace of sorts and sandwich him between us. That might keep him from falling backward. We can move him along the ledge a little faster that way."

Kat nodded. "Great idea, Boss."

"We've got to hurry," said Pastor Will.

Lance motioned to the clergyman. "You and Neida get him to his feet."

Lance and Cory made quick time with the knots and wrapped the sling around Askuwheteau's back. Cory took one side of the rope and Lance the other as he nodded at Kat.

His partner encouraged Neida and the pastor past the light and across the cavern out of view of the crescent opening. At the far end of the room, the trail slanted and narrowed, forcing them to cling to the wall as they inched along the edge over the steep precipice below them. Neida inched along after Kat, and when the three hopped to safety on the higher ridge, Lance, who had watched in tense anticipation, released his breath.

Askuwheteau turned to Lance, gravity carving his face. "You hold a heavy load on your shoulders. But do not worry for Oneida. This is her schoolroom. The ancestors are teaching her what she needs to know, and she will find wings."

Lance peered into his face. A lifetime of wisdom spoke to him from the elder's dark eyes. He nodded and hoped that were true.

Cory and Lance followed the same path over the precipice, but their progress slowed with Askuwheteau between them.

Lance pulled the rope taut, signaled Cory to follow suit. Midway across the ridge, the old man lost his footing, and the weight of his body jolted the sling backward, almost free of Lance's grip.

Neida gasped. Kat hopped back on the ledge and inched to the men, pulled on the juncture of the rope until she could grab the slack at the end. Lance helped Askuwheteau position his feet again. After they secured him, they continued across and helped him to the incline's security, where Neida waited for them, hands wringing in front of her.

The ledge expanded beyond the throne formation, zigzagged, and ascended toward the new shaft. Just as the group reached the entrance, the rustling of whoever was outside fell away. Lance hastened Neida, Kat, and Pastor Will into the tunnel, then guided Askuwheteau after them. They switched on their hat's halogen lamps, four bright lights that illuminated the interior of the tunnel. Lance removed his hard hat and secured it to Askuwheteau's head.

"Move forward; hang onto the wall. Kat, you know the drill. Take caution."

Lance kept Askuwheteau close. Neida's breathing changed into short puffs of panic in front of him, but despite how much he wanted to go to her, he held back his help. He had to get them all through the danger alive—all of them.

"Hold on to me, Hon," echoed Kat's voice ahead.

They proceeded a few feet forward away from the entrance when, without warning, the line halted. Lance peered around Askuwheteau. Neida was bent over, gasping for air. Pastor Will nudged her, but she leaned sideways, and the forward momentum made her knees buckle. The clergyman caught her before she hit the floor.

"What is that smell?" Neida brought a hand up to her nose and mouth as Pastor Will almost jerked her upright again.

"Hey, easy there, Pastor," said Lance as he turned to address Neida. "It's bat guano. It's rather potent. Why don't you put on your mask?"

Kat turned to rub her back. "There's no time. We've got to move."

They'd only traveled a few feet more along the curvature of the cave when the walls jolted, and the cacophony of an explosion echoed around them. The pressure imploded and pummeled a blast through the small space, whisking each of them forward off their feet. Like dominos, Lance rammed into Askuwheteau and the pastor and the pastor into Neida, the impact scattering them across the cold cave floor.

The falling rock smashed three of the lamps. Kat's single light faded under a layer of rubble, plunging them into darkness. The grunts and moans of his companions pierced his ears. Lance brought up an arm to deflect the worst of the debris. He felt around for Askuwheteau with his other hand. All he touched were hard edges and piles of dirt, while the incessant pelting from above kept coming. A rumble vibrated from the depths of the walls. So did the panic in his chest.

"Neida!" Lance cried out against the deafening roar.

He drew his hands up to protect himself, too late to do any good. Something hard hit his head, and the last sensation prevalent before the blackness was the cold floor beneath him and the suffocating reality that he had failed all of them, especially the one he wanted to help the most—Neida.

Reality stopped and started, floated in and out like some specter penetrating the matter of Neida's brain. The sensation hovered for a moment, then disintegrated like a puff of smoke into nothing again. She moaned, a mournful sound in her ears, and as another flash of lucidity grew into something tangible again, even more intense than before, she was aware that her body ached. The silence and the lack of light loitered in the dark, and it conjured up a void of time and space.

Sudden movement beside her made her gasp. The sediment on her legs slid, and a hand clutched her foot.

"Neida, is that you?" It was Lance. "Talk to me."

"I'm okay." The sound rasped from her throat, and she coughed to free her lungs.

Further movement preceded Kat's complaint beside her. Neida reached until she touched a shoulder, followed the shape up to her friend's face. "Kat?"

"Yeah, I'm still here. What about the others?"

"Where's your light, Kat?" asked Lance. "Can you get to your hat? See if you can get your flashlight from your pack too."

"I'll try."

Several minutes' fumbling sounded in the dark. Neida sat up just as Kat uncovered the lamp. The tunnel swelled with light, particles sparking in the beam, and it was the catalyst that bred panic inside Neida's chest once again.

A pile of rubble several feet away crumbled, then another. Cory and the pastor rose from under the debris like quirky apparitions. Cory shook his head and sent an avalanche of dust cascading to the floor. He coughed. "Man, what a ride. Everybody all right?"

"I think so," said Pastor Will. He peered about, his involuntary tic causing him to blink.

Neida whipped around. "Where's grandfather?" She forgot the stifling space and scrambled to a mound several feet away. They all did. They clawed at the dirt and rock, first freed the old man's head then the rest of his body. His face oozed with blood, the wound deep and hideous. "Is he all right?" she asked. They had to get him out of here.

Lance lowered his ear to Askuwheteau's mouth and listened. "He's breathing, anyway."

Seconds later, Askuwheteau heaved with coughing, focusing on the cave ceiling, on Lance, and finally on Neida's face.

"Grandfather, you're hurt. Can you talk?"

"I'm okay," he said, though without conviction. They helped him to sit. His expression pulled with the effort. "My leg hurts."

Situated at his feet, Cory, who had just replaced his hat's light, turned to examine Askuwheteau's appendage. He winced and shook his head. "The bone's protruding. We're going to have to clean the wound and protect the break before we move him."

Lance's lips pressed into a firm line, though he paused for mere seconds before issuing orders. "Kat give Neida your flashlight and take her and the pastor ahead. Cory and I will set the leg. We'll join you when we're done."

"No." Neida spewed the word. She wasn't about to leave her grandfather behind now. He needed her near.

Lance's expression softened, but his retort remained firm. "The cave must open up further on. You'll be able to breathe easier there."

Neida shook her head and emphasized her response. "No ..."

"Please. If you faint, I'll have two victims on my hands."

She peered down at her grandfather, studied his bloodied face. He brought up his shriveled hand and patted her arm. "Listen to him. They will care for me. You must go on."

She hesitated. Panic returned in increments, built ten-fold inside her, muffling her thoughts.

Pastor Will moved first. He stood and clutched her arms, raised her from the cave floor. "They'll fix your grandfather's leg, but the sooner we get out of this tunnel, the easier life will be for all of us."

Kat placed Neida's hard hat on her head, handed her the flashlight, and grabbed her other hand to direct it. "Hang on to my belt. I'll find us a way out of here."

Neida lingered, took a last glance at her grandfather, at Lance and Cory; then Kat led her forward with Pastor Will nudging her from behind.

CHAPTER TWENTY-FIVE

FURTHER INTO THE CAVE, Neida focused on Kat's back, sucked in the stale air. The explosion's sediment still hovered inside the space, forcing her to cough again, which increased her light-headedness.

She hardly remembered time passing. The rush of blood in her temples continued to throb. Every yard or so, she stopped and squeezed her eyelids shut, imagined herself anywhere but the tunnel, but Pastor Will continued his annoying prod from behind.

"Just a few more feet," said Kat, holding Neida steady when she reeled against the cave walls.

Neida spoke between gasps. "I don't want ... to be a burden." Doubts that she could move played with her emotions, but she grasped Kat's belt anyway, and they continued to move forward.

Kat stopped about ten yards ahead, her light catching hold of an obstruction. Upon examination, the cave walls revealed a seam, once an opening, now clogged with piles of rubble. A small gap at the top shimmered with spider webs. Kat climbed the mound and swept them aside, pointed the halogen through the opening so she could peek into the space beyond.

Once she rejoined them, she issued instructions, "Pastor, help me shovel the rock. If we can make a large enough hole, we can all climb through. The other side opens into a chamber."

Pastor Will hesitated. "Are you sure this is the right way to go?"

Kat raised her eyebrows and looked at him like he'd lost his mind. "Well, yeah, considering we've no other course to follow. We've got to get Neida to where she can function again."

The two clawed at the mound and threw chunks of ruin behind them, though Kat seemed to be doing most of the work.

Neida gasped to breathe, but she had to do something. Her grandfather's well-being was at stake, and the sooner they plowed through to the other side, the sooner they could get him to safety. She inhaled, grappled to the edge of the rocks, and started throwing chunk after chunk behind her.

Kat noticed her determination and smiled reassurance, then turned back to her work and quickened her efforts.

Sometime later, they had hollowed out a considerable opening, big enough to venture through.

"It'll be a tight squeeze for your granddaddy, but it's doable." Kat threw a few more rock fragments behind her, then addressed Pastor Will. "Let's get her inside."

They supported Neida's arms and helped her climb the debris, maneuver through the gap, and descend to the chamber within. The uneven rubble was cumbersome under her shoes, put a strain on her ankles, but once her feet hit the ground, she doubled over, closed her eyes, and gasped for air.

When Kat tapped her on the back, Neida struggled to her full height again. Their halogens joined together to push the blackness away, revealing the intricacies of the colossal chamber in front of them. It took Neida a moment to absorb the sight. Though her stability had increased, the magnificence of the depictions in front of her almost forced her to implode. She clutched Kat's shoulder to steady herself, but only for a moment.

Kat plowed toward the three statues that spanned from the cavern floor to the ceiling, at least 30 feet up the rock partition, then busied herself in setting up portable lights to illuminate the cavern. Once the light took hold, Neida gaped in unbelief. Carved from part of the wall, the water-eroded pillars, depictions of Native American men, appeared to support the granite above them. Two of them wore the distinctive costume of the Great Lakes tribes. One wore a turban, a carved bearskin blanket cascading from his shoulder to the floor. On the second, feathers dangled from the swathe of hair flowing down the back of the statue's tunic, almost reaching its fringed leggings.

The third, the figure in the center, wore a costume she couldn't place. Its headdress protruded off the forehead into a worn, duck-like creature. Spanning across its chest, an ornate square breastwork fit over its sack-like, belted robe. The statue's features seemed more Semitic than that of the other two; its countenance regal as though it held a mantle of leadership.

The pastor's frown confirmed the statues were anything but hallucinations. Neida followed him as he scowled past the regal beings and headed toward the painted back wall.

Neida brushed the stone of one of the pillars as she passed, a cool and coarse sensation under her fingers—another check of her senses. In front of her, the mural spanned the rock wall's entirety, the central figure impressive and large. She approached slowly and touched the painted depiction. Her fingers lingered on one of the marked feet, what she could only describe as Christ-like.

Kat nodded at the artwork. "Well, Pastor, what does this look like to you?"

Pastor Will's jaw took a rigid line, his tic convulsing his cheek. "Sacrilege ..." he said, rancor seeping from his words.

"Why?" asked Kat. "Because you think all the ancient nations that lived in America were heathens? That the Spanish, Portuguese, and Italian explorers were the first Christians to find this land? This kind of sheds a different light on the subject, doesn't it? Lance's daddy worked his entire life to prove Christ visited the Native American populations, and I suspect Edward Graham died because someone wanted to conceal such a life-changing philosophy from the rest of us." Kat slipped off her pack, produced an awl, and scraped some paint off a remote area of the mural into a specimen container.

Neida wasn't so sure the explanation could be so easily vindicated. "This can't be the work of an ancient culture, Kat. The artwork is too sophisticated."

Kat whipped around. "Says who? Institutions like the Smithsonian? This kind of evidence baffles scientists and religious men of our day. And when they can't explain the facts, they plow them under or hide them away in museum storage facilities, so no one else can figure out the puzzle either. The minute I get these samples tested back at the lab, I bet you the data will prove this is an original piece of artwork dating from the time of Christ."

Pastor Will rolled and rubbed his neck, exaggerating a slight tremor of his fingers. "No—no one will accept it. It's blasphemy. The Good Book doesn't allow for such a variation of the truth."

"What makes you think the Bible is the only book of scripture?" asked Kat. "I imagine Christians of every ilk recorded sacred events all over the world. And you either believe what you preach on Sunday, or you don't. If the Lord can resurrect himself after lying dead in a tomb for three days, what makes you think anything would stop him from visiting his people wherever their location might be?"

"I don't know, Kat," said Neida.

Kat shrugged. "Why don't you ask your granddaddy?"

Neida stepped back to study the scene. Who else could the individual represent? Bearded and sandaled, the painted figure wore a flowing, white garment. Wounds disfigured his hands, wrists, and feet. And his eyes continued to pierce her from whatever angle she glimpsed up at them. Alongside the central figure, twelve men stood dressed in various headdresses and robes, some in buckskins, which brought another thought to her mind.

"And I suppose the others are his Apostles," said Pastor Will, his trembling fingers gesturing toward the figures on the wall.

Neida nodded. It was almost as if he had read her mind.

"What other interpretation could there be?" asked Kat. "The inference is quite obvious to me."

The theme etched the most unusual view of Christianity ever introduced to Neida. Her mother had never described anything like this to her. Nor had Neida learned such things in her childhood experience at church. If the evidence proved valid, then these Native Americans had seen and touched this individual or at least believed that they had. With the culmination of many other cultures corroborating the event, it was too elaborate a scheme to dismiss such evidence completely. Still, some further explanation had to exist.

Voices from behind made Neida turn. Lance and Cory maneuvered her grandfather through the gap, their arms tucked under him, their upper torsos protecting his splinted leg. Once inside, Lance and Cory faced the front, and with wide eyes and gaping mouths, they froze in place, though her grandfather's expression only reflected reverence. The men hurried to sit Askuwheteau against one of the pillars and gazed up at the giants holding up the ceiling.

Neida joined them and bent to study her grandfather's face. "This looks bad," she said. Her fingers hovered over the bloody wound on Askuwheteau's brow. "I wish I had one of Winona's poultices. What can I do to make you more comfortable?"

Askuwheteau patted his appendage. "The pain is not so bad now, not here, not under the Creator's gaze." His expression transformed as he studied the mural. "I did not think to return to this place again."

Neida gaped at him. "You've been here before?"

He nodded. "In my youth."

Lance peered down at him and asked, "Do you know another way out of here? We've only protected your break, but the severity of your injury requires a hospital, and soon."

Cory's eyes traveled to the top of the statues. "Maybe one of these guys knows a way out of here." He dug a notebook from his backpack, then headed to the other side of the statue, where he examined its base under his hat's lamplight.

Neida slid to the ground next to her grandfather and leaned toward him. "*Is* there a way out of the cave?"

Askuwheteau lifted a feeble arm and pointed toward the mural. "The path to the outside is behind that wall—through the chamber."

Lance's face appeared stern in the low light. He peered behind him at the wall. "One of Granddad's annotations did say the release latch is the lever on Christ's foot." He sprinted off to investigate the mural.

Neida let out a sigh, a sound expressing disbelief and exhaustion. Weeks of searching had little prepared her for this.

Her grandfather patted her hand. "This is a sacred room, Oneida, secured by our people many moons ago." He winced as he tried to adjust his position against the pillar.

Neida frowned at him. "Don't talk. You need to conserve your strength."

He shook his head. "No, Granddaughter. The time for your learning must take place here—now. This is your classroom. The ancestors will give me strength enough to teach you what you need to know."

"But I can't bear to see you in such pain."

"I am well enough. Your tutoring is far more important than a damaged bone that will soon mend."

Neida sighed. *How could he be so insistent under the circumstances? And how can I presume to tax him beyond his strength with all my queries?* But she had so many questions that needed answers. Maybe just a few well-crafted inquiries would help her better understand this place. She locked arms with him and leaned in. "If the Anishinaabe knew about this cave and about the government men who took the artifacts away, how could they dishonor you, especially when it wasn't your fault?"

Askuwheteau peered down at her and shook his head. "The Anishinaabe know nothing about what resides here."

She frowned. "I'm confused. I thought The People asked you to be the watcher of sacred things, and that when the Smithsonian took the artifacts away, the Elders shunned you."

He lowered his gaze to his lap. "No, my shame is my own, the same shame that the generations have passed down because of broken covenants. When your white grandfather desecrated the mound where you live and violated this holy place, I could no longer protect our people's past. Your white grandfather would have taken our sacred stories from our understanding. He would have sold these precious relics to those who cared little about their meaning. Do you understand? To fade from the pages of history is to receive our just reward."

"But how have we faded from history, Grandfather? The Anishinaabe are alive and well."

He grimaced as he turned to her. His dark eyes bore deeply; his grave expression increased the lines in his face so that he looked as ancient as his tale. "Oh, Oneida, *The Awaited One*," he said with solemn tones, "the Anishinaabe are not our people."

She blinked, tried to comprehend the electricity his words shot through her heart. "What do you mean they aren't our people?"

Askuwheteau paused, as though he considered what he should tell her, then turned his despondent eyes toward the mural. "Through the generations, the mounds have told our tale—we, the last of the Mun-dua. Many moons ago, the Great Spirit brought our fair people to this land of promise to retain our religion, our freedom, and our families, but on one condition. We were to never fall to ruin, or to forget our God, like those of the old country."

His jaw drew tense. "But we did not remember our promises, and so the Creator refused to protect us against our enemies.

"At the time of our greatness, we once covered this land," he said, turning back to Neida again. "And when the Creator poured out his wrath upon our people, we lost everything of worth. The Anishinaabe hated us, and, with those who joined them, they destroyed our villages and our sacred lodges, murdered our people until only a few remained. Those remnants of the Elk nation who escaped slaughter found little choice but to submit to bondage under this enemy just to survive."

He sighed long and low. "They destroyed our records. Our people took women from other nations and forgot the past, though my Fathers tried to keep our lineage as pure as possible. The Great Elk nation was not to be forgotten, and, in secret, the chanters recited the stories to remind us of our past. You are of that blood, Granddaughter, something you should never forget. And because you have the blood of the white man also, the Creator has foretold that you and your kind will bring the forgotten stories back to our seed again, so we never forget."

"But I know nothing of our past," said Neida.

Askuwheteau pointed at the back wall with his open hand. "This cave is a monument to our history and what took place among our people before the final battle. It holds the histories of all the nations who have resided upon this land since that time. I thought I would never see this place again. But we are here now because you have listened to the ancestor's pleas. You must engrave the stories deep inside you. Tell others. Only traces of the past yet exist, and they will soon fade if someone does not carry them forward. You were born for this purpose, Oneida. It is up to you now." He settled back against the stone.

Neida shuttered under the weight of his words. "How can you trust me? I'm not sure I even believe in this prophet you embrace."

Askuwheteau leaned toward Neida again. "Open your heart, Granddaughter, for what I now speak to you is truth. Many of the tribes remember the pale Great Master and tell their own story of how he appeared to them. The Anishinaabe covered the Great Master's path with flowers when he visited the temples; our people planted trails of strawberries. He came many winters before most of the Black Robes and Long Knives brought disease and their hatred to this land and changed our nation forever."

Neida felt reluctant to break eye contact or move, desiring the flow of his story to continue uninterrupted.

"The Prophet took many titles," he continued. "The Mundua called him by his boyhood name, *Chee-Zoos*, but names meant nothing to the Prophet."

Neida gaped at him, shocked. "*Chee-Zoos*? Do our people believe the Prophet was Jesus of the Bible?"

Her grandfather paused for a moment, a frown on his face. "Some of our people might have thought so. Other tribes chant legends that agree. But even the white man distorts the *Pale One*'s stories. They describe him in ways I do not recognize, and this troubles me. I struggle to believe their distortions of the truth."

"Then tell me about the *Pale One* you believe to be true, Grandfather."

He adjusted his position again, leaned back against the rock; his face creased with pain.

He needs to rest, she thought, but before she could tell him so, he continued.

"He is *God of the Dawn Light*, the *son of the right hand*, the Creator. He talked of his father, whose business he was about, and though we had forgotten our promises to him before the Creator came to this land, we believed his words when he spoke of them. He said he was the *Giver of Life*, the balancer of nature. He taught us how to make living better, and his kind ways affected us all. We did not want him to leave us, but he said he needed to visit others, so we had to let him go." Askuwheteau closed his eyes, remained silent for some time, as though he had experienced the event personally and now sorrowed in the loss of a friend.

Neida studied the mural's main character. Her grandfather's description sounded very much like the Christian Savior, though his belief seemed much more distinctive in his mind. All the past few weeks' research pointed to a correlation between Native American folklore, Christianity, and even archaeology—all aspects that had escaped an intentional burial or the elements of the ages. The symbols on the Michigan Relics spoken within the Algonquin tribes' lodges today, the Puan name, *Chee-Zoos*, Hebraic inscriptions, and the blatant depiction of Christ on the back wall of the cave held credence. Depending on the viewpoint, all similarities died under a world of semantics, a battle of wills. Even she had to admit her guilt in such behavior. Her determination had set her opinions in stone without regard to the research and evidence before her. From the beginning of time, mankind had tried to prove his point in his particular biased way.

She respected her grandfather, and despite the past misgivings she had entertained about his beliefs, Neida marveled that now she desired to know more and, to her surprise, craved the enlightening. She nodded at the painting. "Is that what the Pale One looked like?" she asked.

Her grandfather opened his eyes and nodded. "Yes. He grew hair on his pale face. His eyes were gray-green as the water, though their hue changed when he spoke to our shaman of important things. His robe flowed long and white. His sandals reminded us of the copper the ancients mined along the Upper Peninsula. And the story of his wounds—etched deep in his palms, wrists, and feet—told of the miracles of his death and of his coming back to life again."

He turned to Neida with a solemn expression. "You must never forget that he gave us our medicine lodges, our rites of purification. He formed churches, changed what we did in our temples, and taught our holy men the priesthood. All these secrets are buried in our mounds of distinction, though few crests are left to tell the tale."

Neida studied his profile. "And this is the story your father chanted to you?"

He nodded. "We used to write our stories in books. The Prophet called priests to read from them, but birch bark and stone crumble and go the way of the dust, so we began to chant the stories instead. Though our chanters forget our history now. If someone doesn't translate what relics remain, the stories will fade away for good."

"What happened to the cities you say were so significant?" asked Neida.

He gazed down into his lap. "They lay decayed, plowed under by the white man, or hidden by the wind under layers of earth."

"Are the Michigan Relics the books you speak of?"

"Among others. We lived at *The Cross of Waters* near Michigan's *Sacred Forest*, where we, and those people who joined with us, left many relics behind. Now we can only read a portion of the language etched on them. We have lost our understanding of the rest. We stored as many of our records as we could find in this place ... for another time ... when someone would know how to read them again. My father taught me about their sacredness, and he asked me always to remember."

Neida lay her hand on his arm and said, "Rest now. You can tell me about this later."

This time, Askuwheteau didn't argue.

She wished for more answers than just what her grandfather could remember. Figuring out the past of those who came before remained a never-ending puzzle. Lance was right, though. They probably would never find all the answers. She sighed and focused on the team and on Lance, who now bent over to study the mark on the *Pale One*'s foot.

The statues, mural, and her grandfather's story had engaged her complete attention for the last few minutes. But as her gaze swept the chamber, she noticed something in a remote corner, far enough behind a rock ledge to be out of the way, yet from her position, protruding just enough to shock her and make her gasp—fully clothed skeletons.

She stood and rushed to them. One sagged against a corner of the sidewall. The other rested nearby, face down.

"Look! Over here," she shouted, without taking her eyes off the discovery.

Lance turned away from the mural and came to where she stood. He focused on the floor and dropped to his knees to examine the remains. "They've been here a while," he said, as he scrutinized the tattered rags, the bony digits resting in what was once the skeleton's lap.

The others gathered alongside these new items of interest, issuing exclamations of surprise.

Neida squatted to brush off a layer of dust from a pack wedged against the wall behind the upright skeleton. She pulled it closer, almost confident as to its ownership. "This might confirm their identity," she said.

Lance hurried to unlatch the flap buttons. Stenciled inside, the name *Graham* stood out in black lettering.

Neida bit her lip.

"Well, I'll be," said Kat.

Lance shook his head. "After all this time." He examined the other skeleton. "And this must be Cory's grandfather. By the condition of the skull, I'd say someone shot him in the head."

Cory didn't say anything, only lowered to the ground and touched his grandfather's remains with reverence.

Lance dug inside the pack and produced a measuring spool, a basic tool kit, and a book with a yellowed envelope jutting from between its pages. He slipped out the vellum and removed a document from inside. A piece of paper caught the air and flitted to the floor in front of Neida. She picked it up and turned it over to reveal the printed side. She could only stare at the evidence in unbelief.

"Holy cow," said Kat, who peered over Neida's shoulder. "That's a lot of zeros. And look who wrote her signature at the bottom."

They all stared at the check in Neida's hand, a draft made out to Edward Graham for $500,000 and the signature that sprawled in an unsteady hand: Lila Fiennes.

Cory nodded at the paper in Lance's hand. "What's that?"

"It's a letter from my grandmother." Lance's jaw tightened as he perused it, then he read the words aloud.

> Edward,
>
> I've tried every other way to sway you from your erroneous opinions of my work. This contribution is my last offer. Here is plenty of money to finance any expedition you fancy to spearhead—with one exception, of course. Come work for me. Forget this quest of yours to find fame and fortune and to ruin my research.
>
> Think about it, man. You could fund more with this gift than with notoriety or what you can earn from those hoaxes. And if you want your reputation to remain intact, you'll listen to me. But if you go ahead with this fetish of yours, I'll hunt you down. I'll stop you. I swear.
>
> L

Lance paused, stared at the missive for several moments, then refolded the letter, and replaced it in the envelope. "Sounds about right," he said with disgust. "It looks like my grandmother tried to bribe Granddad and then killed him before he could reveal his discovery and ruin her career—and no one ever even suspected." His voice tapered off to a whisper.

Kat pressed Lance's shoulder. "Your grandma is a lot of things, Boss, but I don't think she'd stoop to murder."

Lance didn't look up. Still dazed, he seemed to talk to himself. "Yet, she had everything to lose, especially her standing in the academic community."

Cory leaned over his grandfather's bones to study his fractured skull. "And we can assume Lila followed them, and seeing all this, she ended the threat to her career right here."

With a sudden burst of energy, Lance peered up at the group. "But how is Blackhour connected in all this?"

Pastor Will's chin lifted with a jerk, and he looked more than happy to share the information. "He's a greedy man," he said with emphasis. "Thought he'd earn an easy buck, though Blackhour's mistaken if he thinks he's getting away with it. Selling to the elite, spreading these lies to an unsuspecting people."

"I don't buy it," said Lance. "I find it hard to believe that his greed was sufficient motive to kill Fitz and Amanda or to run Neida and me down in the street. He'd have to have far more important reasons to pull stunts like that."

Moisture appeared on the pastor's brow. He pulled the back of his hand along his cheek to quell a spasm and dabbed above his eye before he spoke. "The man will do anything to keep his reputation intact. When Edward's find caught Blackhour's interest, he stole them from him. That's when Lila's husband confronted him and threatened to expose him—to get the artifacts back. Days later, someone knifed Cullen in the street. Poor Lila witnessed the murder herself, and when she tried to bring charges against him, nothing stuck. Nothing ever does with that man. Now that someone is blackmailing him for the return of the relics, he's reacting in desperation. He believes Lila wants to destroy him, and he'll do anything to stop her."

"How do you know all this?" asked Neida. "And why haven't you told anyone until now?" His story was more than fishy. He seemed privy to a little too much information.

The clergyman scowled at her. "Blackhour took over the church a few days ago. He kidnapped me and locked me away in the basement, where I overheard a conversation to support the fact that he's after Lila. It's only a matter of time before he finds her. The woman isn't safe."

Lance shoved his grandfather's tools back in the pack. "We've got to get to her. Even if she did kill my grandfather, we've got to stop Blackhour."

"She's gone home to D.C., but I don't think Blackhour knows," said Pastor Will. "That should give us some time."

Lance stood and placed his grandfather's pack on his shoulder. "We'll come back again later and digest all of this. First, we stop Blackhour. Then we make sure my grandmother pays for what she's done here."

"Once we're out of here, I'll give Robert a call and ask him to meet you in D.C.," said Kat. "He'll get the proper authorities involved."

"We'll have to get this wall open first," said Neida.

Lance examined the barrier again. They all did, though Neida turned to check on her grandfather. He eyed the little group with a strange expression. It filled her with sudden uneasiness.

Lance went back to the painting of Christ and grabbed hold of the depression in the rock. "Stand back, everyone. I don't know what will happen. I suppose I just pull." He tugged the lever forward. A click preceded a cranking behind the partition, but the structure only moaned and faded to silence.

"Something tried to work," said Cory.

"Try it again, Boss."

Lance pulled the control once more, and the apparatus groaned even louder, still without results. He groped along the wall, examining it. "Does something else need to happen first?"

"No, the handle is the only device."

They all turned to Askuwheteau.

Neida rushed to his side. "Are you sure? Maybe your father forgot to tell you all the details."

Her grandfather shook his head. "I have done it myself. The lever must be broken."

"We can blast through the wall," said Cory.

Neida gaped at him. "You're joking, right?"

A sheepish expression touched Cory's face, and he turned away from her scrutiny.

"Our lives are in jeopardy, Hon," said Kat to Neida. "If we're going to get out of this pickle, we've got to plod to the other side in the only way we can."

Though the chamber was big enough for her to breathe easily, Neida still fought down moments of panic at being closed in. She needed to get out of here. Yet, destroying these magnificent antiquities appalled her. She gritted her teeth, weighing the choices. The latter necessity finally won out. "But this mural is a piece of history, a part of my grandfather's culture—of my culture. We can't just blow it into obscurity."

She rushed to the lever and pulled on it, tried a second time when it refused to obey her command. The grating continued behind the mural, but the rock lever broke off into her hand on another attempt. She stared down at the fragment; the shock of it brought tears to her eyes, and she slumped where she stood. Once again, her impatient reaction to frustration had sunk them all knee-deep in disaster. She couldn't bear it. She turned away, away from their expressions of surprise, of horror, even an inkling of blame. Those images only heightened a sick stab of guilt inside her, interring her soul—just like the generations of earth that had buried the vestiges of the past one layer at a time.

CHAPTER TWENTY-SIX

𒌋𒐊

LANCE SKIRTED NEIDA and faced her to study the jagged rock in her palm. He covered her hand with his. "It's ironic, isn't it?" he said, gazing up at the figure above them. "Christ sacrificed himself so others might live. We need to destroy this wall, so that we can survive."

"But not now," Neida said, her throat tight with pain. "Not after what we've been through to get here. We've got to prove or disprove all of this. The world deserves to know the truth."

He took the lever from her. "We'll take samples back. We'll confirm authenticity. But Neida, too much is riding on us getting out of here. And even if we do escape this place, our efforts won't ensure others' convictions. People choose for themselves what and with whom they trust, even though they don't decide the rewards or consequences of those beliefs. But I don't need to tell you that, do I? The evidence we've uncovered along our journey has proven that most verification needs faith to back it up."

Neida stepped back. "Blast my Gran! If she knew what Granddad found and comprehended what this message suggests, she must have realized the opposition we'd face."

"Somehow, I think your grandmother clung to hope and faith that whatever resistance got in the way, you—and possibly the world—would recognize your responsibility and fulfill your duty, no matter what."

Neida rolled her eyes. She was beginning to think that even her relatives were less honorable than that. "Too bad people just don't care anymore," she said.

Lance looked into her eyes. "Then, the task is up to us—to you—to give them another chance, a unique opportunity."

Askuwheteau's words made sense now. She, T*he Awaited One*, was born to reveal the forgotten past, at least in this particular case—so people remembered its lessons.

Lance pushed away the hair from Neida's shoulder. "Maybe Althea's true intention was to introduce you to Askuwheteau, to help you understand who you are. Your father almost robbed you of that chance. And all this—the mural, the Prophet's teachings, and who he is—gives us hard evidence we can't deny. We'd do better to grasp the idea with an open mind and accept the change within us as a result."

Neida nodded. Her father's refusal to accept his heritage—the truth—had left consequences and lost opportunity, outcomes more devastating than he had probably realized. She'd much rather someone give her choices than to deny her increased understanding.

She studied the mural above her. The evidence now chinked away at the disintegrating wall of her resistance. Had this being above her, appeared to her people? Had he manifested miracles while he was on the earth? She'd require lab results, maybe even further convincing. But she couldn't deny his influence had captivated societies, men and women who lived apart from him. They chanted his ideologies, however altered, into their legends, and not merely in the Christian world. Gran's plea, her grandfather's gentle guidance, Lance's tenacity, and unfailing support had all led her here. That had to stand for something.

She returned to her grandfather and knelt beside him. "I'm sorry. Destroying the mural seems our only choice. You need a hospital. Winona and Running Deer are in danger, and Lance's grandmother and Blackhour must answer for their crimes."

Askuwheteau shook his head. "Your path does not change my own. I am an old man, but I have witnessed and believed what others fail to imagine. This is enough for me. The truth resides here." He placed his hand over his heart. "And here," he said as he touched his head. "Now, you must understand what the Creator intends for you. How is your heart, Oneida? Are you ready to fly?"

Neida watched him, speechless. She didn't know the answer—only that she willed herself to soar wherever her new-found wings led her.

Neida stayed with her grandfather as Kat and Lance took pictures of the cave's interior. Cory studied the script on the other side of the statues and made notes before taking images using different light angles shed from his halogen lamp—makeshift, but their only substitute right now. Pastor Will helped Lance and Kat drill holes in the wall and place gunpowder charges at strategic points at one end of the mural. They hoped to spall off the rock in thin layers to keep the damage to a minimum. Within an hour, all seemed ready for the controlled blasts.

Lance approached them and squatted next to Askuwheteau. "We're going to move you further away. We don't know if the explosions will cause falling debris."

Askuwheteau nodded. Cory came to help Lance carry him to the back wall.

When they had settled him, Lance took Neida's hand. "Stay with your grandfather. This shouldn't take too long."

The crew huddled at the statues, crouching low. Neida wrapped her arms around her grandfather a moment before several explosions blasted off in succession. Smoke filtered through the airspace. Lance and Cory bolted from their sanctuary with Kat fast on their heels. Seconds later, the cavern rumbled, and the wall imploded, debris pummeling forward with such intense force, it shook the ground beneath them.

"Lance!" Neida released her grandfather, shot to her feet, and sprinted to the edge of the plume where Pastor Will clung to the stone pillars for protection. The air still smoldered; she couldn't see anything. She coughed as she searched the haze.

The congestion thinned by increments, and forms took shape. Lance, Cory, and Kat huddled in a circle together on the floor, dusted white with sediment. A mound of rock lay on the cavern floor. Only fragments of painted and speckled stone hinted that a mural once occupied the space.

Kat coughed and brushed the powder from her hair as she stood. "Well, this experience should last me a lifetime."

Cory eyed the mess and shook his head. "So much for keeping the damage to a minimum. I don't think anything's left."

"It's a complete wash," said Lance, his voice devoid of enthusiasm. "The wall must have been unstable."

"Sometimes, the Lord's plan is different than our own." The pastor, who emerged from his hiding place, appeared relieved.

Neida stared into the fresh opening, now clearing of dust. "Or maybe he provides something even better. Look.

After a moment's scrutiny, a scramble of bodies plowed into the expanse beyond the ruin. Neida gaped at the walls of this new chamber. Every surface contained a mural, scenes depicting the same Native Americans and central figure of the wall they had just destroyed. Above the Prophet's head, the *Mystic Symbol* of the Michigan Relics embossed the surface. One scene depicted the Prophet healing a sick man. Another showed him teaching from the steps of a large edifice atop a mound—perhaps one of the temples her grandfather had referenced.

"It seems to be a repository of some sort," said Lance with heightened but contained excitement. "There must be hundreds of artifacts here."

Along the walls, cairns of tablets—stone, clay, flint—towered in disarray as though someone had stashed them there on a whim. Bas reliefs of a variety of Native Americans embossed block after block of stone nestled on a ledge under one of the murals. Neida eyed a birch bark scroll that revealed a thick, watertight resin protecting its seams. Copper swords, thick with years of corrosion, leaned against one wall. With every turn of her gaze around her, she found something fascinating to view.

Cory let out a whoop. "Look at this. Can you imagine what these tablets will tell us? We've got our work cut out for us, Lance."

The crunch of rubble sounded where the wall once stood. Pastor Will came through from the other side. His face clouded for a second but cleared when he noticed Neida watching him.

"What's the matter, Pastor?" No doubt, this discovery chaffed the man, and his responses since their confinement inside the cave had only deepened her suspicions about him.

"I'm just worried about your grandfather, Winona, and Lila, that's all. We can't take more time here. Blackhour is leagues ahead of us. If we don't go now, we may be too late to do any good." His face twitched.

"You're right," said Lance, scanning the new room. He pointed. "There's an opening at the end of the cavern. Cory let's get Neida's grandfather. We'll need your help too, Pastor.

His leg is delicate, and whatever is down that tunnel, we'll have to take it slow. Once we reach the outside, I'll hightail it back to Chillicothe and round up a rescue team. Then I'll catch a flight to D.C. and get to my grandmother." He turned to Neida. "You can go with your grandfather to the hospital."

Neida shook her head. "I'm going with you."

"But your grandfather needs you now."

"I have to follow my instincts, Lance, to see this to the end. He'll understand. He expects that of me."

"The pastor and I can stay with her granddaddy," said Kat. "And Cory needs to hurry back to the lab and organize a follow-up. The sooner we move the tablets to a safe place, the sooner we'll figure out the depth of this find."

"I'd like to go to Washington, D.C. with you if you don't mind," said the pastor to Neida.

Kat frowned. "Are you sure, Pastor? I'd appreciate an extra hand."

Pastor Will's mouth skewed in determination. "I have to help Lance and Oneida with whatever they need. It's the least I can do."

Neida found that hard to believe. The only time he had been willing to help was when he drilled holes in the mural wall to ensure they could blow it up. She was sure his anxiousness to go with them encompassed a more devious motive in his mind. Maybe keeping him close was the smarter approach to understanding his intentions. She looked up at him. "We can't promise you'll be safe, Pastor. There might be trouble ahead of us."

"I understand, but I'd like to attend you anyway, that is if Lance doesn't mind."

A sour expression transformed Lance's face, and he looked as though he'd argue the point. Instead, he chuckled under his breath and said, "It seems you've all outnumbered me." He stepped closer to Neida. "But as for trouble, I'm afraid our trouble has only just reared its ugly head."

ᛁᚻ/

The trek out of the cave had proven a less eventful ordeal than had their descent into a moon-shaped fissure leading to a cave full of adventure, especially after Blackhour had almost blasted them down a wormhole toward the room called Sacred. However, carrying Askuwheteau through the narrow passages and then hoisting him through another sinkhole onto a mountainous plateau was far from an ideal circumstance. Her grandfather had looked pale on their expulsion from the cave. He had even passed out for a time when they had, by accident, hit his leg on a ragged rock edge. Kat and Cory had volunteered to stay behind with her grandfather by the creek at their original campsite. Lance, Neida, and the pastor had sped back to Chillicothe to get some help.

By nightfall, Kat had phoned. The ambulance and rescue crew had arrived in due time to transport her grandfather away from danger. He now rested under watchful security in the town's local medical center, and the doctor's prognosis had boded well for him. Cory had caught a flight back to Michigan to set up the lab and arrange for the artifacts to be shipped home. They had to make sure they took the utmost care in the relics handling before they attempted to remove *anything* from the cave.

They'd soon start the long process of inventory and translation, and Neida hoped to delve deeper than anyone had ever attempted into the Hopewell and other Native American cultures who had lived in the area. Kat assured Neida she had called Robert and that he had promised to meet them at Lila's house, where he'd administer justice for all.

Neida sighed with relief at the news. Although she desired more than anything to be with her grandfather, she, Lance, and Pastor Will now focused their attention on just how they were to stop Blackhour from carrying out his malicious agenda.

The flight was gruesome sitting between the two men—Lance, with his nose in his computer, and the pastor blathering on about her relationship with God. He lectured on how the cave artifacts would confuse God's children and lead them further away from the truth. After taking out one of Gran's journals, she excused herself, and reread some of the passages to bide her time. That's when she realized some of the pages had stuck together.

Wondering what she had missed through her first perusal of Gran's words, she coaxed the pages apart with her fingers, massaging them until they obeyed her persuasion. One of the pages ripped at the corner, but once separated, Neida relaxed to find Gran's words still in one piece and legible enough to continue her reading. With each word, heat rose inside her; unbelief took hold of her heart. Written just before Grandfather Graham had left for his last expedition, the revelation that these few passages afforded revealed a scenario she had least expected. She reread them a second time:

> I wish I had never married Edward. I hate him and all that he represents. I've pleaded with him to stop his obsession with finding the stolen artifacts, but he's like a wild man, bent on accusing and mistreating those who are only trying to help him. And now he says I forced him to engage the Smithsonian's participation. He rants like a tyrant, blaming me for keeping him from the ranks of

> local museums, where he desires to exploit the artifacts for profit and personal acclaim.
>
> I haven't a clue what has changed him in the few short years of our marriage. His motives seemed so genuine when we first came together. If I had known his heart from the beginning, I'd have defied my parents' wishes. I'd have refused to become his wife and would have married Askuwheteau instead.
>
> All I can see in my mind's eye is the sad look on Askuwheteau's face and his tears at such desecration of sacred things. I'm desperate to find the artifacts myself before Edward steals them and uses them in opposition to their true purpose. If I can hide them away and thwart his ulterior motives, I might repair some of the damage I have caused by turning my back on my beloved. I must protect Askuwheteau's honor from the likes of my husband. But how? As the legend states, the Awaited One is the one true source who can make this right again.

Neida slammed the book closed and flashed a glance toward Lance. He still concentrated on the computer screen, though, with her abrupt movement, he peered up for a moment, smiled at her and, without saying anything, turned back to his reading.

She glimpsed at Pastor Will and was relieved to see he now slumped in sleep, his twitching eye playing havoc with his face. She rested her head against the seat back and mulled over different scenarios.

Should she ask Pastor Will about Gran and Edward's relationship? *Surely not.* He had already expressed his discontent about Gran's "unsavory business" in town.

What about Lance? Edward was his biological grandfather, and Lance had respected Gran throughout the years. He might resent her if he knew she expressed such strong opinions against his relative. Not to mention, Gran's words might strain Neida's relationship with her step-cousin again, and that thought made her sick inside. After the chaos they had been through over the last few weeks, Lance had become too important to her to chance losing him now.

Her path was clear. For the present time, she'd keep this journal entry to herself. It could only stir up more trouble, and with their current mission at hand, it might complicate the equation far more than she could handle.

CHAPTER TWENTY-SEVEN

THEY STRUGGLED INSIDE THE AIRPORT. The terminal bulged with tourists, which forced them to stand in line to acquire a rental car for what seemed an eternity. Hours later, Lance, Neida, and the pastor stepped out in front of Lila Fiennes Colonial-style estate, where they scrutinized the grounds. Before they had a chance to determine their first plan of action, gunshots blasted from inside the mansion and echoed along the alleyway.

Lance whipped around at the sound. He volleyed a glance down the drive and back again. *Where is Robert?* Kat had said he promised to be here with the local authorities, and they didn't have time to wait for their arrival. Not if they were to accomplish any good.

He leaned toward Neida, forcing harshness into his words. "You and Pastor Will stay here. When the police arrive, insist that they send in the posse."

Neida grabbed his arm. "Don't go inside, Lance. Not without backup."

Pastor Will clutched her shoulders to hold her back. "He's right, Oneida. Blackhour plans to kill Lila if he hasn't already. We still might save her."

She yanked away from the man's grip and leaned toward Lance again. "Wait for the police. Wait for Robert. You don't know what's going on in there."

"I can't wait. You heard the shots. We might be too late already. Pastor, keep her here."

Lance set off, stooping low as he traversed the lot. Near the back of the house, muffled voices and a scream sounded from inside. Several uniformed staff members burst from the house and ran across the blacktop, scattering into the bushes. He listened at the door a moment, then crossed the threshold with caution.

Venturing into each room with his back against the wall, Lance eventually approached a gourmet kitchen, empty of staff. He hurried past rolling carts, refrigerators, burners aflame, and abandoned pans still sizzling to the side. He stopped at the kitchen door and scoped the large foyer beyond. A vestibule of sorts led from the front of the house through its heart. Lavish chandeliers hung like glittering balls of fire from second-story ceilings and reflected in the mirrors that spanned the walls. Greek statues adorned several double-paneled entrances, sparking his memory of the elaborate ballroom that lay on the other side of the wall.

A man's body lay in the center of the hallway. A pool of blood collected on the polished floor beneath him. *Probably one of Blackhour's men*, Lance thought. He hadn't visited the house in years, but he remembered the layout well. Voices drifted into the hallway from the ballroom. He dashed behind the statue outside its doors and glimpsed at the scene inside.

His grandmother conversed with her bodyguard whose back faced Lance. Blackhour sat crumpled on the marble floor, clutching his bloody thigh and eyeing Lila with a scowl. Two other bodies sprawled nearby, face down. Lance stepped back to calculate his next move.

Think, Lance, think.

"Lance."

He jerked in surprise and turned to the voice. Neida and Pastor Will stood in front of him, determination emanating from Neida's eyes. Lance bit back his anger. *Can't she ever listen to me and stay out of danger?*

"I tried to stop her," whispered Pastor Will, his nervous tic complaining again.

Lance sighed and held back a reprimand. Now was not the time or place to argue. He turned around to the situation unfolding inside the ballroom and sized up his chances of surprise. Then something hard and pointed poked into his back. He froze, started to turn.

"Don't move," Pastor Will growled.

Neida hurled past him, evidence that the pastor had shoved her from behind.

"Follow your girlfriend into the ballroom, Lance," he said. "We have some unfinished business inside."

Lila scowled at the three of them as they entered. "It's about time you showed up, Will. I've had enough dealing with the likes of Blackhour, here." A smirk slid across her face. "But things are looking up. With the addition of my grandson and this meddling fool," she nodded at Neida, "we can finally have our little chat."

Lance eyed his grandmother with distaste. "I should have guessed. You and the pastor working together. How long has *this* been going on?"

Lila chuckled. "Will and I go back a long way, even dated in high school. When Edward and his tainted bride started stirring up trouble, we had no choice but to unite and find an avenue that might work for both of us.

"Did you convince him to kill Grandfather, or did you do the deed yourself?" asked Lance.

Lila reared up her chest and leered at him. "You've always thought you were the answer man. Nothing could be further from the truth. Will and I only wanted to destroy those confounded artifacts, blow them into extinction, so people like you would stop trying to undermine my work, and so Will, here, could keep his congregation intact. But someone was forever getting in the way, promising to destroy all we've worked so hard to accomplish over the years. People still are. And I'm not about to let that happen."

She turned to smirk at Blackhour. "And then this murderer, with all his clout and flunkies rallying around him, stole the artifacts and executed my Cullin, just to satisfy his greed. My only goal from that time on was to blackmail him. I want those relics destroyed." She brandished a scowl at the man, "And I want you to pay for taking the only person worth his weight out of my life." She turned back to Lance. "Is that too much to ask?"

Before Lance could answer, Blackhour snorted from his corner. "You can't prove I killed your husband, old woman. I didn't even know who your husband was back then."

"Liar!" screamed Lila. "I saw you kill him myself and heard your reasons too."

Neida looked at Lila. "So, who killed Grandfather Graham, then?"

Lila's eyes narrowed, and she hissed out her words. "Keep quiet. You, Neida Graham, are the reason we're all here today. You and your nosey family. Althea's shame wasn't enough for her. She had to egg Edward on, force him to hire Blackhour to analyze those relics until Edward stepped far too deep into his sky-high mountain of stupidity. He bought the farm because of it, no doubt because of this creature," she pointed her crooked finger at Blackhour, "and I won't rest until he gets a taste of his deserved, filthy slop."

Blackhour sneered, snatched something from under his pant leg. A glint of steel flashed, followed by an explosion that volleyed off the walls. They all watched in horror as Lila lurched back and keeled over on the floor, sputtering until she fell silent. Pastor Will gaped in confusion. Enraged, the bodyguard charged the perpetrator, his bulk and momentum, a projectile of will.

Blackhour shot to his feet, whirled on his one good leg out of reach of the bodyguard's enormous hands. He balanced himself and pointed the gun, stopping the colossus from charging again.

"Don't," said Lance to Blackhour, a feeble effort to soothe the frenzy. "You can't stop the inevitable. There's too many of us."

Blackhour winced, adjusted his hand on his thigh. "That's why I'm going to start with Godzilla here, then you."

Something snapped inside Lance. *Neida! I have to protect her.* He bellowed and sprinted to tackle Blackhour, though too late. A bullet ripped through the bodyguard's chest, hurling him backward to the floor. Reaching his target, Lance sent the man sprawling and tried but failed to stop his own downward momentum. The gun spun like a whirligig deep underneath a sideboard just as Lance's head cracked against the marble. The last memory before the light faded was Neida's horrified scream ringing in his ears.

Neida whipped around to the pastor, whose confused expression morphed into rage. He pointed the weapon at her, determination steadying his hand.

She stepped back and raised her palms toward him in defense. "Think about this, Pastor. If you shoot me, you'll lose your congregation."

He laughed, a wild chortle of unhinged emotion. "Don't be naïve. I already have. Why didn't you stay in California? You Grahams have always been on the devil's errand. But I won't let you spread lies against God. I'll destroy that cave and all its blasphemous falsehoods."

Neida stared up into his face, hovering high above hers like some morbid nightmare. "Did *you* murder Grandfather Graham?" She had to ask.

His face twitched, disgust morphing his features. "You'd be closer to the mark by blaming this lost soul." He flailed the gun at Blackhour, who had risen to his feet again. The pastor's hands quivered, and he rectified his grip. Then he aimed the weapon at Blackhour's chest, ranting his next words with scorn. "And *you*, torturing me into submission. That stops right now."

"What are you going to do?" asked Blackhour. "Shoot me? You're a coward, Pastor. You couldn't have stopped any of this from happening, even if you tried."

The pastor's shuddering intensified, forcing him to shift his stance. He wiped his face on his shoulder and readjusted his sights.

Neida stepped toward him.

He jerked back and pointed the gun at her. His eyes sparked in chaotic frenzy, confirmation of his instability.

She had to do something, reach him in some way. "You're a man of God, not a criminal, Pastor. Why don't we wait for help to arrive and turn Blackhour over to the authorities?"

"Just so you can turn around and share those falsehoods with the world—crucify our Savior all over again? I can't let you do that. I have to destroy those lies."

"Thousands of years of history? The past is the best teacher for what lies ahead of us."

"Never this history."

She sighed, tried another approach, borrowing from what she'd learned over the last few weeks. "But no one has all the answers. If we acknowledge the truth that we can't see, the realities just out of our reach, we can better appreciate the future and each other."

His head thrashed back and forth; tears formed in his eyes. "You're wrong. God won't stand for it. I won't stand for it. You'll not turn Newaygo or my church into a den of misguided scientists and thieves."

The gun exploded, and Neida stumbled back. Her shoulder seared with pain and spurted red.

Pastor Will whipped to Blackhour. His unsteady hand wavered without focus, everything and everyone a target.

Not Lance. Neida didn't think, just lurched forward, stepped to the side of him, and, as hard as she could, kicked at the pastor's knee. Her aim was dead on, hyperextending his joint inward. He screamed and catapulted sideways to the floor, the gun tumbling through the air on its descent. As it hit the marble, the weapon discharged. The grand mirror shattered and sent shards flying everywhere. Neida clutched her shoulder and scrambled to seize the firearm, spun around just in time to halt Blackhour in his furious pursuit for control.

Blackhour let out a disgusted grunt. "Another idiot hero," he growled. "Yet, I'll wager you have even less guts than the pastor, here."

Though her very soul tottered like a ship, Neida centered her core, and, with both hands, adjusted her aim at his head. "Are you sure about that? Or would you prefer proof?" And though her hands trembled on the cold steel, her courage surprised her, filled her with an odd sort of satisfaction she had never felt before.

Like ants, a team of policemen swarmed into the room and surrounded them, several training their guns on Neida. Others shackled the pastor's and Blackhour's wrists behind them in iron-clad restraint.

Robert Graham rushed into the room. "Not this one, boys," he said, referring to Neida, her middle, targeted in their sights. "This lady's one of the good guys."

They lowered their weapons, and one officer pried the gun from Neida's hands with care, her legs and torso still frozen in place.

"It looks like you had the situation pretty much in hand," Robert said with an admiring smile. "But you can relax now, Neida. We'll take it from here."

His comment was like a release switch. Thoughts of Lance spurred her to dash to where he lay motionless on the ground. She fell to her knees, caressing, probing, trying to invoke a response.

He finally moved and groaned.

"Lance, are you all right?"

He didn't answer. Still groggy, his eyes remained closed.

A paramedic appeared, but to Neida's surprise, he planted his body next to her, begged her pardon, then ripped her garment to access her wound and started doctoring her shoulder. So engrossed was she in the situation and in her worry for Lance that she hadn't even felt the pain of the gunshot since she'd kicked the pastor.

"The bullet went right through," said the paramedic. "But the wound looks clean enough. I'll just sterilize it and wrap you up. You should be good in no time."

"But what about Lance? He's been unconscious."

"No worries, ma'am. We'll have him on his feet before you know it."

Several minutes later, they were both on their feet again, though Lance still looked pale and not entirely coherent. He touched gentle fingers to the side of his head, and despite his battered and bruised body, he took Neida into his arms.

She clung to him and let him rock her for some time, then looked up into his chocolate eyes and searched for the solace that had eluded her for weeks. "Is it over?" she asked.

Lance nodded. "More than over."

Hearing the words solidified the intangible into something comforting and real. Neida released an unsteady breath, and with it, weeks of pent-up emotion. She sobbed against Lance, then basked inside the circle of his arms like a lost little girl who had finally found her way back home.

CHAPTER TWENTY-EIGHT

THE TOWNSHIP ARRIVED IN DROVES to repair Hopewell the next week. Robert hired a contractor to repair shelving, furniture, and fit new doors on their hinges, while the Benevolent Society brought in food and helped sweep the last traces of broken dishes and trinkets from the floors. They folded linens, organized filing drawers, library shelves, and supplied listening ears. Even John Warren had rolled up his sleeves to help, although he looked a tad too formal in his slacks and a button-down shirt for dusty, manual labor. The previous couple of months proved one thing—like Dorothy after her stint in Oz—truly, there was no place like home.

Neida wiped at the smudge on the window and watched Lance, with his good arm, throw broken shelving into a bin out on the front lawn. He had sprained his other in the struggle with Blackhour, and he had babied his injury in a sling the entire week. The knot on his head had subsided, and his health was almost restored. He now immersed himself in the clean-up, ignoring his mother's admonition to ease up and rest. Since her arrival, Frances had fussed over all of them like a mother hen who just couldn't stop coddling her brood.

Neida's shoulder still throbbed with pain, but thankfully the Pastor's aim had targeted her less prominent arm, and she could still function almost as usual. She turned to dust the sideboard and the shelf above it, her gaze latching on to the ornate box she had forgotten over the last few weeks. It had been one of the few items in the entire house that had remained untouched in the sacrilege against Hopewell. Even her grandmother's first journal page underneath her nightstand had gone missing. She brought down the box and ran her hand over the delicate scrolls and lavish cutwork. *Where did Gran purchase such a treasure?* But the real question was, what mystery had Gran locked away inside? After the last few weeks' hunt for treasure, she was almost too wary of finding out.

She examined the odd keyhole on the top of the box and thought of the keys in the bureau upstairs. However, on her previous examination, she had seen nothing on the keyring big enough to fit the oblong, heart-shaped hole that gaped up at her like some deformed cyclops eye. And then she remembered the skeleton key inside her father's old cigar box and wondered—just maybe …

Neida scrambled to the cubby in the library window, where she had placed her father's treasures the day she had returned from California. The hidden alcove had proven a safe place during Hopewell's vandalism. Retrieving the dilapidated container, she brought it back and set it next to Gran's box, ignoring the old-world lettering of the bowed lid, the rough, frayed edges of the cardboard—two sights that always stabbed her heart with memories of Dad when she handled them. Instead, she flipped open the lid and rummaged around until she found the key. Her excitement ignited, for the heart-shaped end seemed a perfect fit for the keyhole in Gran's box. She inserted the rusted shaft into place, bit her lip, then twisted until it clicked.

Holding her breath, she laid back the lid. The label inside the top displayed her father's bold, unmistakable handwriting. It read, "To my loving mother, crafted by her loving son."

Neida just stared at the message. What had happened to dissolve such tender feelings between them so long ago? And she hadn't even known her father mastered the skills sufficient to craft such a wonderful treasure because he had never practiced his art while she still lived at home.

A red scarf shrouded the contents of the main portion of the box. She lifted the silk covering slowly, and when she recognized what lay beneath it, her heart plummeted to her feet.

A gun. But whose?

Underneath the weapon sat a folded page, and by the familiar vellum, she surmised it had come from one of her grandmother's journals. She took it out, opened the sheet, and recognized that it was the second page of Gran's missing journal entry due to the date at the top.

Neida searched her memory, thought back, and remembered the last words on the first page. Gran had written, "Only she can ..." Neida held up the new sheet and read on.

> find the artifacts that Blackhour stole from us. Despite the missing items, Edward knew where the map led—to that cave in Ohio, a location I will never forget. He and his accomplice had translated the tablet and, for some shady reason, made plans of their own to sell everything. They hadn't even the desire to study the wisdom that the artifacts contained or that of the treasures inside the sacred room.

> Over the last weeks, before Edward and Rex left on their excursion, I picked their brains about the trip, searched through some of Edward's annotated books for the details, and eventually found a mercenary guide to take me to the cave to find the treasure room. I paid him a lot of money to keep his mouth shut about what I did there. When I saw the sacred place and the host of hallowed knowledge of ages gone by, my duty was clear. The fate of such treasures depended on me. If Edward and Cory planned to deprive the world of an honest understanding of their messages, one that Askuwheteau had protected all his years, I couldn't allow such wanton disregard, not as long as I had breath. Such a tragedy was inconceivable to me. It will forever be. So, I shot them both.

Neida wrestled to endure the flogging of her heart, the tears in her eyes, but she read on anyway.

> I hope those who read this entry spare Askuwheteau the truth of what I did for him. I'm not sure he would have appreciated that I paid for his honor in blood. Nor would Edward's family have forgiven me. And I wouldn't have blamed them at all.
>
> Arthur guessed the whole of it. His finding the gun in the box he had made for me confirmed his suspicions. He loved Edward, but he loved me just as much. I had betrayed him, and, of course,

> that was unforgivable. And so, he stole what he thought was the box's only key, took Neida away, promising he'd never bring her back, and he's kept his word to this day.
>
> I'll bury the box and duplicate key in the mound out back once I lock away this entry. A fitting place to inter the past, I would think. I haven't destroyed the evidence all these years in hopes that I'd find courage enough to turn myself in. But I'm a coward. And despite my folly, I can't destroy the box. It has meant so much to me over the years and is a reminder of my mistake. Both represent Arthur's love, as well as the reason he's buried that love forever in the past. If only he'd understand my efforts were to convey the truth.

Neida glanced at the box, the gun inside. Why hadn't Gran hidden the items before she died? Had she wanted Neida to find them and to accept the revelation the letter contained? She'd never know for sure, and that fact sat like a brick inside her stomach as she read on.

> In recent days, I met with Blackhour. I've warned him I'll turn him in to the authorities if he hinders my granddaughter from her duty. He laughed at me and called me a crazy old woman, said that I had no proof he'd ever done anything wrong. But I think he knows I'm far from bluffing. John has my sealed confession. I've asked him to turn the paper over to the police once I'm gone, or if anything happens to Oneida.

> Today, years after my blunder, I've grown a bit wiser in my old age. To think of oneself as a savior, without authority or creed, only results in the ruination of one's soul. It did mine. How could I have thought murdering someone could right a wrong? How could I have felt such saving was anyone's work but Oneida's? She is The Awaited One, the blood of He Who Watches and is the savior of the prophecy. In the coming days, she'll reveal the wisdom of the artifacts that lie within that cave. She'll bring light back to the world.

The tears were streaming now. Neida clutched her free hand to her mouth, gasped unrestrainable grief into her palm. In her hand, she held the only revelation that had and would destroy all the people that Gran had ever loved. Even Dad and Mom had gone to their graves with this knowledge. They had kept her away, so she'd never discovered such an earthshaking reality as this. And all to protect her heart. She had despised her father for taking her away from Gran. Now all her mistaken emotion dissolved with this single page before her.

John Warren had been wrong about the town knowing everything that went on in Newaygo. As far as she knew, she was the only person privy to the information about Gran, and—right here, right now—Neida vowed she would never tell. And she would think of a way to talk John Warren into giving her Gran's sealed envelope to make sure no one would ever know.

She wiped her eyes with the back of her hand, folded the paper, and placed the trial, jury, and conviction back inside the box, covering it again with the cloth. Locking away the secret, she put the container back on the shelf and slipped the key into her pocket. She promised herself she'd bury both the box and its access in the mound out back as soon as she could. Maybe she'd even destroy it. Gran should have done that long ago.

A commotion from the front lawn clattered through the open front door, and Neida hurried to the window to see what all the fuss was about. A Range Rover had turned into the drive and now followed the path up to the porch.

Neida fiddled in the mirror to repair the damage of the last few minutes. Her eyes still glistened, and her nose had swollen to a puffy bulb at the end. She retrieved a tissue and blew, then hurried to splash cold water on her face at the kitchen sink and returned to the front room where she took a last breath and last look in the mirror. When satisfied, she stepped outside to join Lance and her guests.

The Range Rover had come to a stop. Kat and Cory jumped to the ground with smiles on their faces.

Neida had missed them. She had longed to discuss their upcoming project of examining the tablets and other artifacts, and she looked forward to hashing over the details.

"Hey, you two." Kat waved with a grand gesture and retrieved a wheelchair from the car's storage compartment. She popped open the device on its wheels and rolled it around to the passenger's side, where she waited for Cory to open the door. "I thought we'd never get here," she said. "The traffic out of Ohio was a rat's patootie."

Winona and her grandson emerged from the back, and Lance helped Askuwheteau into the chair as Kat held the handles.

The sight lifted Neida's spirits. She embraced her grandfather and stepped back to study his healthy skin tone and vigor. The bruises on his face, though dark, showed traces of yellow at the edges and hinted he would mend. "You look wonderful, Grandfather. How are you feeling?"

"I am glad to be home," he said, looking to the mound at the back of the property before he turned to Neida again. He studied her face for a moment; a hint of a frown touched his expression before he answered with exaggerated mirth. "I do not care for hospital food, but I can enjoy rolling around in this chair."

Neida chuckled, thankful he hadn't asked her about her red eyes and that his lightheartedness could elevate her mood. "I'll make sure that doesn't happen. I'm determined to get you up and sprinting again." Then to everyone, "Our feast awaits us out back. I expect all of you to stuff yourselves silly."

"I'm more than game," said Kat as she rolled Askuwheteau toward the side of the house. "We stopped out of Detroit, but Cory's belly is fit to be tied. I haven't enjoyed a moment of peace with all that grumbling."

They followed Neida to the back. Frances and the Society members busied themselves and served the company in full view of the Hopewell mound.

Lance, who sat next to Neida, directed his comments at Askuwheteau. "By the way, I hired contractors to repair your door, and we've built you a bigger porch."

Askuwheteau gestured his shriveled hand toward Lance, his life-worn palm pretending to pat him on the head. "You are a good man, Lance Graham. One to be trusted."

Lance nodded his thanks, stared down at the food on his plate, and twisted a curl around his finger. Frances beamed at her son, and Neida couldn't help but smile.

No—never, ever, will I confess that Gran had disappointed them all.

"I'm anxious for you to see our home now, Father," said Winona. "They even planted a lawn in the front yard." She offered cheese to her grandson, who chomped down on the wedge and devoured it with the ferocity of a hungry bird.

"I can't imagine how terrible the ordeal was for you," Kat said. "Protecting a child amid evil men must have taken phenomenal strength."

Winona nodded. "I feared for all of us, especially Father, after they took him away. But when the white authorities stormed the house, it did my heart good to see those lowlifes face down in the dirt. Though Father tells me your nightmare was even worse."

"In all my years of digs, I've never experienced anything like it," said Kat.

Neida paused, a fork-full of casserole hovering in mid-air. She didn't know what had been more challenging, staying one step ahead of Blackhour, almost getting run down or blown up, witnessing a murder, or pointing a gun at someone. Amanda and Fitz's deaths and shattering someone's knee had taken a toll on her most of all.

"We'll soon have our hands full," said Cory. "Ohio just issued the permits, and we start moving the tablets to Kat's lab next week. Then comes the long inventory and translation process. The Smithsonian even offered to help decipher the language."

Lance tsked his disgust. "Well, they can offer all they want. Their indifference over the years disqualifies them. We can more than handle such a significant find."

"I'm glad the world will finally have access to the records," said Winona. "Maybe their translation will give honor to my people. Maybe they'll prove once and for all, we are the ancient ones who once filled this land." She gave her father her only napkin as his had whisked away in the breeze.

"I've translated the passage on the stone box. That might help."

They all turned to Cory again.

He beamed at the gathering like a proud father and explained his findings. "An inscription on the base of the statue corroborates with what we've surmised, though with a slight twist. It translates as, 'Other sheep I have which are not of this fold or the fold of Jerusalem: this righteous remnant shall I support, and they shall hear my voice, and there shall be one fold and one shepherd, for I will return and claim this people.'"

Neida put down her fork. She turned to Lance and met his gaze. Her respect for his faith and forethought increased a notch or two in her mind. He had been right all along.

Askuwheteau raised his chin and said. "We hid the records for years after the *Pale One* walked among us. This was his instruction to our priests. Later, after the Great War with our enemies, our people who survived continued to add other records and artifacts belonging to many other nations. That cave has protected the history of this land and their wise messages for such a time as this."

Cory scratched his newly shaven jaw. "And good thing! We've got a library full of learning to do. It's sure to keep us busy for some time."

"Neida and I will be helping Cory in the lab," said Lance. "We plan to write a book about our findings. We interviewed on a few talk shows just yesterday, and though we tried to steer them away from Blackhour, the pastor, and Lila, we weren't successful. The media are such vultures when it comes to gore." He shook his head and shrugged. "But that doesn't matter. Once we understand the artifacts and what has lain in that cave for eons, the facts will spike plenty of interest about what's important."

"Too bad we're still in the dark about who murdered Edward and Cory's grandfather," said Frances. "From the news feed, I hear Blackhour and the pastor keep accusing each other."

Lance nodded. "We'll probably never know who committed the deed."

Neida looked down at her plate and rubbed the back of her neck. *He has no idea how right he is.*

"Well, I hear you have a new pastor to take Will's place," said Frances.

"Yeah, the Board of Ministers were quick on their feet," said John Warren. "No one ever dreamed Will would act out his savior complex. The pastor thought he was saving his congregation by helping Lila find and destroy those artifacts. But by shooting Neida, he pretty much sealed his fate."

Frances shook her head. "Can you imagine? We put our faith in him all these years. If you can't trust your pastor, who can you trust?"

"He'll spend some time in a mental institution, I'm sure," said Lance.

"I'm just sorry about Lila." Frances put down her fork. "I suppose no one could have changed her mind about the artifacts or Cullen. She was quite a difficult woman, especially when it came to her convictions and her books. But she didn't deserve to die like that, not even if she wanted revenge on Mr. Blackhour."

Winona wiped her mouth on the new napkin that a society woman handed her. "What will happen to him?" she asked.

"Blackhour was responsible for quite a few murders of his own, not just Cullen's," said John Warren. "He was the one who gave the orders to kill Fitz and Amanda. The Smithsonian has added other charges to the mix. He and his band of thugs will rot in jail for the rest of their lives, maybe even receive the death penalty."

Winona nodded. "He deserves the harshest punishment for his crimes against us all." She hugged her grandson, who wiggled away from her embrace.

Kat turned to Winona. "So, what are your plans now?"

"We'll continue at the Lake, I think. Father wants to keep tabs on the artifacts. Just to make sure they never fall into the wrong hands again. He hopes others will learn the language."

"No worries there," said Lance. "We've got the key. As soon as we document the artifacts and the cave's interior, we'll share the information with the world. And we've made arrangements with Ross County officials to close off a portion of the cave system to ensure the preservation of the murals. Once we set up a repository of our own, we'll ensure the treasures are accessible to the greatest amount of people. Perhaps that will make a difference when it comes to this country's future attitudes, despite what went on in the past."

Winona rested an elbow on the table and leaned in. "Your dream may take a while, Lance. The People and the white man still don't trust one another. The past atrocities are still too ingrained in all our minds."

Neida thought back to when she first arrived at Hopewell when her grandmother commented about the past. *Grudges are poisonous bedfellows*, she had said, and Gran had proven that adage beyond any doubt, in a less than noble way. She had believed in an altered reality and had defied the faith and upbringing her parents had taught her to embrace.

Hadn't mankind done the same throughout history? Races, creeds, genders, and institutions had vied for space in the world, just to prove and enforce laws that deemed one group better than another—to prove they held all the answers and to trample over someone else's beliefs in the name of the particular God they worshiped. When all they had to do was peel back the layers of pride, indifference, unbelief, and inequity to discover that they had more in common with each other than they realized.

And the essential reality in all the analyses came down to one vital truth. If a Creator of all mankind existed, he had to be one God, the same being for everyone, despite the mutations people had chosen to imagine or renounce in their modified and limited understanding. And if she eventually came to terms with that precept, then she'd have to admit that this God was the only being who laid rightful claim to her title, *The Awaited One*. Nothing would ever change that.

The chatter continued around her, and Neida gazed at each of their faces, appreciated, more than she could express, the faith they had placed in her, albeit unwarranted. She'd do her best to eradicate the antagonism of the ages, use all the evidence to enlighten and unite the world, at least on this particular subject. But acceptance of these truths was and would forever be left up to the individual. Despite her grandmother's savagery, at least Neida could repay confidence and trust to those who remained with her. And she vowed to always aspire after such things in her future achievements.

"Grandfather, I want you, Winona, and Running Deer to live with me," said Neida, interrupting their stream of words. "I have plenty of room here at Hopewell, and we have a lifetime of catching up to do."

Askuwheteau raised his chin as he gazed at her across the table. His eyes filled with tears. He nodded his assent as those around the table talked all at once, reveling at such an excellent idea.

The company ate in companionable conversation. The wind later picked up, flapping the tablecloth against their knees. A slight chill edged through Neida's sweater. She shivered, and Lance leaned in closer.

"Won't be long till the snows are here," said someone behind them.

Pastor Bob, the new Baptist clergyman, walked across the lawn with a plate of food and took a seat on the other side of Neida. "If anybody wants seconds, now's the time to get them," he said. "The ladies are packing up and will leave in a few minutes. Tomorrow is my first official sermon as Newaygo's pastor, and I need to prepare my words." The minister eyed all the assembled, ending with his gaze upon Neida. "Will any of you join us?"

Bless him for trying. Neida still needed time to recuperate, to refine her feelings about whatever semantics she chose to adopt, and if she could manage to do so, to put her mourning about Gran to rest. "We'll see," she said with a smile.

An hour later, as the last of the sun's rays reflected off the cedar trees and played with the shadows around the mound, Lance and Neida issued hugs and waved their farewells to their guests at the edge of the lawn. Frances hurried off to finish cleaning the kitchen. Kat and Cory packed Neida's loved ones inside the Range Rover again, and Kat skirted the vehicle with a final wave of her hand.

"I'll get your granddaddy and Aunt Winona home safe and sound," she said with a nod. "You two lay off work for the day. You should rest. Heaven knows you deserve it. We all do."

"Take Monday off, Kat," said Lance.

"Is that an order, Boss?" She gave him a wry smile, then climbed inside the SUV and backed down the drive.

Neida waved. She possessed more family than she had ever thought possible—her grandfather, Winona, and Running Deer; Kat, Cory, and John; especially Frances, Robert, and Lance. A lump formed in her throat as the Range Rover darted from view.

As they stood together gazing into the night, the words Lance had said to her outside Chillicothe crept into Neida's mind. *Life is full of promise. Sometimes, you just need to grab onto an idea, believe in the premise ... take a leap, and treasure the possibilities*. He truly was a wise man. Maybe she was ready to follow his advice.

Taking her hand and directing her up the steps, Lance ushered Neida into the house and shut out the cold evening air. They had yet to find a moment alone since their return from Washington, D.C. A pang of nerves rose inside her as she turned on the lights.

Lance secured the bolts and closed the drapes. He twisted around to examine her. "You've been rather quiet tonight," he said with tendernesss in his voice. "Everything all right?"

The loaded question threatened to form tears, but she swallowed them back. She had to be brave. With her new understanding, she'd do anything to keep Lance close.

When she didn't say anything, awkwardness engulfed his expression. He jabbed a thumb over his shoulder. "Uh, I'll just get my mom and go out the back."

She grabbed his arm, kept him in his place. "I'm fine, Lance. Really. I'm just processing everything, I guess."

It would take some time to accept what her Gran had done. Maybe she'd share the revelation with him some day. But not now, definitely not until she had secured his love and loyalty, perhaps never as long as she lived.

She stepped closer to him and stared up into his dark eyes, almost drowned in their reflection, and searched for the right words to say. "Lance ..."

A hint of a smile tugged at the corners of his mouth, but he didn't say anything.

"I ... you said you wouldn't kiss me again unless I wanted it."

He nodded. His gaze almost scorched Neida as he closed in.

"Well, I want you to. I want to explore the possibilities, even if we are ... kind of related." She tried to sound as though the fact were true, but the pounding of her heart was sure to give her away. She desired to explore life with this man. In their childhood, and in the short time she had reacquainted herself with him, he had managed somehow to make her feel whole.

His gaze lingered on her lips, then traveled to her eyes. "Show me one DNA marker that proves we're cousins, and I'll back away."

"Even if proof did exist, I wouldn't believe it. I'm falling in love with you."

He smiled the lazy, lopsided grin so familiar to her now, and said, "My exact sentiments."

Already out of his sling, Lance engulfed her with two strong arms. He placed a gentle kiss on her forehead, resting his cheek against its plane for a moment.

She tilted her head back to meet his eyes. "I think I can get used to this. I'm anxious to start where we left off."

His eyes narrowed. "You don't want proof a future exists for us?"

She slowly shook her head and touched his lips with her finger. "I think I have all the proof I need."

His boyish grin faded, and he slid his warm hand up to cup the side of her face. Then his mouth enveloped hers, shattering all doubt.

Neida melted against him, clung to Lance with every newfound hope gushing up from somewhere inside her. *Possibilities?* Yes, she saw lots of possibilities.

AUTHOR'S NOTE

MANY YEARS AGO, I attended several lectures in Mesa, Arizona, where three researchers introduced me to the Michigan Relics and the mound-building civilizations of North America. I had never heard of the Hopewell or Adena peoples. At the dawn of civilization, these old-world cultures had built over 200,000 earthworks throughout the United States and into Mexico and Canada. They had left behind burial mounds, temple plateaus, places of refuge and fortification, and an abundance of relics that suggested a Semitic and Egyptian origin.

A few Native American populations, like the Ojibwe, Iroquois, Cherokee, and Mi'kmaq, corroborated with such theories, confessing they had entered North America through the St. Lawrence Seaway or the southeastern shores of the Gulf of Mexico by transatlantic voyages from the old world. Their mind-bending stories of the *Pale One*, *Creator*, or *Dawn-God*, known among the tribes from the east to the west coasts of this country, touted similarities to the Christian beliefs of Jesus Christ.

My previous education sparked my uncertainty about this new theory. The history books had failed to suggest that the Native Americans ever arrived from anywhere else than from over the Bering Straits. They had never taught me of eight-foot giants or pits of bones suggesting wars and mass burials, ancient copper mines, or iron-smelting operations. They especially never taught me of relics containing stories of the Garden of Eden, the Flood, or of a man who had visited the people of this country, bearing similarities to Christ.

The information hooked me. Whether by intentional misrepresentation or by ignorance, scholars had hidden America's secrets well.

Academia had dubbed the artifacts, specifically the Michigan Relics, the most significant hoaxes of our history. Sold, burned, plowed under, and forgotten on museum shelves, the relics' authenticity remains futile, even though these relics' first documentation surfaced long before their alleged forger James O. Scotford came on the scene.

Tools, tablets, and pottery laying under ash layers of human remains—some broken by tree roots centuries old—still come forth from the earth to this day. Yet, authorities are still troubled by the crude crumbling clay tablets and the tooth marks that archaeologists claim were produced by present-day saws. Even some scholars from the Church of Jesus Christ of Latter-day Saints, most anxious to find a connection to their belief that Joseph Smith translated the Book of Mormon from ancient plates, have deemed the artifacts counterfeit. And scientists still ignore the prehistoric copper saws and chisels buried deep inside the mounds while underplaying the theology of the relics' messages identical to archaic Semitic ideologies.

Is it possible that Scotford understood the idiosyncrasies of Hebrew formatting or possessed knowledge of Egyptian,

Phoenician, and Greek languages? Scholars might conclude Scotford, an ignorant sign painter, forged some of the plates, but where did he get the information, and at a time when such dogma as found in the *Pistis Sophia*, an ancient Gnostic text, had yet to be translated into English? How could he duplicate most of the 30,000 intricately detailed records in a few years with no signs of forgery? The facts imply someone else created the relics and buried them in the mounds.

The *Manifest Destiny* mindset, the divine sanction for the United States' territorial expansion, seemed key to forming public opinion at the onset of the European influx into this country. Its doctrine encouraged U.S. authorities to classify North America's indigenous peoples as savages and viewed their achievements as lacking worth or qualification for preservation. *The Journal of the Ohio Historical Society* concluded "no subject received more attention and controversy among archaeologists of the 19th century" than the stone tablets discovered inside these ruins. Indifference resulted in the reckless destruction of the earthworks and the artifacts found buried under layers of the past.

Man proves a hesitant customer when buying into matters that veer from tradition. At first glance, the lack of what society deems concrete proof spurs quick criticism at the audacity of such bold research. The resulting spin is the plight of the Michigan Relics and the possibilities surrounding them. Perhaps authentication is left to seekers of truth to explore all the remaining evidence with new eyes. Coupled with faith, our understanding and tolerance of what and particularly who arrived in this country before Columbus may allow us a more authentic look at the past.

November 2020

Another note to the reader: *The statues, artifacts, and cave in this story Vestiges are purely fictional. I have also taken license in the description of Newaygo, Michigan, and the Paint Creek, Ohio, areas for the ease of advancing the story.*

Please visit Peggy's website **peggyannshumway.com** *and join her email list. You'll receive new release and author event information, updates, and access to her blog articles. You can also sign up to receive her free e-book, Fragrance of Thought. Don't hesitate to leave your comments while you're there.*

GLOSSARY

ᛁᚻᛇ

Adena: a mound-building, Native American culture of North America made up of several indigenous groups who arrived here from across the Atlantic Ocean and flourished in the northeast areas of the continent between 1000 B.C. or earlier to about 1 A.D.

Alligewi, Allegan: a white-skinned, blue-eyed Native American culture of great stature, also known as the Talligewi. They came to North America across the Atlantic Ocean from the east and lived around the Mississippi or Ohio River. Many Native American tribes feared them and eventually banded together to battle and destroy them at the Falls of the Ohio near Louisville, Kentucky.

Algonquin: a Native American language group of North America. The Ojibwe, Ottawa, and Potawatomi dialects use a variation of this language. Anciently these people lived on the Atlantic coast, along the St. Lawrence Seaway, and around the Great Lakes region.

Baamaapii: the Ojibwe word that means *later*, *after a while*, or *eventually*.

Bishop Arius: a Christian priest who opposed the Nicene Council of 325 AD and who believed that God, the Father, was a separate deity than that of the Son, Jesus Christ.

Coptic Christians; Copts: Egyptian Christians who believed in a high deity, the greater *Yahweh*, different than that of the lesser deity or lesser *Yahweh*. They also believed in the Satan. Some scientists believe a small group of these Christians escaped persecution from the Nicene Council and came to North America for refuge. Others believe the Michigan Relics are artifacts left by this group.

Cypriot: the Greek dialect used in Cyprus.

Dakota: a Native American tribe who lives in the Dakotas and is a part of the subcultures Santee and Yankton. Also known as the Sioux. Legend states they are of the Turtle Totem, instrumental in leading the Mexican serpent cultures up the Mississippi River to assimilate and conquer the Puan and other tribal nations.

Druze: a close-knit, Middle Eastern, Arabic-speaking group who are Monotheistic.

Esus: a Celtic Deity, portrayed as cutting branches from trees with his ax. Some believe the similarity of his name with that of Jesus and the Welsh god IESU (Jesus) suggests they are one and the same.

Haplotype: an arrangement of tightly connected and specific gene sequences on a chromosome, inherited as a group.

Homoousion: a Christian belief springing from the Nicene Council in AD 325 that explains the character of the Godhead (Father, Son, and the Holy Ghost) as one deity in being and essence.

Hopewell Culture: a mound-building, Native American Woodland culture who lived in the northeastern and midwestern areas of North America to the Gulf of Mexico's shores between 200 BCE and 500 CE. Scientists believe these people were a part of several related indigenous groups, the oldest populations living in the United States' southern regions. These people participated in extensive trade routes into what is currently Mexico and Canada.

Ho Theos: the Greek name for God, the Father.

Iroquois: a Native American confederacy made up of the Mohawk, Oneida, Seneca, Onondaga, Cayuga, and Tuscarora tribes. They made their home in southern Ontario, Quebec, and in the state of New York.

Keweenaw Peninsula: an isthmus located on the northern part of Michigan's upper peninsula, which juts into Lake Superior. The mound-builders mined copper extensively there, which provided the ore for many of their artifacts and tablets.

Khrisna: a primary Hindu deity, the supreme God of compassion, tenderness, and love and who is greatly revered among the Hindu people.

Kyrios: a Greek word meaning *Lord* or *Master*, which refers to the translation of HWHY, Jehovah, or Yahweh.

Manifest Destiny: a 19th-century belief that the United States had a God-given right and duty for a territorial expansion to the Pacific Ocean and beyond.

Michigan Relics: ancient relics that contained Biblical themes and were found at least by the 1840s in 27 counties of Michigan as well as in Illinois. Most scientists believe the artifacts are one of the biggest hoaxes ever invented. However, some believe they were left by 4th-century Coptic Christians who escaped religious persecution and settled in North America.

Mound Builders: various ancient cultures that settled in North America between 3500 BCE to the 16th century CE and were known for their religious, ceremonial, burial, and residential earthwork constructions. Scientists believe at least 200,000 of their mounds existed before the European influx.

Mun-dua: The Ojibwe name for the mound-builders.

Ohlone: This tribe is a Native American tribe of the northern California coast, thought to be a conglomerate of many related populations originally from Siberia.

Ojibwe: a Native American tribe of the Canadian and western Great Lakes areas, allies to and part of the Council of Three Fires with the Potawatomi and Ottawa nations. Their language is part of the Algonquin-speaking groups.

Ottawa: a Native American tribe of the western Great Lakes area, allies to and part of the Council of Three Fires with the Ojibwe and Potawatomi nations. Their language is part of the Algonquin-speaking groups.

Pawnee: a central Plains North American tribe that lived in Kansas and Nebraska before the 16th century until the 19th century. Currently, the tribe lives mostly in Oklahoma.

Phoenician: a Semitic language of the Phoenician culture, written in characters that inspired the Greek and Roman alphabets.

Pistis Sophia: a Gnostic text written in the 3rd and 4th centuries AD. This text was discovered in the 1700s and was translated into English in 1895.

Platform Mounds: flat-topped, artificial mounds of dirt and rock, which were the foundations for temples or other buildings within ancient cultures.

Potawatomi: a Native American tribe of the western Great Lakes area, allies to and part of the Council of Three Fires with the Ojibwe and Ottawa nations. Their language is part of the Algonquin-speaking groups.

Puans: a group that made up part of the mound-builder culture, also known as the Mun-dua.

Quexalcote: the Feathered Serpent, a Mesoamerican deity and descendant of Aztec royalty. He was the god of the Toltec and Aztecs who lived between 400 BC – AD 600 in Mexico and reverenced him.

Talligewi: a white-skinned, blue-eyed Native American culture of great stature, also known as the Alligewi or Allegan, who came to North America across the Atlantic Ocean from the east. They lived around the Mississippi or Ohio River. Many Native American tribes feared them and eventually banded together to battle and destroy them at the Falls of the Ohio near Louisville, Kentucky.

Tetragrammaton: the four-letter Hebrew word (HWHY, YHWH or JHVH) that names the God of Israel.

Trinity: a Christian doctrine that believes God, the Father, Jesus Christ, and the Holy Spirit are one, in essence, being, and nature. The bishops of the Nicene Council in 325 A.D. perpetrated this doctrine at the request of Emperor Constantine and, after much debate, arrived at their final consensus. Many modern Christian faiths continue to support the creed.

Tumulus, tumuli (plural): burial mounds of dirt and rock that are found throughout the world. They are also known as barrows or kurgans.

Yahweh: the national God for Israel's kingdoms, the warrior deity who leads a heaven-sent host against Israel's enemies. At one point in Jewish history, the name was forbidden to be said aloud. The name also refers as Jesus Christ.

OTHER SOURCES

For more information about the Hopewell, Christ in America, and the Mystic Symbol, check out the resources below.

Deal, David Allen, "Complete Translation of a Michigan Clay Tablet," *The Mystic Symbol: Mark of the Mound-builders,* Colfax: Ancient American Archaeology, 2004. (See addendum at the back of the book. The translation of plate 12, on page 176, is David Allen Deal's attempt at deciphering the Michigan Relics' language, and I use part of his translation when I refer to the directions within the Vestiges plot).

Hansen, L. Taylor, *He Walked the Americas*, Amherst: Amherst Press, 1963

May, Wayne N., *This Land* Book Series, Colfax: Ancient American Archaeology, 2004-2009.

Mertz, Henriette, *The Mystic Symbol: Mark of the Mound-builders*, Colfax: Ancient American Archaeology, 2004.

Pidgeon, William, *Traditions of De-Coo-Dah*, New York: Horace Thayer, 1858.

Searching for the Great Hopewell Road: A landmark journey into the mysteries of the ancient Hopewell people. United States of America: Pangea Productions, Ltd., 1998. DVD.

Squire, E. G., *Aboriginal Monuments of New York*, Colfax: Hayriver Press, 2006.

Zimmerman, Fritz, *A Photographic Essay and Guide to the Adena, Hopewell, Sioux and Iroquois Mounds and Earthworks*, Minneapolis: Tasora Books, 2009.

ACKNOWLEDGEMENT

I GIVE MY SINCEREST APPRECIATION to everyone who read and commented on earlier versions of *Vestiges*, particularly Donna Hatch, Pj Switzer, Michaela Stephens, Shaunna Gonzales, and Betsy Love. Their invaluable opinions helped to shape these pages into a workable tale.

Special thanks go to several people. First, Michele Holmes of Precision Editing Group, LLC, a skilled editor and author, guided me through this story's rougher parts and suggested ways to improve this work tenfold. Second, Steve Chugg's artistry in mapmaking added beauty and clarity to the whole. And third, Leann Cordon, who, with her careful eye and patience, line-edited my drafts several times. I cannot forget my dear friend Colleen Moorefield, who always believed I could finish the story, and my parents, who provided me the opportunity to use my faculties in development and scholarship.

My most heartfelt thanks go to a loving Heavenly Father, who endowed me with the ability to put words on paper, as well as the sense to edit out those things that are contrary to his will as I strive to better myself and others.

Finally, a big thank you goes to my readers. Without you, this endeavor of world-building would have culminated in nothing more than a mere fanciful hobby.

Coming Soon

COVENANTS

Faith, Freedom, and Posterity Series, Book 2

CHAPTER ONE

Near the hunting ground below the Sacred City, four hundred twenty-nine years after the sign given of the coming of Christ

BROKEN PROMISES TO GOD, like pottery under a careless hand, are calamities that affect the good of the whole. Ganawenjigi had learned such travesties firsthand. His own people, the ferocious perpetrators and participants of the last great war were the reason he eyed what now sidled forward just below him, a dark form in the bush.

He lay on his belly, low and still, peered down at the warrior from his limestone lookout through the whirled luster of blue-green leaves. He dared not breathe. The tracker's back was to him, his tall and thick frame as sturdy as the trunk of a forest tree, his ocher skin bare except for the multicolored breechcloth and his copper arm and ankle bands burnishing in the sun. The hunter clutched in his free hand a flint-tipped atlatl poised to cast and sink deep inside an enemy. From his belt, he kept close a copper sword to scalp and gut what he would later brandish as his trophy.

The fierce looking man bent forward and riveted his gaze into the undergrowth, parting leaves with his hand as he crept one more step away, and then another, his head swiveling back and forth in his search of the remnant Mun-dua. By the time the warrior was some distance away, Ganawenjigi slowly released the air that burned his lungs and chanced another breath—a mistake, he realized, as a twig snapped beneath his chest.

The tracker whirled. His dark flint eyes, set deep in his chiseled face, fixed upon the ridge. He tiptoed closer until he stopped just below the crest that jutted out above his head. His gaze swept every inlet of rock, every opening through the lacework of branches of the hidden alcove, and he was so close now that Ganawenjigi could smell the man's sweat mingling with the forest decay under his nose.

Can he see me? No, if the tracker had noticed him, he would have finished what he had come here to do. Ganawenjigi clutched the copper knife in his hand, waited, ready for evasive tactics. Finally, the man eased away, hardly a sound issuing from beneath his feet on his retreat away from the niche.

It had been days since Ganawenjigi had finished his solemn work. At the place of gathering, inside the bowels of the earth, he had completed painting the last of the murals, had interred the remaining carvings, tablets, and great circular stones that held the prophesies and promises of his people and those of other nations as well.

He had worked days to carve out the secret hovel within the statue of the Mun-dua warrior and concealed the most sacred prize of all. Its preservation was vital, he well knew—to ensure the sacred items might be spared the wrath and utter destruction of the enemy should they breach the cave's entrance. Within a copper tubing for protection, he had secured the rent fabric of one of their great leader's garments, that which held the most sacred of the written covenants that the Great Elk Nation had made with their Creator. They had passed the covenant down through time by the hands of their prophets. And the prophets, in turn, had taught and warned the people to protect their freedom, their families, and to obey the Great Spirit who had brought them safely across the Sunrise Ocean. Even more vital, if the people failed to uphold their promise to God, that same deity would sweep them from off the face of the land. Hadn't it happened just that way?

With a sad heart, Ganawenjigi had watched friends and family, as well as many stalwart leaders, turn away from the covenant, forgetting their good fortune, and mocking the grace the Creator so abundantly had provided them. The people had turned back to their natural ways like a dog to its vomit. There were but few who were yet alive, Ganawenjigi among them, and if he could escape notice, he might live to tell the tale.

But to whom? The trackers had destroyed his village, along with his family and friends. They had left nothing of what was once a great civilization, their temple a smoking ruin smoldering upward toward the sky. Nothing was left to cherish, and the enemy would forever hunt the remnant of the Great Elk Nation until its people had gone the way of all the earth.

Some of his brethren had joined with their foes, assurance against an otherwise cruel death. He could not commit to such a traitorous act. The promise Ganawenjigi had made to his father was far more important than his own life. He was to preserve the sacred records and messages of the covenant for future generations. Those who would possess this land would need to know that God would hold them under the same obligation—that of keeping their promises to Him. The covenant would always be attached to the land, and those who disobeyed the Creator would inherit the same destructive end as had his own people.

He had ensured the cave's obscurity for months, had finally heaved the heavy boulder into its place and readjusted the vines and scrub to mask the entrance. Waiting days to ensure no one followed him and under the cover of night, he had sloshed through the undulating blue-gray stream past opossum and raccoon and had, with great effort, clamored up and down and up again the rolling, timbered wilderness to draw his enemy far away from the repository, in case they found his trail. But Ganawenjigi well knew that his discovery was likely, and because of his enemy's hatred and relentless pursuit, it was only a matter of time before they discovered him.

He picked up the pace, hustled down the crest of saplings, grandparent trees, and the gnarled roots and shrubbery that scraped at his arms and legs—pushing on further still toward the bottom where the terrain rose high around him, creating a chasm. He found a crevice in the rockface and maneuvered between the great granite walls to cover from the elements for a much-needed rest.

Barely situated in the hovel, he heard the cracking of a limb close by. Ganawenjigi grabbed for his dagger, inched toward the slivered opening, his heart racing in his chest. His ears strained to listen. Only silence met his ears. With cautious observance, he edged his head barely past the rockface opening, his gaze snagging on the distraction of a large orange moon that rose from a ledge in the distance from behind slow-moving clouds.

A lethal mistake. A shadow moved on the ground, then a swoosh of metal sounded from above. Ganawenjigi whirled toward a perched form above him, a second's glance, before a blade dropped down toward his neck, severing his last horrified gasp.

Present

The sound of water throttling through copper pipes against the cave ceiling was such a relief, especially after a year of cutting through Graham County, Ohio's governmental red tape to secure the required construction permits. Oneida Graham clutched the lead rope and swung her harnessed body across the massive Native American statues of the cave's archaeological find of the century. She examined the intricate watercourse above her. Her colleague and boyfriend, Lance Graham, had worked for days attaching the elaborate system amid bugs, bats, and mold of every kind. There appeared to be no leaks, and the pipes would divert the water outside, away from the damaged relics of the room called *Sacred*. Hopefully, their handiwork would preserve the statues and muralled walls, which were only a small part of the repository's multifaceted treasures.

The statues were magnificent creatures, spanning from the cavern's ceiling to the floor. She swung to one of the Native American colossi wearing a turban and bear-skin robe cascading from its shoulder. After a brief pause, she pushed off again and planted her boots against the Semitic-looking Mun-dua's chest. Peering up at the headdress adorning its head, Neida imagined the prominent nostrils just below the adornment were large enough to suck her entire body into oblivion if perchance it came to life.

"Hey there, Mr. Anas, the love of my life," she said. "Are you ready for your makeover?" Neida had named each of the three statues—cornball titles that made Lance roll his eyes—Mr. Anas, meaning duck, for the statue's duck-like headdress, Mr. Fimbria, from the Latin, denoting fringe because of one of the giant's fringed leggings, and Mr. Tam O'Shanter, because of the turban embellishing the last statue's head. She carefully examined the rough surface for cracks with her gloved hand. There were quite a few. Even a fissure, carved by centuries of water torture, marred the base of one statue's neck. Neida retrieved the silicone gun from the pocket of her tool belt and started filling the material into the severest of flaws.

At that moment, Lance swung from his work on the ceiling pipes around the third statue that sported fringed buckskins and hair down its back. He stopped alongside Neida and planted a kiss on her cheek. "Are you declaring your admiration for this guy again?" he asked. "I thought I was the love of your life." He feigned a frown at Neida as he waited for her answer.

"Only when you're watching your Ps and Qs, Lance. Mr. Anas and I have become quite close over the last few days. You know what they say about patients falling for their nursemaids, and vice versa."

"Well, if it's that easy for a rather handsome but severe fellow to turn your head, maybe my effort to get you where I want you was better spent working in the lab with Cory."

Cory Willett, their resident paleographer, was at present translating a multitude of tablets they had discovered inside the cave a year ago.

Neida raised an eyebrow. "Right where you want me, huh?"

He nodded with his boyish grin and leaned in to kiss her full on the mouth. After she basked in a pleasant moment, he pulled back and winked at her.

"I've got you dangling from a rope as my captive audience," he whispered and then nuzzled her ear. "A fitting place to present a brave declaration."

Neida pushed his ticklish advances away with her shoulder and raised an eyebrow. "A brave declaration? You mean you're ready to confess I've got a better chess strategy than you?"

Lance ignored her quip and suddenly squinted at the hollow at the base of the statue's neck and frowned, "What is that?"

Neida peered up in the direction of his gaze and noticed something she had never seen there before. She took hold of her rope and inched up the Mun-dua's chest until she had a better view inside the hollow. A blue satin-covered box sat precariously wedged inside the nook. Her mouth dropped open, and she reached for the mysterious addition just as Lance crept up the rock chest to join her.

She spun toward him. "Is this what I think it is?"

"Why don't you open it and find out," said Lance with exaggeration and wide eyes.

Neida adjusted her ropes and locked her position. Gently, she pulled back the cover and gasped as she gazed upon a solitaire diamond ring—at least two-carats of an exquisite princess cut, gleaming in the reflection of the portable lights surrounding the cavern's interior.

Tears formed in her eyes, and she turned to Lance, unable to speak.

"So?" he said. "Was dangling at the end of a rope in the presence of the most beautiful woman I have ever known—both inside and out—worth my effort?"

She couldn't take her gloves off fast enough. "Yes, yes," she sputtered and fidgeted until Lance had removed the ring from its moorings and slid it on her finger. She stared at the jewel adorning her hand, then grabbed each side of Lance's face and said, "Oh, how I love you, Lance Graham. To the moon and back."

"Only that far?" he asked, a hurt look on his face, then he smiled. "I love you too, Oneida Woodward Graham. I find it quite satisfying that at least you won't have to change your last name." He reached for her rope, swung her closer, and enveloped her to him.

Although they were considered cousins, she felt grateful that the connection was only through her grandmother's marriage to Lance's grandfather. She showered his face with kisses—his eyes, his nose, his temples—until her lips found his mouth, and she savored his warm, unequaled ardor that she had failed to experience in her 33 years of dating other men. It filled her with joy.

"Hey, you two," came a voice from below. It was Kat Stewart, her newest and closest friend and Lance's partner at Graham & Associates archaeological firm.

They parted, but Neida couldn't stop staring into Lance's eyes, stroking his cheeks, smiling as the tears streamed down her face.

"I take it she said yes," shouted Kat from below.

Neida peered down at her friend. "You knew about this?"

Kat nodded up at her. "Who do you think arranged for the crew to take an early lunch?" Kat bent to remove a pink box from the bag she had lugged inside the cave. "The guys should be back at any time. I brought some champagne and this yummy cake. We can have a little *part-tay* as soon as you two come down from the far reaches. Mr. Anas can wait another day for his plastic surgery."

Lance pulled her close again and nibbled on her neck, talking between kisses. "I don't know, Kat. I rather like it up here." Then he spoke close to Neida's ear. "I'd rather keep you all to myself, even if the competition at this level is rather stiff."

Neida laughed at his pun and patted the statue's hard chest. "And I imagine Mr. Anas's heart is rather cold too, not exactly the type of guy I'm looking for."

Lance smiled and kissed her again. "Race you to the bottom."

He started his trip to the cave floor, and after Neida replaced one of her gloves, she followed suit. Seconds later, she realized Lance had stopped his descent and was frowning at Mr. Anas's gigantic hand resting palm up at the end of a folded arm against its ribs.

Neida leveled her position and moved toward Lance. "At this rate, I *will* beat you to the bottom. What are you looking at?" She leaned in closer.

Lance pointed at the small granite door where the statue's palm and torso met.

The rugged partition recessed into the statue's body, but she could clearly see it was unattached on all four sides, as though the piece were removable. Engrained on the outside of the square stone was the Mystic Symbol.

"I'm not surprised we've overlooked this," said Lance. "You wouldn't be able to see it from the floor. And this sign of the Creator on the outside gives me the idea there might be something hidden behind it."

"I was thinking the same thing," she said. "Do you have something to remove the stone?"

Lance took out some flat-nosed pliers and needled their tips between the top and bottom slits of the statue's inlaid stone, accidently damaging the granite just to get the ends far enough inside. He glanced at Neida, then shimmied the piece carefully toward them. The fragment slid forward without hindrance. When he had freed the block completely, he set the slab aside.

The construction lights around the cavern diffused enough light across the recess's entrance and Neida perceived that something lay within.

Lance grabbed the treasure's edge and slid it from its vault, revealing a foot-long copper tubing, opened at each end. Traces of fabric still clung to the ends, suggesting the contents had once been completely enclosed.

Neida retrieved her flashlight and shined it into the hole. "The insides are totally solid. Only the slits around the stone would have allowed air to get inside, though I don't think the seam was big enough to allow vermin or moisture to hitch a ride. I don't see any bugs at all."

Lance nodded. "This is just like the tablet we found inside the stone box last year. I think whoever put the tube here meant to protect whatever's inside."

"What's going on up there?" asked Kat from the floor. "You two coming down, or what?"

"We've discovered something," said Lance without looking down.

"Oh? Can you bring it down?" Kat peered up at them and squinted at Lance to see what was in his hand.

"Give us a second," he said.

Neida and Lance completed their rappel to the bottom, but before they were off the ropes, noise from the tunnels filled the cavern. The technicians, returning from their lunch break, appeared and looked to Lance with wide eyes, three anxious faces waiting for his announcement. Obviously, Kat had already spilled the beans.

"So, what's the verdict?" asked one of the technicians.

Lance put his arm around Neida's shoulders. "You're looking at the soon-to-be Mrs. Lance Graham."

The cave echoed with good wishes, accompanied by back slaps and hugs.

Neida felt her cheeks burn at such gregarious outpourings of joy. Although she was used to the technicians after a year of working with them, their lavish expressions and boisterousness still caught her off guard at times.

Another technician interrupted the fray. "What a relief! I thought for sure Neida had turned you down—that you were going to hit her over the head with that pipe in your hand and drag her to your lair until she agrees."

They all laughed.

"Very funny, Jeremy," said Lance. "I'll have you know that Neida thinks me a rather wonderful catch."

"Don't put words in my mouth," said Neida, raising her eyebrows and placing her hands on her hips.

Her response brought another roar of laughter and teasing.

"And what did Mr. Anas hand you up top?" asked Kat after the ruckus had died down.

Lance held up the newly found prize for all to see, shrugged his shoulders, and squinted to examine the pipe's interior. "That all depends on what's inside. But as far as I can tell, it looks like some kind of fabric, and because of the chemicals from this copper tube, the relic might be in pretty good shape."

Kat perked up. "Then let's take this celebration to the lab, shall we? We just might have more to commemorate than your future nuptials. Besides, Cory was fit to be tied that he couldn't participate in all the excitement."

Lance nodded. "I'm right there with you, Kat. Let's not keep my best man waiting."

ABOUT THE AUTHOR

PEGGY ANN SHUMWAY has always been enthralled by the individuals, stories, and mysteries of the past, which led her to years of historical and archaeological study and exploration. She loves family history and has compiled several genealogical works for herself and others. She holds a bachelor's degree in multimedia, which she uses for cover design and video production, and she often blogs about writing. Her archaeological mystery adventure debut, *Vestiges*, allowed her to delve into the Hopewell civilization and combines her love of history with her passion for world-building. Peggy lives amid the rustic background of Arizona.

Made in the USA
Coppell, TX
08 September 2021